Praise for the Shetland series

'Ann's characterization is worthy of the best writers in the field . . . Rarely has a sense of place been so evocatively conveyed in a crime novel' *Daily Express*

'Like a smoky Shetland peat fire, this elegantly written, slow-burning intrigue shrouds you in mystery and crackles with inner heat' Peter James

'A clever whodunit . . . as always, it's the wonderfully evoked island atmosphere that steals the show' *Mirror*

'The best living evoker of landscape' Mark Lawson, *Guardian*

'I'm a big fan of Cleeves' complex crime novels and this is no exception . . . Atmospheric, compelling and ultimately satisfying' *Woman & Home*

'Cleeves' setting is beautifully evoked . . . this is as finely crafted and satisfying as a well-made piece of furniture – just look at the workmanship' *The Times*

'A most satisfying mystery set in an isolated and intriguing location. Jimmy Perez is a fine creation' Peter Robinson

'Cleverly plotted, with a brilliant evocation of the Scots islands' *Sunday Mirror*

Praise for the Vera Stanhope series

'Nobody does unsettling undercurrents better than Ann Cleeves'
Val McDermid

'Ann Cleeves is a skilful technician, keeping our interest alive and building slowly up to the denouement. Her easy use of language and clever story construction make her one of the best natural writers of detective fiction'   *Sunday Express*

'An excellent, atmospheric mystery. Ann Cleeves is our Queen in the North'   Mick Herron

'Cleeves weaves an absorbingly cunning mystery'   *Daily Mail*

'A fine writer'   *Sunday Telegraph*

'Great sense of place, well-rounded characters and a cracking plot'
Woman & Home

'Ann Cleeves . . . is another fine author with a strong, credible female protagonist . . . It's a dark, interesting novel with considerable emotional force behind it'   *Spectator*

'If you're a fan of ITV's crime drama *Vera*, you'll love the books that inspired the series'   *S Magazine*

Praise for the Two Rivers series

'As a huge fan of both the Shetland and Vera series of books, I had high expectations for Cleeves' latest. She easily exceeded those expectations with *The Long Call*. Matthew Venn is a keeper. A stunning debut for Cleeves' latest crimefighter'   David Baldacci

'Had me hooked – a promising beginning to another fine chapter in the Ann Cleeves story'   *The Times*

'Clever, compassionate and atmospheric, with a great cast of new characters to love. I am already a Matthew Venn fan'

Elly Griffiths

'A triumph that cements Cleeves' status as one of Britain's best crime writers'   *Daily Express*

'Ann Cleeves' new series gets off to a terrific start with *The Long Call* – her native Devon is wonderfully evoked, and Matthew Venn is a very appealing new detective. Another sure-fire hit'

Martin Edwards, author of *Gallows Court*

'A traditional mystery of the best sort'   *Guardian*

'Brilliant – a page-turning and sensitively told tale, with a vividly evoked North Devon setting, a powerful emotional heft and a new detective hero in Matthew Venn who you will want to follow for book after book. Wonderful!'

Chris Ewan, bestselling author of *Safe House*

'Cleeves combines a flair for evoking sense of place with a thoughtful, complex plot'   *Mail on Sunday*

THIN AIR

Ann Cleeves is the author of over thirty critically acclaimed novels, and in 2017 was awarded the highest accolade in crime writing, the CWA Diamond Dagger. She is the creator of popular detectives Vera Stanhope and Jimmy Perez, who can now be found on television in ITV's *Vera* and BBC One's *Shetland*. The TV series and the books they are based on have become international sensations, capturing the minds of millions worldwide.

Ann worked as a probation officer, bird observatory cook, and auxiliary coastguard before she started writing. She is a member of 'Murder Squad', working with other British northern writers to promote crime fiction. Ann is also a passionate champion for libraries and was a National Libraries Day Ambassador in 2016. Ann lives in North Tyneside near where the Vera books are set.

Ann Cleeves

THIN AIR

PAN BOOKS

First published 2014 by Macmillan

This edition first published 2021 by Pan Books
an imprint of Pan Macmillan
The Smithson, 6 Briset Street, London EC1M 5NR
EU representative: Macmillan Publishers Ireland Ltd, 1st Floor,
The Liffey Trust Centre, 117–126 Sheriff Street Upper,
Dublin 1, D01 YC43
Associated companies throughout the world
www.panmacmillan.com

ISBN 978-1-5290-5023-3

7 9 8 6

A CIP catalogue record for this book is available from the British Library.

Typeset by Palimpsest Book Production Ltd, Falkirk, Stirlingshire
Printed and bound by CPI Group (UK) Ltd, Croydon, CR0 4YY

Visit **www.panmacmillan.com** to read more about all our books
and to buy them. You will also find features, author interviews and
news of any author events, and you can sign up for e-newsletters
so that you're always first to hear about our new releases.

For Joseph Clarke.

And his beautiful mother.

Acknowledgements

THANKS TO EVERYONE WHO HAS HELPED make this book better: my agents Sara Menguc and Moses Cardona and my editor Catherine Richards. I'm grateful to the Pan Macmillan team of Jeremy, Becky, Emma, Sam and all Andy Belshaw's group. Thanks to my friends in Shetland, specially Ingirid Eunson and Jim Dickson for great food and company, Mary Blance for advice in all things Shetland, Steven and Charlotte for giving me the idea and everyone else who's provided tea, beer and stories. Any mistakes are my own – I do know that it's impossible to send an email by iPhone from Unst, but this is a story. Finally, let's raise a glass (of champagne) to my fairy godmother Elaine.

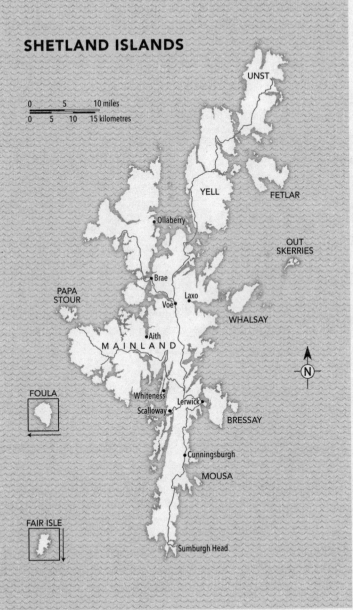

SHETLAND ISLANDS

0   5   10 miles
0   5   10   15 kilometres

UNST

YELL

FETLAR

OUT
SKERRIES

Ollaberry

Brae

Laxo

Voe

WHALSAY

PAPA
STOUR

Aith

MAINLAND

FOULA

Whiteness

Lerwick

Scalloway

BRESSAY

Cunningsburgh

MOUSA

FAIR ISLE

Sumburgh Head

N

Chapter One

THE MUSIC STARTED. A SINGLE CHORD played on fiddle and accordion, a breathless moment of silence when the scene was fixed in Polly's head like a photograph, and then the Meoness community hall was jumping. Polly had spent thirteen hours on the overnight boat from Aberdeen to Lerwick and when she'd first come ashore the ground had seemed to shift under her feet, and this was another kind of illusion. The music appeared to bounce from the walls and the floor and to push people towards the centre of the room, to lift them onto their feet. Even the home-made bunting and the balloons strung from the rafters seemed to dance. The band's rhythm set toes tapping and heads nodding. Children in party clothes clapped and elderly relatives clambered from their chairs to join in. A young mother jiggled a baby on her knee. Lowrie took the hand of his new bride, Caroline, and led her onto the dance floor to show her off to his family once more.

This was the hamefarin'. Lowrie was a Shetlander, and after years of courtship Caroline had finally persuaded him, or bullied him, to marry her. The real wedding had taken place

1

close to Caroline's home in Kent and her two closest friends had followed her to Unst, Shetland's most northerly island, to complete the celebration. And they'd brought their men with them.

'Doesn't she look gorgeous?' It was Eleanor, crouching beside Polly's chair.

The two women had known Caroline since they were students; she was their voice of reason and their sister-in-arms. They'd been her bridesmaids in Kent and now they were dressed up again in the cream silk dresses they'd chosen together in London. They'd made the trek north to be part of the hamefarin'. They'd followed Caroline round the room for the bridal march and now they admired again her elegance, her poise, and her very expensive frock.

'It's what she's wanted since she first laid eyes on Lowrie during Freshers' Week,' Eleanor went on. 'It was obvious even then that she'd get her way. She's a determined lady, our Caroline.'

'Lowrie doesn't seem to mind too much. He hasn't stopped beaming since they got married.'

Eleanor laughed. 'Isn't this all such fun?'

Polly thought she hadn't seen Eleanor so happy for months. 'Great fun,' she said. Polly seldom relaxed in social situations, but decided she was actually rather enjoying herself tonight. She smiled back at her friend and felt a moment of connection, of tenderness. Since her parents had died, these people were the only family she had. Then she decided that the drink must be making her maudlin.

'They'll be setting out supper soon.' Eleanor had to shout to make herself heard over the band. Her face was flushed and her eyes were bright as if she had a fever. 'The friends of the bride and groom have to help serve. It's the tradition.'

The music stopped and the guests clapped and laughed. Polly's partner, Marcus, had been dancing with Lowrie's mother. His dancing had been lively, even if he couldn't quite follow the steps. He came over to them, still following the beat of the music, almost skipping.

'It's supper time,' Eleanor said to him. 'You have to help put out the trestles. Ian's weighing in already. We'll come through in a moment to act as waitresses.'

Marcus dropped a kiss onto Polly's head and disappeared. Polly was proud that she hadn't asked him if he was having a good time. She was always anxious about their relationship and could tell that her need for reassurance was beginning to irritate him.

The men had set out tables and benches in a smaller room, and Lowrie's friends were handing out mugs of soup to the waiting guests. Eleanor and Polly took a tray each. Eleanor was enjoying herself immensely. She was showing off, flirting with the old men and revelling in the attention. Then there were bannocks and platters of mutton and salt beef. *Bannocks and flesh*, Lowrie had called it. Polly was vegetarian and the mounds of meat at the end of her fingertips as she carried the plates from the kitchen made her feel a little queasy. There was a sense of dislocation about the whole event. It was being on the ship for thirteen hours the night before and spending all day in the open air. The strangeness of the evening light. Eleanor being so manic. Polly sipped tea and nibbled on a piece of wedding cake and thought she could still feel the rolling of the ship under her feet.

When the meal was over she and Marcus helped to clear the tables, then the band began to play again and, despite her protests, she was swung into an eightsome reel. She found

3

herself in the centre of the circle, being passed from man to man and then spinning. Lowrie's father was her partner. He had his arms crossed and braced and the force of the movement almost lifted her from her feet. She'd thought of him as an elderly man and hadn't expected him to be so strong. There was a fleeting and astonishing moment of sexual desire. When the music stopped she saw that she was trembling. It was the physical effort and an odd excitement. There was no sign of Eleanor or Marcus and she went outside for air.

It must have been nearly eleven o'clock, but it was still light. Lowrie said that in Shetland this was called the 'simmer dim', the summer dusk. So far north it never really got dark in June and now the shore was all grey and silver. Polly spent her working life analysing folk tales and she could understand how Shetlanders had come to create the trowes, the little people with magical powers. It must be a result of the dramatic seasons and the strange light. It occurred to her that she might write a paper on it. There might be interest from Scandinavian academics.

From the hall behind her came the sound of the band finishing another tune, laughter and the clink of crockery being washed up in the kitchen. On the beach below a couple sat, smoking. Polly could see them only as silhouettes. Then a little girl appeared on the shore, apparently from nowhere. She was dressed in white and the low light caught her and she seemed to shine. The dress was high-waisted and trimmed with lace and she wore white ribbons in her hair. She stretched out her arms to hold the skirt wide and skipped across the sand, dancing to the music in her head. As Polly watched, the girl turned to her and, very serious, curtsied. Polly stood and clapped her hands.

She looked around her to see if there were any other adults watching. She hadn't noticed the girl in the party earlier, but she must be there with her parents. Perhaps she belonged to the couple sitting below her. But when she turned back to the tideline the girl had vanished and all that was left was a shimmering reflection of the rising moon in the water.

Chapter Two

WHEN THE PARTY ENDED THEY COULDN'T SLEEP. Caroline and Lowrie had disappeared back to Lowrie's parents' house. Polly, Eleanor and their men had booked a holiday cottage called Sletts within walking distance of the Meoness community hall, and now the four of them sat outside it on white wooden chairs and watched the tide ebb. No background noise except the water and their own murmured conversation. The occasional echoing splash of wine being poured into large glasses. Polly felt the dizziness return and thought again that she'd had far too much to drink. She turned back to face her friends and realized they were in the middle of a conversation.

'Did you see Lowrie's cousin's kiddie?' The envy in Eleanor's voice was palpable. 'Little Vaila. Only four weeks old.'

Eleanor was thirty-six and desperate for a baby. There'd been a late miscarriage, and the child would have been a girl. None of them knew what to say. There was a long silence.

'I saw something really weird when you were all out for a

walk this afternoon,' Eleanor went on, obviously deciding to change the subject. Perhaps she understood that talk of babies embarrassed them. 'There was a young girl dancing on the beach. She was all in white. A kind of old-fashioned party dress. She seemed a bit young to be on her own, but when I went out to talk to her she'd disappeared. Into thin air.'

'What are you saying?' Her husband Ian's voice was teasing, but not unkind. 'You don't think you saw a ghost?'

Polly didn't speak. She was remembering the girl she'd seen dancing on the sand.

'I'm not sure,' Eleanor said. 'I could easily believe in ghosts in a place like this. All this history so close to the surface. Some of the research I've been doing for Bright Star has been compelling. Really, I think a lot of the people I've talked to believed they've had a supernatural encounter.'

'I bet they were all weirdos.'

'No! Ordinary people who'd had extraordinary experiences.'

'You're on holiday now,' Ian said. 'You don't need to think about work, or the company or the new commission. You'll make yourself ill again. Just relax and let it go.' The others laughed uneasily, hoping that he'd dealt with the awkwardness and they could enjoy the evening once more.

It occurred to Polly that Ian had only agreed to come to Shetland because she and Marcus would be there. He couldn't quite face his wife on his own, even though her depression seemed to have lifted a little in the last couple of months. After the miscarriage he'd believed that she was unravelling, that he was losing her. Polly didn't know if he'd even wanted a baby. Perhaps he just wanted Eleanor back the way she was when they'd first met. Stylish and uncomplicated, full of pranks and larks. Fun.

Eleanor flushed. She'd been drinking since early evening. She worked in television and usually she could hold her booze, but tonight even she seemed a little drunk. 'Perhaps you think I'm going mad again, that I should be back in the loony bin.' She stared out at the water. 'Or perhaps you believe I'm inventing things. To get attention.'

There was another silence. For a moment Polly was tempted to speak, to say that she'd seen a child dressed in white dancing on the beach too, but still she stayed silent. A sort of betrayal.

'Only when you claim to have seen spirits from the other side.' Ian was dismissive. He was a sound engineer. A bit of a nerd. He clearly thought the whole conversation was ridiculous and he was feeling awkward, way out of his comfort zone.

It was as dark now as it would get and a mist was rising from the sea to cover the remaining light. Polly shivered. She was wearing a padded jacket, but it was cold. 'We should go in,' she said. 'I'm ready for bed.'

'You believe me, don't you, Pol?' Eleanor had been a beauty when she was a student, in a grown-up, voluptuous way that had made Polly look like a grey, malnourished child. Ian leaned forward and lit a fat white candle on the table. The light flickered and Polly saw lines under her friend's eyes. Stress and a kind of desperation. She was wearing a theatrical black evening cloak over her bridesmaid's dress. 'There was a little girl just outside the house here when I woke up from my sleep this afternoon. When you were all out walking. And then she disappeared. She just seemed to walk into the sea.'

'Of course I believe you.' Polly wanted to show her support for Eleanor, to stop her talking about children and embarrassing herself. She paused. 'I probably saw her myself this evening, when I left the hall to catch my breath just after supper. She was playing out on the beach. I don't think she was a ghost, though. Just a local child dressed up for the party, and this afternoon she probably ran home up the track.' Polly didn't say that the girl *she'd* seen during the hamefarin' had also disappeared while she was looking away. That would have encouraged Eleanor in her fancies, and she wanted her friend back too. The closeness they'd had. The laughs and the silliness.

She stood up and carried the glasses into the house. The men followed. She wondered what Marcus was making of all this. He was Polly's new man – newish at least – and she was still amazed that they were a couple. She felt like a giddy teenager when she thought about him. He'd agreed to the party immediately when she'd tentatively asked if he fancied it. 'Shetland in midsummer? Of course.' With the huge schoolboy grin that had attracted her in the first place. 'And if we're going north, where better than to go to Unst, the *furthest* north it's possible to be and still be in the UK.' For him, it seemed, life was nothing but new experiences.

Through the kitchen window Polly saw that Eleanor was still sitting outside. The mist had slid as far as the house now and the image was blurred. It was as if Eleanor was made of ice and was slowly melting. Polly went to the door and shouted out to her.

'Come in, lovely. You'll catch your death.'

Eleanor waved. 'Give me a few minutes. I'll be there very soon.' She blew out the candle.

Turning to go to her room, Polly thought she caught sight of a white figure dancing along the tideline.

Chapter Three

JIMMY PEREZ WALKED CASSIE DOWN THE hill to Ravenswick School. Some days he let her go by herself, but then he watched from the house, picking out the red Fair Isle bonnet knitted by his mother and worn by Cassie whatever the weather, until it disappeared inside. His paranoia was the result of guilt and the fact that Cassie wasn't his child. He'd been charged to care for her and he felt the duty like an honour and a burden.

He was on late shift, so he walked slowly back to the converted chapel that had once been Fran's home, and thought again that he should do something with his house in Lerwick. He wasn't sure that he could bring himself to sell it, and besides he had it in his head that it would provide some sort of security for Cassie if anything should happen to him. Her natural father always seemed to have money, but Perez thought he was feckless. The Lerwick house would see Cassie through university perhaps or give her the deposit for her first home. Properties in town fetched more than those in the country. But it seemed criminal that it should be lying empty when folk needed places to stay and, with nobody living there, it would soon get damp. He decided to call into an estate agency in the street before he started work, to see about getting it rented out. When Fran had died the year before, small tasks like that had seemed insurmountable and he felt a stab of pride that he could consider dealing with the business now.

He was opening the door when his phone started ringing. Sandy Wilson, his colleague. It was only recently that Perez had started thinking of the man like that. Before that he'd seen Sandy as a boy to be instructed and protected.

'There's a woman gone missing in Unst.' Even now, it seemed, Sandy was incapable of giving detailed information without being prompted.

'What sort of woman?' A couple of months ago Perez would have been angry and would have let his irritation show. He could still get moody. Late at night when he couldn't sleep, eaten away by grief and guilt, he hated the world, but when he made breakfast for Cassie he had to be sane. And, like everything, sanity came more easily with practice.

'A tourist. Name of Eleanor Longstaff. Aged thirty-six and from Battersea.' A pause. 'That's London. She was staying in a holiday let in Meoness with her husband and another couple. They'd been at Lowrie Malcolmson's hamefarin', then went back to the cottage for a few drinks around midnight. The others left Eleanor sitting outside when they went to bed, and when they woke up this morning there was no sign of her. She'd disappeared into thin air.'

Perez considered. 'Her husband didn't notice that she hadn't come to bed?'

'I did ask that.' Sandy could be touchy; he was always thinking he was being criticized. 'He's a heavy sleeper. And, like I said, they'd all had a bit to drink.'

'Could she have slept in a spare room? On a sofa? And just gone out this morning?' In which case there was no reason to panic. Even if they couldn't find Eleanor in Unst, the ferries would be operating by now. Perhaps she'd just felt the need to be on her own, or the wild hadn't suited her and she'd run back to the city. Perhaps there'd been a row with the husband. But if she'd disappeared late at night there would be no ferries; no escape from the most northerly island in the UK. In the early hours of the morning a woman who'd been drinking could wander away from the path and lose her way on the cliff. The strange light of the simmer dim could be almost hallucinatory.

'I don't know about that,' Sandy said. 'I spoke to the husband, Ian. He said she hadn't been herself lately. She'd been depressed. Something about losing a baby.'

'He's thinking she might have committed suicide?'

'He didn't say that, but I think it's on his mind. He sounded upset. He wanted us there straight away.' Sandy paused. 'I told him we'd be with them as soon as we could. It's Mary Lomax's patch, but she's away south, so I've asked the coastguard to start a search. Was that OK?'

'Perfect.' Perez was thinking it was a good day for a trip to the North Isles, clear and still. 'Book us onto the ferries and I'll pick you up in Lerwick on the way through.'

The ferry was already at Toft when they arrived and theirs was the second car in the booked lane, waved aboard almost immediately. They drank dreadful coffee from the machine in the passenger lounge, and Perez watched the fulmars flying low over the water. It felt like a day off. Truanting. He looked at his phone and asked Sandy to check his. Reception came and went here, so they might not hear even if the woman had turned up. He hoped that when they arrived at Meoness she would be there. He pictured how she would be, offering them coffee or lunch to make up for their inconvenience. Embarrassed to have caused so much fuss. A little angry with her husband for overreacting. He and Sandy would turn round and drive back to Lerwick, with only half a day wasted. But even when they arrived at Yell and the phones were working again there was still no news. Perez drove north across the island very quickly, feeling a strange sense of urgency. When they got to Gutcher a ferry was pulling out from the pier and they had to wait for the next one to arrive. He could feel the tension mounting in his forehead and across his shoulders. Fran had been thirty-six when she had died.

When they landed at Belmont in Unst a group of children was waiting to board the ferry south. He thought they must be on their way to Lerwick for some end-of-term outing. Some of them were in fancy dress. They giggled as they boarded the coach to take them to Shetland mainland. Perez was going to ask Sandy if he knew what it was about – Sandy read the *Shetland Times* as avidly as a gossipy woman – but the sergeant had a map open on his knee, concentrating on getting them there, and Perez thought it better not to interrupt.

The holiday house was long and low and whitewashed, and sat right on a beach with a crescent of sand and pebbles at its back. Once perhaps it had been a croft house with a byre attached, but the renovations had been well done, with the holiday market in mind. There was wooden decking between the house and the beach and a couple sat there, waiting. Perez looked at them as he got out of the car. The woman was skinny and pale. An interesting angular face, which Fran would have wanted to draw. Long hair tied back at her neck. Jeans and a cotton jumper. She walked out to greet them. 'Is there any news? Ian has taken the car out to look for her, but that was ages ago and we haven't heard anything since.' Her eyes were grey and slanted like a cat's. She had a faint north-of-England accent.

Perez introduced himself.

'Polly Gilmour. This is my partner, Marcus Wentworth.'

'And you were staying here with Mr and Mrs Longstaff.'

'Yes, we came for Lowrie and Caroline's wedding party. The four of us thought we'd make a holiday out of it, a kind of retreat.' The eyes were almost unblinking.

'Did Mrs Longstaff need a retreat?' Perez had reached the deck and took a wooden chair on the other side of the table from Marcus. Sandy leaned against the wall of the house and tried to look inconspicuous.

There was a silence. Perhaps it wasn't the sort of question they were expecting.

'I mean,' Perez said, 'was there any reason why she might have taken herself away? If she'd been going through a bad time?'

Polly hesitated. 'She had a miscarriage late in pregnancy,' she said. 'She's been a bit low lately and had a spell in hospital. Ian thought it would help her to get away from London.'

For a while Perez didn't speak. He'd been married before he met Fran, and his wife had suffered three miscarriages. He'd been devastated by each one, but determined to hold himself together. Sarah had thought him uncaring and had walked away from the marriage.

'Is Eleanor still seeing a doctor for the depression?'

Polly shook her head. 'She signed herself out of hospital and has refused treatment since. She said it was natural to feel sad at the loss of a child; you'd be ill if you didn't. And she's been much better recently. Almost back to her old self.'

There was another silence. Perez could sense Sandy's impatience. It seemed Marcus was unnerved by it too, because he stood up. 'Coffee? It's a long drive from Lerwick. I don't think I realized the scale of the place before we arrived – how much distance there is between communities.' He sounded easy, confident, a man who'd been to a good school and expected to get what he wanted.

'Coffee would be grand.' Perez waited until he'd disappeared into the house and then turned again to Polly. 'Tell me about Eleanor.'

Now the woman did blink. 'We're friends. Really close. There are three of us: Eleanor, Caroline and me. We met on our first day at university. Eleanor took me under her wing. You could tell that she would do well, even then. She was always beautiful, of course, and that still helps, doesn't it? Especially if you want to work in the media.'

'What was her work?'

'She did drama at uni and found work in television as soon as she left, first as a runner, then as a script editor. Recently she's set up her own TV production company. Mostly documentaries for Channel 4 and the BBC.'

'Sounds stressful.' Perez gave a little laugh. He couldn't imagine what it must be like to run a company or live in London. Through the open door into the kitchen he smelled coffee. Good coffee still reminded him of Fran.

'Nell thrived on the stress. It was what made her feel alive. And, as far as I know, the company was doing well. But not getting pregnant was different. Outside her control. And I think it was the first time she'd ever failed at anything.'

'Do you think she's killed herself?'

The question seemed to stun her, but the response was immediate. 'Not for a moment. Nell's a fighter. She wouldn't give up. She's in the middle of a project at work and she would never leave anything half-finished.'

'What's the project?' Perez felt that he was out of his depth. He knew nothing about the media and only watched TV with Cassie. CBBC or Disney.

'A film about ghosts. Contemporary hauntings. That's why she was delighted when I told her the story of Peerie Lizzie.'

'How did you know it?' Perez hadn't realized that anyone outside Shetland had heard of the ghost of Peerie Lizzie.

'I'm a librarian,' Polly said. 'I specialize in folk stories, British myths and legends.' She paused. 'Nell never stops working. I guess she's kind of obsessive. She thought that while she was here she could interview people who'd seen the girl. She even brought a digital recorder with her.'

Peerie Lizzie was a little girl who was supposed to haunt the land around Meoness in Unst late at night. It was claimed she was the spirit of a child, the daughter of the big house, who'd been drowned close by in 1930. The child had been especially precious because the parents had been middle-aged when she was conceived, and some stories had it that her appearance foretold a pregnancy. Perhaps that was why Eleanor had been so interested. Perez was a sceptic. Most people who reported the sightings were young men with a few drinks inside them, or attention-seekers looking to get their name in the paper. As far as he knew, nobody had got pregnant as a result.

He had the sense that Polly was going to say more, but she

turned away and looked at the beach, so he resumed the conversation.

'Do you think she might have wandered up the road last night in the hope of seeing the ghost?'

Marcus appeared with a tray, a pot of coffee and four mugs. Polly waited to answer until he'd set them on the table.

'It's more likely than a notion that she would have killed herself.' A pause. 'As I said, she was obsessed with the idea of the documentary, so yes, it's just what she might have done.' The woman looked up at her partner. 'Don't you think so?'

'I didn't know her. Not like you did. A couple of supper parties and then a night together when we came up on the boat from Aberdeen . . . But I certainly wouldn't have had her down as a potential suicide risk.'

'Do you have a photo?' Perez still couldn't get a handle on the missing woman and thought that a picture in his head might make her more real for him. 'It would help, if we need to widen the search.' He'd show the boys who worked on the ferry to Yell. If she'd been out early in the morning, and on foot, they'd have noticed her.

'Not a print,' Polly said, 'but there are some on my laptop. I took some pictures on the boat from Aberdeen, so they're recent. The house has Wi-Fi. Come inside.'

The interior of the house was tasteful and simple. Only the sheepskins in front of the wood-burner and the prints of puffins and gannets on the walls reminded visitors they were in Shetland. And the spectacular view from the window. Polly's laptop was open on the coffee table and she switched it on. With a few clicks she'd reached the file of photos.

Eleanor Longstaff was dark-eyed. Long hair was being blown by the wind away from her face. She could have shared ancestors with Jimmy Perez, whose forebears were ship-wrecked off Fair Isle during the Spanish Armada. The photo had been taken on the deck of the NorthLink ferry. Eleanor was dressed in a waterproof anorak and was leaning back against the rail. She was laughing. No sign here, at least, of stress or depression.

'I can email you a copy, if that's any good,' Polly said.

Perez nodded and handed her his work card with his contact details. He'd get the photo printed in Unst's small police station. Mary Lomax, the community police officer, might be away, but Sandy had brought a key to the building.

Polly's narrow fingers were tapping on the keyboard when she stopped suddenly and looked round at them. She seemed paler than ever. Horrified. 'I've had an email from Eleanor. It arrived this morning. Sent at two a.m., so not that long after we went to bed. It must be from her iPhone.'

'Open it!' Marcus was looking over her shoulder.

She looked at Perez for permission. He nodded and moved so that he had a better view of the screen. Polly double-clicked on the message and it opened.

No greeting and no sign-off, not even the obligatory x. Just one line. *Don't bother looking for me. You won't find me alive.*

Chapter Four

OUTSIDE THERE WAS THE SOUND OF a car moving slowly down the track. Ian's 4x4. Polly turned off the laptop. She didn't care what the policeman thought; she couldn't bear the idea that Ian would walk in and find them all staring at a message from his wife. A message that could be read as a suicide note. She still couldn't quite believe in the email; thought if she opened her in-box again it would have vanished, a figment of their collective imaginations.

Ian was a techie, a geek, not given to emotion of any kind; and even now, as he stood in the doorway frowning, it was hard to tell what he made of the situation. Polly had always thought that he and Eleanor made an unlikely couple. How could Eleanor, who needed so much love, who wanted to be touched and hugged and kissed, fall for a man so stony and unresponsive? It had occurred to Polly that her own reaction was selfish: perhaps she just hated the idea of losing her close friends of university days, of being separated from them. But Caroline had married Lowrie, who was sympathetic and uncomplicated, and Polly was entirely happy for *her*.

In contrast, Eleanor's engagement to Ian had made Polly anxious from the start. The night before Eleanor's wedding the three of them had got drunk together in Polly's flat. The bride and the bridesmaids and too much fizzy wine. An essential ritual.

'You do realize that it's not too late?' Polly had said, after Caroline had fallen asleep in a chair in the corner, her mouth open, snoring. 'You don't have to go through with it. Pull out now and I'll sort out the practical stuff for you.'

'Of course I don't want to pull out.' Eleanor had been horrified, had looked at Polly as if she hardly knew her. 'Ian's what I want and what I need. I can't imagine not spending the rest of my life with him. What's wrong with you? Can't you be happy for me? Are you jealous that I've found someone special at last?'

That had been three years ago and it still seemed to Polly that their friendship was strained. Caroline hadn't noticed, but Polly had been aware of the tension, of having to choose her words carefully. She couldn't spill out her feelings to Eleanor as she had in the old days, when they'd both been single. She'd hoped this trip to Unst might make everything between them right again.

Of course Eleanor's wedding to Ian had taken place and Polly had been there as the witness, smiling for the camera outside the registry office on a breezy March day. Eleanor had changed her name to her husband's, although few of their friends did that any more. In the afternoon they'd gone up in the London Eye and had drunk a toast in champagne to Mr and Mrs Longstaff. Then Eleanor had sent the guests away to party without them. 'My husband and I want to be alone.' A radiant smile.

Caroline's marriage had brought back all the memories of that time, and Polly remembered Eleanor's wedding again as Ian stood, solid and angular, in the doorway of the house. She had a brief and ridiculous idea. *Two weddings and a funeral.* She realized that the start of a grin was appearing on her face and knew it was caused by stress, but was horrified all the same.

The police officer with the Spanish name spoke first. He stood up and introduced himself to the newcomer. 'You didn't see anything of your wife on the island?'

Ian shook his head. He was always a man of few words. Now he seemed frozen. 'I went up to Lowrie's house, but there was nobody there. I tried phoning, but it went straight to voicemail.'

'Our volunteer coastguards are out looking,' Perez said.

Ian nodded, but didn't move from his place by the door.

'Let's walk,' Perez said. 'I always find it easier to think when I'm walking.'

Polly thought that he was a sensitive man. He wouldn't want to tell Ian about the email from Eleanor in front of an audience.

Ian turned and the two men left the house. Polly and Marcus stayed in the living room with Perez's younger colleague. Marcus got up to make more coffee. He collected the tray from outside and walked with it to the kitchen. Polly wanted to apologize to him. *I should never have brought you here. I thought it would be fun and a good way to get to know my friends. Now it's turned into the worst sort of nightmare.* But Wilson, the young sergeant, was watching and listening, and in these circumstances anything she said might be misinterpreted.

She still felt insecure when strangers were in the room, socially awkward, despite her two degrees and her brilliant job at the Sentiman Library. It was to do with her voice and her modest suburban background, a fear of the educated classes learned from her parents. Sometimes she was convinced that Ian suffered in the same way; they were both from the north and they both lacked the confidence that Marcus and Eleanor had inherited along with their clear voices and their savings accounts. Perhaps *they'd* have been better suited together, leaving Eleanor and Marcus to make a stylish celebrity couple.

'It'll have been a fine wedding,' the police officer said. It was the first time she'd heard him speak and though he spoke slowly she struggled to understand. Lowrie had been in England since university. They laughed at his accent sometimes, but it wasn't as dense as this. 'Unst folk always throw a good hamefarin'.' Polly thought he sounded wistful, as if he wished he'd been invited.

'I don't think Eleanor came inside again last night,' she said. 'The door was still unlocked. If you're from London you always lock the door. It's a habit.' She'd been thinking about that.

'These midsummer nights some folk find it hard to sleep,' Wilson said. 'And the weather's so fine your friend might have gone for a walk. You see the stars here in a way you can't in the city. Lowrie and his family will be back tidying up in the hall at Meoness now. Perhaps she's there.'

'But the email?' Polly cried. 'Why would she send that?'

'A kind of sick joke? Or maybe someone else hacked into her account?'

Polly shook her head. Eleanor loved mischief and practical jokes, but she wouldn't put her friends through this kind of anxiety. If she'd sent the email she'd have been watching through the window and would come bursting in with a *Ta-da, that had you fooled* grin on her face before they had time to be worried. The email disturbed Polly almost more than anything else. She supposed it was possible that Eleanor's account had been hacked.

'Is it OK if I go and check in the hall?' she said. 'We never thought that Lowrie and Caroline might be there.'

Sandy Wilson looked confused. She could tell that he didn't know what to do – he wasn't a man used to making decisions and he wanted to ask his boss. So she took the responsibility from him by grabbing her jacket and leaving. 'Thanks. Tell Marcus where I've gone.' And she walked out of the house.

Outside it was clear and the sea was sparkling with reflected sunlight. Polly saw that Ian and Perez were still strolling along the beach, deep in conversation, but she turned in the opposite direction, away from the shore, and neither man noticed her. The road was narrow, with a fence on one side and occasional passing places on the other. A sheep wandered into her path. She could smell the grease on its fleece before it scrambled away, and the scent of crushed grass. A great skua, sitting on the hill, hook-beaked and scary, seemed to be staring at her. Meoness was a sprawling community of croft houses with land attached and an occasional newbuild. Between Sletts and the other houses there were skeletons of old buildings, walls and boundary dykes half-hidden by cotton grass and wild iris. Where the track joined a slightly wider road, there stood an old red telephone kiosk and the community hall. A couple of cars were parked outside and there was the noise of a Hoover coming through the open windows. She pushed on the door and went inside. Lowrie stood on a stepladder in the main hall and was taking down the bunting. In London he worked as an accountant for a big retail chain, and was always very respectable in jacket and tie. Now he was wearing a sweatshirt and jeans and a round Fair Isle hat shaped like a pork pie. He grinned and waved. The sound of the vacuum cleaner came from a smaller room, where they'd eaten supper the night before. It stopped and Caroline came through.

'So you've come to help at last!' she said. 'About time too. We've nearly finished.' She was big-boned and blonde. 'We were just about to have a drink to celebrate clearing up. Apparently that's traditional too.'

'Is Eleanor here?'

'No! Isn't she sleeping off her hangover?' Caroline took the string of bunting from her husband and started to wind it into a ball.

'She didn't sleep at Sletts last night,' Polly said. 'We don't know where she is. Ian was so worried that he called the police. A couple of officers came from Lerwick and the inspector's talking to him now. The coastguards are doing a search of the cliffs.'

Lowrie climbed down the ladder. 'She'll surely not have gone far.' He sounded so matter-of-fact that Polly could tell he thought they were overreacting. City people, so sensitized to crime that they saw it everywhere. Perhaps he was embarrassed that they'd caused this fuss, dragging police officers across two islands and two ferries because a woman had wanted to experience the strange Shetland night alone. But now it was lunchtime and there was still no sign of Eleanor. And she'd sent that weird email.

'She sent me this message,' Polly tried to keep her voice calm, 'saying not to bother looking for her. Saying that we'd never see her alive again.' And at that point she began to cry.

They took her into Lowrie's parents' house and sat her in a tall wooden chair in the kitchen and made her tea. After the sunshine it seemed very dark in the house, all shadow and dust. There was a rack over a Rayburn where dozens of tea towels were folded and hanging to dry. Presumably they'd been used the night before and already washed. The room seemed to Polly to be impossibly cluttered. How could they find anything in the chaos of fading magazines, knitting wool and vegetables? There was a faint smell of sheep and mould. She hated disorder and found it physically repellent. Weren't they embarrassed to bring guests to a house that was so untidy?

There was no sign of Lowrie's parents.

'I know,' she said, 'that it's ridiculous, and I'm sure there's a rational explanation. But Eleanor's been so fragile lately. Losing the baby and all that talk of haunting and ghosts. When the policeman said you'd all be in the hall, I thought, *Of course, she'll be there*. I couldn't stand being in that house any longer. And then, when you hadn't seen her, I knew something dreadful must have happened.'

The room was very warm and she felt that she might fall asleep in the hard chair, and when she woke up all this would be a dream.

'I'll walk back with you,' Caroline said. 'There might be some news.'

Her voice sounded hard, detached, as if she didn't care about Eleanor at all. Why wasn't she more upset? Polly had the idea that Caroline just wanted her out of the house before her in-laws returned. Perhaps a hysterical friend would reflect badly on her. Caroline was an academic, always measured and precise. It also occurred to Polly that Caroline might not believe her story and that she wanted to check out the facts of Eleanor's disappearance for herself.

They took a different route back to the holiday cottage. Caroline led the way through the garden where hens scratched behind wire mesh, over a stile and onto short cropped grass. She seemed very at home here.

'Would you ever live in Shetland?' Polly asked suddenly. 'Would Lowrie want that?'

'Maybe. If I could think of something to do all day. We've talked about it. I wouldn't want to bring up kids in the city.' Caroline gave a sudden grin. 'He has this idea about setting up a business here. Soft fruit grown in polytunnels. High-end jams and preserves.'

'And you wouldn't mind that? Leaving behind your friends. And everything that goes with being in town. Theatre on your doorstep. Shops and bars and restaurants. Even Lerwick's miles away.' Polly found herself distracted from her anxiety by this new Caroline, who wore wellingtons, could negotiate a barbed-wire fence with ease and could contemplate making a home in this barren landscape where the seasons were so extreme.

'Ah, we might have to compromise on the exact location. Unst might be a step too far for me. And I love Grusche and George to pieces, but I wouldn't want to be next door to the in-laws.' She paused for a moment and looked back over the croft. 'Sometimes Grusche treats Lowrie as if he is nine years old and can't clean his teeth without being reminded.'

They came to the brow of a low hill and Polly got her bearings. She could see the track to their house and the beach ahead of them. Ian and Perez were still on the sand, but they were heading back to Sletts. There was a view south of cliffs and headlands.

'If Eleanor fell over a cliff,' she said suddenly, 'she could lie on the rocks below for days without being found.'

Ahead of them was a drystone circle with a gap in the side. A skua, which seemed to Polly as big as an eagle, suddenly dived at them straight from the sun. Polly shrieked. She could feel the air of its wing-beat on her face. Caroline gave a little laugh. 'It's only protecting its nest. If you put your hand in the air, it'll aim for that and miss your face.' She pointed at the stone circle. 'That's a planticrub. People used to grow cabbages in there as food for the sheep. I suppose the wall sheltered the plants from the salt wind.'

She was about to walk on and Polly could see that her friend had made the decision that this would be her home. She was buying into the history and the culture already. But Caroline's subject was human geography, and Polly thought she'd always be an outsider here, an observer. She'd regard her neighbours with the same amused objectivity as when she was studying migrant workers for her PhD.

Polly couldn't imagine life in the city without her friends. Because they'd always been there, she'd never felt the need to build a wider social circle and somehow, at this moment, Marcus didn't matter. The shock of the diving bird had provoked a panic that was unlike anything she'd experienced in everyday life. At work she was a competent professional, choosing stock for the private subscription library where she worked, advising the historians and students who used it. But here the faintness of the day before had returned. She bent, rested her hands on her knees and felt the blood come back to her head.

'Do you want to rest for a bit?' Caroline was solicitous, but smug too. She was fit and she could have continued walking for miles. Polly thought again with surprise that the woman had no real concern for Eleanor's safety. Her head was full of her new husband and her plans for the future.

They sat with their backs to the wall. The sun had heated the stones and they were out of the wind.

Polly felt herself falling asleep again and wondered how she could do that when Eleanor still hadn't been found. She stood up, shaking her limbs to feel more awake, and for the first time looked into the planticrub. No sign that anything had been grown there for years. Cropped grass and a scattering of sheep droppings. And an iPhone with a distinctive pink case, which Polly recognized as Eleanor's.

Chapter Five

Jimmy Perez could sense the tension of the man walking beside him. He seemed rigid, like a robot. Each footstep was heavy and, looking back over the sand, Perez was surprised that their prints weren't very different, that the ones left by Ian Longstaff were no deeper than his.

'You've been married for three years?' Here on the beach they could be miles away from the tasteful holiday house of Sletts; Perez felt they were contained in a bubble formed by the natural sounds. There was a breeze blowing from Norway and the tide was sucking on a bank of shingle close to the water. A faint heat haze blurred the distant horizon.

'Just over three years. I was doing the sound on one of her shows.' Ian looked at him. There was a barely contained frustration that was turning into anger. 'But we're wasting time here. We should be looking for her.'

'People *are* looking,' Perez said. 'Local people who know the land. We'd just be in the way. Now talk me through everything that's happened since you arrived in Shetland. You arrived on the ferry from Aberdeen yesterday morning?'

'I wanted to bring my car,' Ian said, 'so we decided on the ferry instead of flying. And in the end Marcus brought his too. We didn't know what it would be like here. Whether there'd be shops. You know . . .'

'Oh, we're almost civilized these days.'

Ian stopped walking and grinned, despite himself. 'Yeah, well. Neither Nell nor me really does country. We weren't sure what we'd find.'

'Did you stop in Lerwick at all? For shopping? Breakfast?'

'We had breakfast on the boat and decided to head straight north. We'd stocked the boot with enough food and booze to last for months, and Caroline had said she'd sort out milk and bread. I'd looked on the map. Before then I hadn't realized how far it would be.'

'Two long, skinny islands and two ferries – and that's after you get to Toft on Shetland mainland,' Perez said, as if he had all the time in the world.

'It was late morning by the time we arrived. We'd arranged to get into the house early, and Polly made lunch.' He stopped again and stared at Perez. 'Do you really want all this stuff?' Terns screamed overhead.

'I do.'

'Eleanor hadn't slept much on the boat from Aberdeen. She's like a kid when she's excited. Hyper. When we'd cleared up lunch she said she wanted to rest before the wedding.'

'Was she really excited?' Perez asked. 'Not anxious and depressed?'

'They've told you about the baby.' He stared out towards the water. 'It was her second miscarriage. She wants a child. Of course she was upset and angry. Eleanor has always got what she wanted.' He paused. 'That makes her sound horrible, but things have always come easily to her. Liberal, arty family with enough money to indulge her. She's bright enough to pass exams without too much effort. Then this happened. Something that couldn't be put right with money or hard work. It floored her.'

'She spent some time in hospital?'

'Just to please me,' he said. 'I felt so helpless. I wanted my wife back. I'm an engineer and I'm used to fixing things if they're not working properly. I got her into a private place.'

'But she refused to stay there?' Perez wondered what that must do to a relationship, a husband sending his wife to an institution because she was sad.

'She said she wasn't ill and it would only take time. She said that I should trust her.' Ian paused. 'She was right. On this trip she was much more herself again. Focused on a new project at work. Excited about the trip and about the wedding.'

'And ghosts,' Perez said.

'That was work. A project about contemporary hauntings. We teased her. She teased us back.'

'So after lunch your wife had a snooze,' Perez said. 'What about the rest of you?'

'We went for a walk to get the lie of the land. There's a footpath that goes south along the cliffs. The weather was lovely and the views were spectacular. There were puffins so close that you could reach out and touch them. Eleanor would have loved that. At one point I wondered if I should go back for her. It seemed a shame that she was missing it.' Ian frowned.

'But you didn't go back?'

'No. I decided to let her rest. We knew it would be a late night and we're booked into the house for a week. Plenty of time for her to explore.' He started walking again and his words came in breathy bursts. 'When we got up she was awake and sitting on the deck. Later, after the party, she claimed that was when she'd seen a ghost.'

'Peerie Lizzie?' Perez kept his voice even. This man wouldn't like to be mocked. Underneath the steel Perez sensed a fragile ego.

'Yes, a child. A girl in an old-fashioned white dress with ribbons in her hair. Eleanor said that she watched her for a while, then she was worried that there were no parents around and that the girl was getting very close to the water. But when she approached her, the child vanished. That was the story, at least.'

'You didn't believe it?' Perez wasn't sure how this could be relevant. He remembered the kids in fancy dress at the ferry – perhaps Eleanor had seen one of those.

'Eleanor loved practical jokes, taking the piss. I wondered if she was winding us up. But Polly and Marcus took it seriously and started coming up with practical explanations. Polly's always been a tad earnest – I could never quite see how Eleanor and she were such good friends. Though Nell has always collected admirers – she makes people feel as if they're special. I just let the whole ghost thing go.'

'You didn't consider that it might be a sign that Eleanor's depression had returned?' Perez had been depressed after Fran's death and he'd imagined all sorts.

'Hearing voices and seeing things, you mean? Nah, I didn't think that, though she accused me of believing she was mad, when we were discussing it after the party.'

'And after you returned from the walk you prepared for the dance?'

'Yes, we got there a bit early to help out.'

'Of course,' Perez said. 'As friends of the bride and the groom, that would be your role. Tradition.'

'So we were told.' Ian didn't sound as if he was much impressed by tradition.

Perez could picture just how it would have been. They'd be there to set out the bar and greet older friends and family as they arrived, to organize the food. Later there'd be huge pots of tea, the milk already added, trays of home-bakes, and the young people would wait on the other guests. 'How did Eleanor seem during the party?'

'Well! Lively. She was dancing. The girls had gone to classes in London to learn the steps so they wouldn't be left out. It was great to see her so happy.'

'And afterwards?'

'Afterwards we came back to the house,' Ian said. 'It was gone midnight, but we were still buzzing and nobody was ready to go to bed. We opened a couple of bottles of wine, wrapped up well and sat out on the deck.' There was a silence. Perez waited for him to continue. 'Eleanor talked about some cousin of Lowrie's who'd just had a baby. A tiny girl. She'd been there at the party, passed around for all the relatives to admire – her mother the centre of attention.' Another pause, then a sort of confession. 'I don't know if it was the baby Eleanor was jealous of or all the admiration, the fuss.' Again Perez said nothing.

Ian seemed to be concentrating, replaying the evening's events in his head. 'Then Polly said that she'd seen a child in a white dress on the beach outside the hall. It's the same beach as here, of course, just further north. And suddenly Eleanor seemed to go weird on us. All theatrical and melodramatic.

33

She accused me of not taking her seriously, of thinking she was mad. Maybe she'd just had too much to drink. The rest of us went to bed and she waited outside. I thought she was making a point. Perhaps she expected me to go out again and apologize, fetch her in.' He stopped again. 'But I'm a stubborn bugger. I went to bed. And I've never had any trouble sleeping, so I went out like a light. When I got up this morning there was no sign of her.' For the first time he seemed to lose control. He stopped walking and put his head in his hands.

Perez waited for a moment. 'She definitely didn't sleep with you? Even for a while?'

He shook his head. 'She must still have been wearing the clothes she wore to the party. Nothing else is missing. Not even her trainers. She hadn't taken off her make-up, because her cream and wipes were still packed, and she'd do that even if she was too drunk to stand.' He gave a little laugh. 'She'd love this: playing the lead in her own ghost story. Disappearing into nothing.'

By now they were halfway along the beach and Perez could see the Meoness community hall, where the night before there would have been music and dancing, bunting and flowers, and a big glittering sign with the newly married couple's name on it. They turned and had almost reached the house when they saw Sandy Wilson, standing on the deck and waving. The sun was so bright behind him that Perez couldn't make out the expression on his face. It was impossible to tell if this was a wave of celebration or an urgent call for Perez's presence. Perhaps Eleanor had been found by the search party, with nothing more serious than a broken ankle. Perez hoped so. He would like to meet her. Ian broke into a run.

On the deck Sandy had been joined by Polly.

Now Ian was close enough to shout. 'Where is she? Have you found her?' Perez sensed the desperation in his voice.

Sandy didn't reply.

The women had left Eleanor's phone in the planticrub, with Caroline to keep guard of it. At least the spate of US crime shows had made people aware that a possible crime scene shouldn't be disturbed. Walking along the sheep track on the top of the cliff, Perez tried to work out what the discovery of the phone might mean. Ian had told him that he'd tried to call Eleanor as soon as he'd realized she was missing: 'Of course I tried to get in touch with her. It was the first thing I thought of. And I've been trying ever since. But there was no answer.'

Why did the woman no longer have her phone? And did this mean that someone other than Eleanor had composed the email to Polly Gilmour? Perez repeated the words in his head. *Don't bother looking for me. You won't find me alive.* He ran through explanations for the message, which grew wilder and more improbable: a killer setting up the scenario that Eleanor had committed suicide; someone playing a tasteless and elaborate joke. One thing was certain. Eleanor was still in Unst, whether she was alive or dead. The ferry boys had already told Sandy that nobody matching her description had left the island that morning.

Lowrie's new bride was sitting on the grass outside the crub, but scrambled to her feet when she saw him approach. She looked to Perez very English, strong and healthy, with curly fair hair and good white teeth. He could imagine her running up a hockey field and cheering her team on. And when she spoke there was a no-nonsense tone to the voice.

'Is Polly OK? I didn't want to send her off on her own, but I thought someone should stay here. Scare off the sheep. And any stray walkers.' If she was upset about Eleanor's disappearance there was no sign of it. But perhaps not showing emotion was part of her character too.

'Polly's with Marcus.' Perez paused. Marcus had been comforting the woman as if she were a child, offering to wrap her in a rug, to make her herbal tea. 'She's distressed of course, but she seems fine.' He looked over the wall. 'You're sure that belonged to Eleanor?'

'I haven't touched it to look at the call records,' she said, 'but it's certainly the same model and colour.'

He put on gloves and reached over the wall to retrieve the phone. It came to him suddenly that he was treating this as a potential murder scene and that he had no expectation of Eleanor being found alive. If the phone had lain here for most of the night in a heavy dew there'd be little chance of fingerprints, though, and any of her friends could have touched it over the previous few days. The battery was low, but there was sufficient signal to see the email to Polly in the Sent box and the record of missed calls from Ian. There'd been no other calls or emails sent or received since.

He looked at the woman, who stood watching him impassively. 'I suppose you don't have any idea what might have happened to her?'

Caroline stared at him, considering the words before saying them. He thought that was how she would always be and, before she had a chance to answer, another question came into his head.

'What do you do for a living?'

'I'm an academic. Human geography. UCL.'

'So are we all part of your study?'

She gave a little laugh. 'It would be interesting research. The effect of isolation on island communities under stress. Though I'm sure it's been done before.'

'And perhaps you're too close to the subject to be objective.'

'Ah,' she said. 'Objectivity – that's a whole new area of research in its own right.'

'Are you sufficiently objective to tell me what happened to your friend in the early hours of this morning?'

There was another brief pause and then she did reply. 'I think Eleanor might have been trying to run away from her husband.'

Chapter Six

CAROLINE LAWSON TOOK PEREZ BACK to her parent-in-laws' house. She, it seemed, had not changed her name with marriage. The name-change business wasn't something he and Fran had ever spoken about, but he supposed that if his fiancée had lived and they'd had the wedding they'd been planning, she would have kept her own name. She was an artist with a growing reputation and it would have been crazy to lose that. Except that Hunter wasn't the name she'd been born with, but the name of her ex-husband Duncan, who was Cassie's father. They were part of a complicated modern family. Perez wasn't sure what he would have made of Fran using Duncan's name when she was married to *him*, then thought that he would have gone along with it for Cassie's sake.

The door was unlocked, but the house was empty. There was a note on the table in the kitchen: *We've joined the search party to look for Eleanor.* Caroline moved the kettle to the hot plate of the Rayburn to make tea.

'You seem very at home here in Shetland,' Perez said.

'I love it.' A pause. 'Lowrie wants to move back. I might be persuaded.'

'Could you find work?'

'Not in my field. But I've always wanted to make time to write my research up into a book.'

'So,' Perez said. 'Tell me about Eleanor.'

The kettle whistled and Caroline made the tea, then sat down at the table opposite him, shifting a pile of the *Shetland Times* to make room for the mug. Perez had grown up in such a kitchen as this. A working space with a wax-cloth on the table, a place for baking and knitting and filling in subsidy forms. Not for showing off to the neighbours. A cat wandered through and sat on the windowsill in the sun.

'Four of us met at Durham University,' she said. 'Lowrie was in a different college at Durham, but Polly, Eleanor and I were freshers together and in the same hall of residence. On the same corridor, sharing a kitchen, excited and scared shitless, all at the same time. You know . . .'

Perez nodded, but what could he know of life in a smart English university? The nearest he could come to it was being sent from Fair Isle at the age of eleven to board at the Anderson High in Lerwick. Then Duncan Hunter had been his ally and protector, but he couldn't imagine being friends with the man now. They rubbed along together because of their responsibility for Cassie.

Caroline continued to speak. 'We shared a flat in the second year and a house in the third. One night at a party Eleanor named us the Three MsKeteers – she was going through a feminist phase – and that stuck. I was going out with Lowrie then, but I carried on living with the girls and he was a kind of permanent fixture. We were all very close.'

'And you kept in touch even after you left university?' Perez had never made those sorts of close friendships. He wasn't the kind of policeman who used colleagues as a surrogate family.

'When we graduated the three of us were based in London. Polly started her postgrad training – she's a librarian – and I was doing my PhD. Eleanor found work as a runner with ITV. So we just went on living together, sharing a grotty flat. Lowrie got a job in Edinburgh, but he came down when he could. We were poor as church mice. It wasn't very different from being students.' She gave a little smile. 'Though Nell was subsidized big-style by her mother and, when she got fed up with slumming it, she'd go home for a weekend of comfort. Lowrie was earning, so I got treated to nights out when he came to stay. I suppose it was really only Polly who found it tough going financially. Not that it stopped the rest of us moaning.'

Perez listened and tried to picture these three young women in their flat in London at the beginning of their careers. He said nothing to hurry on the story. He was more use here than he would be out helping the search team.

'We did well in our own fields,' Caroline continued. 'Moved out of the slummy flat. Lowrie got a promotion to London and he and I set up home together. Eleanor was a rising star in ITV. Polly qualified and got a job first in a local-authority library, then in the Sentiman, where she still works. That's a weird place in Hampstead. It keeps the records of the UK Folklore Society, tales of morris men and legends of the Green Man. You know the sort of thing.'

Perez thought he had no idea. 'And ghosts?'

Caroline looked at him sharply. 'I don't know anything about that. You'd have to ask Polly.' She paused before continuing her story. 'For a while she and Nell shared an apartment, but then Ian Longstaff swept Eleanor off her feet and into his house in South London and Polly found a nice little flat of her own not far away.' She paused. 'I suppose we grew up.'

'But you were still friends?'

'Yeah, when we moved out of our shared home we made a pact that we'd meet up at least once a month. We kept to it at first and then it became more difficult to find a time when we were all free. I have students to supervise and, since she set up in her own business, Eleanor is abroad a lot. Even when she's home Ian seems to demand all her time. I suppose only Polly has the diligence and determination to make the commitment work. She's the one to email the rest of us, negotiating times and places to meet. And since Marcus came on the scene even she's been less organized.' Caroline paused. 'That's why I was pleased that everyone agreed to make the trek north for the hamefarin'. It was a chance for the three of us to spend some time together away from London.'

'Why do you think Eleanor would want to run away from her husband?' It was where the conversation had started. Perez wasn't frustrated by the time it had taken to get back to the question. He had a much better sense now of these women as successful, professional friends.

For the first time Caroline seemed unsure of herself. 'I have no evidence.'

'Sometimes I have to pursue an investigation without evidence,' Perez said. 'The purpose of my work is to obtain it, but it's not where we start from.'

'It seems disloyal speculating like this.' She frowned.

Perez said nothing.

'For the past six months Eleanor has been very low. More unhappy than I've ever known her.'

'She'd lost a child,' Perez said gently. This woman with her strong bones and her clear thinking might not understand how that would feel. He didn't see Caroline as the most imaginative of women. Or the most maternal.

'Yes, and Ian hasn't been any support to her. He stuck her in a private psychiatric place so that she wouldn't be a nuisance and then he started lecturing her to sort herself out. He lost patience with her.' She paused again. 'I think Eleanor might have found comfort elsewhere.' The words sounded oddly prim, and Perez again had a sense of the schoolgirl she had once been.

'Another man?'

'I think so.' Now Caroline sounded wretched, as if she regretted having started this conversation. 'But, as I said, I have no real evidence. And Nell didn't discuss it.' She paused again. Through the window they saw a very elderly man walk down the road outside. He was dressed in his Sunday best – black trousers, polished shoes and all-over knitted jersey – and was bent over a walking stick. Caroline waited until he'd disappeared from sight before she started talking. 'I saw her one evening with a guy in a restaurant. I was walking past and although they weren't sitting in the window I saw her quite clearly. She stood to pick up the scarf that had fallen from her chair. The man had his back to me, so I saw nothing of him except the back of his head. Eleanor reached out and touched his hand on the table. There was a look on her face . . . I don't know how to describe it. Mixed-up. Guilty perhaps.'

'Did she see you?' Perez tried to picture the scene in the restaurant and thought that Caroline was making too much of it. Eleanor could have been reassuring a young colleague about a problem at work. A touch of the hand could be a gesture of friendship. It didn't have to be intimate.

'No,' Caroline said. 'It was a few months ago. She had her second miscarriage just before Christmas, and this was March or April. Late enough for it to be dark outside. One of those drizzly days that feel more like midwinter. She hadn't long sprung herself from the hospital. She wouldn't have seen me.'

'Did you discuss it with her?'

'Yes.' Caroline paused. 'She lied. *You must have been mistaken, Caro. I was in Brussels that week. I wasn't even in London.* Her voice all brittle and tense. I let it go. But I wasn't mistaken. It was definitely her.' She looked up at Perez. 'That was when I knew this new man must be important, you see. If the dinner was just a work meeting, or even if she was having a fling or a one-night stand, she'd tell me and swear me to secrecy. But she lied and she'd never done that to me before.' There was another pause. 'Since then Eleanor seems to have been trying to avoid me. I think she's met up on her own with Polly a couple of times, but I've only seen her when other people have been around.'

'If Eleanor were planning to leave her husband,' Perez said, 'I don't quite understand why she would wait until she was in Shetland to do it. It's so much more inconvenient here.'

Caroline gave a tight smile. 'Eleanor's never planned to do anything in her life. It would have come to her in the middle of a dance; or maybe when she saw Lowrie and me together she realized that her life with Ian was impossible. That she couldn't stand it any longer. Then she would have walked away. Without thinking through the consequences. Have you tried the guest houses in Unst? If she hasn't left on the ferry, she might be fast asleep on a comfortable bed. Eleanor has always liked her comfort.'

'Without taking her toothbrush or her moisturizer?'

For the first time Caroline looked a little shaken. 'Ah,' she said. 'That doesn't sound so much like the Nell I know.' She reached for the pot in the middle of the table and poured out more tea.

Outside there was a noise. The bark of a dog and running footsteps. A man crashed through the door into the kitchen. He was wheezing from running and his face was red. He bent double and tried to catch his breath to speak. Caroline stood up and stroked the hair from his forehead. She could have been comforting an anxious child.

'We've found her! I need to tell the police.' Then he noticed Perez, sitting in the shadow. 'Who are you?'

'He is the police.' Caroline's voice was impatient. 'You've found Nell? Where is she? Is she OK?'

Lowrie Malcolmson straightened. He ignored his new wife's questions and directed his words to Perez. 'Eleanor's dead,' he said. 'You need to come with me.' Then he put his arms round Caroline's shoulders and pulled her to him. 'I'm so sorry.' Perez saw that he was crying. 'I know how much she meant to you, and this shouldn't happen to anyone. I'm so very sorry.'

Caroline wanted to go with them, but Perez told her to stay where she was. 'If this is a suspicious death we need the locus contaminated as little as possible.'

She nodded, as if she could see that made sense. 'Can I go to Sletts to tell the others?'

'I'd rather you didn't tell anyone yet. Not until we have something specific to say.'

She nodded again.

'Are you OK here on your own? Should I get someone to be with you?'

'No,' she said, and he thought again how strong she was. She could be an island woman from a previous generation, doing all the work on the croft and bringing up a family while her man was at sea; coping alone with the news that he'd been drowned in a storm. 'Lowrie's parents will be back soon. I'll be fine.'

Eleanor's body lay on the headland south of Sletts. A murderer would have taken the most direct way from the scene, so Perez took a circuitous route to avoid further contamination. He thought the English people would probably have walked within a hundred yards of here during their exploration of the cliffs the day before. Just away from the marked footpath was a standing stone formed from granite. At its base a small peaty lochan. The stone was reflected in the water, with the colour of the sky and a small white cloud. But the reflection was disturbed by the shape that lay in the shallow pool. Eleanor Longstaff was on her back. Her feet were bare and Perez saw that the toenails were painted. She still wore the bridesmaid's dress of the night before: full-length cream silk, which seemed to move when a breeze blew across the surface of the water. Her eyes were open wide and stared at the huge sky.

Chapter Seven

SANDY WILSON WAS STILL WAITING IN the holiday house when the call came through from Jimmy Perez. He was hungry and wondering what they might do about lunch. And he was uncomfortable. These people had turned Sletts into a little piece of London, with their ground coffee and their English voices, the fancy food on the cupboard shelves. *He* was the Shetlander and yet he felt like a stranger. He went outside to take the call.

'Meet us there, will you, Sandy, once you've found someone to sit in with the witnesses?' Then a list of directions that Sandy jotted on the back of his hand, because he remembered nothing when he was flustered. 'And while you're waiting for someone to relieve you, see if you can track down James Grieve and Vicki Hewitt. This is a suspicious death and we want the pathologist and crime scene manager here. I know it's Sunday, but work your charm, eh? It'd be great if we could get them in today. If not, first thing in the morning.'

'What should I tell the folk in the house?'

'Tell Eleanor's man that she's dead. He deserves that. He

can decide whether or not to tell the rest of them. If Mary Lomax is back on the island, get her to sit in with them.' Mary was the North Isles community police officer, middle-aged, motherly and perfect for the job. She'd grown up in Glasgow, but had taken to island life immediately. Apart from the accent, you'd have her down as a native Shetlander.

Sandy phoned Mary. She said she was back in Unst and that she'd be at Sletts in half an hour. Then he turned his mobile to silent and hesitated, rehearsing in his mind the words that he would use to tell the Englishman with his square face and his hard eyes that his wife was dead. When he walked through the door they all stared at him and his mouth went dry.

'Could I have a word outside, please, Mr Longstaff?' Speaking slowly so the man would understand his accent. Knapping.

He expected questions, a refusal to comply, but Longstaff stood up and followed him onto the deck. As they left the house the other couple continued to stare at him in silence.

'They've found her.' It wasn't a question. Sandy nodded. 'Is she dead?'

'I'm sorry, sir.'

Sandy was about to offer his condolences, say those words that always sounded false to him, even though he meant them, but Longstaff interrupted. 'I knew she must be. She wouldn't have gone like that. Not all night without a word. She'd know that I'd be worried. It's been a difficult time, but we loved each other. In a way that other people can't understand.' He looked up. 'Can I see her?'

'I'm sure that can be arranged,' Sandy said. 'But maybe just not yet.'

There was a sound of a car coming down the track. Mary

Lomax climbed out. She hadn't taken time to change into her uniform, was wearing tracksuit bottoms and an elderly fleece that smelled of her collie. She'd taken on a small croft to work in her spare time. Sandy waved at her, felt the kind of relief that had always marked the end of the school term for him.

'I'm sure that you've urgent things to be doing, Sandy. I can look after things here now.' She put her arm around Ian Longstaff's shoulder. Sandy expected him to push her away, but he curved his head towards her and clung onto her as she led him inside.

Perez was waiting on the hill, a good distance from the body with his back to it. He'd sent everyone else away and was looking south. The land sloped down towards Springfield, the old laird's house that had been turned into a hotel. Sandy knew better than to approach the crime scene and stayed where he was, by the fence. He thought this must be hard for his boss. Another dead woman, much the same age as Fran had been. He never knew what to say to Jimmy Perez these days, or whether he *could* say anything to make him feel better.

'James Grieve will fly in on the last flight from Aberdeen.' The words shouted because he was still a distance away. And that seemed to work, because Perez gave him a smile and walked towards him.

'I'm hoping to get the Chief Inspector in this evening too.'

'Who have you asked?'

'Willow Reeves.'

Sandy gave a little smile at the name. 'Would you like me to stay here to keep the walkers and gawpers away?' He didn't mind dead people. He couldn't offend them.

'Nah, I'll do it – I've called in reinforcements from Lerwick.' Sandy thought Perez liked the idea of a silent vigil. He had turned in the other direction now and was staring out over the water. Maybe he needed the time on his own. 'Find us some accommodation, would you, Sandy? We can't be traipsing back to Lerwick every night. See if you can find somewhere big enough for us all. Didn't I read that Springfield House has new owners? It might be worth trying there.'

So Sandy was back in his car driving away from Meoness and the few miles to the big house further south. Springfield had been empty for years until an English couple had turned up to renovate it. The house had a special place in Shetland mythology because it was where Peerie Lizzie had been living when she drowned.

When Sandy arrived one of the owners was showing a family into his car. He was still standing at the door, the keys in his hand. 'Can I help you?' He was in late middle age and a shock of grey hair stuck up at the front, like the crest of a bird, giving him a comical, cartoonish appearance.

Sandy explained who he was and that he needed as many rooms as the hotel could provide.

'I'm just about to drop these people at the ferry. Is that OK? Call into the bar and ask Billy to make you a coffee or a sandwich and I'll catch up with you as soon as I can. My partner's out for the afternoon.' His voice was deep and somehow familiar.

The bar was reached from a courtyard at the back of the house. Once it had been a stable or a garage. Sandy had seen pictures in the museum of the house in Peerie Lizzie's day – grand men and women in fancy clothes, arrived from the south for a week of fishing and shooting. Perhaps this was where they kept the rods and the guns. Inside the bar Billy Jamieson was polishing glasses. Sandy had done him for drink-driving about a year before, but the man didn't seem to bear a grudge. 'Sandy, what can I do for you? Is this work or pleasure?'

'Work.' No details, though news would get out soon enough. Had probably got out already and Billy was just fishing for more information. 'I'm here to book some accommodation, but your boss is away to the ferry with some guests. He said to give me a coffee and a sandwich while I wait.'

Billy nodded, played with the coffee machine and disappeared into a small kitchen at the back, only sticking his head round briefly to ask if ham would do because they didn't have much else left.

'I'm starving,' Sandy said. 'I'd eat you in a sandwich, if there was enough mustard to go with it.' He sat at the bar with his coffee. The room was empty apart from a couple of foreign tourists in a corner and a local man nursing a pint. 'What are they like to work for then?'

Billy understood what the question was about. A couple of gay men taking over the place had been a topic of conversation all over the islands. Nothing too unpleasant – Shetlanders considered themselves above prejudice these days. But a lot of interest and a few unfunny jokes. He shrugged. 'Fine enough. David's a good cook and he does most of the work. Charlie's the front man.'

And on cue the owner appeared at the door, a silhouette against the sunlight outside. He walked in smiling, his hand outstretched. 'Sorry to keep you waiting. I'm Charles Hillier.' As if the name was important, as if Sandy should recognize it. And something did stir in his memory: Saturday-night television in his grandmother Mima's house in Whalsay. He and his brother there for a sleepover because his parents were away. Some variety theatre or game show, and the three of them laughing because the humour was the sort that bairns could enjoy too. Now he felt awkward because the memory was so sketchy, but the man obviously thought he was still famous. Sandy decided it was best to stick to the business in hand. He'd look the hotelier up on Google later.

'We'll have a team based in Unst for a few days at least. Could you provide some rooms for us? Bedrooms and maybe a meeting room.'

If Hillier was disappointed not to be recognized he didn't show it now, but switched into professional mode, leading Sandy into the main house and showing him into bedrooms, throwing open doors with the air of a conjuror. He was flamboyant, a showman. In his head Sandy was counting up what all this would cost and was wondering what Jimmy Perez would say. 'Would there be a discount? As we'll be taking so many of your rooms?'

Hillier laughed. 'Let's see what we can do, shall we? We'd want to do all we can to help our friends in the police.' He took Sandy into a small lounge and brought a tray of tea, with little home-made shortbread biscuits.

'What's this about?' he asked. His head bobbed forward and Sandy was reminded again of a bird, a parrot maybe. His eyes were beady and bright. 'Are you allowed to say?'

Sandy thought that by now there'd be no point in keeping secrets. 'A visitor to the island died,' he said. 'It's a possible suspicious death.' He was expecting more questions, but the man dipped his head again towards his tea and said nothing.

Chapter Eight

WILLOW REEVES WAS AT HER PARENTS' place in North Uist when the call came from Jimmy Perez. The commune had come together for a working lunch and they were sitting round the long table in the old barn. Time had snapped like elastic released from tension and she was a kid again. Everything was the same – the taste of home-made bread and vegetable stew, the murmured voices that hid dissent and frustration under a veneer of politeness. Except that there were no children at the table. The individuals she remembered as being strong and flexible now had grey hair and arthritic joints. No new members had joined since she'd signed up for the police service. There were no families to boost numbers for the island school. The communal ideal of shared ownership and shared beliefs seemed to be unappealing to Thatcher's children.

She muttered an apology and went outside to take the call. Her mother, Lottie, had been delighted to see her and Willow had enjoyed her time here, felt better for the mindless physical exercise and the organic food. And she'd banished the guilt that had bothered her every time she'd phoned them and heard her mother's wistful but undemanding enquiry about when she might be planning a visit. Her relationship with her father had always been more problematic and now, after a fortnight, she was ready to leave. The unexpected contact with the outside world came as a relief.

'I'm sorry to bother you.' Perez's voice sounded distant. 'I know that you were spending some time with your folks.'

'Is it work, Jimmy?'

'We've got a suspicious death. A woman from the south here for a hamefarin' in Unst. No obvious cause of death, but she's kind of posed, so I don't see it as natural causes. James Grieve is booked onto this evening's flight.'

James was the pathologist, based in Aberdeen. She'd met him in Shetland on a previous case. Another investigation featuring a posed body.

'I know that you're on leave,' Perez said, 'but I thought I'd contact you first.' A pause. 'I thought that you'd want to know.'

There was a moment of pleasure because she could tell that he wanted her there; she was his first choice. She was already calculating flight times and possibilities. She should get the next plane from Benbecula if she left in ten minutes. 'Can you book me onto the last flight from Glasgow, Jimmy?'

'For today?'

'If that's all right with you, Inspector.' Mock-stern because, in theory, she was his boss when it came to serious crime in the Highlands and Islands.

'I won't get to meet you from Sumburgh,' he said. 'I'm thinking that I should stay here in Unst tonight. You know what a trek it is back to the mainland. I'll arrange for a hire car to be waiting for you at the airport and book you onto the last ferries up. Will you bring James? I'll sort out accommodation for you both too.'

When she told her parents that she'd been called back to work they said they were disappointed, but she thought they were as relieved as she was to see her go. She reminded them of the time when the commune was thriving, when there was the noise and clutter of children running through the yard. They saw how supple she was when she worked in the field, and they saw themselves thirty years before. Her father waited at the airport until her plane took off. She saw him, still and impassive as it taxied along the runway.

James Grieve was short and smart, and every time she saw him she was reminded that once he'd been a medic in the army. His plane had arrived into Sumburgh before hers and he was waiting for her, a leather holdall at his feet and his coat folded over one arm. His shoes were so highly polished that they glinted in the sunlight.

He gave a tight little smile. 'Chief Inspector, we meet again.'

She drove north over smooth roads, past the places that reminded her of her previous visit to Shetland. Jimmy Perez had been on sick leave then, unbearable at times, angry and uncommunicative. He'd sounded better on the phone. She thought they'd work well together and was aware of another emotion too, a kind of anticipation, but knew better than to think in that way. She was always disappointed in her relationships with men and it was best to remember that this visit was just about work. Perez could have contacted her sooner if he'd had a more personal reason; besides, he was still grieving. They bypassed Lerwick and continued north, had ten minutes' wait for the ferry at Toft and were the last car aboard the boat from

Gutcher to Unst. She'd looked at the map in the plane and knew where she was going.

Perez was waiting for them at the side of the road by a telephone kiosk. She'd phoned him when they'd arrived in Unst. He was dark and untidy, his hair just a little too long. When she pulled in he directed her to park beside the community hall. 'We can walk from here.'

They climbed out of the car and there was a moment's awkwardness. 'So,' he said. 'Here we are again.'

Then James Grieve began asking questions about the dead woman and the scene, and Perez was leading them across sheep-cropped grass and she had to pay attention to his detailed description of what had happened. Willow found that she'd lost all track of time. Midsummer in the Uists was light enough, but here they were much further north and although it was already evening there was a clarity that made it feel like early afternoon. Sandy Wilson was waiting by a stile in a gap in a drystone wall. He'd caught the sun and his face was freckled like a schoolboy's. He grinned at her and she thought that he, at least, was pleased to see her.

'I've tracked down Vicki Hewitt,' he said. 'She'll be on the first flight tomorrow. I'll go out early and pick her up.' Vicki was the crime-scene manager and had to come in from the mainland too.

'Follow the sheep track,' Perez said. 'That's the route we've all used.'

She saw the standing stone first. It was enormous and shaped into a point, and Willow found her attention wandering. She was thinking about the people who'd worked the monumental lump of rock and fixed it into the peat and was wondering what significance it might have had for them.

She thought too that there'd been a settlement on this land more recently than the stone had been erected. Crumbled drystone dykes marked field boundaries and two higher walls formed the corner of what might once have been a house. The land had supported many more families in previous generations in Shetland.

As they got closer Willow saw the woman in the water. She was dark-haired and pale-skinned, and Willow saw what Perez meant about the body having been posed. Even if the victim had been taken ill or tripped into the water, she wouldn't be lying like this, flat on her back, with her head pointed directly towards the stone. And she couldn't see how it might be suicide. 'You say there was a note?'

'An email,' Perez said. 'Sent to one of her friends. *Don't bother looking for me. You won't find me alive.*'

'You could read that as a suicide note.'

'Except that the iPhone from which she sent it wasn't with her. It was found on the hill close to where you left your car.'

'So the murderer is playing games then, you think?' Willow thought it was the time of year for games.

Perez shrugged to show that he was reluctant to speculate. She was reminded of the old Perez and wanted to snap at him, *And don't you play games with me, mister. Just give me an opinion.*

James Grieve was taking photographs, completely focused on his work and apparently unaware of any tension between them. He looked up suddenly. 'You do realize that I can't give you any cause of death until we move the body. I could have had a good night's sleep in my own bed and come up first thing tomorrow morning.'

'But then you'd have been deprived of our company this evening.' Willow thought *she* could have stayed in North Uist, and felt again the relief of being away from the place, where she sensed her father's disapproval eating into her confidence from the moment of her arrival.

'Time of death?' Willow knew she was wasting her time, but couldn't help asking.

James Grieve glared. 'Tell me when she was last seen, and when her body was found, and it'll be somewhere between the two.'

'You can't blame a girl for trying.' She flashed a grin at him, never quite sure when she was pushing him too far. 'We'll leave Sandy here, shall we, Jimmy, and have a word with your suspects?'

He led her down a slope and pointed out a low white house at the end of the track and right by the sea.

'That's Sletts, the holiday let where they're staying,' Perez said. 'They were two couples, in Unst for a friend's wedding. Professional thirty-somethings from London.' He paused. 'I haven't given them any details yet, though they know that she's dead. Mary Lomax, the community officer, is sitting with them. Perhaps I should have gone in earlier. They'll be tense with waiting for information. Hostile. But I'm not sure where to start with them and so I waited for you. It's almost as if they speak a different language. As if they're aliens from a different world.'

'And you think I'll have more in common with them than you? You're joking, aren't you?' She looked down at her jeans, bought from a charity shop and the hem let down so that they fitted, at the hand-knitted sweater with the hole in the elbow.

'You won't be intimidated.' His voice was serious. 'I can't imagine you being intimidated by anyone.'

The compliment took her breath away for a moment, then

she almost ran down the slope to the house below, her face turned away from him so he couldn't see that she was blushing.

Inside three people sat round a dinner table, though it seemed that the meal had been more like a picnic. There was half a French loaf, some cheese still in its wrapper, a tub of hummus. They weren't speaking. Willow understood what Perez meant about them being members of an alien species. It was the cut and shine of the hair and the quality of the casual clothes. There'd be no Oxfam-shop jeans here. She knocked on the door and walked straight in through the immaculate kitchen. This holiday house was far better equipped than her flat in Inverness. They turned round to stare at her. Still speechless. Then they saw Perez behind her and the questions came tumbling out, one after another, the voices a chorus of well-bred noise. A motherly woman sat in the corner knitting hand-spun yarn.

Willow held up her hands and the noise faded away. The Englishwoman, Polly Gilmour, stood up. She was blonde and pale. And fraught. 'We've been here for hours with no news. No communication. Mary knows as little as we do. Somebody turned up an hour ago and took our mobiles and our laptops, and he said that you'd explain. We've been sitting here waiting for someone to come.' She paused. 'Oh God, someone needs to tell Cilla.'

'Cilla?'

'Eleanor's mother.'

'If you give us the number,' Willow said, 'we can do that.'

A solid bruiser of a man stood up. 'What happened? Did she kill herself? There wouldn't have been this fuss if she'd had an accident.'

'And you are?' Willow turned to him.

'Her husband. Ian.'

'I'm so sorry, Mr Longstaff. You shouldn't have been asked to wait for so long without any information, but it's hard in the islands when we have so few officers. I'm so sorry about the death of your wife.' Willow looked for a reaction. None came. His face was blank. He was the sort of man who wouldn't show emotion, and he'd had time to take in the information of his wife's death. Willow wished she'd been here when he'd first been told.

'How did she die?' The words were as flat and hard as slaps.

'We don't know yet. The pathologist has flown in from Aberdeen. He'll take her south tomorrow for a post-mortem.'

'Was it suicide?'

'It's impossible to say at this point.' Willow saw now that the three English people were out of their depth. They were accustomed to being in control of their lives. *They* were the ones who felt as if they were in alien territory. They'd come to Shetland expecting a great cultural experience, to meet the locals and experience the traditions. Then they'd expected that they'd all go home. They'd be full of stories to share with their friends in the smart cafes and wine bars, but like visitors to a zoo they'd be untouched by the stay. Instead when they returned to London their lives would never be the same again.

'Who are you, please?' It was the man who hadn't yet spoken. Polly Gilmour's partner. He had dark curly hair and an unfashionable beard, the sort of voice that made you think of public schools and smart universities. Polite enough, but confident that he'd be answered. His face was tanned and she wondered if he'd just come back from holiday.

'My name's Willow Reeves. I'm a chief inspector with the

Serious Crime Squad based in Inverness, and I'll be in charge of this investigation.'

'You think Eleanor was murdered?' It was the husband, aggressive now, his head thrust forward towards her. The regional accent was stronger. She wondered if he felt like an outsider in this company too.

She kept her voice calm. Grief took people in different ways. 'It's an unexplained death,' she said. 'We won't know until Dr Grieve does the post-mortem what the cause might be.'

'Where is she now?' Polly asked.

'Where she was found.' Willow turned slowly to face the woman. 'By the standing stone on the hill behind the house. She'll be moved in the morning.'

'Are you sure it's her?' It was the husband again. 'We walked that way this morning looking for her.'

'She was found by Lowrie Malcolmson,' Perez said. 'He could identify her. And if you searched along the cliff you wouldn't have seen her. She's lying in a small loch, hidden from the footpath.'

Willow thought Eleanor had probably been lying there since the early hours of the morning; even if the search party *had* looked in that area they must have missed her. On a fine Sunday in June a murderer wouldn't take time to arrange the body so carefully when there might be walkers around. 'We'll need to take detailed statements,' she said, 'but that can wait until the morning. Try to get some rest.' These people had already had time together to prepare any story. Another night would make no difference.

Out on the deck the light was fading. It was nearly midnight. Inside, Polly had lit candles on the table where they'd been sitting. Looking in at them through the window, Willow saw the English people as a beautifully composed painting. It could be a scene from a Parisian bar: Marcus Wentworth, with his dark hair and beard, leaning back on his chair to one side of the table, faced by the woman whose hair looked silver in the candlelight. The clutter of bread and fruit on the white cloth. And staring out, squat and brooding, the dead woman's husband. What might the title be? *Three Friends*. Except, Willow thought, that Eleanor had been the person who had held the friends together and now they were almost three strangers, caught up in their own preoccupations.

Chapter Nine

GEORGE MALCOLMSON DIDN'T LIKE CHAOS. He'd been a keeper at the Muckle Flugga Light until it had been automated in 1995 and that had suited him well. Lighthouse work was all about routine. There were seasons for painting and seasons for maintenance. A time for being sober, when you were on duty, and a time for drinking, during the month onshore. The helicopter had brought them to the rock for their shift every four weeks and had taken them away at the end of it, as long as the weather allowed. George had always been more upset about being grounded onshore than about being stranded on the rock. In Muckle Flugga the keepers had worked in threes. If you had two men on their own in a small space that could be the recipe for disaster – for ill will, fighting and madness. George had a reputation as a peacemaker because he was controlled and never lost his temper. The other men had liked to work with him. He was calm, methodical.

The patterns and rituals of his lighthouse life had made him superstitious. It had pleased him that the rock was the most northerly station in the UK. There was clarity about the fact and that gave it special significance. He still thought that three was a lucky number, didn't whistle in a boat and sometimes planted his crops at full moon – he knew the power of the tide.

Now he sat in the bar of Springfield House with a pint on the table in front of him. His house at Voxter was in chaos because a woman, a friend of his son, had died. He tried to work out what might have been behind the death. George hated random tragedy and looked for patterns here too; for whatever could lie behind Eleanor Longstaff's dying. He couldn't imagine that anything they'd done could have led to the woman being killed, but it was a difficult time and he couldn't be certain. Lowrie had been influenced by the woman when he was a student, but surely all that nonsense was long finished. George went over and over the events of the previous day in his head, searching for a reason, for any small episode that might explain what had happened.

His wife couldn't understand his need to organize his life into patterns and rhythms and he no longer tried to explain his obsession to her. Grusche would have liked more children, but he'd known that three was a good number for a family and had made excuses to stop after Lowrie was born. He'd tried to discuss his worry that another child might not be healthy, that she was getting on in years and he feared for her safety too, but she'd laughed at his anxiety. In the end, though, she'd stopped trying to persuade him. He could be stubborn and his wife had had to come to terms with what she called his ridiculous superstitions. And she was so close to Lowrie that perhaps she realized that another child might feel left out.

All the strangers in Voxter and the break in his routine had made George jittery. The fuss of the hamefarin' had been disruptive enough, but he'd been prepared for that. It was the death of the woman with the dark hair and the flashing eyes that had disturbed him. If he'd stayed in the house he'd likely have taken more drams than were good for him and that would have got him into bother, so he'd mumbled an excuse and come here, driving very carefully up the track because he suspected he might still be a little drunk from the night before. He'd been told that Mary Lomax had gone south and so there'd be no police officer to stop him, but he didn't want an accident. That would only provide another reason for his wife to be angry with him. He loved Grusche and he didn't want to hurt her.

Then Sandy Wilson, the young detective from Whalsay, arrived in the bar and George had felt uncomfortable all over again. He got up to leave when he heard the man say that his team were looking for accommodation in Springfield. Suddenly there were too many associations with the past, with this building, and George wasn't quite sure what to make of them. Driving slowly back to Voxter, he wished again that the lighthouses had never been automated, that he was back with his old life of whitewashing the tower and polishing the lenses, of taking his shifts with his pals. Of returning each month to his exotic foreign wife and his growing son. Back then his world was much simpler.

Chapter Ten

WILLOW WAS SURPRISED BY THE OPULENCE of their temporary accommodation. Sandy had found rooms for them in a hotel just south of Meoness. The house was Georgian, large and very grand, beautifully restored with period furniture and paintings. Peerie Lizzie had grown up here, not far from the cliff where Eleanor's body was found, and she'd drowned in the voe, the inlet that cut into the land from the sea. The legend was that she'd been caught out by the tide in a thick fog. Now it was the darkest part of the night, the stars were out and the water reflected a sliver of moon. The house stood on a slight rise and had a view of water and, in the distance, the standing stone, breaking the line of the horizon. Lizzie's father had been an English laird and now it was mostly English tourists who pretended to be masters of their island universe, or at least this house and its surrounding garden. Locals came here too, but to the public bar that had been built in the old stables at the back of the house, and on special occasions to eat in the dining room.

Sandy was apologetic. 'It's a bit pricey, but everywhere else was full. I got them to give us a discount.'

Willow could see that he was uncomfortable in this house, overwhelmed by its grandeur. 'Hey, it's fab. Really convenient and enough space for us to set up a base if we need to. Good choice!'

It was past midnight and they had the lounge to themselves. The owners had left food for them in the kitchen, and Sandy brought in trays of sandwiches wrapped in cling film and a plate of cakes and biscuits. Willow had been given a double bedroom. It had brocade curtains, a huge ornate mirror and delicate chairs that looked as if they would snap under her weight. She'd always been clumsy and had a horror of breaking things. She'd dumped her holdall there and pulled out a bottle of the island malt whisky that always reminded her of home. She'd brought some to the islands with her when she was last in Shetland and had thought it might be the start of a good tradition.

In the lounge they switched on a couple of table lamps and began to eat. Willow found glasses in a sideboard and poured out the whisky. James Grieve raised his glass to her. 'I've spoken to the funeral director. We'll get the body south on tomorrow evening's ferry.'

'And you really have no idea about the cause of death?'

She always felt untidy and awkward in comparison to him. Unsophisticated and gawky. She suspected that he regarded her with amused resignation, as if he saw her as an example of how the police service had deteriorated in the time he'd been working as a forensic pathologist.

'Are you asking me to speculate, Chief Inspector?'

'I wouldn't dare, Doctor.'

He laughed. 'If I were a betting man I'd guess that we'll find some form of blunt-force trauma on the back of her head.'

'And that's why she was posed in that way?' Willow was talking almost to herself. 'So she still looked perfect.'

'Ah, that's psychology or some other magic, and beyond my area of competence.' The small man drained his glass. 'I just can't see any other cause of death until we move her.' He stood up. 'I'm away to my bed. I'll see you bright and early in the morning.'

Sandy Wilson seemed to have been drowsing throughout the conversation and he stood up and left the room too. Willow reached out and tipped a little more whisky into Perez's glass and then into her own. 'So how have you been, Jimmy?' She thought she wouldn't have had the nerve to be so personal without a drink inside her. 'And how's Cassie?'

'She's well,' he said. 'Fewer nightmares at least.'

'And are you sleeping better these days?' When she'd last been in Shetland Perez was still on sick leave, depressed and struggling to survive after the death of Cassie's mother.

'I'm fit for work,' he said quickly. 'Signed off the sick months ago.'

'You've always been fit for work, Jimmy. I've never been teamed with a better detective. But that wasn't what I asked you.' She should have been tired, but her brain was still fizzing. It was almost like having jet lag. Two island groups and you'd think they'd be similar, but arriving in Shetland she always felt that she was in another, more distant country.

He shrugged, a kind of apology for being so sensitive. 'There are good days and bad days. More good now.'

'And you're OK with working on this? Eleanor Longstaff

would be about the same age as Fran when she died.' She looked at him, wondering if she'd overstepped the mark again, trespassed into his personal grief.

'Yes,' he said and smiled at her. 'There'll be no tantrums this time, I promise. I'll behave myself.'

Willow wasn't sure how to answer that. They stood and climbed the impressive stairs and at the top turned to go their separate ways.

The next morning she returned to Sletts. Perez's colleague Mary was still there. She'd made up a bed for herself in a small box-room that had been advertised in the holiday brochure as being ideal for children. 'It was quiet all night,' she told Willow, 'but I'm not sure how much sleep they had. They all look exhausted this morning.'

'Where are they?' The house seemed empty. 'Are they out?'

'No, they're having breakfast outside. Not quite sure why when there's a perfectly decent table in here. But they're English. A thing about fresh air maybe. I guess they don't have so much of that in London.'

Willow found them on the deck. They were arranged much as they had been the night before, with Polly and Marcus on either side of the white picnic table and Ian in the middle, staring out at the water. She thought he was built like a bull, with all the weight in his shoulders and neck. His legs and feet were almost dainty.

'We don't know what to do,' Polly said. 'We were thinking that we might go home.'

'That's what *you* were thinking.' Ian Longstaff's words were brutal, even cruel. It was as if he despised the woman. 'I'm staying here until I know what's happened.'

There was a moment of shocked silence. 'Then we'll stay too,' Polly said. She seemed close to tears. 'Obviously. We won't leave you here on your own.'

Ian put his head in his hands. 'I'm sorry,' he said. 'That was rude. But I can't think straight. Everything's so crazy and out of control. We came for a party, and now Eleanor's gone.'

To Willow the words didn't sound entirely convincing. She'd had him down as a strong, silent type and wouldn't have thought it was his style to apologize.

'We'd be grateful if you'd stay for a couple of days,' she said mildly, 'until we have more information about Eleanor's death. We've set up a base in Springfield House on the island here and I'd like to start taking statements there this morning, if that suits you. You haven't made any other plans?'

'I keep expecting her to appear,' Ian said. 'Like those ghosts that seemed to fascinate her in the last weeks of her life. She'll wander down the beach in the dress she was wearing on Saturday night, and she'll pull me by the hand and expect me to dance with her.' There was a moment of silence and then he turned to Willow. 'Of course we'll all help you if we can. Who do you want to speak to first?'

'Mr Wentworth.' She turned to the dark man. 'If you wouldn't mind, sir.' She'd thought about it on the way to Sletts and had decided that he'd be the most objective witness. He might be shocked that a woman he'd known had died, but he wouldn't be as emotional. They'd been almost strangers. 'In half an hour, if that would suit you. Would you need a lift?'

He shook his head and said he had his own car. She gave him directions, and when she left the English people were still sitting in silence.

He arrived at Springfield House at exactly the agreed time. She'd taken over the small morning room as an office. The sun shone directly in through the large sash window and the room was filled with light. There were cut flowers in a glass bowl on the mantelpiece and she felt like a Victorian lady of the manor sitting at the mahogany table. Jimmy Perez was with her, but they'd agreed that she would lead the interview. Perez seemed subdued and distracted and she wondered if he was actually sleeping as well as he'd claimed the night before. Or perhaps he was anxious about Cassie. He'd arranged for her to stay with her natural father for a few days, and Willow knew the relationship between the two men was difficult.

Marcus Wentworth sat on a yellow brocade sofa. He seemed quite at ease and not to mind the silence that followed his entrance in the room. Willow saw that as a kind of arrogance.

'Tell me how you fit into the party at Sletts,' Willow said. 'You didn't know Caroline or Lowrie well, yet you were invited to the hamefarin'.'

'I didn't know Caroline and Lowrie at all actually,' he said. 'I think Polly swung the invitation. You know how it works. *Do you mind if I invite Marcus along?* That must have been how it happened. And I was delighted. I'd never been to Shetland, and a wedding this far north was always going to be something special, wasn't it?'

'How long have you known Ms Gilmour?'

'About six months.' He paused, looked up and smiled. 'We've become very close, though. She's quite reserved and I'm only just getting to know her properly. Polly's a very gentle person, actually. I love that in her. Rather shy too. I hope you'll remember that when you talk to her. And the fact that she's just lost a very dear friend.'

Willow decided he was one of those public-school boys who never really grew up. He'd be given to sentimentality, to ideas of honour and protecting his woman. She'd gone out with an army officer once who had a similar view of the world. The relationship had been destined to fail from the start. 'How well did you know Eleanor?'

Marcus looked across to Perez. 'I explained to your colleague that I was very much the outsider of the group. The four of us had dinner a couple of times, and of course we spent time chatting on the ferry from Aberdeen. She seemed lovely, but she was Polly's best friend, so I was disposed to like her.'

There was a pause. Willow wondered why she'd taken such a dislike to the man. Perhaps it was just because he reminded her of a former lover and she should learn to be more objective. 'Tell me a little bit about yourself, Mr Wentworth. What do you do for a living?' She made her voice warm to compensate for the antipathy.

'I run my own tour company. Specialist travel to North Africa and the Middle East for people who want to stray off the beaten track, but are a little nervous about doing it on their own.' He paused. 'Sorry, that sounds like a sales pitch. I took a gap year before university and got the travel bug. Worked for other people for a while, then I set up for myself. I don't need to advertise these days. Most of my work comes from word-of-mouth recommendation. I specialize in elderly Americans.

Very wealthy elderly Americans.' He gave her a quick grin, but she didn't respond.

'How did you meet Ms Gilmour?' Willow thought they made an odd couple: the rangy tour leader and the quiet librarian.

'She came on one of my holidays. Morocco. Taroudant and the Atlas Mountains. The rest of the group had an average age of seventy and didn't want to wander much from the hotel pool or the minibus, so we spent a lot of time together. She's a kind woman.' He looked up suddenly. 'Kindness is very attractive, don't you think?'

Willow didn't know how to answer that. She was beginning to feel impatient, but she was aware of Perez in the corner. His skill was patience. Letting a silence stretch until it was filled by a witness.

And eventually Marcus continued talking. 'She's not my usual type actually. I tend to go for girls who are more extrovert. Perhaps more like me. But something about Polly has got under my skin. I even took her to meet my mother a couple of weeks ago. Mother usually hates my girlfriends, but they got on like a house on fire. Perhaps it's about time I considered settling down.' He paused, suddenly embarrassed, and gave a little laugh. 'Sorry, you don't want to know all about my love life. But I was pleased when Polly asked me to this wedding. I thought she must like me. I mean, you wouldn't want to spend a whole week with someone if you couldn't stand their company. Would you?' This time it was Marcus who waited for the silence to be filled.

Perez spoke. 'What did you make of the relationship between Ian and Eleanor?'

Marcus seemed startled by his question, almost as if he'd

forgotten that the Shetlander was in the room. 'Oh, I hadn't known them long enough to have an opinion.'

'They're your partner's two best friends. You'd have discussed it, surely. Especially as Eleanor had been going through a hard time.'

'I don't think Ian was Polly's friend,' Marcus said carefully. 'They don't have much in common. He's very ambitious, very driven. *She* treats her work as a vocation. I'm sure she'd do it even if she wasn't being paid.'

'That doesn't quite answer my question,' Perez said. 'If your partner was ambivalent about Mr Longstaff, all the more reason for you to discuss him.'

Marcus looked up sharply. 'I don't think Ian killed Eleanor, if that's what you're implying. They were a couple who enjoyed drama. The excitement of falling out and making up. Polly isn't like that. She couldn't understand it. She had a very safe and secure childhood. Her parents have probably never rowed since they were first married. Not in her presence at least. We tend to give a moral weight to the things with which we're most comfortable, don't you think?'

Willow found herself staring at him. She'd first thought him stupid, a public-school buffoon straight out of Wodehouse. Now she wondered how she could have reached that opinion.

'Do you have any other insights into Polly's friends?' Perez asked. 'Lowrie and Caroline, for example. What did you make of them?'

'I only saw them at their wedding and then at the party!' Marcus said. 'They seemed at ease with each other. At home. It occurred to me that they might settle in Shetland. And they both seemed very fond of Eleanor. I can't imagine either of them would have wanted to hurt her.'

'The night Eleanor disappeared,' Willow leaned forward across the table, 'did you leave the house for any reason?'

'Of course not. Why would I?'

'You're as far north as you can get in the UK and it's midsummer. That makes people behave strangely. And you like wild places. Perhaps you took the opportunity to explore on your own.'

'I was tired,' he said. 'Too tired to wander around on my own. And I can sleep anywhere. I wouldn't be able to work as I do if I couldn't drop off in planes, in a camp in the bush, in strange hotels. The light doesn't bother me. I slept very well.'

'And Polly?'

'Ah, Polly's quite different. She takes sleeping tablets when she travels away from home. She worries about being shattered the next day. She is rather a worrier altogether, I'm afraid. I'm hoping I'll cure her of that. But when she takes the pills she doesn't stir.'

Chapter Eleven

POLLY HATED BEING IN THE HOUSE with Ian. He'd shut himself in the room that he'd shared with Eleanor, but even through the walls she sensed his desperation and imagined a suppressed rage, pictured him pacing up and down across the stripped wooden floor. She thought she should offer him some comfort, but was nervous about approaching him. Once Marcus had left to give his statement to the police officers she made a pot of coffee and sat outside.

A young girl came onto the beach. The girl carried a bucket and a spade; she took off her socks and shoes, squatted on the sand and began to dig. Very tidily and with concentration. She seemed old enough to be at school and Polly wondered what she was doing there. Perhaps she was on holiday with her parents, though there was no adult with her. In London it would be a matter of concern to see a child alone, but here perhaps it would be less unusual. It was only when the girl stood up and ran towards the sea that Polly recognized her as the child who'd been dancing on the sand on the night of the hamefarin'. There was the same long hair and skinny limbs.

But this time, instead of the white dress, she wore a red pinafore printed with blue butterflies over a blue blouse. It still looked a little old-fashioned and formal for the beach. For a moment Polly couldn't believe her eyes. It was almost as if she'd started to believe in Eleanor's notion of the girl as Peerie Lizzie.

She ran into the house to get her jacket. Away from the shelter of the building there was a breeze that felt cold to her, though the child seemed oblivious to the chill. When she reached the shore the girl was still there, but walking away from her towards the Meoness community hall. Perhaps an adult was waiting for her there. She seemed to have covered a considerable distance, though she stopped occasionally to pick up a shell or a piece of driftwood, before dropping it into the bucket. Polly hurried after her without any real idea what she would do if she caught up with her. What would she say to the girl's parents if they were waiting for her? *My dead friend thought your daughter was a ghost.*

The girl turned away from the water and took the path from the beach. Polly thought she would catch up with the child when she got to the road. She would surely stop to put on her socks and sandals, and then Polly could pass her and make a friendly comment that might lead to a conversation. Perhaps she lived in one of the houses along the street between Sletts and the hall. Polly realized that she wanted to confirm Eleanor's account of what had happened on the afternoon before she died. Suddenly it seemed overwhelmingly important to prove that her friend hadn't imagined the girl on the beach and her apparent disappearance into the sea.

A sandy path ran beside the Meoness hall and joined the street by the telephone kiosk. Polly came to the corner of the hall and had a view of the road in both directions. She'd expected to find the child there, sitting on the verge, cleaning her feet, but there was no sign either of the child or of any waiting adults. Polly hadn't heard a car. The girl had completely disappeared from view.

There were two houses on the road that led back to Sletts. Polly walked fast, peering into each building, hoping to catch a glimpse of the girl inside. Lack of sleep and confusion about Eleanor's death were making her question her own judgement. It was as if the silver light of the simmer dim was seeping into her brain, drowning her reason. Had she imagined the girl with the bucket and spade, the dancing child at the wedding party? The first building was single-storeyed, modern, but built to the same pattern as the older homes on the island: a storm porch in the front, with rooms to either side. On the grass to the back of the house there was a climbing frame with a swing attached to it. A rotary washing line had a pair of men's jeans hanging from it. This was a family home. The obvious explanation was that the girl had hurried along the road and gone inside. Polly thought that she'd overreacted, running out of Sletts and chasing down the beach. The girl must have noticed her and might even have thought she posed some kind of danger. News of Eleanor's death would have got out by now and children might have been told to be wary of strangers. Perhaps that was why the girl had disappeared so quickly. What could she do now? Eleanor would have knocked at the door and charmed the residents so that they'd have invited her in, made tea for her and laughed when she explained that she'd thought the child might be a spirit. But Polly was more timid.

Her phone rang. She'd checked it occasionally, but there'd been no signal. It was Marcus, apparently frantic.

'Where are you?' Anxiety made him sound almost angry.

'I've just come out for a walk.' She turned her back on the house where the child might live. 'I felt locked up in that house. Like it's a prison.'

'There's a murderer out there.' He was almost stuttering. She was surprised. She'd thought that she suited him because she was so undemanding and had made an effort to be kind to the mother he so obviously worshipped. She hadn't thought he cared for her so much. Why would he, when everyone adored him. He could choose from anyone She loved *him* with a passion that took her breath away and shocked her, but had never imagined that the emotion might be reciprocated. 'You could have put yourself in danger. Where are you? I'll come and meet you. The detectives want to take your statement.'

She wondered briefly if that was why Marcus was so disturbed: she'd inconvenienced the detectives. But he wasn't the sort of person to be concerned about that sort of thing. He didn't usually care what people thought of him.

She told him she would meet him on the road and continued her walk. The next house was much older, dilapidated. The roof was made from turf and she thought nobody could live there. There was an out-house attached, with broken windows, and the garden was overgrown with long weeds. But as she walked past she thought she saw a white face staring out at her. The glass was so grubby she couldn't make out any other details, and as soon as she saw it, it vanished. Then she saw Marcus's car approaching.

Polly didn't mention her chase across the shore. She would

have looked foolish. When she climbed into the passenger seat beside him he took her hand and gripped it tight. 'You made me so worried,' he said. 'Don't ever do that again.'

He dropped her at Springfield House and said he would wait for her in the car outside; he had a book. Polly thought that he too was finding the atmosphere at Sletts, Ian's grief and his fury unbearable. It seemed to her that this tall, symmetrical house, so out of place on the bare island, was very similar to the place where Marcus had grown up. He'd taken her there about a month before. She'd expected him to have been brought up somewhere grander than her own parents' home, of course. She'd imagined a detached house in a leafy suburban street – stockbroker belt, with a local golf course and perhaps a view of the Thames. But his family home was even more distinguished: a small manor house set in a couple of acres of its own grounds, a mini-version of the National Trust properties she'd been dragged to as a child. As Marcus had opened the door to let her in she'd heard her own mother's voice in her head, the same words that had been spoken at every visit to a new stately home: *Mind, lass, this would take a bit of cleaning.* Instead there had been *his* mother, very gracious, offering tea in the drawing room. And as she'd found herself flattening out her accent and taking care not to use dialect words, it had felt like a betrayal, though her parents had always wanted her to get on and would have been as proud as punch to see her there as a guest.

The two police officers – the tall, scruffy woman and the dark, still man – were waiting for her in a sunny room at the front of the house. They offered her coffee from a Thermos jug and home-made biscuits. It felt a bit like the interview she'd had for the job at the Sentiman Library, although then the people asking the questions had been elderly trustees, eccentric and wanting her to do well.

'Sorry to take you through all these details again.'

Polly hadn't caught the woman's name when they'd first been introduced and felt too embarrassed to ask now. She loved her work in the library because there she avoided the small humiliations that had seemed to make up her life before she was appointed to the post. She wondered how other people faced them. Marcus was so confident that he sailed through life convinced that everybody loved him. Now she smiled and said that it was perfectly fine and she realized why they had to ask.

'You and Eleanor have been friends for a long time,' the detective said.

'Since our first day at college. I'm not quite sure how we got on so well. We were very different. I was so scared – the first one of my family ever to have gone to university. And she took it all in her stride, a star in the University Dramatic Society from the first audition, universally popular. I'm not sure how I would have survived that first year without Eleanor and Caroline.'

'She confided in you?'

Polly thought about that. 'Certainly she used to. Boys and affairs, and worries about work. I was never any competition, you see. Once she married Ian, of course we didn't see quite as much of each other.'

'And she had him to confide in then.' The detective smiled. It hadn't been quite a question, but still Polly felt compelled to answer.

'Yes, I suppose she did.'

'Or perhaps you don't think Ian was as sympathetic about Eleanor's problems as you would have been?' The female detective smiled again. And waited.

Polly felt herself blushing. 'A miscarriage is sometimes difficult for a man to understand,' she said. 'Eleanor had a horrible experience, especially the second time.'

'And she talked to you about it?'

'I went round to her house as soon as I heard.' Polly remembered the evening. It had been raining. The sort of monsoon rain that got her drenched as soon as she left the car, and bounced off the pavements and spilled over the gutters. Ian had opened the door to her and at first she'd thought he wouldn't let her in, that he'd keep her waiting, soaking, on the doorstep, but he'd stood aside eventually. Eleanor had been in her dressing gown on the sofa. No make-up and looking old, so in the first instant Polly had thought that Cilla, Eleanor's mother, had been sitting there. She looked up and Polly saw that she'd been crying.

'Oh, Pol, it was *horrible*. I had to give birth to it. The pain of labour and nothing to show at the end.'

'She was upset,' the detective said. Another almost-question interrupting the memory.

'Of course she was upset.' Polly knew she was being waspish. 'She'd carried the baby through the difficult, dangerous time. She'd allowed herself to believe that everything would be fine. She'd had a scan and knew that it would be a girl, and had started designing a fancy nursery. She was enjoying being pregnant. Then suddenly, without any warning, there was no child. At least there was a child, but it was dead.'

'So no wonder she fantasized about seeing little girls disappearing into the sea.'

'No!' Polly was becoming outraged on her friend's behalf. She paused for a moment. 'I'm sorry, what's your name?'

The woman seemed unfazed. 'Reeves. Chief Inspector Willow Reeves.'

'Then let me explain, Chief Inspector Reeves. Eleanor was depressed after the miscarriages, but she wasn't psychotic. She wasn't seeing strange images or hearing voices. There *was* a girl on the beach. She didn't disappear into the sea, but she was dancing on the beach. I saw her at the party in the last of the light, just as Eleanor had described her. And again this afternoon, playing on the sand. So she was no figment of Eleanor's imagination.'

There was a silence. Motes of dust floated in a shaft of sunlight. In the corner Inspector Perez was writing notes. After her outburst the room seemed very peaceful. Polly fought back the desire to apologize for overreacting.

'Last night,' Willow said, 'did you leave the house for any reason?'

Polly shook her head.

'You were the last person to see her alive, and she was still sitting outside?'

'Yes.' Polly looked at her and wondered if she should mention the figure she'd seen in the mist on the tideline. But then the detectives might think she was psychotic too. 'I expected Eleanor to follow me into the house.'

'But you didn't hear her? You don't know if that happened?'

'No,' Polly said. 'I didn't hear anything until I woke up the next morning.' She paused because she was embarrassed by the admission. 'I don't sleep well. Occasionally I take sleeping tablets.'

'And Mr Wentworth?' Willow seemed to be staring out of the window. 'Was he still there when you woke up?'

'Of course he was! He went to bed with me.'

'In the same bed?'

'No, there were two singles. One room was a double and the other a twin. We tossed a coin for the double, and the Longstaffs won.' Polly thought that seemed like an eternity ago. Their arrival at Sletts, bursting into the house and checking out the space. Laughing as they fought over who would get the double bed.

'So he might have left the room without you hearing. To get a glass of water perhaps, or to see the sun coming up.' The detective gave a gentle smile, the sort Polly might have given to encourage a timid reader to ask more detailed questions about the background to a story.

'I'm really not sure where you're going with this.' Polly felt a mounting anger. The trivial questions seemed to have nothing to do with Eleanor.

'I'm saying that you're assuming Mr Wentworth was in bed all night, but really we can't be certain, can we?' Willow paused. 'Any one of you could have left Sletts that night without the others knowing.'

Chapter Twelve

THE ROOM WAS HOT BECAUSE IT was in full sunlight. Perez sat in the corner listening to Willow and Polly talking and for a moment he struggled to concentrate. He was thinking about Cassie and hoping that Duncan had seen her all the way into school. Then he told himself he was being ridiculous: Cassie would be perfectly safe and he should stop being over-protective; she'd end up resenting him. He returned his focus to the woman who was being interviewed. Polly puzzled him. She was timid, so much the stereotypical librarian that it was hard to believe in a friendship between her and the exuberant film-maker. Had she felt frustrated at always being in the shadow of Eleanor, with her beauty and her powerful personality?

Perez was just about to ask the woman about her work when Willow put the question for him, as if she'd been reading his thoughts. 'What do you do for a living, Ms Gilmour?'

'I'm a librarian, with a special interest in British myths and customs. I work for the UK Folklore Society. They have a library in Hampstead that is open to the public and I run it for them.' Her voice was suddenly enthusiastic. 'I was assistant librarian in a busy public branch for a while, but that didn't suit me nearly so well.' She gave a little self-deprecating smile, so that Perez caught a glimpse of what Eleanor might have seen in her. She did have a sense of humour after all. 'I'm much better at stories than I am with people. It's my dream job.'

'Perhaps Eleanor consulted you then. About her ghosts.'

'Not really. I told her about Peerie Lizzie when we decided that we'd come up for the hamefarin'. That was when she explained that her company had been commissioned to produce a documentary about people who claimed to have experienced the supernatural. I offered to look out some material for her, but by then her staff had already made their contacts. It was clear she was more interested in contemporary sightings than in the origins of the stories.' Polly looked up and smiled. 'Eleanor never had the patience for detailed research.'

The room fell silent. Outside there was the call of an oystercatcher in the distance. Willow looked at Perez to see if he had any questions.

'Do you know if Eleanor had an affair recently?' As soon as the words were spoken he thought that he should have been more tactful. Half his mind was on Cassie still, wondering if it would seem odd if he phoned the school to check that she'd arrived there safely. Polly blinked at him as if he'd slapped her.

'No!' she said. 'I'm sure she hadn't.'

He wondered again at the uneven relationship between the women. Polly's attitude felt more like hero-worship than a friendship between equals. But perhaps that was always the way in a relationship – one person was always more dependent than the other.

'She had moral qualms about sex outside marriage?'

85

She stared at him. 'We never discussed it in those terms.'

'You think such a thing would have been impossible for her?'

'No,' Polly said at last. 'I don't suppose it would. She didn't have moral qualms about anything much. But she would have told me about it. We didn't have secrets. Not about a big thing like that.'

'When was the last time the two of you met alone?' Perez wished he'd seen the two women together when Eleanor was alive. He remembered Fran with *her* friends in London and in the islands. She'd been easy and relaxed with them all. They'd laughed and drunk too much wine and gossiped, and he was struggling to imagine this woman behaving like that. But perhaps Polly was strained because she was grieving, and he thought again that he was being unfair to her.

'Thursday evening. The day before we left London.' Polly looked up at him. 'It was to check last-minute details for the trip. Eleanor met me from the library and we walked back to my flat. I cooked her supper and we talked through the final arrangements.'

'How was she then?'

'Fine.' The answer came too quickly and he waited for her to continue. 'Really fine. Excited. About work – this documentary that she was making. It was a big deal for her company. A new departure. More popular than the stuff she'd made before, and if everything worked out it would be shown on BBC1. She was fizzing. More excited than I'd seen her for years. I thought that she'd finally moved on after losing the baby.'

'But she didn't talk about a new man in her life?'

Polly shook her head. 'I don't know where that idea has come from. Have you been talking to Cilla? She never thought

86

that Eleanor's marriage would last. She's an intellectual snob and Ian was never good enough.'

'Cilla is Eleanor's mother?'

'Yes, she's an art historian. She works for the British Museum. Very grand. A character.' She paused and Perez wondered if Cilla had considered that Polly wasn't quite good enough for her daughter too.

Later they were eating lunch in the kitchen of Springfield House. James Grieve had been fretting all morning about missing his flight and had already left. Sandy had gone with him to collect Vicki Hewitt, the CSI, so again it was just Perez and Willow Reeves sitting across a table, sharing food. Perez felt comfortable working with her, but ambiguous about the effect she had on him. Another woman in his life, even if she were a colleague, felt like a kind of betrayal to Fran. And Willow was tall and big-boned with tangled hair and scruffy clothes. Her parents were hippies living in a commune in North Uist. He'd never met anyone quite like her before.

'So what do we think?' Willow leaned forward across the table. They were eating lentil soup and home-baked bannocks. 'It must be one of the three friends, mustn't it? None of the locals would have met Eleanor Longstaff except at the wedding party. They'd certainly have no reason to kill her.' She dipped the corner of a bannock into the soup and reconsidered. 'We need to check the alibis of the Malcolmsons, of course. They've known her for years too. So our murderer must be one of those five.'

'Don't we have to be sure that Eleanor hadn't been in touch with anyone here?' Perez spoke slowly. 'I know it's unlikely, but if she'd started work on that ghost programme, she might have contacted people who'd claimed to see Peerie Lizzie. It's even possible that she set up a meeting with them.'

'At two o'clock in the morning? And then pissed them off to the extent that they'd decided to kill her?' Willow was scornful.

'It's unlikely, I know, but it would be interesting, don't you think, if Eleanor had been talking to islanders and hadn't told her husband or her friends.'

There was a moment of silence. Charles Hillier wandered through and offered cheese and fruit. When he'd bought the big house with his partner there'd been rumours. Not just about a gay couple taking on the place, but something else. Perez struggled to remember the details. Something about a celebrity past?

Charles lingered close to the table and then seemed to realize he was intruding: 'Just help yourselves. I'll make myself scarce. David's in Lerwick all day, so he won't disturb you, and I've told the guests that the morning room's out of bounds. They know better than to come into the kitchen. Health-and-safety regs. A nightmare!' He hesitated for a minute as if he was hoping they'd include him in the conversation, but when they only smiled at him he disappeared.

'So where do we go from here?' Willow cut a large slice of cheese. 'Sandy will be tied up for most of the day with Vicki, and I'd like to be at the scene when the body's removed.'

She was being thoughtful, Perez decided, keeping him away from the crime scene because he might be distressed by another sight of the body, but he made no comment. He was past the stage when he railed against people who were being kind. 'Do you want me to talk to the Malcolmsons – Lowrie's folk – this afternoon?'

'Please.' A pause. 'And someone should go to London to see Eleanor's mother and her colleagues. If Eleanor was having an affair with someone at work, I bet one of them will know. I'd ask you to go, but I understand that's tricky because of Cassie.'

'It's not necessarily a problem.' And immediately his head was full of plans. He found himself strangely excited about a trip south. 'It might even work out well. Cass can come with me and stay with Fran's parents. They'd love to see her. They miss her.'

'So you'll do it?'

He nodded.

'Oh, Jimmy Perez, I didn't know you were so keen to run away from me.' She smiled to show that it was a joke, but still he felt awkward, as if he might have offended her.

It seemed that Lowrie and Caroline had taken the ferries into Lerwick, just as Hillier's partner David had done, but Perez left a message with them to contact him when they returned. Then he tracked down Charles, who was mending a dripping tap in one of the grand bathrooms upstairs.

'Any chance I could use your PC?'

Charles showed him into the office and switched on the computer so that Perez could book his flights to London online. The screensaver was a photo of Charles onstage dressed in Victorian costume, brandishing a big saw and heading towards a barrel with a beautiful blonde inside.

'Of course, you were a famous magician!' Vague memories of watching a television show with his parents came back to Perez. His father had loved it, but Perez had found the old-fashioned showmanship embarrassing. 'Do you miss it?'

'Not now. By the time I retired it was all about being disappointed. Driving miles to an audition, only to be told that the act was outdated. Days of being scared to leave the house in case my agent called. And there's only so many ways of cutting a woman in half and making a rabbit disappear. It was time for me to give up, before all the money ran out, and let the young men take over with all that Houdini stuff. I'm too much of a coward to go in for that. Must admit that I'm enjoying this bit of melodrama, though. A bit of excitement in our dull and dreary lives, and it's not as if I knew the poor woman.'

'What brought you to Shetland?'

Charles looked up. 'David. He's always been an outdoors nut and he's been visiting this place since he was a kid. He supported me throughout my stage career. Now it was my turn. I love it. Buying this place and moving north was the best thing we ever did, though it's certainly been more work than I'd imagined.'

Charles went back to the dripping tap, and Perez phoned Fran's parents from the office landline. Fran's mother answered the phone.

'How exciting! Of course Cassie can stay, Jimmy. And you too. It'd be great to catch up.'

He said that the offer was very kind, but he'd be working and needed to stay closer to the centre of town. The couple had never said anything, but he suspected they blamed him at some level for Fran's murder. If he hadn't dragged their daughter to Fair Isle the previous autumn, then she'd still be alive. He liked them well enough, but felt awkward in their company. The guilt that he managed to keep at the back of his mind when he was working took over all his thoughts when he was with them. He booked himself a hotel close to Eleanor's office in King's Cross for the following night and went out onto the island.

It was a breezy day with a gusty wind blowing little clouds across the sun and the water in the voe into white-topped waves. On his way to the Malcolmsons' croft Perez ran through what he knew of Lowrie's parents. George had been one of the last lightkeepers at Muckle Flugga before it was automated. Perez remembered that time in the mid-Nineties. There'd been a photo of George and his colleagues, all very smart in their uniforms, in the *Shetland Times*, accompanied by tales of his life on the rock. Perez had been still at school in Lerwick then and he'd been very taken with the stories. George had moved onto his father's croft when he lost his work with the Northern Lighthouse Board. His wife Grusche was a German woman who'd come to cook in the work camps when the oil was first discovered. They'd met at a dance when George was on shore leave, and gossip had it that he married her because she didn't mind being alone when he was away at the light. He'd had other girlfriends, but they'd all wanted him to give up his work.

Perez knew Grusche better than her husband. She'd signed up to one of the art evening classes that Fran had run and the women had become friends. Occasionally Grusche had stopped overnight with them in Ravenswick, if she'd been in Lerwick for a film or a concert and had missed the ferries back to Unst. She'd just retired as cook at the island school, and she baked for Springfield House. Perez knew all these facts without having to check them. In the islands such domestic histories were known by everyone.

When Perez arrived the Malcolmsons were in the kitchen. Grusche was making bread, kneading the dough on a board on the table. She was a tall woman, with strong features, striking rather than attractive. She saw him as he passed the window and waved him to come in.

'Caroline said that you were here,' she said. 'I'm glad it's you looking after this business, Jimmy.' Her accent was German mixed with North Isles Shetland. She turned to her husband, who was in a low chair by the range, half-asleep. 'This is Jimmy Perez, Fran's man. I told you about him.' She paused. 'George didn't get much rest last night. He and the bairns were up most of the night talking about what had happened.'

Perez wondered what Lowrie and Caroline would make of being described as bairns. He held out a hand to George, who half-rose in his seat to take it. 'I need to ask some questions. Intrusive questions. You understand.'

'Of course, Jimmy. That's the work that you do. Just give me a moment.' She rolled the dough into a ball, lifted it into a cream china bowl and covered it with a clean tea towel, before setting it on the Rayburn. He wondered if she always answered for the two of them. 'Do you want tea, or are you swimming in it?'

'I'm fine.' He sat with her at the table.

She smiled. 'So, drowning in tea already, Jimmy. The Shetland way.'

'How well did you both know Eleanor Longstaff?'

'We'd met her a few times.' Grusche still seemed to do the talking for them both. 'In Durham, when Lowrie was there. And more recently when they were all living in London. They were good friends, I think. They were all at Lowrie's wedding

92

in Kent a few weeks ago and Eleanor was one of the brides-maids. Such a bonny young woman. She almost stole the show.'

'What made your son decide on an English university?' For many Shetlanders Glasgow or Stirling seemed enough of an adventure.

'Me!' She grinned. 'I'd always brought him up to believe that there was a big wide world out there for him to explore. And I'm ambitious for my son. You know these women with only children, Jimmy – how ferocious we are on their behalf! I'd planned for him to go to Oxford or Cambridge, but he thought he might be out of his depth there. Durham was a compromise.'

And George? Perez wondered. *What did he make of having his only son so far away?*

'What did you think of Eleanor Longstaff?'

'I liked her! She was full of fun, a performer. One of those people who are always acting. Entertaining. I enjoyed talking to her about art and politics.' She paused. 'But I was glad when Lowrie went for Caroline.' Another pause. 'Some people are like a rich chocolate cake, don't you think, Jimmy? You'd only enjoy them in small mouthfuls. I could never imagine Eleanor setting up home in Unst.'

'But you think Lowrie and Caroline will come back?'

'Maybe. We'd like that, wouldn't we, George?'

The man smiled from his chair. 'Yes, it'd be good to see our grand-bairns growing up. And to have some help on the croft.'

'We could make no assumptions about either of those things.' Grusche's voice was sharp. 'Not about children, or what Lowrie and Caroline would do when they were here. But I missed him when he left home and it would be wonderful to see him back.'

'Was there ever a possibility that Lowrie would settle with

Eleanor then? Did he go out with her?' Perez hadn't been told about that. Did it mean the English people were keeping information from him? Or had it happened so long ago – a brief student fling – that they'd forgotten about it? Perhaps Shetlanders had longer memories than other folk.

Grusche shrugged. 'He went out with Eleanor a couple of times. She was an attractive woman.'

George stood up and leaned his back against the range. 'Yon woman broke his heart,' he said. 'We need to be honest with Jimmy. He'll find out these things anyway. It's impossible to keep a thing like that hidden.'

'Lowrie was nineteen,' Grusche said. 'A boy. Away from home for the first time. It's not surprising that he took rejection so seriously.'

'But he came home threatening to leave the university,' George said. 'You even thought he might kill himself! You called her a witch.'

'I was overreacting,' Grusche said. 'And so was he. He found Caroline, who is sensible and not given to games.'

'But that was the sort of woman Eleanor was, Jimmy.' It seemed to Perez that George thought carefully about every word before he spoke it, that he was trying to convey a special message hidden behind the words. 'She was a generous person and warm and funny. But she wasn't very kind. She wasn't aware of anyone's pleasure but her own, and she was always after excitement.'

Perez looked at the man. He thought George had been brooding about all this since Eleanor Longstaff's body had been discovered. 'Is there anything else you think I should know?'

The man hesitated and then he shook his head. 'No. But when I heard that someone had killed her, I wasn't surprised.'

Chapter Thirteen

WILLOW REEVES WATCHED THE HEARSE from Lerwick drive away with the body, past Sletts, until it disappeared behind the Meoness community hall, where two days ago the victim had been dancing. From this distance the vehicle looked like a shiny beetle, and sunlight bounced from its black paint. Eleanor Longstaff would be in the boat south tonight and in Dr Grieve's Aberdeen mortuary tomorrow.

She turned to look at Vicki Hewitt at work. So far the crime-scene manager had found little to excite her close to where Eleanor's body had been lying. The ground was too dry for footwear marks and the heather grew right to the edge of the loch. No mud or sand. When they'd lifted the woman from the water they'd seen the blow to the head, just as James Grieve had predicted. There'd been bloodstains on the back of the expensive silk dress, spatters that had remained even though the body had been underwater for some time and the material was soaking. And there were other marks that might have been grass or soil.

'Does this mean she was killed elsewhere and carried here?

That the blood dried into the fabric before she was placed in the loch?' *If so, why? Because the place had a special significance? To make Eleanor look perfect?*

'Dragged rather than carried.' Vicki's words were muffled by her mask. She pointed to where the heather had been flattened in places, the stalks snapped. 'Not conclusive of course, because the vegetation damage could have been caused by walkers in heavy boots any time in the last couple of weeks, but it's possible, don't you think? Dragging would explain the grass stains on the back of the dress. And I don't think she was murdered very far away. I didn't see any damage to the vegetation near the stile.' She began moving in slow sweeps, bent almost double, parting the bog grasses and heather with her gloved hands. She stopped where the grass was shorter, cropped by sheep, then bent again and picked up an object so small that Willow couldn't make it out, and slipped it into an evidence bag.

'What have you got?'

'Not sure yet. Wait a minute.' Vicki continued her fingertip search and crouched again to slide a scrap into a different bag.

Willow was wearing overshoes, but she waited where she was until Vicki called to her. Here they were close to the edge of the cliff and the noise of breaking waves and the onshore breeze were suddenly exhilarating. There was sea pink and blue squill. Vicki laid the bags on the palm of her hand so that Willow could look inside.

'Torn scraps of paper.' Willow was disappointed. 'Could be anything.'

'Not ordinary litter,' Vicki said. 'Not sweet paper or crisp packet. And anyway, why tear them into pieces?'

'What then?'

'It's stiff, shiny. My guess is it was a photo.'

Willow thought about that. Who printed out photos these days? People took digital pictures and then posted them on Facebook or Twitter. 'So somebody up here tore up a photo. A fit of rage perhaps? It would be good if we could find the rest of it.'

Vicki laughed. 'With this breeze the rest will be halfway to Norway by now. These pieces were caught in the longer grass.'

Close to the cliff edge, stones – round and smoothed by the water – had been thrown up by violent storms. Some were as big as a small child, too heavy almost for a man to lift, yet during gales the tide had tossed them like marbles from the shore below. 'One of those could be your murder weapon.' Vicki stretched her hands above her head and then rubbed her aching back. 'Though if I was the killer I'd have thrown it back over the cliff, once I was done.'

'Not premeditated then.' Willow was talking almost to herself. 'The killer didn't bring a weapon with them.'

'Unless they knew these rocks were here and arranged the meeting. And the victim would have been walking away. Or turned away. This wasn't self-defence or a scrap that got out of hand.'

Willow couldn't imagine the immaculate Eleanor in a catfight. 'Would there have been blood on the killer's clothing? We've bagged what her friends were wearing that night and sent it south. No results yet.'

'Not from the original blow perhaps, but it'd be hard to avoid it if you were dragging the body and then arranging it.' Vicki frowned. 'I'll collect some samples of heather. I'd hope to find small traces of blood on the grass too, especially if the killer dragged Eleanor by her feet, in the hope of keeping themselves clean. And you'd expect the shoes and socks to be wet. You couldn't place the body so accurately without getting into the loch.'

'Unless the killer went barefoot too.' Willow paused. 'Sandy did a quick search of the area yesterday.'

Vicki snorted. 'Have you ever known a man search properly for anything? My husband's hopeless. A quick look then it's "Vicki, what have you done with my football kit?" and, like a mug, I find it for him because it's easier than getting him to do it for himself.'

'You think they'll be somewhere here then?' Willow hadn't known that Vicki Hewitt had a husband and was distracted for a moment, wondering if there were children too.

'It's possible.' Vicki was already bent double again, feeling among the boulders with gloved hands. Then she was lying flat on her stomach reaching into the holes in the sandy soil close to the cliff edge. But she found nothing and stood up and stretched again.

Willow wondered what her husband did for a living, if he didn't mind these strange call-outs to crime scenes. She herself had never found a man prepared to put up with the frequent and sudden disappearances.

'I'd get a search team in to look properly,' Vicki said, 'but if the killer had any sense the shoes would be at the bottom of the cliff and swept away by the tide by now.' She walked to the edge of the cordon and began to take off her paper suit, pushing her mask from her face so that she could talk properly.

'So the killer didn't panic,' Willow said. Out at sea a trawler was pitching and tipping over the waves. She felt slightly nauseous watching it. 'They didn't hit Eleanor over the head in a blind rage and run away. They threw the murder weapon, the cloak that she was last seen wearing and the sandals into the sea. And perhaps they tore up a photograph and scattered the pieces in the wind. Then they walked back to the road as if nothing had happened. It would have been early in the morning and already light.'

'How did the phone get to the hill by the hall?' Vicki was packing up now and had started walking down the hill with the big silver box in which she kept her equipment.

'I'm not sure. It wasn't left there to throw us off track. The murderer wanted the body found. Otherwise why not tip Eleanor over the cliff with everything else? If the body had been discovered on the boulder beach at the bottom of the headland we'd probably have put it down to an accident. She'd been drinking, after all. There were lots of witnesses to that. One head wound wouldn't show up among the others, and nobody would survive that fall.' Willow thought it would have been no further to drag the body to the cliff edge than to the loch. And it would have been easier because the grass there was so much shorter.

'Perhaps Eleanor had dropped the phone earlier in the evening?' Vicki turned to wait for Willow at the stile.

'But someone sent that email at two o'clock in the morning. What was Eleanor doing wandering around in the early hours? And why go from the stone enclosure near the hall and then walk in the opposite direction to the loch? Too many questions and nothing that makes sense.' Again Willow thought that there'd been a meeting here. It had been planned. She tried to imagine the scene. The strange half-light of early morning, Eleanor waiting, shivering perhaps, wrapping her cloak around her party clothes to keep warm. Had she dozed? Been surprised in the end by the visitor for whom she'd been waiting? Or had the murderer moved silently over the grass like one of Eleanor's ghosts and killed the woman without warning?

Later, on her way into the grand entrance hall of Springfield House, Willow bumped into Perez. 'How did you get on with the Malcolmsons?'

'It was interesting . . .' He paused, shot a glance behind him and only then did she see Ian Longstaff waiting for them in the shadows of the hall. 'But I'll explain later.'

They sat in the yellow room with its flashes of sunshine. Willow asked Perez to lead the interview; he'd already formed a relationship with the man and she could tell that Longstaff viewed her with distrust. Most of the women he knew worked in the media and were fashionable, well groomed and neurotic. They didn't have unmanageable hair or charity-shop clothes. She settled carefully on a low spindly chair out of his line of view.

'I understand that this must be difficult for you,' Perez said. 'I'm sorry.'

'You understand nothing!' Longstaff leaned forward. 'I loved Eleanor from the moment I saw her. I might as well be dead myself.'

There was a silence. Willow became aware of sounds outside the room. Curlews on the hill. The inevitable sheep. Inside, the tension became so uncomfortable that she wondered if she should intervene. Perez was an intensely private man and wouldn't explain that the love of *his* life had been murdered too. She couldn't do that, but she might ask a harmless question while Perez recovered his composure. In the end she waited. It wasn't her place to interfere.

'Of course,' Perez said at last, 'it's the guilt that's the hardest thing. The idea that you might have done something different. The rerunning of various scenarios in your head.'

Another silence before Longstaff nodded. 'I should have gone outside to fetch her in, that night after the party. I should have protected her.'

'Did she *need* protecting? Were you aware that she might be in danger? She worked in the media, and high-profile people can attract unwanted notice.' Perez's voice was so low that Willow had to listen carefully to make out the words. 'You're a sound engineer and you work in the same business. You'll understand that.'

'You think she had a stalker?' Longstaff looked up at him sharply. 'No, there was nothing of that sort. She never appeared on television herself. And she would have told me if she was getting any hassle.'

'This project she was working on – the project that seemed to trigger the . . .' Perez hesitated and seemed to be searching for the right word, 'disagreement between you, when you were drinking with your friends after the wedding party. Can you tell me a little about that? Were you working on it too, on the sound?'

'There wouldn't have been a role for me yet,' Longstaff said. 'The show was still in pre-production. Eleanor had decided on a scriptwriter, but she wasn't sure exactly what form the broadcast should take yet. She was researching stories. Intelligent, rational people who were convinced they'd seen a ghost. She said she didn't want an hour full of weirdos and loonies.'

'And she'd heard the story of Peerie Lizzie.' Perez was looking down at the water from the small window by his side, as if he expected to see the ghost of the child rising up from the sea. 'A girl who grew up in this house in the 1920s, who was drowned in a high tide and who comes back to haunt the childless.' *And drunk young men.*

Longstaff waited a beat before replying. 'Is that the story? That only the childless see her? Eleanor didn't tell me that.' Another beat. 'Or perhaps she did, but I wasn't listening. I'd begun to lose patience with her. That seems cruel now – cruel and wasteful. I'd give anything to have her back and prattling about her favourite projects.'

'There are lots of stories.' Perez gave a smile and turned slightly to include Willow. 'That's the way of ghosts.'

'I've never believed in the supernatural,' Longstaff said.

'And now?'

'Now I can see why people might *want* to believe. We're grateful for anything that might maintain that contact.'

'Had Eleanor been in touch with anyone here in Unst about Peerie Lizzie? Had she arranged to meet someone who claimed to have seen the ghost?'

Longstaff shrugged. 'She probably talked to Lowrie about it. They're old friends from her uni days. He'd be a good local contact.'

'Had she met Lowrie to discuss it? In London perhaps, when the project was still in its initial phase?'

Willow wondered where Perez was going with this. Perhaps he thought Lowrie was the man with whom Eleanor had been seen in the restaurant. But surely Caroline would have recognized her lover, even from the back in a crowded bar?

'I don't know.' Longstaff's original impatience had returned. 'And I don't know how these questions will help us find out who killed Eleanor.' He had his legs crossed and one foot was twitching, tapping the polished wooden floor in a strange Morse code.

Perez seemed unbothered by the noise, which had set Willow's nerves jangling, or by the man's words. 'Because I understand that Eleanor and Lowrie were very close when they were at university. They had a relationship, didn't they? So perhaps it would be natural for her to go to him with her questions.'

Longstaff gave a harsh little laugh. 'Nell had lots of relationships when she was at university. The way she tells it, she worked her way through the whole dramatic society. Lowrie might have thought they had a special thing going, but from her point of view he was just another recreational shag.' He paused. 'I still don't understand how this will help us find her killer.'

The foot began tapping again.

'I'm sorry to press the point,' Perez said, 'but it's important to find out if Eleanor had made any local contacts – someone she might have arranged to meet, perhaps on the night of her death.'

'She wasn't crazy enough to go wandering around in the early hours of the morning to meet a total stranger!'

'Really?' Perez gave that smile again. 'Most of us think of Shetland as a safe place. We leave our doors open and we feel happy to go out alone at night.'

'One of you killed her!'

'Really?' The question repeated itself like the chorus of a song. 'Most homicides in the UK are committed by people we know. Much more likely, I'd think, that she was murdered by one of her friends.'

Longstaff looked up sharply, but didn't answer. They sat for a moment staring at each other in silence.

The interview over, the three of them stood outside Springfield House. The breeze tugged at Willow's hair, until she pulled it out of her eyes and her mouth and tied it in a knot at the back of her head.

'I don't believe any of her friends killed her.' It was clear that Ian Longstaff had been thinking about Perez's last comment, and the words came out without warning. 'They adored her.'

Neither of the detectives answered him. They watched him climb into his large car and drive away.

They ate that night in the kitchen, while the B&B guests sat in the dining room. Charles's partner David had arrived back from Lerwick with fish from the Blydoit shop and he cooked scallops, quickly seared while they waited at the table, and followed it with a rich lamb stew. He was an intense man, very quiet and dignified. He'd taught classics in a provincial university and Willow wondered what had brought the pair together; the scholar and the stage magician seemed to have little in common. He left the casserole on the middle of the table so that they could help themselves. There was a home-made loaf and Shetland butter to complete the meal.

'The bread's Grusche Malcolmson's,' he said, on his way out of the room, unwilling to claim credit for another person's work. 'She does all our baking.' He paused. 'If anyone asks, you're our family. We're not supposed to have guests in the kitchen. Health regulations.' He gave another tight smile.

Willow gave an absent-minded nod, but she was preoccupied. Grusche was the mother of the bridegroom at the hamefarin'. Another witness. Another possible suspect. In these islands there were too many connections. It would be just the same at home in the Western Isles.

'So, Sandy.' She looked at the young man over the table. 'You got Eleanor's body onto the ferry for James Grieve. Do you have any other news for us?'

He looked like a schoolboy asked to stand up in front of the class to show what he'd learned, uncertain and flushed. 'Just confirmation of what Eleanor's friends told us. I checked with the ferry terminal and they were booked on the boat on Friday night. Two executive cabins and two cars. None of them has a criminal record. I've got details of her next of kin and her work colleagues. Her mother, Cilla, was informed of Eleanor's death yesterday. She's expecting Jimmy to visit. She'll be at home, not at work.' He paused for breath and looked up from the stew.

Willow wondered if it would be patronizing to tell him that he'd done very well and resisted the impulse. 'And you, Jimmy? Did you get anything new from Lowrie's mother and father?'

There was a moment's pause. 'Lowrie was in love with our victim when he was a student. A grand passion, apparently. He came home one holiday threatening to leave university, and his parents even worried that he might kill himself.'

'A young man being melodramatic, do you think? Or is it still significant after all this time?' Willow thought she must have been a cold and heartless girl herself, for she couldn't remember having lost sleep over a man. There were men she'd fancied and had enjoyed being with, but after a few months she'd grown impatient with them all, had made an excuse and moved on.

Perez shrugged. 'Maybe it says more about Eleanor. Perhaps she enjoyed provoking that sort of reaction.'

'So if she was having an affair,' Willow said, 'it had less to do with needing comfort after the miscarriage than with putting some excitement and danger into her life.'

'Perhaps.' He considered the idea. 'Or needing to be loved. When I've spoken to her family and her friends in London I might have more idea what was going on.' He paused. 'Do you think it might be worth trying to trace this child that Eleanor saw on the beach the afternoon she died, and that Polly saw at the party?'

'Are you believing in ghosts now too, Jimmy?' Willow kept her voice light. She hoped he wasn't going all flaky on her.

'I wondered if she might be a possible witness,' he replied. 'If Eleanor wandered out to look for her.'

'Good point.' She nodded towards Sandy. 'Will you look into that while Jimmy's on his jaunt to the south? See if you can track down Peerie Lizzie for us.'

She'd meant it as a joke, but she noticed that Jimmy didn't laugh.

Chapter Fourteen

POLLY HAD NEVER DEALT WELL WITH STRESS. Sometimes she felt fragile, like one of her mother's favourite porcelain vases, as if it would only take a loud noise or an unintentional jolt for her to crack, or to topple and smash into pieces. She'd never been to see a doctor about her anxiety and had rather admired Eleanor for having submitted to treatment, even for a short while. There seemed such a stigma to a psychiatric hospital, even the private places full of celebrities struggling with addiction.

The worst time had been straight after she'd graduated. An inner-city public library where youths had gathered round the computers as if they were in an amusement arcade full of gaming machines. Where the reading-group members had demanded edgy contemporary fiction instead of the classics that Polly offered them. Her boss had been a loud woman who despised weakness and pretension and accused Polly of both. She'd had grey teeth and body odour and they'd disliked each other immediately.

It was Eleanor who'd seen the advertisement for the

Sentiman job in the *Guardian. You like all this strange stuff, Poll. Why don't you go for it?* Another reason to be grateful to her.

They were gathered in Sletts now, and Polly could feel the tension as pressure on her forehead and squeezing against her eyes. Mary Lomax was no longer camping out with them, but the three felt constrained, choosing every word carefully as if there was still someone listening in. The landline rang. For a moment they stared at it. Were they expecting another message from the dead Eleanor? Polly reached out and answered it. It was Caroline, her voice normal, almost cheery. Again it seemed strange to Polly that Caroline could be so cool and restrained when her best friend was dead. 'Grusche wonders if you'd like to come to dinner here in Voxter? Get you all out of the house for a bit.'

Walking down the track towards the hall they found that they were chatting freely for the first time all day. About Willow and Perez, what odd police officers they were and nothing like the detectives you'd find in London, comparing notes on the interviews in Springfield House. And about Eleanor. Snatches of anecdote and pieced-together memories of the times they'd spent together. Even Ian seemed to be able to escape his anger for a moment. At one point in the conversation he stopped in the middle of the road. 'The thing about Eleanor was that she could be *so* sodding annoying.' Marcus and Polly gave a surprised laugh of agreement and they all continued on their way.

Walking past the houses, the old, apparently derelict croft and the newbuild family home, Polly was tempted to say something about the little girl. *I think Nell's ghost lives in one of these. I saw her playing on the beach. Not a ghost at all.* But in the end she stayed silent. It would have felt disrespectful to

Eleanor's memory, and she didn't want to remind the others that the last hour they'd shared with their friend had been odd and a little embarrassing. She sneaked a look in through the windows as she went past, though. Still it was impossible to see anything through the mucky glass of the old house; she thought there might be a faint warm light in the corner of the room – the embers of a fire perhaps. And, looking at the chimney, there was a drift of smoke, the smell of peat. No other sign of life.

There was more washing on the line of the new house. Casual women's clothes and a row of baby jumpsuits and tiny cardigans. Nothing that might belong to a girl aged about ten. A pushchair stood in the front porch. Polly lingered while the others walked on. It was still a fine day and the window was open. From inside the house came the sound of a radio playing country music, then of a baby crying and a woman's soothing voice.

In the Malcolmsons' kitchen there was the smell of meat cooking, and Polly was sure there'd be the awkwardness of reminding everyone that she was vegetarian and then a scramble while they found something she could eat. The inevitable omelette or lump of old cheese. But it seemed that Caroline and Lowrie had explained, and Grusche pulled out of the oven an open tart with leeks and mushrooms and home-grown chives, which she left to stand on top of the Rayburn while drinks were poured and the table was laid.

For a while during the meal Eleanor wasn't mentioned at all. Ian and George were drinking steadily, both intent, Polly thought, on getting drunk. All she knew of George was that he'd once been a lightkeeper. Lowrie had talked of growing up with the ritual of his father disappearing for four weeks out of eight. 'The Lighthouse Board flew him out to Muckle Flugga in the helicopter and sometimes the weather was so wild that he couldn't get home.'

'That must have been tough,' she'd said. She and Lowrie were both only children, and her father had doted on her. She'd looked forward to him coming home each day from the factory where he was a supervisor, the sound of his key in the door. She couldn't imagine having grown up without him.

'Not at all.' Lowrie had laughed. 'My mother spoilt me rotten. And it wasn't so unusual then. Lots of kids' parents were at sea or worked on the rigs. It was almost easier when he was away. He's found it hard to adjust to life with more than two other people. If he seems a bit odd just now, that's the reason for it.'

Polly wondered if George had developed the habit of heavy drinking when he worked on the rock. There'd surely be no drink allowed in the lighthouse, so perhaps he'd made up for it when he was at home and that had formed a ritual too. Lowrie's parents seemed a strange couple to her. Grusche was cultured. She knew about books and films and talked about her weekly treat – a trip to the matinee movie at the Mareel arts centre in Lerwick. 'It's not all blockbusters from the US, you know. We get our share of art house too. I can't wait until I'm a pensioner and then I'll get a free cup of tea at the afternoon viewings.' George seemed entirely absorbed by the work of the croft and had no interest in any life away from the islands. It had always been Grusche who'd come to visit Lowrie when he'd been at university, dragging him off to plays and art exhibitions, exhausting him with her energy. Polly could only remember seeing George once. He'd been there for Lowrie's graduation, uncomfortable in an old suit that didn't quite fit, while Grusche had been splendid in a dress that she'd made herself. And as soon as the ceremony was over George had taken them all to a pub and stood a round of drinks for the whole crowd. Her own parents had stood awkwardly beside her; it had been the first time they'd been in a bar for years.

It was Grusche who first brought up the subject of Eleanor's murder. 'You're very lucky to have Jimmy Perez working on the case. He's a good man. I knew his girlfriend, Fran. She was a fine painter.' The table fell silent and everyone looked at her. She seemed not to notice, though, and began to clear the plates. Then she paused. 'Of course Jimmy will understand what pain you're going through. Fran was murdered too.'

Then there was another silence until Grusche dished out the pudding, a fool made with rhubarb from the garden and Shetland cream, and Marcus shifted the mood by beginning one of his stories – this one about walking through the desert in the Yemen with an elderly American botanist.

Polly tuned out Marcus and watched the others instead. She'd heard the story before and she'd always been an observer. This felt like a traditional family meal, with George and Grusche as the parents. It occurred to Polly for the first time that most of her friends had been only children, in one way or another. Caroline had a much younger sister, and Eleanor had half-brothers whom she rarely saw, but Marcus and Ian had no siblings. Like her. *We made our own family.* She wondered what relevance that might have had to Eleanor's murder.

Time moved on, but outside it was still light. Grusche made coffee and the men used that as an excuse to get out the whisky. They'd shifted seats so that they were all at one end of the table, the bottle between them. Polly caught Marcus's eye and he winked at her. She wondered if he saw this tragedy as just another of his adventures, a story he'd tell to his customers when they'd made camp in the mountains somewhere and were sitting around the fire as darkness fell. A tale about the time he went north to celebrate a wedding and ended up as a suspect in a murder inquiry. Because she realized now that they were all suspects.

At the women's end of the table Caroline was talking about their plans of moving to the islands.

'You're still thinking of that then,' Grusche said. 'I wondered if Eleanor's murder might have put you off.'

'There's a lot more violence in London than there is here!' Caroline's voice was matter-of-fact and Polly wondered if Caroline was capable of grieving for Eleanor at all; if she herself was the only person who cared. Even Lowrie, who had been so close to Eleanor at one time, now seemed engrossed in a conversation with his father. Of course Caroline worked with statistics and objective proof. Emotion seemed to have no place in her life in any situation. Caroline went on, 'In fact, this has made me more determined that this is the right decision. When dreadful things happen it's good to have a close community around you. Of course I have wonderful friends like Polly in London, but somehow that's not quite the same.'

And so I'll soon have lost all my companions. My surrogate family. Polly felt suddenly like crying. She loved Marcus and when she looked at him now, holding the men spellbound with another traveller's tale, she was almost faint with longing, but that contact would never be the same as her relationship with her old girlfriends.

Perhaps Caroline realized that she'd been tactless because she said, 'And of course Polly will visit. Every summer during the long days. She'll have her own room in our new house in the islands.'

Polly smiled, but she'd already decided that she never again wanted to come back to Shetland.

'So have you made any practical decisions?' Grusche asked. 'Do we have a time-frame here, for example?'

Polly thought Grusche was delighted at the notion of having her son home and was desperate for details, but didn't like to seem too excited. She didn't want to come across as a pushy mother-in-law.

'We went into some estate agents while we were in Lerwick today.' It sounded a bit like a confession, and Caroline looked over to Lowrie. Perhaps they'd decided to keep this news secret and she was hoping to get some tacit permission. But Lowrie was talking to Ian now and didn't see her. Her voice was suddenly shrill with excitement. 'There's a house in Vidlin that looks absolutely perfect. Sheltered, and plenty of garden for horticulture; the possibility of buying a field next door. And compared to London, prices are cheap! We went to look at it on the way home this afternoon. Grusche, it's gorgeous. I loved it.'

How can you be so happy? Polly thought. *Eleanor's dead.*

'So you'll put in a bid then?' Grusche looked at Polly to explain. 'In Scotland that's mostly how house-sales work. Sealed bids.'

'No. Actually,' Caroline took a deep breath, 'they were happy to take an offer. And they accepted it. It's been on the market for a while, so as long as we can sell our place reasonably quickly – and there's a colleague of Lowrie's who's been coveting the house since we first moved in – we should be here by Christmas.' She gave a little laugh, then put her hand

over her mouth as if she realized at last that the excitement
was inappropriate.

*What is it that Caroline's so eager to escape? Her work? London?
Me?* Polly felt the resentment burn and grow.

'Oh, Caroline!' Grusche gave a mock-pout. 'You dreadful
woman. What will I do now when I want to visit London for
a fix of culture? Where will I stay?'

'With me, of course,' Polly said. 'When Marcus is away on
his travels I have the flat all to myself and it would be lovely
to see you.'

Grusche clapped her hands. 'So there we are. All settled.'
She called across the table to her husband. 'Listen, George.
Have you heard? Some good news at last, after these terrible
days.'

Polly looked at Ian, expecting him to share her anger, but
he looked up from his glass and seemed not to care that
Eleanor had been forgotten in the conversation about the
newly-weds' move north.

When they walked back to Sletts the sun was on the horizon
and the shadows were so long that they made the road almost
dark. They didn't speak. It was as if they'd felt the need to be
entertaining companions in return for a fine dinner, and now
they could mourn Eleanor again in the silence of the evening.
The new house by the track was quiet, the curtains drawn,
the washing all taken in. Marcus and Ian were strolling ahead,
deep in conversation. Although they were very different person-
alities, it seemed that they'd become friends and Polly was
pleased about that. It was too dark to tell if there was smoke
coming from the chimney of the croft with the turf on the

roof. Coming closer, Polly saw there was a faint light inside. From a candle or a lamp. She crossed the grass to look in through the window. The light caught a small figure dressed in white. A child dancing, spinning like a top – her feet clad in silk slippers – fixed to a spot. Then, as Polly watched, the girl ran from the room. The draught from the door seemed to blow out the candle and everything was dark again and she couldn't believe what she'd seen.

Chapter Fifteen

GEORGE WALKED WITH HIS SON'S FRIENDS out into the still night to see them off. It had been a good evening and he was mellow and full of fine food and drink. Grusche had always been a splendid cook and he was lucky that she'd agreed to wed him. Sometimes he thought it was the life of an islander that had attracted her, rather than him as a man, but maybe after all these years that didn't matter. They made a good team and she'd brought their boy up to be a decent man. He saw the three English people to the road and stood for a moment at the gate, enjoying the peace and wondering why he felt this sense of unease.

It was good to be alone for a while after all that talk in the house about the woman who'd been killed. He couldn't pretend to be sorry that Eleanor Longstaff was dead. Lowrie had married Caroline, who was straightforward and strong. A bit bossy like Grusche, but sometimes that wasn't such a terrible trait in a woman. Sometimes women had more energy than men and encouraged them in new ventures and kept them focused on what was most important. George suspected that

Lowrie still dreamed about Eleanor, and he thought that was a bad thing. Perhaps now she was gone the couple could move on. They could buy this new grand house in Vidlin and start thinking about starting a family of their own, without the dark woman from London intruding in their lives. If Peerie Lizzie should appear to *them*, it might mean that his first grandchild was on the way.

George had grown up in Meoness. From where he stood, leaning over the gate beyond the community hall, he could see the house at Utra where his father had been born. It was almost derelict now, though it still had its turf roof. But soon the walls would crumble and folk would use the stone to repair their dykes, and all memory of what had gone on there would be lost. He thought of his life as a boy in the islands. Most of his friends had left years before. Many had become merchant seamen and had travelled the world. George could count on the fingers of one hand the times he'd left Shetland. Grusche wanted to plan a foreign holiday now that she'd retired from the school. With Lowrie back in Shetland to keep an eye on the croft when they were away, perhaps that might be possible. George thought he'd like to go to Canada to see where some of his relatives who'd joined the whaling ships had landed. Perhaps there were other Malcolmsons on the far side of the world, who still remembered Utra when lots of people lived there.

He turned and walked back towards the house. There was a little moonlight to show the path, but it wouldn't have mattered if it was dark. He knew every inch of his land and could have made his way around it blindfold. Through the kitchen window he saw that Lowrie was clearing the dishes. Caroline was at the sink, washing up. They must have persuaded

Grusche that she'd worked hard enough, because she was sitting in a chair by the Rayburn, knitting. Three people in the room. It occurred to him that, since Lowrie's marriage, there were now four in the family and that perhaps he himself had become the outsider.

Chapter Sixteen

SANDY WASN'T SLEEPING. IT WASN'T THE light night. He'd grown up in the islands and was used to the simmer dim. He was kept awake by laughter and talking just outside. His room was at the back of the house, small, the only one without its own bathroom. When he'd shown him round Charles had been apologetic. 'It's the only single in the house and there's usually a child in here. There's a door through to the adjoining room; it's a kind of family suite.' Sandy had taken it anyway and had given the better rooms to Willow and Jimmy. But it looked out on the courtyard and towards the bar, and tonight the noise seemed to go on well past normal closing time, the smokers all gathering in the yard chatting.

In the end he got up and dressed. He fancied winding down a bit, a couple of pints with people who spoke the same language as him. Jimmy Perez was a Shetlander, but since Fran's death he'd been distant and no fun at all. Sandy made his way through the quiet house. There was still a light in the hotel office. He saw it under the door. But there was no sound from inside. Outside the air was still, but cold. He let himself into the courtyard and could hear rowdy laughter, someone singing the end of a song.

When he walked into the bar there was a moment of silence. Even those who didn't recognize him would know now who he was and what he was doing there. Only three people were making the noise: a group of men in their late twenties who were kind of familiar. He ordered a pint. Draught Belhaven, not the island's bottled beer. Billy nodded, but didn't speak. Now Sandy recognized the drinkers as boys from the ferry. The most sober held up his hands.

'Did we wake you? It's Frankie's birthday and we were just having a few drinks. To celebrate, you know how it is. Sorry, pal.' He held out his hand. 'Davy Stout.'

'Will you be fit to take out the ferry early tomorrow? My boss'll be out on the first boat.' Sandy grinned to take the sting out of the words. No point coming in and throwing his weight around.

'We're all on the late shift and we'll be fine by then.' But Sandy's presence seemed to have made the group more subdued. Billy came out from the bar to collect the last glasses and wipe the tables. He looked at his watch. He expected them to be leaving once they'd finished their drinks.

'You're here investigating that holidaymaker's death,' Stout said.

'Eleanor Longstaff. She was up for Lowrie Malcolmson's hamefarin'.'

'I was there. It was a fine do. You think someone killed her?'

Sandy shrugged. 'Did you see her at the party? One of the bridesmaids. Dark hair. English.'

'You wouldn't miss her.'

'Anyone showing any special interest?'

This time the ferryman shrugged. 'She wanted people to look at her. You know the sort. Never happy without an audience. Most of the men in the room obliged.'

'Nobody gave her any hassle?' Sandy drained his glass and raised it to Billy to show that he wanted another. The barman seemed disappointed.

'Nah. It wasn't that sort of party. You've been to the hamefarin's. It was for families. Elderly relatives and bairns.'

'Did you know all the people there?' Sandy asked.

'Apart from the English folk.'

'I'm interested in a peerie lassie. Aged around ten. She was out on the beach, and her parents could have been in the hall. Do you mind who that might have been?'

The man considered and seemed to be running through possibilities in his head. 'Sorry, I can't think of anyone like that at all. But I didn't know everyone. Besides the couple's English friends, there were other relatives from the south.'

'Any lasses of that age live in Meoness?'

This time he answered more quickly. 'Nah. Some of us have bairns, but they're all boys.'

The drinkers drifted away then and Sandy was left to finish his beer alone. When he returned to his room the light in the office had been switched off.

Chapter Seventeen

PEREZ LEFT UNST THE NEXT MORNING on the first ferry to Yell. Sandy got up to see him off and watched him go, as if it was a sort of desertion. There were a couple of families on the boat, holidaymakers heading south after a spring break. Perez wondered if he'd see them again at Sumburgh. The rest were local, in cars with the blue-and-white Shetland flag on their bumpers, making the long commute to Lerwick for work or shopping.

Cassie was waiting for him at Duncan's house, her small overnight bag already packed. He could tell she was excited, but that she was fidgeting about missing school. Cassie had always been one for following rules, and since Fran's death it had become a kind of compulsion. A neurosis. Perez could understand that. It was about security. Playing it safe.

'I've told her,' Duncan said, 'a few days away from lessons will do her no harm. I was always bunking off, wasn't I, Jimmy?'

'I've talked to Miss Price.' Perez directed his words to Cassie, not to her father. 'She's given me some work for you to do when you're staying with Grandma. And she wants a story all about the trip to London, when you get back to school.'

On the way south to Sumburgh they talked about London. 'Grandma wants to show you the sights,' Perez said. 'She's talking about a boat trip on the Thames and all sorts of treats. They can't wait to see you.'

'Will you be there?'

'I have work to do in the city,' Perez said. He paused. 'Anyway I think Grandma and Grandpa would rather have you to themselves for a while. Then they can spoil you without me seeing and stopping them.'

'Is it dangerous work?'

'No! It's talking to people, to women mostly. Routine. Background stuff.'

'But you're a boss,' she said. 'Sandy should be doing routine work.'

'I wanted an excuse to take you to London.' And that, at last, seemed to satisfy her.

It was a clear day and, on the flight south to Aberdeen, Fair Isle appeared suddenly beneath them, with the iconic shape of Sheep Rock to the east. Perez wasn't sure whether he should point it out. *That's where I was born. And where your mother died.* But Cassie saw the island below and mentioned it herself. 'You said you would take me soon,' she said. 'When can we go?'

'This summer. When school's finished. We'll stay for a few days.' He realized that the idea made him uncomfortable. Was it impertinent to think of Cassie as belonging to his family now? What would Fran's parents in London make of that?

Cassie seemed to pick up his ambivalence. 'What should I call your mother and father when I see them? They're not quite grandparents, are they? Or are they? I never know, so I end up not calling them anything.'

'They think of themselves as your grandparents,' he said. But call them whatever you like. James and Mary? You could ask them.'

She peered out of the window until the island disappeared from view. There was a quick connection at Aberdeen and then they were arriving into Heathrow, into the crowds and the noise. Everything giant-sized and everyone yelling. Cassie went very quiet and held onto his hand. She looked smaller here where the buildings and the buses towered above her. He wanted to scoop her up in his arms and take her back to Shetland, where he could keep her safe. Then he thought that a woman had just been killed in Shetland and that people were much the same wherever they were.

Fran's parents were waiting for them, had probably been looking out for the taxi for hours. Cassie was their only grandchild, but it was more than that. She was all they had left of their daughter. Perez could understand why she was so important. They glimpsed traces of the girl they'd known and the woman they'd lost in Cassie's eyes, in the way she ran, and in her stubbornness and her fierce independence. They lived in a neat little house in a tree-lined suburb, which had become more fashionable since they'd bought it. There was a new coffee shop on the corner. A woman in an extravagant floral dress walked down the street clutching a small white dog and ignored them.

Fran's mother took Cassie to the room that had once been Fran's. It smelled of paint. Perez wondered if the couple had been up all night decorating it. There was a view over city gardens, and everything was green and lush.

'You'll stay for an early supper, Jimmy? I thought we'd eat soon because Cassie will be tired.' She smiled and he thought she was a very good woman. She made such an effort to keep the blame from her voice.

'I'm sorry,' he said. 'I'm pushed for time. You know.'

'But you'll have a cup of tea at least.'

So he agreed to a cup of tea. He had to respond in some way to her generosity of spirit. Downstairs Fran's father already had the kettle on. They sat in the tiny garden on uncomfortable wrought-iron seats, balancing the cups on a wobbly wrought-iron table, while Cassie played with the neighbour's cat and they all tried to pretend there was no tension or awkwardness. He thought even Cassie was relieved when he took his leave. He stood on the doorstep and said he would be there early on Thursday morning to take the girl home. That provoked the only crack in the mask of cordial civilization.

'So soon, Jimmy?' Fran's mother cried. 'Is that all we have? One full day?'

'I have to be back in the islands for work.' The words mild. 'And Cassie has school.' He understood that deep down they wanted to capture Cassie and bring her up themselves. How could they entrust her safety to the man who'd allowed their daughter to be killed? But Fran had bequeathed Cassie to him and they all had to respect her wishes.

'Of course.' She'd already recovered her composure. 'You said that it would only be a flying visit.'

'Why don't you come up and stay with *us*?'

'We will.' But they'd only been in Shetland once since Fran had died and he knew they'd found the experience distressing. It reminded them of how far she'd grown away from them, even before her murder.

★

125

He checked into his hotel and phoned the number he'd been given for Cilla Montgomery, Eleanor's mother. No reply. Then he tried Bright Star, Eleanor's production company. It was five o'clock and he'd expected that the staff would be preparing to leave work for the evening and thought he'd be forced to make an appointment for the following day. But a young man said everyone would be around for a couple of hours yet, if Perez wanted to call in, and went on to give crisp directions. Perez found the office in a converted brewery close to King's Cross station. Bright Star took up half the ground floor. In the rest of the building there was an architect's practice, a literary agency and a firm of lawyers. Perez was buzzed into an open-plan office where five people sat in front of PCs. Most seemed very young and all were casually dressed. He'd been expecting a place where films might be made – a studio with cameras and spotlights – but this had the air of a well-appointed sixth-form common room. The atmosphere was sombre. Perez supposed that Eleanor's death would mark the end of Bright Star Productions and these people might now find themselves without work.

A tall, dark man dressed in jeans, Converse boots and a loose sweater of the kind that Willow Reeves might have worn came up to him with his hand outstretched.

'Inspector Perez. We've been expecting you. You found us OK?' He smiled as if the inspector was a valued client. Perez wondered if Eleanor's team had been appointed for their charm. He supposed that it would be part of the job to be appealing to broadcasters and commissioners. 'I'm not quite sure how we can help, though. We're in a state of shock.' He shook Perez's hand. 'My name's Leo Whitehouse. I was Nell's assistant.'

Perez sat on a desk and felt like a college lecturer trying to be one of the gang. 'Eleanor was working on a documentary about ghosts,' he said. 'Can you give me the background to that?'

'There'd been a survey about contemporary belief systems for one of the national papers and it seemed to indicate a spike in the number of younger, educated individuals who claimed to have had supernatural experiences. Our documentary planned to look in more detail at what might have provoked the increase. It wasn't about debunking the reports, but about considering what might lead apparently rational people to become convinced that they'd seen a ghost or that a medium had been in contact with a deceased loved one. A need for the spiritual in an irreligious age. That was the angle we were going for.' The words came easily. He'd obviously described the project before. He paused before continuing. 'Actually we were all thrilled when we got the commission. Things had been looking a bit tricky recently. Financially, I mean. It looked as if there might have to be some redundancies. The ghost project was just what we needed.'

Perez made a mental note to ask Willow to get a search on the Bright Star accounts. 'What was Eleanor's take on the subject?'

'I'm sorry?' The lanky young man frowned.

'Did she believe in ghosts?'

'Oh, I don't think so!' Leo gave a sudden grin. 'Nell believed in good red wine and expensive shoes. I don't think you would have called her a spiritual woman in any sense.'

'Even more recently? I understand that the loss of a child had affected her very deeply.' Perez looked out at the young, unmarked faces and wondered if any of them had faced tragedy. In the weeks after Fran's death *he'd* been convinced that he'd seen her standing at the foot of his bed. If a medium had promised that she could set up a line of contact with the dead, he'd have jumped at the chance.

'That was a few months ago,' the man said. 'She'd been more her old self lately. Excited by her friend's wedding and the trip north. The whole ghost thing.'

'Were you all working on that?' Perez looked around the room, at the nearly grown children who'd lost their boss and their surrogate mother.

'No,' Leo said. 'Just me and Alice at this point.' A small, dark young woman dressed in black waved from a desk in the back row. 'The others are winding up a couple of smaller projects. Eleanor did the important stuff, setting up meetings with potential directors, working out budgets. We were making the initial contacts, weeding out the loonies.'

'Were there lots of those?'

'No,' Leo said. 'Surprisingly few.'

'Had you talked to anyone in Shetland about sightings of Peerie Lizzie?'

There was a moment's silence in the room and in the end Alice spoke. 'I found out about Peerie Lizzie on the Internet,' she said, 'and tracked down one couple who'd claimed to have seen her. The others weren't very credible. Though Eleanor had already heard about Peerie Lizzie from a friend and she said she'd follow up that story because she was going to Shetland anyway. It was a bit of a bummer actually! I was hoping I'd get a trip to the islands out of it. I've never been further north than Derby.'

'Did Eleanor set up a meeting with the couple?'

'I don't know,' Alice said. 'Nell went a bit weird and

mysterious on us actually, about Peerie Lizzie. I mean usually she was very open and sharing about her work, but she started shutting her office door when she was on the phone.' She pointed to a glass box in the corner of the room. 'It was odd. She hasn't minded us listening in before, even to quite high-powered discussions with execs.'

'Are you sure all her secret conversations were work-related?' Perez was trying to make sense of this. If Peerie Lizzie had the reputation of appearing to the childless and helping them to become pregnant, he could see why Eleanor would want to follow up the story herself. But he couldn't understand why she would want to keep her interest private. Perhaps she'd be embarrassed to admit that she might be taking the claims seriously, but she had a legitimate work-related excuse for her questions, so why be worried about her team eaves-dropping? It occurred to him that there might be another explanation for the closed door.

Alice seemed to be following his train of thought. 'You think she might have been having an affair?' She laughed. 'Nah, really I don't think so. We always said that Nell was married to Ian and her work, and we weren't sure which was most important to her. She wouldn't make time for another man in her life.'

'Do you have the contact details for the Shetland couple who claimed to have seen the ghost?'

'Sure, I've got them on my system. I'll print them out for you.' She tapped on the keyboard, the printer whirred and she handed him a sheet of paper with a name and an address.

'Neil and Vaila Arthur, Spindrift, Meoness, Unst.'

The words obviously meant nothing to the people in the room. But they were of great significance to him.

Chapter Eighteen

PEREZ STOOD ON THE PAVEMENT AND felt the heat reflect from it. After his meeting with the team from Bright Star Productions, he couldn't face seeing Eleanor's mother that evening. He'd had an early start and the travel and the encounter with Fran's parents had left him restless and lacking in concentration. He knew that his decision to keep custody of Cassie was purely selfish – she was all he had left of the woman he'd adored – but it had been Fran's wish and, no matter what her parents thought, there was no way he would change his mind. He found himself walking through the streets until he came to a quiet coffee shop. It was eight at night and he marvelled that the place was still open. A couple of students with laptops sat at the tables. He ordered tea and a toasted sandwich and perched on a high stool at a counter near the window and watched the passers-by. He phoned Eleanor's mother.

'Yes?' An imperious voice, but one that sounded old and exhausted.

He asked if he might visit her the next morning.

'I suppose so, but I'm not sure what good it will do. My daughter wasn't killed in London, after all.'

'But you might have some questions for me,' Perez said. 'We could have a conversation about Eleanor.'

There was a pause. He imagined her sipping from a glass by her side. Perhaps he even heard the faint sound of her pouring more wine. 'Yes,' she said. 'I'd like that.'

'What time would you like me to come?'

'Whenever you like. I won't be at work. They've forced me to take compassionate leave, though I think I'd be better off there.' She paused. 'Not too early, though. I've never done early mornings.'

'Eleven o'clock?'

'Fine. Whatever.' The teenage slang sounded strange coming from her. She'd lost interest in the conversation now, he thought.

'I'll see you then.' But he thought she might have cut off the conversation before he'd even finished speaking.

Willow Reeves answered her mobile so quickly that he wasn't ready to speak to her and he wasn't quite sure what to say.

'Jimmy? Are you there?' Amused rather than irritated by his failure to speak, when he'd been the one to make the call. 'Do you have anything useful?'

'It sounds as if Eleanor's company wasn't doing as well as her friends led us to believe. Maybe this ghost show was just about keeping it solvent. It might be worth getting the forensic accountants to check out the figures.'

'I can certainly organize that.' Her voice was suddenly very clear. He could imagine her in the next room.

'Eleanor had made contact with a couple who'd claimed to see Peerie Lizzie,' he said. 'They're called Arthur, and they live in Unst.' A pause. 'The address is Meoness.'

'Well, there's a coincidence.'

He wasn't sure how to react to that. 'The house is called Spindrift.'

'I've seen the name somewhere.' He could sense her excitement down the line. 'The new bungalow on the way to Sletts. They've carved the name on a bit of driftwood and stuck it on the front wall of the garden. I'll go and talk to them tomorrow and see if Eleanor visited. Maybe she was there on the night she died, sitting up waiting for the spirit to appear.'

He could tell she was being flippant and didn't bother answering.

'Jimmy?'

'Yes.'

'We're all missing you. Come back soon.'

Again he wasn't sure what to say. He switched off his phone, climbed down from the stool and continued walking until he reached his hotel.

He woke early and, instead of going straight to see Eleanor's mother, headed instead to Hampstead and the Folklore Society library, where Polly Gilmour worked. It was an ordinary house in a leafy street, standing out from the others only because it was shabbier. When he pushed open the door, a bell rang and a middle-aged woman with long grey hair fluttered down the stairs to greet him. She wore a long skirt and a silk tunic and many silk scarves.

'Can I help you? If it's anything *terribly* esoteric I'm afraid you'll have to come back later. Our fabulous librarian is away on holiday.'

He explained who he was.

'Poor Polly! She was so looking forward to her trip north with her friends.' The woman wrung her hands. She was shrouded in so much fabric that there seemed to be no real substance to her.

'How had she seemed in the last few weeks?' Now that he was here Perez wasn't sure what he had expected from the visit. Perhaps only to feel that he understood Polly Gilmour a little better.

'Well, excited of course. Being a bridesmaid at the wedding in Kent and then going to Shetland for the party. And having a new man in her life. There were times when we'd given up hope of her ever finding someone. And Marcus does seem such a nice chap.'

'Did you ever meet Eleanor Longstaff?' He'd already turned for the door when the question occurred to him.

'Oh yes, a few times. They were almost like sisters.'

'When was the last time you saw her?'

'She came to meet Polly the day before they set off for Shetland together. Last-minute plans, I suppose. Polly was in a meeting, and I made Eleanor tea in the members' room while she waited. Her phone rang, so I hustled her into the staffroom. We're still rather old-fashioned here about mobile phones, and the members detest them.' She hesitated. 'Of course I wasn't eavesdropping, but Eleanor was very angry and even from the office I couldn't help hearing.'

'What exactly did Eleanor say?' Perez appeared to be taking no more than a polite interest.

'Of course I can't be certain of the exact words, though I do pride myself on my memory.'

'If you could just do the best you can.' He smiled.

The woman smiled back, obviously charmed. 'The gist was:

"How can you expect me to go away with you, with this hanging over us. Just sort it out!"'

Perez nodded, as though to compliment her memory. 'That's very helpful. You have no idea who was on the other end of the line?'

The woman shook her head. 'I assume that it was her husband, but from the office of course I couldn't hear anything from the other end of the line.'

'Of course.' Perez thought they'd be able to trace the call from Eleanor's mobile records, though that would take time. 'Have you ever met Mr Longstaff?' It was hard to imagine the dour man in this whimsical place, but perhaps he'd come along to a social event with Eleanor.

The woman shook her head. 'Just the lovely Eleanor. We'll all miss her.'

Perez left the building. Walking down the quiet street, he was still not sure what he'd achieved by the visit.

Eleanor's mother lived in an apartment in a large white terrace in Pimlico. Ringing the bell, which was an old-fashioned pull, Perez felt momentarily overwhelmed. It came to him that there might be another door, a tradesmen's entrance, and perhaps he would be expected to use that; he even wondered if he might be greeted by a housekeeper. But when the door was opened, it was by a woman who could only be Eleanor's mother. The hair was a different colour – it had been immaculately cut and dyed various shades of dark blonde to make it look almost natural – but there were the same nose and cheekbones as he'd seen in Eleanor's photo on Polly Gilmour's computer.

She led him into a wide hallway. The walls had been painted a deep green and there were pictures everywhere. The art was unfamiliar. Some looked like prints of cave paintings, scratched images of animals and birds. Primitive, but also amazingly lifelike. There were photos of strange dwellings growing out of a hillside, a collage made from scraps of woven cloth and two large abstract oils. He would have liked to spend more time with them, but she'd already moved on and had settled on the windowsill in a room that seemed half-sitting room and half-study. There was a desk and the walls were hidden by bookshelves. In one corner an armchair was covered with a batik throw and next to it stood a coffee table made from animal hide. There was a glass on the table and Perez thought that she'd been sitting here when he'd phoned the night before. Now she was framed by the window, so she looked like a piece of art herself. The background was a small courtyard garden, where the sun had been trapped by a brick wall. In the corner stood a tree covered in pink blooms in a pot.

She pointed him to a chair on the other side of the desk, but didn't offer him tea or coffee. To a Shetlander that seemed so odd that for a moment Perez was unsure how to proceed.

'Well,' she said with a touch of impatience, 'I suppose that you have questions.' The voice threw him too. It was the voice of the old-fashioned upper classes, of the Queen's Speech on Christmas Day and 1950s radio recordings. Over the phone the cut-glass accent had been less pronounced.

'I'd like you to tell me about your daughter,' he said.

That obviously wasn't what she'd been expecting. 'Can you be more specific?'

'No.' He paused. 'You'll know what's important about her. And what might have led to her murder.'

A moment of silence. From the window behind her he began to hear faint sounds. The distant hum of traffic. A blackbird's song.

'She was always a headstrong girl,' the woman said at last. 'People said she took after me. Bright, of course.' As if that went without saying.

'An only child?'

'My husband left me soon after Eleanor was born,' she said. 'He was a child himself and couldn't bear the fact that he no longer got my full attention. I had other male partners to share my life, but nobody with whom I'd have contemplated parenthood.'

'And now?' But Perez thought he already knew the answer. This flat was Cilla's territory. Nobody else stayed here.

There was a brief pause. 'There are occasional distractions, but now I live alone and I'm grateful for that. I've discovered that I'm too selfish to share my home.'

'Did Eleanor keep in touch with her father? Had they met lately?' Perez wondered if this might have been the man in the restaurant seen by Caroline Lawson.

'I doubt it. Oriental art is his subject and he travels a lot. He's seldom in London and he has a new young family of his own. By his third wife.' The last phrase was spat out like venom.

'But you never discouraged contact?'

Cilla shrugged. 'If I had, Eleanor would have taken no notice. As I've told you, she was headstrong. I think she had Richard's email address and they might have met occasionally when he was in town, but she never discussed him with me.'

'What did you make of her marriage?'

'Ian Longstaff wasn't the sort of man I would have expected her to marry, but he seemed to make her happy. She claimed that he did.' Cilla Montgomery smoothed her skirt. 'Of course he couldn't give her children, and that was a disappointment.'

Perez wondered how a man could be held responsible for a miscarriage in late pregnancy, but didn't respond. Cilla continued, 'I thought she made too much of it. These things happen, and men expect women to get on with it. A child isn't everything.'

'There was some tension within the marriage?'

'She never said that.'

'But you felt it?'

Another silence. Somewhere in the distance a car alarm had been triggered. The wailing drilled into Perez's brain and then stopped as suddenly as it had started.

'Not tension exactly. She could have lived with tension. Eleanor enjoyed excitement and challenge. Like me she was most scared of being bored. Even the drama of the miscarriages had its element of satisfaction for her, guaranteeing that she would be the centre of attention at least for a while.' Cilla turned briefly to look out of the window to the courtyard beyond. 'Ian began as a challenge. His background and skills were very different from my daughter's. She found his solidness and his working-class family interesting, almost exotic. And he stood up to her in arguments. But, as time went on, he loved her too much and gave in to her too easily. Not his fault. How can you fight with a woman who has just lost a baby? I think she began to despise him just for those qualities that another person might admire: gentleness, compassion, loyalty.' She paused again and gave a strange little laugh that jarred on Perez's nerves in the way that the car alarm had done. 'I'm not painting a very flattering picture of my daughter, am I, Inspector? But I understood her because she was so much like me.'

'Do you think she was having an affair?' Perez wondered how this mother could be so dispassionate and clear-eyed about a daughter who had died so recently. If anything happened to Cassie, he'd be howling at the moon and incapable of carrying on a rational discussion.

'She never mentioned anything of the sort to me, but I wouldn't be surprised.'

'When did you last see Eleanor?'

There was another brief pause. 'The day before she set off to Shetland,' Cilla said. 'She phoned me at work and asked if I might be free for lunch.'

'Where do you work?'

'The British Museum. I'm an art historian. My speciality is Africa.' There was a sudden spark of passion and for a moment he thought that her work was the most important thing in her life. 'I arranged to meet Eleanor in a Turkish restaurant not far from the museum. It was rather a nuisance actually, because I was in the middle of putting together a proposal for an exhibition. But Eleanor seldom asked to meet up, so I reorganized my day.'

'And was there something specific that she wanted to talk about?' Perez was suddenly tense. Perhaps he was catching the mood from the small woman, who was still leaning against the windowsill. The light from the garden behind her meant that her features were indistinct, but he sensed a stress in her too. Maybe she was deciding how much she should confide.

'Perhaps.' She leaned forward and wiped sudden and unexpected tears from her eyes. He saw for the first time how tired and sad she was, the lines between her mouth and her nose, the sagging jawline. It occurred to him that her choice of seat was a habitual vanity; she presented a younger face looking into the room. She straightened, dry-eyed once more. 'It was an odd encounter. Usually Eleanor was very direct, but that day she was . . .' she paused to find the right word, 'elliptical. As if she wanted me to guess what was going on. It was clear that she was troubled about something. I could see that she was excited about her work. She was ambitious from a young age and work has always been important. But her mood was strained too. I should have asked her what was wrong, but I chose not to. It seems terribly petty now, but we were always competitive and I didn't want to give her the satisfaction of knowing that I was curious about her life.'

'Can you remember exactly what she said?' Perez struggled to imagine the conversation between the two women. They'd be seated across the table from each other picking at plates of spicy food. A glass of wine each perhaps. And they'd be batting words back and forth, a peculiar game of verbal ping-pong. Eleanor must have wanted *something* from the meeting. She'd be busy, if it was the day before she set off for Shetland. What had been so important that she'd insisted on seeing her mother for lunch?

Cilla frowned. 'She said that she was setting off on a great adventure and asked if I planned anything similar myself. Clearly she wanted me to ask what she meant, but I pretended not to understand. I told her that Shetland was a long way north, but it was hardly a journey of a lifetime. After all she's used to foreign travel. I used to take her with me on field trips.'

'And what do you think she meant?'

'Well, not a long drive and an overnight ferry,' Cilla said.

'Clearly the adventure she spoke of was more metaphorical than geographical.'

Perez thought there was nothing clear about the communication between the mother and daughter. Their relationship seemed to involve a strange game of second-guessing and pretence. 'Could you be more specific?'

'It might have been a new man, I suppose,' the woman said. 'That would be the most prosaic explanation. Or a spiritual journey. She was very lit up. Perhaps she'd even started to believe in her ghosts. Or it could just have been her work. In the end that was always what meant most to her.' She stood up. 'We said goodbye on the pavement and she hugged me. She was always very touchy-feely with her friends, but never with me, so I was taken aback by that. Then she walked away. I nearly called her back. I had the words in my head. *What was that all about, Nell? What did you really want from me?* But then I thought about my project at the museum and how I was already behind schedule. I stood for a moment and watched her climb into a cab. And then I went back to work.'

They looked at each other. Perez got to his feet too. He knew that was what was expected of him. 'What time did she leave you?'

'I'm not sure. About two-thirty.'

So what had Eleanor done between having lunch with her mother and meeting Polly in the library in Hampstead? Had she gone back to the office?

Cilla was looking at him impatiently, but he stood his ground.

'Did Eleanor get in touch when she was in Shetland?'

'Just a text on the Saturday afternoon to say they'd arrived safely and that it was a beautiful place.' The woman had walked into the hall full of images. 'I texted her back and told her to have a lovely time. Put an "x" on the bottom, with one of those ridiculous smiley faces.' She turned to see that Perez was following her. 'I'm glad I did that at least. I hope she knew how much I cared for her.'

'Do you have any questions for me?' he asked, remembering his promise when he'd phoned the night before.

Her hand was on the door handle and she was frozen for a moment. 'No,' she said. 'I don't think I do.'

Again he was shocked. Most relatives wanted to know if their relatives had suffered. He walked down the street expecting her to call him back to ask the question that was obviously in her head. But when he turned to look, the door was already shut. As at her last meeting with her daughter, she was too proud to change her mind.

Chapter Nineteen

On Wednesday morning Willow woke to fog so thick that she could hardly see the grass outside the bedroom window. Her first thought was that she was glad Jimmy Perez wasn't scheduled to return from London to the islands until the following day and hoped the weather would clear to let him in. Then she wondered why that mattered so much to her. The day before she and Sandy had been out visiting, taking statements from everyone who'd been at the party, asking about Eleanor. Most of them remembered her. 'She danced like a demon,' one elderly man had said, his eyes twinkling. No one had remembered seeing a girl in a white dress on the beach or admitted to being part of the smoking couple whom Polly had mentioned. Willow felt that the investigation had got stuck and hoped that Jimmy Perez would bring a new energy to it on his return. *Of course that's why I want him back here.* But she was too honest to be taken in by the thought. *Yeah, right. He's got under your skin, lady. Just let that go and concentrate on work. You really don't need the complication.*

Sandy was already in the kitchen eating breakfast and

Charles and David were there too. They were sitting at the table, drinking tea. David jumped up as soon as he saw her, offering eggs from the Malcolmsons' croft. She'd told him when she arrived that she was vegetarian. *All that I have left from a childhood in a commune. Yoga every morning and a refusal to eat meat.*

'Yes, please, to the eggs.' When she was working a case she always felt hungry. 'Scrambled. With toast made from Grusche's bread, if there's any left.'

He pulled a pinafore over his head and moved to the stove to start cooking.

'I hope the weather changes before tomorrow.' Sandy looked up from his carnivore's dream-start to the day. 'There's no way the planes will be moving in this. Jimmy and Cassie will be stranded in Aberdeen.' He sounded anxious, lost without Perez too.

What is it with the man that he's made us all dependent on him?

Charles looked over from his side of the table. 'It could be quite clear in Sumburgh, and you know how quickly it can change. Four seasons in a day here.' He was already accustomed to reassuring visitors about the weather. There was the sound of footsteps on the stairs and he got up to serve his guests in the dining room.

Willow drank some coffee and thought there was a perfectly logical explanation for her anxiety to get Jimmy back. He was her reference point in the islands and she depended on his judgement.

She took Sandy with her to talk to the Arthurs in Spindrift, their new house close to the community hall. The couple might end up as suspects and, if they ever came to court, a single interviewer's evidence wouldn't be admissible. Besides, Sandy was a Shetlander and about as unthreatening as you could get. He'd always put people at their ease. Outside the fog was still as thick as when she'd woken up and her coat was covered in drops of moisture by the time they reached the car. In the distance there was a strange diffuse light, which suggested that eventually the sun would burn it away. In this weather anyone might believe in ghosts.

In the bungalow's porch there was a pram with a tiny baby sleeping inside it. Sandy was ahead of her and saw it and backed away as if it were a bomb. They walked round the side of the house looking for another way in. At the back door he gave a quick knock, then opened it and shouted inside. 'Anyone home?'

A young woman appeared. She was carrying a mug of coffee and was dressed in pyjamas and dressing gown. Willow introduced herself. 'I hope we didn't wake you.'

'Not at all. I was up and just about to get dressed. We had such a bad night with Vaila. My husband was working in Yell today anyway, so he got up early and took her out in the pram to walk her to sleep, and I took the chance for a lie-in. Come away in. I'll put the kettle on and go and make myself decent. You'll be here about that poor woman who'd come north for Lowrie's hamefarin'.' Still talking as she was setting out cups and heading into her bedroom. So chatty and friendly that Willow found it hard to consider her as a potential killer. And she was tiny. It was unlikely she'd have had the strength to move Eleanor's body and position it in the loch.

They sat in a living room, which could have been in suburban England: patterned paper on one wall and furniture from IKEA. The woman cleared a pile of baby clothes and a rattle from the leather sofa so that they could sit down. The fog made the room so gloomy that she switched on the light.

'Your baby's named Vaila? That's pretty.' Willow took the offered coffee.

'I'm Vaila too. Named after one of the off-islands. I thought it might be a bit confusing, but Neil liked it, and it's always been a tradition in Shetland to keep names in the family, so we thought *Why not?* She can use her middle name if she doesn't like it when she's older.'

Willow looked at Sandy. She'd asked him to begin the interview. He looked panic-stricken for a moment, then cleared his throat.

'You were at the hamefarin' on Saturday night?'

The woman stared at him. 'Don't I know you? Weren't you in Anderson High? The year below me. You were a Whalsay boy, and you stayed in the hostel too.' She paused. 'Well, I'd never have had you down as becoming a detective.'

'Perhaps you could tell us about the hamefarin'.' Willow thought the garrulous Vaila was about to launch into a series of school reminiscences, and interrupted before she had the chance. Sandy would be too polite to stop her in mid-stream. 'Did you meet Eleanor Longstaff there?'

'Yes, but I'd met her before that. It was supposed to be secret, but now she's dead that's not important, is it?'

'When did you first meet her?' Sandy made another attempt to control the conversation.

'That afternoon. The afternoon of the party. It was all arranged by phone. I went up to Sletts. She said that would be better, because if her friends came back from their walk we could make an excuse about why I was there. If she came here it would be more difficult to explain where she'd been.'

'Why was she so keen to talk to you?' Again Sandy asked the question.

'Because of Peerie Lizzie, of course. Eleanor was making a film about her, and we were going to be in it. We were going to get paid. An appearance fee, she said.' Vaila paused. 'Do you think it'll still be made? Neil was a bit shy about it, but I was dead excited about being on the telly. It wasn't just the money . . .'

'Why was it so important to keep the meeting secret?' Willow looked outside. She thought the fog might be clearing. There were denser shadows in the distance that might have been the Meoness community hall and the Malcolmsons' croft house.

'Eleanor said her friends wouldn't understand. Because she really believed the story and her husband wasn't the sort to accept that it might be true. So that afternoon I went to Sletts and I told her what happened. How I saw the lassie and then I fell pregnant, and we'd been trying for years. We were planning on another round of IVF, but in the end we didn't need to.'

Willow thought Vaila must be in her early thirties, but she still spoke like an excitable schoolgirl, the words tumbling out without thought. Vaila paused for a moment to catch her breath and then continued talking. 'I thought Eleanor was hoping to see Lizzie herself. You could tell that she wanted a bairn. Later, at the party in the hall, she was all over the baby.'

'So you went to Sletts that afternoon,' Sandy said. Perhaps all this talk of babies was making him uncomfortable. 'And Eleanor was expecting you.'

'Nothing much happened,' Vaila said. 'There were no cameras or anything, but Eleanor had this little recorder and asked me to speak into it. To tell the tale of when I saw Peerie Lizzie. She said it was better than her taking notes.'

Willow shot a look at Sandy, but he seemed so focused on keeping Vaila on track that he appeared not to understand the importance of the information. No recorder had been found in the search of the holiday home.

'And what was the tale?'

'Well.' The woman settled back in her chair as if she were about to tell a bedtime story to a child. 'It was a misty sort of day much like this, but a bit earlier in the year. February and late afternoon, so it was already getting a bit dark. I work as a classroom assistant in the school in Meoness, only I'm on maternity leave just now, and I was on my way home. Then there she was on the track in front of me. A girl of about ten, all dressed in white. Kind of old-fashioned, you know, with white ribbons in her hair. And she danced. Like she was performing just for me. Like it was a sort of sign. Then she disappeared into the fog. I shouted and ran up the track after her, but I didn't see her again.'

Willow was sceptical. 'Couldn't it just have been an island girl dressed up? Things look so weird in the fog.'

'I know all the kids in this part of Unst and I didn't recognize her. But it was more than that. I *knew* she wasn't real and that something important was happening to me. It was a kind of religious experience. And she just vanished in front of my eyes.'

Willow knew there could be a number of explanations for the disappearing child, but she didn't say anything. If she challenged Vaila too hard, she might be offended and clam up. She'd convinced herself that she'd seen an apparition. Willow had met people in the commune who'd believed that trees had spirits, and that a guru from Wolverhampton would save the known universe; she hadn't been able to persuade them that their ideas were irrational, either.

The woman went on, 'Besides, there was no fog the next time I saw her.'

'You saw her again?'

'That was late July. One of the still, sunny evenings you get sometimes in the summer. I'd spent the evening down with Grusche and George. He's a relative, a kind of uncle, and when Neil's working away I sometimes go down to see them. I'm not good with my own company. It was such a fine evening that I took the path along the beach to get home and I saw the lassie again. This time she was quite a way off, just a silhouette up by the standing stone on the headland. I dashed back to George's house because I wanted someone else to see her. They'd all made fun of me when I said that I'd seen her in the mist. But when we got on the shore and looked up towards the stone there was nothing to be seen.'

'And that was what you told Eleanor Longstaff?' It was impossible to tell from Sandy's voice whether he believed every word or thought it was a load of nonsense.

'Yes. I spoke it all into her little machine, and then she replayed the first bit to make sure it had recorded properly.'

'What did she say?'

'She asked whether my husband believed me,' Vaila said. 'And I told her that my Neil wasn't the sort to believe in ghosts, but he knew I wasn't making it up, so he kind of went along with it.' A beat. 'He's a plumber.' As if that explained everything.

'Did you see what Eleanor did with the machine when she'd finished?' Sandy's voice was calm and easy. Willow thought he was brighter than he always made out. 'She wouldn't want it left where all her friends might see it. If she was trying to keep your meeting secret.'

Vaila screwed up her face in an effort to concentrate. 'I think she just put it in her pocket. She was wearing a knitted jacket over jeans, and the jacket had a patch pocket. I think she stuck it in there.'

Sandy glanced across at Willow and she gave him a nod of approval. He always needed to be encouraged.

'But that wasn't the end of the story.' Vaila was beaming and Willow thought again how young she seemed. 'And not the important part really. It was about a month later that I found out I was pregnant! So it must have been Lizzie, mustn't it?' She looked round at them for confirmation as if the logic were inescapable.

Sandy and Willow looked at each other, but said nothing. On cue the baby began to cry and Vaila went into the porch and gathered her into her arms.

They drove to the end of the track near the footpath that led to the murder scene and sat in the car watching the mist shifting, so that the cliffs in the distance began to appear.

'A bit of a coincidence that Eleanor claimed to have seen the girl on the afternoon that Vaila was telling her story.' Willow wiped the condensation from the inside of the windscreen with a mucky handkerchief.

'Wishful thinking? She was desperate to get pregnant, so she convinced herself that some random girl was a ghost?'

'Maybe, but it seems more calculated than that to me.' And Willow wasn't sure if a woman of Eleanor's background would be so impressionable, however desperate she was for a baby. 'I wish I knew what game she was playing.'

'Is it relevant that her body was found where Vaila saw the girl?'

'I don't know. It's certainly an odd coincidence.' Willow paused. 'I wish I knew what had happened to that digital recorder. Vicki Hewitt did a thorough search of Sletts before she left and she wouldn't miss something like that.'

'I thought ghosts were supposed to be scary,' Sandy said. 'Vaila Arthur didn't give you the impression that she was frightened. Maybe it's because we've all grown up with stories of the trowes, so we take weird things in our stride.'

'Trowes?'

He shifted in his seat. 'Little men who live under the ground. They can lure you down to their halls with fine music and, when you wake up, you find that you've lost a hundred years.' A pause. 'Nobody believes it, of course. It's just stories for bairns.'

'Naturally.' She kept her voice serious. 'So what do we do now?'

'Talk to those English folk and find out if they have any idea why Eleanor might have kept her research secret?' He sounded as if he didn't like the idea much.

'I suppose we should.' She wondered why she was as reluctant as Sandy to talk to the people at Sletts. She turned in her seat. 'Did you believe Vaila? Did she see her ghost?'

He paused for a moment. 'I'm with her husband. I don't believe in ghosts, but I don't think she was making it up. Not deliberately. She was desperate for a baby and she saw what she wanted to see.'

Chapter Twenty

IN THE HOUSE ON THE SHORE at Meoness, Polly thought she was unravelling just as she'd suspected Eleanor of doing when anger and depression at the loss of a child had made her so low. It was the fog closing them in, and the sense that they were all trapped. Her nerves were fraying and she was finding it impossible to sleep, even when she took pills. She was haunted by the light nights and by the horror of all that had happened. She couldn't understand why the men didn't make more fuss about the possibility of their leaving. Now she was desperate to return to London, to busy streets and colour, to daily newspapers that arrived on time and regular visits to the gym. To the comfort and routine of the Sentiman Library.

They sat in Sletts, looking occasionally out at the grey world beyond their window. The detectives had returned their laptops and phones and the men both seemed to be engrossed in the screens. Marcus was planning a trip for another rich client who was obsessed with climbing Kilimanjaro before he died, and she supposed that Ian was working too. He was checking his emails and suddenly turned into the room, frowning. 'All these ghouls sending messages about how sorry they are that Eleanor's dead. It's nonsense, of course. They just want to be part of the drama. She'd upset half of them, and the other half were embarrassed when she had the miscarriage.'

Polly thought that was probably true. She was trying to read, but couldn't concentrate and sneaked a look at Marcus's screen. He was putting together information for his client and there were images of lush vegetation and stunning views from his previous trips to Tanzania. She wondered again what this man who was so well travelled and attractive could have seen in her. Now he was leaning back and had his feet on the rungs of a dining chair. He was wearing the sandals he'd had on when they first met, and his feet were brown, long and bony. She longed to reach out and stroke them, but realized how insensitive that would be when Ian must be coming to terms with the idea that he'd never have physical contact with Eleanor again.

Marcus had burst into her life like a being from a different planet. She'd booked the trip to Morocco in the middle of the winter. An impulse when she'd been with Caroline and Eleanor one night, and their lives had seemed so much more exciting than hers. It had been just before Eleanor had lost the child and her friend had been full of fun and mischief: 'Go on, Pol! What have you got to lose?' One click of the mouse sent her credit-card details into the ether, and a fortnight later she'd arrived at Agadir airport and there was Marcus, holding a card with her name on it, leaning against a pillar and grinning in a way that was ironic and welcoming at the same time. *I'm just playing at this tour-leading shit, but I'll make sure that you have a good time.* And he did. The other members of the party were elderly Germans who went to bed at eight-thirty every evening and spoke little English. In the warm evenings she and Marcus explored the walled city of Taroudant and watched the swifts soaring overhead, and it felt quite natural when he put his arm around her shoulders on the way back to the hotel. She was dazzled by the place and the man. And by the fact that she'd had the courage to respond to him. Her boyfriends at college had been shy and earnest and she'd always imagined that she'd end up with someone like that, an academic or a research scientist who spent his working life in a lab coat. Not an adventurer with brown, bony feet who wandered the world. Someone who'd been to public school and who'd grown up in a grand country house.

She'd returned to England at the end of the holiday with no expectations of seeing him again. This was a holiday fling and she'd be grateful for the memories. She imagined telling the girls about Marcus and showing them her photos. 'This is the night we stayed in the Berber village. Here we are on a trek through the mountains.' He'd bought her earrings in a souk and waited while she had henna painted on her hands. 'So that you don't forget me.' As if she ever would. At his request she'd entered her mobile number into his phone, but she'd put his asking down to a form of politeness. Or the collection of trophies. Perhaps he had a list of numbers of the women with whom he'd slept when he was leading his tours.

He'd phoned two days later. 'That's spooky,' she'd said, making every effort to keep the excitement from her voice, 'I was just thinking about you.' And that was quite true, but it would have been so whenever he'd called. She couldn't *stop* thinking about him.

'Would you like to meet up?' His voice had faded away at the end of the sentence and it had occurred to her for the first time that he might be nervous too, that phoning his customers out of the blue for a date wasn't his usual way of operating.

'Yes.' Because what else was there to say; and he'd told her one night, sitting outside in the warm darkness, that he loved the fact that she never wasted words.

And a few weeks later he was practically living in her flat when he was in England, and she became used to him kissing her goodbye in the early mornings, and returning from work occasionally to find that his rucksack was parked just inside the door and he was sitting on the little balcony outside her flat, his brown feet on the rail, drinking tea or beer. He'd jump up to greet her and begin asking her about her work. Only when he'd listened to her tedious stories of eccentric researchers into rural English myths would he begin his travellers' tales.

She'd thought at first that he might be with her for her money, the security of a London crash pad when he was in the UK. She had no confidence in her ability to attract a man. Her parents had died one after the other within six months, leaving her the house in Manchester, so she had some savings as well as the flat in London. His tours were pricey, but he wasn't travelling continuously and sometimes he only had a couple of clients. They provided a way for him to see the world, but would never make his fortune. Then he'd taken her to see his mother and she'd seen that money probably wasn't an issue. There were paintings on the wall worth more than her parents' suburban home.

'What's wrong with you?' Marcus said, amused, when she asked one day what he saw in her. 'What will it take me to persuade you that you're a wonderful woman? I've never met anyone so compassionate and wise. You're just fishing for compliments. There are women you play with, and women you settle down with. I want to be with you for the long term.'

When she'd suggested that he might like to come with her to Shetland she wasn't sure what his response would be. He'd have to take a couple of weeks off work, and in the summer he sometimes organized lucrative day trips for American visitors to the UK, but he'd agreed without hesitation. Now, holed up in this house, she longed to have him to herself. She felt cheated because she'd imagined the stay in Shetland would be a romantic time for them. That was why Marcus had brought his own car, so that they could explore on their own, find empty beaches for picnics, ancient historical sites. She'd even had the wild fantasy that he might propose to her. Instead they were locked up in this place on the beach, haunted by the memory of Eleanor, shut in by the weather and the hill where her body had been found. It rose behind the house and its shadow was always with them.

The knock on the door surprised them all. The fog was so dense that it was hard to believe any world existed outside the house. Ian got to his feet and flung open the door. Two police officers. Not the dark detective this time, but the tall, untidy woman and Wilson, the younger man. Without a word Ian stood aside to let them in. Marcus put his feet on the floor and stood up. The officers' clothes and hair were covered with fine droplets of water, so they looked grey too, as if they'd brought the drizzle in with them.

'I'll make some coffee,' Polly said. 'Would you like some?' And she escaped into the kitchen before they could reply.

When she returned to the living room the officers had taken off their jackets and looked more human, though the woman's wild hair made Polly think of a mermaid from a kid's story book. There was an awkward silence and she realized they'd been waiting for her before they started any meaningful conversation.

'We've discovered that Eleanor had made contact with some local people to discuss her documentary,' Willow Reeves said. They'd settled around the dining table. It was as if the discussion required something more formal than the easy chairs. 'I'm wondering why she never mentioned that to you. As she was so excited by the project.' When nobody responded she probed again. 'Why the need for secrecy, do you think?'

'She might have mentioned it to me,' Ian said. 'She talked about her work all the time, but I didn't always listen. I have my own work. Sometimes she seemed not to realize . . .'

'But she lied to you.' Willow's voice was gentle. Polly thought she might have made a good psychiatrist. 'That afternoon when she claimed to be tired and the rest of you went for a walk, she met up with a woman who said that she'd seen Peerie Lizzie. The spirit of a drowned child.'

There was a moment of stunned silence. The detective looked at them each in turn. 'She didn't discuss this with anyone?'

They looked at each other and Polly could see that they were all trying to readjust to the idea of a different Eleanor. That the straightforward, upfront Eleanor they'd all known might have told lies.

'Nell might have been embarrassed.' Polly reached out to pour more coffee. 'I mean, she knew we could never believe in stuff like that.' Though now, she thought, she could sense irrational ideas drifting into her own brain like flotsam swirling around in the tide. Now she might be more sympathetic to Eleanor's talk of ghosts.

'And you thought that Eleanor might believe it?' The detective's voice was non-committal, but Polly could sense the scepticism.

'Six months ago I'd have said it was impossible.' Ian tapped his fingers impatiently on the table. 'But recently? I don't know what to think. She'd been behaving so strangely. I should have been more sympathetic about the baby. I should have given her my full attention. Insisted, at least, that she stay in hospital until they were ready to discharge her.'

'How did she seem when you came back from the walk that afternoon?' Again Willow addressed the question to the whole group.

Ian's fingers still rattled on the table. Polly wanted to put her hand over his to stop the noise, to calm him.

'Fine. Didn't she?' Polly tried to remember. They'd come in, full of the walk and the things they'd seen. Puffins flying onto the ledges of the cliffs. Being dive-bombed by the skuas. Seals. Eleanor had seemed rested, better than she'd been for months. 'We were all looking forward to the party. It was like being kids again preparing for a night out. She and I sat in her bedroom and painted our nails.'

'So that would have been a time when she might have confided in you,' Willow said. 'When it was just the two of you together.'

'Yes.' Polly paused. 'But she didn't.'

Willow turned towards Marcus. 'You haven't said much, Mr Wentworth. Do you have anything to add?'

'I didn't really know her. We met properly for the first time on the boat from Aberdeen. My sense was that she seemed . . .' He paused. 'Playful, perhaps. That everything was coming together for her and she was determined to have fun.'

Looking outside, Polly saw that the fog had almost disappeared. It was possible to see as far as the horizon and a milky sunlight was catching the water. She felt a bubble of gratitude to Marcus for bringing the old Eleanor back to life for her.

The younger detective's phone rang. A ridiculous call sign: the *Captain Pugwash* theme tune. He blushed and hurried outside with a muttered apology. The rest of them grinned, enjoying the break in the tension. Willow Reeves took one of the biscuits that Polly had set out on a plate.

'When can we go home?' Polly asked suddenly. Again she had a longing for her ordinary life, for popping to the local Waitrose for a treat for their supper, and for evenings of theatre or the cinema. For her and Marcus walking along their street on the way back to her flat. Knowing that when they arrived they'd make love lazily and lie in bed afterwards listening to the sounds of the city. That's what she loved about London: everything was familiar, but anonymous.

'Whenever you like,' Willow Reeves said easily. 'We have no power to keep you here. It makes life easier for us, of course, if you stay locally in case we have more questions.'

'I'm staying,' said Ian, pugnacious and determined. 'For the week that we'd booked at least. Maybe for longer than that. Until we know what happened.' He hesitated. 'I can't stand not knowing. I can live with anything else.'

'That would be helpful.' Willow smiled towards Polly as if she sensed her restlessness and discomfort. 'Of course there's no need to stay in Unst. Do some trips to Shetland mainland and to Lerwick. After a few days in the sticks it will seem truly metropolitan. A good cappuccino and a restaurant meal and you might not feel so eager to get home.'

The young detective came back into the house, still apologizing, saying he thought he'd switched off his phone. He stood, making it clear that he thought they should leave, and when Willow made no sign of moving he leaned towards her. 'That was Jimmy.'

Now the woman did get to her feet and they both trooped outside into the pale sunshine. Polly thought that Willow Reeves might be the senior investigating officer in the case, but if anyone was to find out who'd killed Eleanor it would be Jimmy Perez.

Chapter Twenty-One

AFTER SPEAKING TO ELEANOR'S MOTHER, Perez thought he had no reason to stay in London. He'd done all that Willow had asked him. He could get on a plane and be home that afternoon, ready to drop Cassie back at Duncan's before arriving in Unst by the last ferry. And ready to share a glass of whisky with Willow before she disappeared to bed. The thought tempted him. But he'd promised Fran's mother a whole day with their granddaughter and knew he couldn't leave the city yet.

He was walking away from Cilla's grand apartment, thinking that he might wander along the Thames and take some time to explore the city, when his phone rang.

'Inspector?' A young voice, female. He tried to remember where he'd heard it before. 'This is Alice from Bright Star. We met yesterday evening. I worked with Eleanor.'

'Of course.' To his left there was a large Victorian church with a black smoke-stained steeple and an overgrown grave-yard. He slipped through the gate to get away from the traffic noise and landed on a wooden bench in the shade. A bunch of dead flowers lay next to a tilted headstone by the path. They were brown and shrivelled and must have been there for weeks. The young woman was still speaking.

'I've been going through Nell's records. I should have thought of that yesterday. She kept notebooks, hard copies. She'd been researching the history of the Unst ghost and had been in touch with other people on the island. I thought you'd like to know.'

'Can I come and collect the books from you?' The idea of action made him feel brighter. He hadn't realized that the conversation with Cilla had left him so low. It was as if the lethargy of his depression had descended while he was in the Pimlico flat. A black magic, bringing with it the old guilt and the memories of Fran.

'Sure. You know where to find us now.'

He picked up the dead, brown flowers and threw them into a bin as he walked through the church gate.

In the Bright Star office Leo and Alice were waiting for him. Now that the immediate shock of Eleanor's death was over, the staff were excited to be involved in the investigation, eager at the thought that they might be helping. Murder sometimes took young people that way. They had no sense of their own mortality. Alice had set out the notebooks on Eleanor's desk and had one open at the relevant page. 'Look,' she said. 'Nell obviously phoned these people to ask about the history of the girl who died in 1930. She'd tracked down the present owners of the house where Lizzie was supposed to have lived. There's a phone number and some scribbled notes, which I can't quite make out. Her handwriting was always indecipherable. But it certainly looks as if she contacted them.'

Perez would have liked to look at the notes on his own, but the young woman had been so helpful that he didn't have the heart to ask her to leave. Outside in the main office people were pretending to work, but were obviously fascinated too. He sat at Eleanor's desk and pulled the books towards him.

There was, as Alice had said, a phone number. Then an address: *Springfield House, Unst.* And two names: *Charles Hillier and David Gordon.* Then some squiggles that might have been the record of a telephone conversation. It seemed that Eleanor had devised her own form of shorthand and Perez thought it would take time and patience to decipher the code.

'Thank you,' he said. 'That's very useful.' He'd never owned a briefcase, but used instead a canvas bag that he'd collected from a stall when the Tall Ships Race had ended in Lerwick one year. He put the notebooks into that. As the young people let him out into the street he paused again. 'Did Eleanor have a favourite restaurant? Somewhere she might take clients or colleagues for dinner?'

'There's a French place in Bloomsbury that was her regular haunt for everyday,' Leo said. 'They knew her there and said she was like their daughter. It wasn't smart enough for clients she wanted to impress, though. Then she'd go flamboyantly upmarket and choose somewhere like the Savoy. Even when she knew the company couldn't really afford it.'

Perez jotted down the name and address of the French restaurant. Outside on the pavement outside the production-company office it felt sweltering. The sun was bouncing off the concrete again and onto his face, making his eyes water. He was never prepared for how warm it was in the south and how little breeze there was. He always dressed in the wrong sort of clothes. From the Bright Star office it was an easy walk to the restaurant. On the way he dialled Willow's phone number, but there was no answer. He hesitated for a moment and then tried Sandy instead. The Shetlander answered just as Perez had given up hope. He sounded flustered.

'We're just at Sletts talking to the English folk. Seems Vaila Arthur met up with Eleanor the afternoon before the murder. Eleanor recorded the interview for her TV programme, but we can't find the machine.'

'Are you getting anywhere with the people at Sletts?'

Sandy hesitated as if it was a trick question. 'They claim not to have known about the meeting with Vaila. I'm not sure how it's going. The boss is still in there with them.'

Perez wondered if he should wait until Willow was free, to pass on the information about Charles and David, but Sandy was more reliable these days. 'There seems to be evidence that Eleanor made more contacts in Unst than we'd realized. She'd been in touch with Charles and David about the history of Peerie Lizzie Geldard's time at Springfield House, for example.'

'Why didn't they say anything about that to us? They'd surely have recognized the name.'

This time it was Perez who paused. 'You'd think so, wouldn't you? That's the question that's been bothering me too.'

The restaurant was small and unpretentious. Perez stood outside for a moment pretending to look at the menu and imagining Caroline walking past on a gloomy day and catching sight of her friend inside with a strange man. He thought that he'd check the restaurant's name with Caroline when he returned to Unst, but he suspected this was the right place. There were tables close to the window and it wasn't far from the university, so it was feasible that the academic could be wandering past after work. Caroline could easily have caught a glimpse here of Eleanor with her mystery man. Now it was two o'clock. The lunchtime rush was over and the elderly waiter found him a table looking out into the street. 'So that you can watch the world go by, huh?'

Perez realized he was hungry and ordered onion soup and steak. He propped Eleanor's notebook in front of him and tried to read as he ate. In a clearer hand there was the history of Lizzie Geldard and her death. Then the first sighting of the ghost. That had come during the war, when Peerie Lizzie had appeared to a Yell woman visiting her sweetheart who was stationed at the RAF station in Unst. The next day he was killed in a raid over Germany, and a week later the woman discovered that she was pregnant. So it seemed that a sighting of Lizzie didn't only foretell a new birth, but death as well.

By now the restaurant was empty apart from him. The waiter cleared his plate and offered dessert or coffee.

'Coffee would be wonderful. Unless you're wanting to close.'

'We're open all afternoon. In this climate we need all the business we can get.' He was French certainly, but the accent was less pronounced now. Now that Perez was the only customer this was more of a conversation than a performance.

'I was recommended your restaurant place by a friend,' Perez said.

'Oh?'

'Eleanor Longstaff.'

A pause. 'Poor Eleanor.' The man's grief seemed genuine. 'She's dead, you know. Murdered. It was in the newspaper.' He hurried behind the bar and returned with a page from a tabloid from two days earlier. The headline ran: *TV boss killed in the land of the midnight sun.* Which wasn't quite true, Perez thought. The simmer dim wasn't quite the same as full sunlight. The piece was heavy on sensationalism and light on facts. Perez suspected that the journalist hadn't made the trek north. Few editors would have the budget for last-minute air fares to the islands.

'Did Eleanor eat with you often?'

The man had made Perez coffee. Now he disappeared again and poured one for himself. He sat at the next table, not presuming to join Perez, but willing to gossip at a distance. 'She was a regular. She came for coffee and pastries sometimes on her way to her office. She worked here on her laptop. Or with her writing.' He nodded to the notebooks on the table. 'Just like those.'

'I'm a police officer from Shetland,' Perez said. 'I'm investigating her death.'

'So not her friend then?'

Perez paused. 'I didn't meet her while she was alive. But I feel as if she's almost a friend. That I'm responsible for finding out who killed her.' He wondered where that had come from. The waiter would think he was mad. And he'd only had a small glass of sharp red wine with his lunch.

The man nodded again to the books. 'Do you think they'll help you?'

'I'm not sure. Perhaps.' Perez drank the coffee. He thought Fran would have loved it here. She'd have charmed the waiter, as Eleanor obviously had. 'Did she come here with her husband?'

'A couple of times. Mostly for lunch, not dinner, and then they were always in a hurry. No time to drink coffee and chat.' The waiter smiled.

'And you're sure that it *was* her husband?'

The man nodded. 'Strong man, square face. Very short hair. Besides, Eleanor introduced him.'

'Did she come here with any other men?'

This time there was no immediate reply.

'It's important,' Perez said. 'I'm trying to find out who killed her. If it's not relevant nobody else need know.'

'She came one evening with a man,' the waiter said. 'Could have been anyone. A colleague from work.'

'But she often came with colleagues.' Perez drained the coffee. 'This must have been different or you wouldn't have remembered.'

'*She* was different. Like a little girl. Nervous.' He smiled again.

'And the man? What can you tell me about him?'

The man shrugged in a return to the Gallic performance. 'It was very busy. Bad weather, and everyone wanting to get out of the rain. I didn't notice.'

'You were fond of her. You would have noticed.'

They were both looking out of the window rather than at each other, but the tension increased.

'I think he was younger than her. A good-looking man. And she was nervous to be with him. Or anxious, perhaps that's a better word. That's all I can tell you.'

Perez wasn't sure that was true, but he knew it was all he was going to get today. He stood up and paid his bill. 'Who paid that night?' If the man had paid there might be a record of his credit card.

'Eleanor.' The waiter paused. 'When they were leaving they argued about it and Eleanor said, "Just think about it, will you?" It seemed to matter very much to her, whatever she was asking him. Then they went out into the night. He held an umbrella over her head, but she walked ahead of him into the rain.'

'Did you ever see him again?'

The man shook his head. 'Eleanor came in after that. The last time was a week ago and she had her breakfast as usual. But I never saw him again.'

Perez spent the rest of the evening in his hotel, reading through the notes. He went out and bought another notebook, hard-backed just like Eleanor's, and transcribed her words into that, leaving dashes for each letter he couldn't quite read. At eight o'clock he phoned Fran's parents' house to make arrangements to collect Cassie the following morning. He explained that he'd be coming in a taxi, which would go on to take them to Heathrow. 'I won't be able to come in, I'm afraid. It's such an early flight to Aberdeen.' An elaborate arrangement to avoid too much contact with them. Hating himself for the duplicity because they were good people.

'Of course, Jimmy. We understand. She'll be ready.' Fran's mother was excited because they'd had such a fine day and she was willing to be kind to him. He asked to speak to Cassie.

'I bet you've had a wonderful time.'

There was a rush of words as the child described the trip down the river, seeing the Tower of London and eating out. 'Real pizza in a real Italian restaurant.' A pause and then she added in a whisper so that her grandparents couldn't hear her, 'I'll be glad to go home, though.'

'So will I, Cass.' He whispered too and then clicked off the phone and went back to his notes.

Chapter Twenty-Two

ON THURSDAY MORNING SANDY LEFT Springfield House without talking to Willow. He could see her in the yellow lounge that had become her office and she seemed engrossed in a phone call. He didn't want to disturb her. He'd already said that he'd finish the interviews of the party guests and would call again on the people who'd been out when they'd done their first round of canvassing. Caroline had given them a list of everyone invited. Her family had left for home in Kent the day after the party, and before Eleanor's body was found. Willow was talking to them on the phone. Sandy was pleased to leave that to her. He didn't understand the southern accents.

He found that he'd become obsessed by the child on the beach, the little girl seen by both Eleanor and Polly. He didn't believe in ghosts, so she must either be real or a figment of the women's imaginations. And he couldn't see that both women would have conjured up the same vision from nowhere. Yet the girl wasn't on the guest list and nobody else had noticed her. Willow said that people often wandered into island events – friends of friends, who hadn't been formally invited, but who would be made welcome just the same. That was probably true, but Sandy was stubborn and needed to pin this down. And though he would never have admitted it to himself, he wanted something concrete to hand to Jimmy Perez when he returned. He wanted Jimmy to tell him that he'd done well.

Outside he looked anxiously up at the sky. It was grey and there was drizzle, but it was surely clear enough for the planes to get in. Sandy drove carefully out of the courtyard and towards Meoness. The school was tiny, one of those scheduled for closure, and only saved after the community made a fuss. Perhaps because there'd been doubt about its survival it was still in the original stone building that looked more like a kirk than a school. There was a view of the voe and the open sea. When he arrived it was playtime and the children were yelling and chasing in the yard. Less than a dozen of them, and most of them boys. Sandy hesitated outside. It wasn't just that schools – even peerie schools like this – made him uncomfortable. He knew the teacher. They'd been friends once. She'd been his first teenage crush. She'd gone away south to university and had worked in Edinburgh for a while and he'd heard that she was back. There'd been a piece in the *Shetland Times* about it, about her giving up her post as deputy head in a big school in the city to take on Meoness primary. Head teacher. Sole teacher.

A woman came out into the playground and rang an old-fashioned hand bell. He recognized her immediately as Louisa Laurence. He hadn't seen her for ten years, but she hadn't changed so much. A bit skinnier maybe, her hair shorter and smarter. The children filed inside, giggling and pushing. Sandy thought he'd timed this badly. She'd be busy now. Perhaps he should come back at lunchtime when she might be free to talk.

But then he thought he'd look foolish if he just drove away. Someone might have seen him from inside the school and, besides, Jimmy Perez wouldn't have done that.

He knocked at the classroom door and went in. There was a smell of poster paint, clay and floor polish. They were sitting around tables in rough age groups. The older ones were working from maths sheets. Louisa was squatting with the little ones, helping them build a model from cardboard tubes.

'Yes.' She got to her feet. Then she saw him. 'Sandy Wilson, what are you doing here?' Her voice was cool. He might have been one of her seven-year-olds misbehaving.

'I'm working on an investigation into a serious crime,' he said. 'Perhaps you've heard about it.' He was aware that the older children were listening in.

'I'm not sure how I can help.' She had smooth, dark hair and he thought she had more in common now with the English people in Sletts than she did with him. He was pleased that she'd known him at once, though. He'd wondered if she would have forgotten him.

'Perhaps I should come back later,' he said, 'when you're not so busy.'

'No need for that.' She watched a car pull up outside. 'That's Mr Rickard. He's here to take music – that's one subject I can't teach, even to the little ones. You remember me, Sandy, always tone-deaf, always told to stand at the back and mime.' She turned her attention back to him and smiled. 'If you're lucky I'll make you a cup of tea and you can tell me what this is all about.'

She asked the children to finish what they were doing and he looked around the room. As Davy Stout, the ferryman, had said, there was a preponderance of boys. He couldn't see any girls with long, dark hair. This would be a waste of time and he'd have nothing to tell Perez to make him proud.

They drank tea in a little room that acted as her office.

'What brought you back?' he asked.

She shrugged. 'My father died last year and my mother's on her own. Guilt, I suppose.'

'You had nothing to keep you south?'

'I don't have a husband or a family, if that's what you're asking.'

He thought she'd always had a sharp tongue. It'd be a brave man who took her on.

'So what are you doing in Unst, Sandy Wilson? And in my school?'

'The woman who was killed, she had a thing about Peerie Lizzie.'

'What sort of thing?' She took a biscuit from the tin that stood between them and dipped it into her tea. Her teeth were very sharp too.

'She was a TV producer and she was making a film about ghosts. But maybe she believed in them. She claimed to have seen a dark-haired girl, aged about ten, on the beach by Sletts, the holiday home on the shore. I'm trying to work out what really happened, but I didn't see any bairns to match that description in your class.'

'Perhaps she dreamed the whole thing up,' Louisa said, 'to make her television show more interesting.'

'I don't think so. Another woman saw the lass too. I'd like to find her.' He thought again. 'Do you know Vaila Arthur?'

'She works here part-time as classroom assistant, but she's on maternity leave.'

'What do you make of her?'

Louisa smiled. 'She's helpful enough. Chatty. Loves the kids.'

'She claims to have seen Peerie Lizzie.'

'I know that.' Another smile. 'I've heard the story many times. It gets a little bit more dramatic every time she tells it.' Louisa paused. 'I wouldn't have her down as the most reliable witness.' There was another hesitation before she continued, her voice confidential. 'Grusche Malcolmson was the cook here until she retired. She was an old pal of my mother, so I've known her for years. Vaila's a kind of niece of hers and she drives Grusche crazy with her silliness.'

This was classic Shetland, Sandy thought. Everyone connected one way or another. 'If you know Grusche and George, maybe you were at Lowrie Malcolmson's hamefarin'?'

Louisa shook her head. 'Grusche asked me, and I'd heard all about the wedding. I think she only retired because it was taking up so much of her time. I'm hoping to lure her back as cook. We still haven't got anyone permanent and she was brilliant. But I live in Yell with my mother and she hates being left alone all night. I'd have missed the last ferry home.'

He saw then how constrained Louisa's life was. She'd come back to the islands from her responsible job in Edinburgh, leaving behind her friends and her freedom, to care for a mother who made demands on her.

'So you can't help me in my ghost-hunting?'

'I'm not sure.' Louisa smiled at him. 'The girl you describe certainly isn't one of my pupils, but I might have seen her.'

'When?'

'Last Saturday. The day of the party.' She paused. 'I'd left behind a pile of marking, so I just popped back to Unst to collect it from the school. I had a bit of a wait for the ferry in Yell. It was a lovely day, so I didn't want to stay in the car. There was a young girl with a woman and they were waiting in the sun too. She had long, dark, curly hair. I didn't recognize her, but then she could have belonged to anywhere in the North Isles, or she could have been visiting.'

'Did you speak to her?'

'No. I'd been speaking to kids all week and I was angry with myself for leaving the paperwork behind. Making conversation with a ten-year-old was the last thing on my mind. My thoughts were running to a big glass of Pinot and a deep bath.'

'Did you see what they were doing?'

'I think they were taking photos of the seals that swim around the pier there.' Louisa was frowning, trying to concentrate. 'Maybe looking out for otters.'

'And they came to Unst in the ferry with you?'

'I think so. But I wasn't really watching. I was just thinking of getting back to the school and home again as soon as possible.'

In the classroom the children were singing. Scottish folk songs that Sandy had been taught as a bairn. Their voices were sweet. 'Perhaps I could come and visit you,' he said. 'When all this is over. Perhaps I could see you at home. Your mother might remember me. I used to make her laugh.' He remembered Mavis, Louisa's mother, as a shopkeeper in Lerwick. Stern on the outside, but given to giggles.

'So you did, Sandy. But my mother doesn't laugh much now and she doesn't remember anyone. Not even me, on her bad days. Dementia. She was older when she got me, if you remember, and the illness came on suddenly soon after my father died. At first I just thought she was grieving for him.' Louisa turned away.

'Then I could come to see you?'

The song stopped and there was a moment of silence.

'Why don't you do that, Sandy? You could make *me* laugh. I often need cheering up.'

Chapter Twenty-Three

SHETLAND SEEMED GREY AND GLOOMY WHEN they got out of the plane. And cold, as if the summer was already over. Perez dropped Cassie at school and watched for a moment from the corridor as she took her place in the classroom. She caught sight of him waiting and waved impatiently to send him on his way.

Driving through Shetland mainland to get the ferry to the North Isles, he wondered what the young people from Eleanor's company Bright Star would make of the space and the distances. The chill weather. Willow had said that she'd wait for him to arrive before talking to Charles and David, before asking the men why they hadn't mentioned that Eleanor had been in touch with them. She was looking out for him at Springfield House and then led him to the yellow lounge that they'd used as an interview room.

'It sounds as if you had a useful trip south.' She smiled, looking up from her laptop for a moment.

'I'm glad to be back.'

'What was Eleanor's mother like?'

175

He thought about that for such a long time that he saw she was wondering if he'd ever answer. 'Very elegant,' he said at last. 'Sophisticated. But not a happy woman even before Eleanor died, I think. They didn't have an easy relationship. And she couldn't throw much light on the investigation. Eleanor had lunch with her just before the trip north, and Cilla thought she was different. Unsettled. But there's nothing concrete. Nothing helpful.' He hesitated again. 'Anything to report here?'

'The techies have blown up the images that were on the two scraps of paper Vicki found at the scene.' Willow clicked on her laptop and turned it so that he could see the screen. 'They were definitely photographs, but it's difficult to make out anything helpful from such small pieces.'

Perez stared at them. One of them was of a corner of a building. Wood and glass. Contemporary. It must be in the background of the shot to contain even that much detail in such a small fragment of photograph. He wondered if it was familiar, but the perspective was strange and he couldn't quite make it fit anywhere he knew. The other was a slice of a face. An eyebrow and a strand of dark hair. 'Is that Eleanor?'

Willow looked up from the computer. 'I wondered that. So the killer ripped up a photo of his victim just before or after the murder? What does that tell us?'

Perez shook his head. 'Not much, except that the murderer knew Eleanor well enough to have a picture of her, but I think we'd already worked that out.'

Willow nodded. She seemed distracted and he saw that her attention had already moved elsewhere. 'What do we do about David and Charles?'

He paused again and wondered if he'd been this indecisive

before Fran had died. 'If Eleanor had been in touch with them, why wouldn't they tell us?'

'Just keeping their heads down, do you think? People have all sorts of reasons for not wanting to get involved in a police investigation. Even these days a gay couple might not want to draw attention to themselves.' She stood up. 'Sandy's done a check and neither of them has a record. Not even a traffic offence. Let's just talk to them, shall we?' He thought everything seemed very simple and straightforward to her.

They found David in the kitchen garden at the back of the house. It was surrounded by a high drystone wall and entry was through an arched wooden gate. Inside only part of the ground had been cultivated, the vegetables there planted in straight rows. The rest was overgrown, almost a meadow, and at the far end a lean-to greenhouse had its glass missing and the metal frame was rusting away. David was digging potatoes. He wore wellingtons and a checked shirt. They watched as he sifted the potatoes with his fork, shaking the sandy soil from them before sliding them into a bucket. He must have sensed Perez and Willow behind him, because he stuck the fork into the ground and turned.

'Tatties for tonight's supper,' he said. 'We should have our own broad beans soon too.'

'It's well sheltered here.' Perez couldn't think what else to say.

'We have to grow all we can. The transport costs are outrageous, and folk don't realize why everything imported is so pricey. The house seemed very reasonable when we bought it, but we hadn't factored in that all the repairs would be more expensive than they'd be in the south. And there's almost full employment here, with everything that's happening with the oil and gas. It's hard to get good men to do the work.' It was the longest speech he'd ever made. Perez saw that worry about the business was always with him.

'It's hard coming into the islands from outside,' he said. 'You have to start from the beginning making contacts.'

'I feel responsible.' It sounded like a confession. 'This was always my dream, not Charles's. If things don't work financially either, I'm not sure how we'll manage, whether we'll survive.' He was talking about his relationship with the other man and not just about the hotel.

'We need to talk to you.' Willow was brisk, businesslike. It was as if he hadn't spoken. 'Charles too. When's a good time?'

'I'll be in for tea in ten minutes.' The man seemed puzzled by the request, but quite relaxed. 'I haven't seen Charles since lunchtime, but he'll be there too.' He bent again to return to his task.

When they went to the kitchen later he was washing his hands under the tap, scrubbing his nails. The potatoes were in a colander on the bench and Charles was pouring boiling water into a teapot. For the first time Perez noticed how big Charles's hands were, very long and flexible. When he set down the kettle he waved them about, fingers together, so that they reminded Perez of a seal's flippers cutting through the water.

'To what do we owe the pleasure?' He was one of those men who hide their anxiety with joviality and bad jokes. 'You'll have a cup of tea?' Again waving the hands first towards the chairs at the table, then to the mugs.

Perez remained standing. But Willow nodded and sat down at the table. 'Eleanor Longstaff phoned you,' he said. 'A couple of weeks ago. About Peerie Lizzie. The Geldards owned this house.'

David looked blank. 'I didn't talk to anyone.' He was drying his hands on a paper towel and threw it into the bin.

Perez was watching Charles.

'What about you, Mr Hillier? Did you talk to her?'

There was a moment's silence. Charlie poured tea and went to the fridge for milk, which he tipped from the carton into a jug. This seemed to take a long time. At last he was back, facing them again. 'I spoke to someone,' he said. 'I can't remember her name. I suppose it could have been the poor woman who died.' He sat down and his big hands settled flat on the table in front of him.

Perez caught Willow's eye. 'When was this?' His voice was very quiet.

'About a month ago.' He looked up. 'You must realize, Jimmy, that we get a lot of enquiries.'

'But this was a television production company. A chance for some publicity. For you and for your business. That would have been a bit exciting, I'd have thought. You'd have remembered that, maybe researched the company on the Internet to see what they'd done before.' *Talked to your partner?*

'I told you, Jimmy, my days in show business are long over.' Charles gave a rueful smile.

'But you'd be glad of some media exposure for the hotel. David was telling me how difficult it is to make a decent living up here. And I understood that Eleanor was offering a performance fee.'

Charles lifted the hands, a gesture of incomprehension, and looked at David. 'Really, I don't remember anything of that sort.' The explanation more for his partner than for the detectives.

'So what exactly did Eleanor want from you?' Perez asked.

'Information, Jimmy. Nothing more than that. She wanted me to tell her the story of poor Peerie Lizzie. David had done the research. We'd put it all into a little brochure for any of the guests who might be interested. There was a child called Elizabeth, only child of Gilbert and Roberta Geldard. She was born in 1920 and died just ten years later. She was playing out in the garden under the care of a local woman, one of the Malcolmsons. Elizabeth slipped away from her minder to go to the voe and she must have wandered out onto the sand. Then the fog came down and the tide came in and she was drowned. They found her body the following day, washed up onto the shore. She was lying on her back with her hands by her side and she seemed quite perfect, although the story is that she'd been in the water all night.'

'There was no possibility that it was foul play?' Perez directed the question to David, who seemed a more reliable source of information.

'I found no suggestion of that at the time,' David said. 'I looked up the report of the death in the *Shetland Times*. The implication was that the young nursemaid should have been more careful, but nobody was ever charged. I tried to trace her – the nursemaid, I mean – but she died in 1993. I hadn't really expected to find her alive.'

'This was quite a project for you,' Willow said. 'Time-consuming when you have so much other work in the hotel.'

'History's always been a passion. I loved doing it. And, as you said, I thought the ghost story might bring in punters. We charge more than the other B&Bs on the island. We need to give our guests something extra.'

Willow turned to Charles. 'How did you leave things with Mrs Longstaff? You passed on David's research. Anything else?'

'She said that she'd be in Unst in a few weeks' time and might get in touch then.'

'And did she?'

'Of course not.' His voice had become shrill and high-pitched and he turned towards Perez as though he considered him to be more sympathetic. 'I would have told you, Jimmy. I would have realized how important that would be.'

Willow left it at that, but Perez didn't quite believe him. The hoteliers disappeared from the room, Charles seeming relieved to be let off the hook.

'Well?' Willow had finished her tea and had her elbows on the table. 'What now?'

'I think I could do with a bit of a walk to clear my head after all my travels.'

Willow looked at him quizzically and he thought she didn't quite believe *him* either.

He left her sitting in the kitchen and walked out of the main gate and down towards the voe, imagining a ten-year-old child escaping down this path many years before. This was a precious child conceived in middle age. Spoilt perhaps, doted on, used to getting her own way. The nursemaid would have had problems containing her. Lizzie must have played here before surely, and she would know the shore and the tides. This wasn't a stranger from the south come to visit relatives in the big house. But if the fog came down suddenly, as it could in the islands, it wasn't impossible that she lost all sense of direction. Even if the nursemaid followed her down to the beach and shouted for her, sound could be distorted by the mist. Then voices seemed to swirl in all directions, just like the fog itself. It wasn't the death of the girl that had sparked questions in Perez's mind, though, but the condition in which she'd been found.

She was lying on her back with her hands by her side and she seemed quite perfect. Almost posed, he thought. Just like Eleanor. And a body that had been in the water, even for one night, wouldn't look like that. Sea creatures would have nibbled at it; she'd be bloated and covered in weed and sand. Of course it could just be a story. Like the story of the ghost. The idea of a perfect body might have been a fiction created to provide comfort for the grieving parents. Besides, he wasn't here to solve a case that was nearly a hundred years old.

He walked back to the house and found himself sitting in his car. Here he paused for a moment. He should find Willow and tell her what he was doing. She'd be angry if he just drove off without telling her what was in his mind. That would be bad manners. But he started the car anyway and drove up the single-track road to Meoness. Outside George Malcolmson's croft he paused again and thought that he was being distracted and should concentrate on the present investigation. Then he opened the car door and went to the house. Grusche was in the kitchen ironing. In the laundry basket were clothes that obviously belonged to her son and daughter-in-law.

'Are you looking for Lowrie and Caroline, Jimmy? They're away south to Vidlin. They've put in an offer on a house there and want to measure up some of the rooms.' Her eyes were shining.

'So they're coming home?'

'Isn't it exciting? I couldn't let myself believe that they might come back here.'

'It was George I was after.'

She looked up sharply, but didn't ask what he might want with her husband. 'He's out on the croft somewhere. This time of year he can't bear to be inside. It's like a disease for him.

A sort of claustrophobia. Maybe it was all that time he spent in the lighthouse. On a rock station you'd be cooped inside for most of your shift. Having to get on with the other men. Sometimes I think it's given him strange notions about things, made him almost compulsive.'

'In what way?'

'Oh, nothing harmful, Jimmy. Nothing that would lead to murder. He always sits in the same chair, uses the same knife and fork and gets put out if I give someone his mug. If we go into town he has to check three times that the hens have been shut away. In the lighthouse everything was routine. Perhaps there's a thin line between that and ritual. Superstition. It gets worse as he gets older. Sometimes I think I should get him to see a doctor.'

Perez didn't know what to say and Grusche seemed not to expect an answer. He just nodded at her and went outside.

George was working in his vegetable garden just like David. Like everyone in the islands with a bit of land at this time of year. He was hoeing between lines of plants, his movements easy and regular and seeming to take no effort.

'Aye-aye.' He stopped and rested the hoe against the fence.

'I don't want to disturb you.'

'You're not doing that, Jimmy. I was ready for a rest.'

'These stories of Peerie Lizzie. It was your niece who was supposed to have seen her.'

'Vaila,' he said. 'She was last in the line when they were handing out the common sense. Not a bit of malice in her, but she was always kind of daft, even as a bairn.'

'You don't believe in the ghost then.'

He didn't answer for a moment. 'I was brought up to go

to the kirk every Sunday,' he said, 'but I'm not sure I believe in miracles, either. Only in what I can see with my own eyes.' But he turned away as he was speaking. Perez remembered what Grusche had said about his superstition and wasn't sure that he was telling the truth.

'You'll have been brought up with stories of Peerie Lizzie too,' Perez said. 'Was it one of your relatives who was supposed to have been minding the girl when she wandered off to the shore? I was told she was a Malcolmson.'

'She was my Aunt Sarah, my father's older sister.' He paused. 'She was only a girl herself when Elizabeth Geldard was drowned. Fifteen years old, taken into the big house to mind the child.'

'Did she talk about what had happened?'

'She left the islands soon after the accident,' George said. 'When she came back she was an old woman, very frail, and that part of her life was forgotten. There'd always been folk who claimed to see Peerie Lizzie, but by the time she came home nobody realized that she'd been involved.'

'Why did she leave?' Perez thought that sudden accidental death couldn't have been so uncommon in those days in the islands. Not sufficiently rare to force a young girl to flee.

'The Geldards blamed her,' George said. 'And they had money and influence. It would have been hard for her to stay. She went to work for a family in Inverness and married a boy down there. The relationship didn't last very long, but it seems that she had a child nobody had known about. A woman turned up to her funeral, claiming that my Aunt Sarah was her mother. You can imagine the gossip it caused here.' He gave a sudden grin. 'Every woman in the family wanted to invite her into their home to get the full story, but she was very dignified. She drove straight back to Lerwick and got the last plane south. We never heard from her again.'

He took up his hoe and began to push it between the seedlings.

But Perez followed him along the strip of grass left between the beds. 'Did Eleanor Longstaff contact you about all this? She'd been doing some research into Peerie Lizzie.'

'She never talked to me about it.'

'Lowrie then? She might have asked him. As they were such old friends.'

'If she did, he never mentioned it. You'd need to talk to him about it.' And George walked away to show that the subject was closed.

Chapter Twenty-Four

THE FOG CAME AND WENT ALL afternoon. There was no wind later in the day, but the mist seemed to thin occasionally as if by magic and then, for no apparent reason, returned and was as thick as ever. Polly and Marcus took a trip into Lerwick as Willow had suggested. At first Marcus hadn't been keen.

'We don't have a lot of time. By the time we get there we'll have to come back. Why don't we wait until we have a full day to explore?'

But Polly thought she'd go completely mad if she didn't leave the island. 'I'd like to look at the museum,' she said, 'have a dig around in the archives. We have time enough for that.'

He'd smiled then. 'Isn't that a sort of busman's holiday?' But he'd gone online to look at timetables and book ferries very quickly and they left almost at once. She thought that he was always happier when he was moving. He talked about settling down and finding a job that would keep him in the country for more than a month at a time, but she thought he'd soon get restless. They'd asked Ian if he'd like to join them, but he refused and Polly sensed that he was pleased to see them drive away. In the house on the beach they were like rats crammed together in a cage.

Lerwick felt like a big town after Unst. The boat to Aberdeen was moored at the ferry terminal. It looked huge, a reminder of the mainland, real-scale cities and real-scale transport. Polly looked at Marcus, wondering if he'd had the same thought as she'd had: they could just drive aboard and escape completely. But he seemed not even to notice it and had his eyes on streets and road signs, and was triumphant when he brought her straight to the new buildings of the arts centre and the museum looking out over the water.

'What will you do?' She knew that the museum would bore him. He was only interested in the exotic present.

'I'll explore the town. Meet you in the cafe back here for tea? Then I suppose we'll have to get back.'

'We could book into a hotel for a night.' The thought of returning to Unst and the house by the shore already made her feel panicky. She imagined a solid town house in Lerwick, a meal in a good restaurant, then frivolous television in their room. Something to banish thoughts of Eleanor.

He looked at her and she could see that he found the idea appealing too. For a moment she thought he might agree to the plan. 'Perhaps we'd better not,' he said at last. 'We don't want the police to think we're being difficult.'

In the main body of the museum there was a small display about Elizabeth Geldard and an oil painting of the girl, sitting at a window, with her hands on her lap looking very demure. She wore winter clothes, a knitted cardigan and a hat, and it was only the long hair that made Polly think of the girl she'd seen on the beach. This child looked rather staid and dull, and Polly couldn't imagine her twirling on her toes or skipping across the sand. There was no mention of the acquisition of the work, whether it had been a donation or been purchased. A small display board explained the legend of Peerie Lizzie, but Polly learned nothing new from it, except that a song about the girl had been written by Marty Thomson, a local musician.

From the car she'd phoned the archivist, Simon Barr. He'd heard of the Sentiman Library, shared her fascination with folk tales and agreed to see her at once. She found him upstairs in a big, open-plan office, with a view of the Hay's Dock. She decided this constant presence of water was adding to her unease. She'd never learned to swim and as a child she'd had nightmares about drowning. She hadn't thought about the dream for years, but since Eleanor's death it had recurred, just as she was waking, so it stayed with her all day. Now she pictured the sea eating away at the islands, nibbling them piece by piece until there was no land left and the water overwhelmed her. She sat with her back to the window facing Barr's desk.

'So you want to know about our Peerie Lizzie,' he said. 'Of course it's quite a recent legend, as these things go. My grandmother worked at Springfield House when she was a girl, though she's been dead for many years now.'

'Did she tell you what happened the day Elizabeth was drowned?'

'She told me her version of the story, but I couldn't say how much was true and how much she'd made up over the years. She was full of tales and, like a lot of old people, she mixed up the fact and the fiction in her mind, I think.'

'Did she believe in the ghost?' Polly found that she was holding her breath.

'Oh, she claimed to have seen her. She spent all her life in Unst. Before its present owners took it on, Springfield House was empty for years and local folk treated the land as their own, taking their children to picnic in the gardens. According to my grandmother, Lizzie appeared to her when she was picking raspberries there one summer. It was late in the evening and she was on her own. The child was dressed in white and seemed to walk towards her in the walled garden; then she disappeared although the gate was shut.' He paused and grinned. 'But don't believe a word of it. As I told you, my grandmother loved making up stories.'

'What did she tell you about the child's death?'

'She said everyone blamed Sarah Malcolmson, but it wasn't really her fault. She'd been given the day off to help her mother with a new baby, and she was only there when Elizabeth ran down to the shore because she'd stopped to chat to the lad who worked in the gardens on her way home. If anyone was responsible for the accident it was Lizzie's mother, Roberta.'

'Are there any reports into the accident?'

'Nothing unbiased. Gilbert Geldard was a landowner and a gentleman. The authorities were always going to accept his version of events. David Gordon, one of the owners of Springfield, has put together a pamphlet about the story for his guests. You're very welcome to look at the *Shetland Times* account of the tragedy, and I can let you have a copy of David's paper. He's a historian, so it's well put together.'

He'd told her all she'd wanted to know, but still she lingered in his office. It was new and light, but the atmosphere reminded her of her shared office in the Sentiman. She felt safe here, and all the horror of their stay in Unst was left behind. Of course there was no ghost. The stories were like the ones she worked with – you could trace them back to an original source, made more elaborate over the years. Soon they would return to London, and she would go back to work and everything would be well. She stood and took her leave.

She found Marcus in the museum cafe drinking tea and eating home-made cake. He caught a glimpse of her across the room and waved and smiled as if he'd been away on one of his trips.

'What did you make of Lerwick?'

'It was fun,' he said. 'Everyone knows each other. Which is comforting, but a bit scary. You wouldn't get away with anything here.' He reached into his pocket and brought out a pair of hand-knitted Fair Isle gloves. 'A present.'

She leaned across the table to kiss him.

Back in Unst they stopped twice on their way to Sletts. Once to look at the famous bus shelter, decorated like a piece of installation art, and once for Marcus to take photographs of seals hauled up onto the rocks. Perhaps because of the mist the animals seemed unafraid and allowed them to come very close before sliding into the still water. They groaned like people in pain and the noise echoed around the bay. They reminded Polly of fat, glistening slugs, grey and blotchy, and she wondered why people were so fond of them.

'There's a folk tale about the seals,' she said. 'Selkies. They steal the souls of women.'

'Do you think one of them could be Eleanor? Perhaps that sly-looking one with the long eyelashes.'

She looked at Marcus, horrified. She'd never thought he could be so hard-hearted.

'Sorry.' He put his arm around her. 'That was crass. But all this is so bizarre, isn't it? I'm having problems taking it seriously. If I stay here much longer I think I might go mad. Having that couple of hours away made me realize how stressful it's been. That house with the water on one side of it and the hill on the other. Ian so screwed up.'

She thought that she might be mad already. 'Do you want to leave?'

'I think we should stick it out until Saturday,' he said. 'That was the deal, wasn't it? After that you have to be back at work, and so do I. We leave Ian to it then. If he wants to stay, that's fine, but he's on his own.'

She nodded, relieved because she had something to look forward to, an escape back to London. She realized that it had been the open-ended nature of their confinement that had become such a problem for her. 'What do you think Ian will do?' She thought his determination to see the investigation through to the end had become a kind of obsession. Perhaps he believed he'd lose his sense of Eleanor if he moved away from the islands.

'He'll come too, won't he?' Marcus said. 'He'll see that no good will come of his staying here. I think he's someone who needs to work. He'll be better off in London with his colleagues. We just remind him of Nell.'

Polly wasn't so sure. Ian had always been stubborn. As Marcus drove back along the track to Sletts she looked into the windows of the houses. It had become a habit now, this searching for the child in the white dress. But the visibility was so poor that there was nothing but shadow.

It seemed that Ian had decided to escape from Sletts too, because when they got back the house was empty and his car was gone. Polly switched on the lamps in an attempt to cheer up the room, but the sulphur light bounced back from the fog, only adding to the sense of isolation. She peered through the window into the gloom. 'We could be the only people alive in the whole world.'

Marcus was back on his laptop, engrossed in answering a new bunch of emails from customers and didn't seem to hear her. She tried to read, but found it impossible to concentrate and stood behind Marcus and began to stroke his neck. She hadn't liked the idea of making love when Ian was around, but at last they had the house to themselves. Marcus turned and smiled at her in a distracted way and continued to tap on the keyboard. He was lying back in one chair, his feet on the rungs of another, completely relaxed, and she had the impulse to shake him.

'I might go out for a walk,' she said at last. 'I can't settle to anything.' She hoped to provoke the same reaction as she had when she'd gone out alone before. *Don't be stupid, there's a killer out there. Wait until I've finished this and I'll come out with you.*

But he just looked up briefly from the screen. 'OK. Take care.' It was as if he was so wrapped up in his work that he'd forgotten about Eleanor's death altogether and seemed to have no sense of danger.

It was the first time Marcus had made her angry. Previously he'd always been so solicitous and she couldn't see what could be so important on the screen. There was a brief flash of jealousy as she even wondered if there was an email from another woman that was holding his attention; perhaps that was why he seemed so engrossed, the reason for the self-satisfied smile. She picked up her jacket and went outside. There was a chill that she hadn't been expecting and she was tempted to return immediately into the warm. But she could be stubborn too and instead she walked back down the track towards the old croft house. The garden was overgrown, but the grass on the way to the front door had been trampled. There was no other sign of life. No smoke from the chimney this time. No face at the window. She knocked. The paint on the door was peeling and came off in blue specks on her fist. No answer. The door wasn't locked – there might have been a bolt inside, but there wasn't a hole for the key. She pushed it and was surprised at how easily it opened.

'Hello!' But she knew nobody could be living here. From the faint light coming from the open door she saw that the place wasn't habitable. Ahead of her was what had once been a tiny scullery. A bench with an enamel bowl standing on it. To the right the room where she'd imagined having seen the girl dancing in the candlelight. A beaten-earth floor. In one corner a small stove. She opened it and saw that there were blocks of peat inside, but the stove was cold and she couldn't decide if any of it had been burned. She walked to the window and thought that perhaps the dust had been disturbed on the sill and there was a drop of candle wax.

Looking in at her was a face. Pale and blurred by the dirt on the glass and the gloom of the fog. She screamed. The face disappeared, there were footsteps on the scullery floor and a man appeared in the doorway.

'What are you doing here?' He was middle-aged and his grey hair was too long and stuck up at the front, giving him a faintly clownish appearance. Something about the silhouette he presented, the angular body and that ridiculous hair were familiar.

'I was just looking,' she said. 'I'm so sorry. I thought the house was derelict.' Apology and politeness had always been her default positions.

'Oh, nobody lives here.' She realized now that he was English. He stepped further into the room and she backed away from him. 'Who are you?' he said. It was hard to tell whether he was angry or amused. The voice was flat.

'My name's Polly Gilmour. I'm staying at Sletts. My partner will be looking for me, if I don't go back soon.' She hoped that was true, but remembered Marcus as she'd last seen him, determined to be normal, to communicate with the outside world, and she wasn't sure if he would be bothered to come after her. She found that she was shaking.

'So you're one of Eleanor Longstaff's friends?'

'Yes.'

He looked her up and down as if she were a sort of biological specimen, then gave a sly smile. 'I think I've seen you around.'

'Who are you?'

'Charles Hillier. I run Springfield House. The detectives are staying there.' He seemed about to say more, but suddenly headlights lit up the room.

'That'll be Ian,' she said. 'Eleanor's husband. I should go. It's my turn to make supper.' The inanity struck her as crazy. She'd imagined seeing a ghost in this house and now some strange man had her penned inside it and she was talking about cooking a meal. She judged the distance between them and darted past him into the scullery. But he shut the front door with his foot and stood with his back to it, blocking her way again. She was trembling and found it impossible to think clearly at all. It felt like the worst sort of nightmare. With the front door shut, the small room was almost dark.

Suddenly someone was banging on the living-room window with the flat of his hand. 'Polly, is that you?' It was Ian. He must have caught sight of her in his headlights and stopped his car.

'Yes, I'm here.' She was surprised at how strongly the words came out: now she sounded defiant rather than scared. Hillier moved away from the door as Ian Longstaff came in. The three of them stood very close together in the tiny room. There was the smell of damp, but something else. Alcohol. Polly thought Ian must have taken off to a bar somewhere and had been sitting nursing pints and brooding. She wondered if Lowrie had been with him and, if so, how the man could have been so stupid as to let him drive back.

'Who are you?' Ian glared at the older man. Polly thought he looked like a gorilla picking a fight with another male for supremacy of the troop. Eleanor had always called him, with amused affection, her alpha male.

Hillier barked back his name. 'I own Springfield House hotel. Your friend here was trespassing.'

'So you own this place too, do you?' Polly could tell that Ian longed for a fight and realized he'd wanted to hit someone ever since he'd been told that Eleanor was dead.

'I know the owner.'

'And that gives you the right to throw your weight about, does it? To intimidate women?' Ian was bristling with aggression, so now she was almost more frightened of him than of Hillier.

'I'm not intimidated,' she said. 'It was a misunderstanding. Let's go.' She squeezed past the older man and out of the front door, pulling Ian after her by the sleeve of his jacket. He resisted for a moment, then the fight seemed to leave him altogether and he followed her.

Hillier stood in the doorway watching them. He was still smiling and called after them. 'Do you know who lived in this place?'

Curiosity got the better of her. Ian was walking back to his car, but she paused for a moment. 'Who?'

'Sarah Malcolmson,' Hillier said. 'The girl who was blamed for Peerie Lizzie's death. This was her family's house.'

Chapter Twenty-Five

TIME STRETCHED AND HAD BECOME UNIMPORTANT. The long-case clock in the corner had just struck eleven, but it was light and the team was still working, sitting in the yellow morning room in Springfield House. Occasionally they heard the drinkers in the public bar coming out to the courtyard to make their way home. Willow was uneasy. Just being here made them compromised – they were enjoying the hospitality of potential suspects after all. The remains left on the sideboard were of the supper provided by Charles and David. And earlier Perez had wandered off on his own to talk to George Malcolmson and that was unforgivable. Any information that the man provided would be uncorroborated, but it wasn't the breach in protocol that made her so angry, it was the attitude of Jimmy Perez. His driving away on his own had felt like a personal affront. Why hadn't he discussed his ideas with her first?

Sandy sat between them and seemed to have been infected by her anxiety. He looked at them like a child sensing tension between parents and wondering if he was to blame.

'I went to the school this morning,' he said. 'Just on the off-chance. I thought I might find the lassie Eleanor saw on the beach. If her mother was with her that day, she might have seen what was going on at Sletts. We know that Vaila Arthur turned up to see Eleanor the afternoon before the party; a witness might have noticed someone else.'

'Any luck?' Willow was glad to be distracted.

'No one in the school meets that description, but the teacher thought she saw the child with a woman coming off the ferry on Friday afternoon.'

'Just holidaymakers then,' Willow said. 'Probably not relevant.'

Perez looked up and she thought he was about to contradict her, but he said nothing. He had Eleanor's notes spread on the table between them and was occasionally writing in a book of his own.

'So what did you get from the Malcolmson house, Jimmy?' Willow finally found the silence unbearable. 'Did you speak to Lowrie again? We still don't know if Eleanor contacted him for more details of Peerie Lizzie before heading north.'

Perez looked up. 'No. Lowrie and Caroline were down at Vidlin, looking at the house they're planning to buy. I spoke to George, though.'

'Anything?' *Don't go all brooding and mysterious on me again, Jimmy Perez. I can't stand it.*

'The young maid who was looking after the Geldard child was a relative of his,' Perez said. 'Her family had lived in Utra, that derelict croft on the way to Sletts. After the tragedy she was sent south. She married a man from Inverness and there was a child apparently, who turned up for Sarah's funeral, surprising them all.'

'It should be possible to trace her. We should be able to track down Sarah's married name. Sandy, will you get on to that tomorrow?'

Sandy nodded. 'You think it might be important?'

'We won't know until you speak to her!' Immediately Willow felt guilty, because it wasn't Sandy who had provoked her anger. 'And, Jimmy, perhaps you can talk to Lowrie. It's become more important now to know what contact he had with Eleanor before the party. If she spoke to Charles Hillier before she came here, she'll have known that the nursemaid in the Peerie Lizzie story was Lowrie's relative. She would surely have wanted to talk to Lowrie about that, either in London or here.'

Perez nodded and returned to the notebook.

A silence. Now the light was fading. Willow wondered how Perez could possibly see to read. She reached out to switch on a lamp and his face was transformed into a series of planes and shadows. She felt an irrational urge to touch his forehead, because in the artificial light it looked hard and smooth like metal. He looked up and caught her eye and she turned away. She'd been caught staring like an awkward teenager.

'I wonder if Eleanor had already found Sarah Malcolmson's daughter,' he said. 'There's a name here on the page after she'd contacted David and Charles. Monica. No surname even. I can't see how she might feature here, other than as a part of the Unst ghost story.'

'Any contact details?' Willow leaned forward, but found Eleanor's handwriting impossible to read. Perez must have spent hours working through the book, becoming accustomed to its eccentricities.

'No, perhaps she'd only got as far as tracing the name.'

'Something else for us to work on tomorrow.' She stretched,

suddenly exhausted. 'I'm away to my bed. I wake up so early here and I need some sleep.'

Perez didn't move. She saw that the notebooks had become an obsession. 'Jimmy,' she said, 'you need to rest. It'll wait until tomorrow.'

Then he did look at her and, like an obedient child, he got to his feet.

She woke early, as the sunlight filtered through the crack in the heavy curtains onto her face. So at least the fog had cleared. She made tea and showered. Yoga, a ritual from her childhood in the commune, and then she felt ready for the day, suddenly full of energy and optimism. Today there would be a break in the case. The kitchen was unusually quiet. No David. No smell of coffee. Willow had a sudden panic that the men had run away, packed a few things into their car and taken the first ferry out; even that they had left the night before. Perhaps their questions about Eleanor had frightened them off. She hadn't seen them since dinner; later in the evening she'd collected a supper tray from the kitchen herself. They could be south to the mainland by now on the first plane to Aberdeen. Though she couldn't conceive what reason either of them might have for killing Eleanor Longstaff.

It was still too early for the real guests to appear for breakfast, and downstairs the house was empty. She walked through the grand entrance hall and tried to imagine what the place had been like in Gilbert and Roberta Geldard's day. There'd have been more servants. Someone would already be up sweeping the floors, lighting a range in the kitchen, and the big front door would be thrown open to let in the air. Perhaps Elizabeth had been unable to sleep because of the bright sunshine, even so early in the day. And she'd run out through the open door down to the shore to play. Then a mist had rolled in from the sea without her noticing and the tide had come in and surrounded her. She'd been stranded on a sandbank and drowned.

Willow followed in Peerie Lizzie's path, through the wide front door and out into the garden. No mist today. Bright sunshine and a gusty wind blowing the shadows of the clouds across the water. There was, though, a figure on the shore. A silhouette against the light, not identifiable at this distance. She thought it was probably Jimmy Perez, that he hadn't slept either and was standing looking into the middle distance and brooding about his lost love. She supposed she shouldn't disturb him, but decided she'd made allowance enough for his grief.

She walked down the grass track and through the big stone pillars. Wide flagstone steps led to the shore. The man was crying. His back was turned to her and he was quite silent, but she could tell from the movement of his shoulders. An oystercatcher called from the sandy grass as she disturbed it by walking to the beach. She'd known as soon as she'd left the garden that this wasn't Perez. This man was older and his hair was shorter, lighter. She hesitated for a moment, reluctant to intrude on his private grief. He must have sensed her watching him, because he turned suddenly and stood quite still until she reached him. It was David Gordon, tears and mucus streaming down his face. He'd always been so private and dignified that the sight was shocking. She supposed Charles had left him. Nothing else would account for such disorder, the filthy face and dishevelled clothes.

'Chief Inspector.'

'Mr Gordon, I'm sorry. I didn't realize at first that it was you. Would you rather that I left you alone?' She was tempted to mention the possibility of breakfast – yoga always left her feeling hungry – but decided that might be insensitive.

'No! Come with me!' He sounded completely distraught and she wondered if he was having some sort of breakdown, thought this was the very last complication that she needed.

She saw a line of his footprints in the sand. He was wearing rubber clogs and the prints were quite distinctive. He'd obviously come from further along the shore and now he set off back in that direction quickly, like a dog following a scent. She followed, stopping briefly when the sand was very wet, to take off her own shoes.

Charles Hillier was lying on his back, staring up at the sky, close to the tideline. It was not long after high water. His hair and his clothes were dripping. He was fully dressed in the trousers and shirt he'd been wearing the evening before. There was no immediate sign of injury, but he was clearly dead.

'You see!' David cried. 'I was coming to tell you, and then suddenly it hit me that I'd be alone for the rest of my life and I broke down. So selfish. So dreadfully selfish. Not to be crying for Charles, but for myself.'

Willow took in the scene. There was no chance they'd get Vicki Hewitt or James Grieve to Unst before the next high water, so they would need to move the body – Vicki was fastidious about maintaining the integrity of the crime scene, but even she would accept the need for action if the alternative was the corpse being sucked away into the North Sea by a particularly big tide. She pulled out her phone. Miraculously there was a signal. She phoned first Perez and then Sandy. She told Sandy to ask the remaining two guests to find alternative accommodation and to suggest that they leave Springfield House as soon as possible. They were an elderly couple from Bedfordshire; she already had their contact details and they were too frail to walk as far as the beach. Certainly they'd have been incapable of killing Charles Hillier, if this turned out to be murder. She asked Perez to join her on the shore. Sandy was full of questions, which she ignored. Perez asked none.

So she and David Gordon stood on the sand waiting. She didn't want to send him back to the house alone, and she couldn't leave Charles's body to the mercy of gulls, rats or dogs. He stood staring out at the water. 'I should never have forced Charles to come here,' he said.

'He seemed perfectly content, happy even.' She supposed this was what the man wanted to hear, but she thought it was true too.

'He was an actor,' David said. 'That was why he made such a good stage magician. He could make people believe whatever he wanted them to. He wanted me to believe that he was pleased with the move. But I knew he was bored. He needed more drama in his life than Shetland could give him.'

'Perhaps it was enough for him to know that *you* loved it here.'

There was a silence. David didn't respond to that. 'How did he die?'

She thought he must realize that she could have no more idea than him. 'Was he ill?'

'No. Horribly fit. I was the one who did all the exercise and was careful about what I ate, but he'd never had a day's illness.'

'Then we'll need to wait for the post-mortem.' In the far distance Willow saw Perez appear from the front door of the house and lope down the stone steps. She felt like the sheriff in an old cowboy movie, waiting for the cavalry to appear on the horizon. 'When did you last see Charles?'

'Last night. I went to bed early. There was live music in the bar, but our manager deals with that. He's local and he's very good at running the Thursday events. I assumed that perhaps Charles had popped in to see how things were going. I'd been working in the garden all day and I was exhausted. I went straight to sleep. When I woke early this morning I realized Charles hadn't come to bed and I came looking for him. I searched the house first. Then I came out into the garden and saw something on the shore. It was that blue shirt. I recognized the colour, but I couldn't believe it was him until I got here.'

'Was it unusual for him to be up all night?' Willow knew all this should wait until she had another officer with her and could talk properly to David as a witness, but it would be unbearable to stand here in silence, and all information was valuable. A small fishing boat came round the headland followed by screaming gulls.

'Yes, but it wasn't unheard of. He loved popular old television – it probably reminded him of his glory days – and if there were repeats of obscure sitcoms on BBC4 he'd sit up and watch until the early hours. Sometimes he'd fall asleep in the armchair and still be there in the morning . . .' David's voice tailed off.

'And last night?'

'Last night he went out after dinner. Sometimes he was restless. Perhaps he felt trapped here and just needed a sense of movement. He took the car and came back about an hour later.'

'Did he say where he'd been?' Willow tried to understand

this relationship. Had these men discussed what they wanted from the partnership, or had each been so careful about his partner's privacy that they'd simply tried to guess what had made the other happy?

'He said he'd been for a drive. The fog had made him feel trapped and he needed to get out for a while. When I went to bed early I hoped he might follow me up and that we might talk.' At last David turned away from the sea and faced her. He'd stopped crying. 'For a while I've had the feeling that he's been keeping secrets from me. Making plans. When I woke and he wasn't there, I wasn't surprised. I thought he'd run away.'

Like Eleanor, Willow thought. *Caroline thought that she was planning to run away from her partner too.* She couldn't think what else the two dead people might have had in common.

Chapter Twenty-Six

PEREZ WALKED BACK TO SPRINGFIELD HOUSE with David Gordon and wondered what he might say to provide comfort. Certainly nothing about his own experience of bereavement. When Fran had died and people had shared their own stories of grieving he'd wanted to hit them, to scream, *I don't care if someone close to you died. Don't use my tragedy to wallow in your own. You cannot come close to knowing how I feel.* But he *had* wanted to talk about Fran and to say her name.

'Where did you and Charles meet?'

David spoke without looking at him, to a background sound of waves breaking on the sand. 'Quite by chance in a cafe in York. It was the summer and the place was busy with tourists. I was living there, and Charles was performing at the theatre. His television career was already finished by then, but he was still able to pull in the crowds in provincial venues. There was a seat at his table and I asked if I could join him. "Excuse me," I said. "Don't I know you?" He was thrilled to be recognized, though honestly I don't think I'd ever seen him on TV. Later I realized that he looked very like a colleague from Leeds,

206

and that was who he reminded me of. But we talked and there was an attraction even then. He offered to leave a complimentary ticket for me at the theatre for his performance. I thanked him, never really intending to go. Not my thing. Charles always said I was a snob. But I was at the box office an hour beforehand and I knew I'd be devastated if the ticket wasn't waiting for me.

'After the show we went for a meal. And I suppose that was it. We've been together as a couple ever since. I carried on living and working in York, but Charles stayed with me whenever he wasn't working. Then he was offered fewer tours and I found teaching increasingly less attractive, so we decided on early retirement and a move north. Charles loved the drama of the grand gesture. And for a man used to life in the city, running off to Unst was pretty dramatic. He was passionate about the house and enjoyed supervising the refurbishment. But when that was complete there was just the everyday tedium of running and maintaining a place the size of Springfield. He was starting to be bored. We'd always planned to leave Shetland in the winters and do some travelling, but the house soaked up all our spare cash and I'm sure he felt trapped here.'

They'd reached the steps that led through the terraced garden. David paused for a moment, not to catch his breath – he was obviously very fit – but to remember. 'I've never told anyone else that story.' Another pause. 'But then nobody has ever asked.' They stopped at the front door. 'What will happen now?'

'Willow has already contacted the funeral director in Lerwick,' Perez said. 'Charles will go south for post-mortem. You met James Grieve, the pathologist. He's great at what he does.' He hesitated. 'Very respectful.'

'What do you think killed him?' It came out as a strangled cry of pain.

'Dr Grieve will help us to know that.' Perez remembered a conversation with the pathologist, late one night. Another case. They'd had dinner together and shared a bottle of wine. *My patients aren't the dead, Jimmy, but the living relatives. My responsibility is to them.* At least there was no mystery about what happened to Fran, he thought. I was there. He had a sudden flashback: the lightning glint of a knife in moonlight. A scream. He thought not knowing how she'd died would have been the worst kind of torture.

Sandy was waiting for them inside. 'I found rooms for the other guests in a B&B in Yell and booked them onto the ferry. They left five minutes ago.' His voice was almost a whisper, but David wouldn't have heard if Sandy had shouted. He was lost in memories of his lover.

'What should I do?' David asked. It was as if he was a stranger in his own home. Perez thought the roles had reversed now. The police officers were in charge of the place and David was more like a guest. 'I want to help.'

'We'd be really glad of some coffee, if you're up to making it.'

David looked grateful to have something specific to do and disappeared towards the kitchen. Perez sent Sandy to the beach to relieve Willow. Hillier's death must be linked to Eleanor Longstaff's, and he wanted to speak to the group at Sletts before news of the tragedy leaked out. But he knew better than to go without speaking to Willow first. The only time they'd really fallen out on an earlier case was when he followed his own line of investigation. And the previous evening he'd pushed his luck by talking to George without her permission.

He stood by the front door and watched Sandy's progress across the beach, then waited as Willow walked towards him. He saw her as if for the first time, the long, tangled hair and the easy stride, and thought she looked more like a Viking than most Shetlanders. He could imagine her rowing a longboat with the strength of a man. The thought made him smile and the image stayed with him until she reached him.

'Jimmy, do tell me there's a reason why you're looking so happy, because I don't have a clue where we should go from here.'

He shook his head and could feel himself blushing. 'I was thinking we should go and talk to the folk at Sletts before the news of Hillier's death is generally known. I'd like to see their reaction when they hear of it.'

'Could we get Lowrie and Caroline there too, do you think? They seem to have avoided our questions until now, and we can't rule them out of Eleanor's murder just because they were celebrating their marriage on the night of her death.'

'I could phone them,' he said. 'And it might be worth contacting the English people too to warn them that we're on the way. We don't want them deciding this is their day for a trip into Lerwick.'

'You do that, Jimmy. But tell them we'll be there in an hour. I haven't had breakfast yet and I don't work well on an empty stomach.'

When they arrived at the holiday house all the friends were there, taking up the chairs in the living room, so Perez had to drag two garden seats in from the deck. Caroline was sitting on the arm of Lowrie's chair.

'This is very mysterious, Inspector.'

He wondered if anything would penetrate her skin of efficient good humour. He couldn't imagine her ever crying, for example. Had something in her past led to her forming this protective shell or was it a feature of her age and class?

'There's been another death.' They'd all been looking to Perez for an explanation and when Willow spoke they stared at her, surprised. He watched them, but the shock seemed real.

'Who?' It was Polly Gilmour, as pale as a ghost herself, Perez thought.

'A hotelier called Charles Hillier.'

Perez thought he saw the woman flash a glance at Longstaff. 'You knew him?' he said.

There was a pause before Polly answered. 'We had a . . .' Another pause. 'An encounter yesterday.'

'What happened?' Willow leaned forward. They were similar in age and she could have been an old friend from university, encouraging gossip.

'I'd wandered into that derelict house on the way to the hall. Just nosy, I suppose, to see what it looked like inside. And Mr Hillier turned up to ask what I was doing there.'

'As if it was any business of his!' Longstaff seemed to have aged since Perez had first met him; to have turned into one of those angry, red-faced middle-aged men with a short fuse and a tendency to fall victim to a heart attack.

'You were there too, Mr Longstaff?' Willow again, keeping it calm and cool.

'I was driving past and I saw them in the house, just shadows in my headlights. A woman's been murdered here, and it looked as if Hillier was keeping her there against her will. Of course I was going to check that Polly was OK. She should never have been wandering around on her own.' He looked at Marcus. Accusing: *You should be taking better care of your woman.*

'And was Mr Hillier being unreasonable?' Willow again.

Polly shook her head. 'He was just being weird. I probably shouldn't have been there, but I wasn't doing any harm and he seemed to overreact big-style. Then Ian turned up and things started getting a bit fraught, so we just left.' She hesitated. 'Hillier said there was some connection between the house and the ghost that Eleanor claimed to have seen.' She turned to Lowrie. 'Did you know anything about that?'

Lowrie shrugged. 'The croft house was in our family,' he said. 'The lass looking after Lizzie Geldard lived there. Then my grandfather built our house on a bit of the land, and later Vaila and her man built their new place next door, and the old house was just left to ruin. It was a shame. I thought Vaila's husband might renovate and extend the old place, but I suppose it would have cost more in the end than starting from scratch.' He hesitated. 'And there's always been a kind of superstition about the building. Maybe they thought it would be bad luck to tear it down.'

'Is it ever used?' Willow asked.

'Maybe for storage, but probably not even for that now, it's such a damp old place.'

Perez thought Polly was about to speak again, but she turned towards the window and said nothing.

'What did you do last night when you got back here?' Willow asked.

'I cooked supper,' Polly said. 'There was heaps, so we phoned Lowrie and Caroline and asked them to join us. It was good to get together to remember Eleanor. Somehow she seems to have got lost in all this.'

'And then?'

'Then the others wanted to go out. I stayed here.' She paused and smiled at Ian. 'Ian was worried about me, but I felt quite safe. There are locks on the doors and my mobile has reception. I promised I'd phone if anything worried me. We've all been shut in together since Eleanor died and I longed for some time on my own.'

'Where did the rest of you go?'

'To the bar at Springfield House.' Lowrie took up the story. 'Ian had been round to our place in the afternoon and we'd had a few beers. I thought it might be good for him to have some company. Then after dinner I could see that he wanted to carry on drinking, so I suggested going to the bar. I didn't like the idea of him being in his room on his own with a bottle of whisky. I mean Polly and Marcus have been fantastic, but being here in Sletts must just remind Ian of Eleanor. There's sometimes music at Springfield House on a Thursday night, and I thought the noise and the people might help release the tension for a while.'

'And did it?' Perez remembered the days after Fran's death. He'd felt like drinking himself unconscious, but he never had. Too guilty. He hadn't felt he deserved to escape the pain.

'Yeah,' Ian said. 'But I've got a bloody awful hangover this morning.'

'How long did you stay in the bar?'

Ian shrugged and looked at Caroline. 'You drove us home. When was that?'

'I'm not sure.' Caroline turned to Perez. 'It was getting light again. Maybe two o'clock.'

'Were you in the bar with the men?'

'I stopped for one drink,' she said. 'Then I saw that it was going to turn into a session, so I came back to Meoness in our car and told Lowrie to give me a ring when they wanted to be collected.' She paused. 'It was obviously going to be a boys' night out and I had the feeling that I'd be in the way.'

'You didn't come back to Sletts to keep Polly company?' That seemed odd to Perez, if the two women were such good friends.

'No. I wanted to speak to the solicitor handling the sale of our house. He's an old friend and I knew he wouldn't mind me calling late. Now that we've made the decision to come north we want to get things moving as soon as possible.' Caroline hesitated. 'I've already handed in my notice to the university, and Lowrie's told his employer that he'll be leaving soon. It's a little bit scary that we won't have any real income for a while. We need to be planning our new life.'

Perez had the uncharitable thought that Caroline seemed to be viewing her friend's death as an interruption to her business plans. 'Were George and Grusche at home?'

'Are you asking me to provide an alibi, Inspector?' The question was sharp and angry.

'I'm just trying to get a picture of everyone's movements.'

'Grusche was at a book group in Baltasound. I'm sure her friends will corroborate her story. George was working outside, I think.'

Perez directed his next question to the men.

'When you were at Springfield did you see Charles Hillier?'

Lowrie shook his head. 'The owners hardly ever come into the bar. It's managed by a local guy, a pal of mine. Ian told me that he'd run up against Charles, but I didn't think there was any danger that they'd meet there.'

'Did any of you leave the bar for any length of time?' The

question came from Willow. 'Of course we'll be talking to the other drinkers.'

'By that time I was so pissed I could hardly stand,' Ian said. 'I didn't think much of the local band – the folk thing doesn't really do it for me – and I might have gone out to escape the music, but I don't remember anything about it.'

'I left for about half an hour,' Marcus said. 'It would have been around eleven. I phoned Polly. I wanted to make sure she was OK. She said she was fine, just going to bed and not to make too much noise when I came in. Then I phoned my mother. I hadn't been in touch for a few days and we chatted for quite a time.' He gave a wry smile. 'You know mothers.'

'If you were in the garden at Springfield you'd have had a view down to the shore,' Perez said. 'Did you see anything? Hear anything?'

Marcus gave a little laugh. 'The fog had come in again. It was eerie. There was a foghorn somewhere in the distance. Moaning like the seals we saw earlier in the day. But no, I didn't see anything.'

Chapter Twenty-Seven

BEFORE THEY'D ARRIVED AT SLETTS, Willow had discussed tactics with Perez. 'See if you can get Lowrie on his own afterwards, Jimmy. Talk to him about Eleanor. She must have asked him about Peerie Lizzie before she arrived for the party. Why hasn't he told us? Some last-minute fling with his first love before he tied the knot, do you think? Seems to me Eleanor would have been up for that. It would have amused her.'

Now they were all trooping out of the holiday house and Perez wasn't sure how he would manage to separate Lowrie from Caroline. The woman was so forceful and competent that she intimidated him. But it seemed she had plans of her own: a trip to a gallery in Yell to look at some pieces for the new house. 'Are you OK to walk home, Lowrie? If I take the car now, I should be back before supper.' So in the end it was quite straightforward and Perez joined Lowrie as he set off along the beach towards Voxter, his parents' croft.

'This is a terrible business, Jimmy.'

'Worse for you, perhaps. You were very close to Eleanor at

one time, I think.' Perez remembered Lowrie, red-faced and distraught after finding the woman's body.

'Has my mother been gossiping to you?' The tide was on the ebb now and the sand was hard where they were walking. It was hard to tell what Lowrie made of Grusche's interference. Or what he made of Eleanor's death after the first dramatic reaction.

'As Marcus said, you know what mothers are like.' *My mother wants me home too. She'd like me and Cassie in a croft in Fair Isle, where she can keep us safe.*

'I fancied myself in love with Eleanor when we were at university,' Lowrie said. 'It seems like a kind of madness now. But I was young and homesick and I'd never met anyone quite like her. She was like some exotic creature from another planet. For the first six months in Durham she filled all my dreams.'

'What happened?'

'She slept with me a couple of times for fun and then moved on to more interesting men. Men with more style and influence.' Lowrie stopped suddenly and looked out to the horizon. 'She said that I was very sweet, but she was ready for a grown-up.'

'A bit harsh.' Perez kept his voice light. He didn't want to make too much of this and frighten the man into clamming up. 'But you stayed friends?'

'I adored her. Better to stay friends than to lose contact altogether, I thought. One day she might need me, and I'd come rushing to the rescue like a knight on a white charger and she'd realize that I was the man for her all along. Then I came to my senses and saw that living with her would be a nightmare.'

'Ian managed it, though, did he?'

Lowrie hesitated. 'Ian's a very different kind of man.'

'In what way?' Perez was genuinely interested. He thought that of all the incomers Ian was the person he understood least.

'He's very certain. There are no doubts with Ian. Once he knows where he stands on an issue there's no moving him.' Lowrie slowed in his walk and turned to Perez. 'He was like that when he decided that Eleanor was ill and needed to be in hospital. The rest of us couldn't see it. We knew she'd hate it.' He paused. 'I went to see her in there. I didn't tell the others, but I just slipped in on my own after work. It looked pleasant enough, like a kind of hotel, but she was so miserable. It was making her more crazy than losing the baby. I told her she should leave. She was a voluntary patient. There was nothing to stop her.'

'And did she take your advice?'

'Yes. She signed herself out the next day.'

'What did Ian make of that?'

'I didn't tell him I had anything to do with it.' Lowrie grinned briefly. 'Too much of a coward. Ian has a lousy temper. I'm not sure what Nell said to him.'

'Did you see her on her own after that?'

There was a pause. Perez wondered if Lowrie was preparing to lie. 'Once,' he said at last. 'Ian was working away and I went to her house. She seemed better. She thanked me for giving her the confidence to leave the hospital. I asked how Ian had taken it and she said he'd realized she wasn't ill, just sad. And she'd decided not to get so hung up on the baby thing. *Maybe it's just nature telling me I'd be a crap mother. I've got a wonderful man and that should be enough.*'

'Did you believe it would be enough for her?' Perez asked.

'I think I did. She seemed calmer, better than she'd been for ages.'

'Did she talk to you about her ghost project?'

There was a long pause and Perez expected another confidence. 'No,' Lowrie said. 'She didn't talk about her work at all.'

'It seems odd that she didn't ask you about the project before she headed north for the party. We know she researched the background to Peerie Lizzie. She'll have known that the nursemaid in the story was a relative of yours.'

Lowrie continued his walk. 'Maybe she realized that Caroline and I were too wrapped up in the wedding to have given any time to her. Sensitivity wasn't exactly Eleanor's strong point, but she'd have seen we'd be too busy to help with a TV show.'

Perez thought about that. The Eleanor who'd been described to him was self-centred and passionate about her work. He couldn't believe that she'd turned away from a useful source of information just because Lowrie was planning his wedding. It wouldn't have taken more than a quick phone call after all.

'Did she ask to meet you at all in the last few weeks? More recently than when you met her for that drink?'

'Not to discuss her work!'

'But to discuss anything?' They'd come to a piece of driftwood. It was huge and twisted, white as bone. The trunk of a tree, sculpted by the water. Perez sat on it, forcing Lowrie to stop too.

'The six of us had dinner together about a month ago, to make final arrangements for the wedding in Kent and to talk about their trip north. You'd have thought they were trekking to the South Pole, the fuss they all made about it.' He sat beside Perez. 'What are all these questions about, Jimmy?'

'Eleanor met a man sometime before you were married. We're trying to trace him. It might not be important, of course, but it's a loose end.'

'Is that the guy Caroline saw her with in the restaurant in Bloomsbury?' Lowrie gave a little laugh. Perez thought he sounded almost relieved. 'Well, that wasn't me. Caroline rushed straight home that night and told me she'd seen Eleanor with a stranger. She made a big drama of it. I said if Eleanor was having an affair I wouldn't be so surprised, but it was none of our business.'

Perez wondered about the implications of that. Only the day before he'd been in London, but now he found it hard, looking out at the North Sea, to imagine himself back in the little French restaurant in Bloomsbury and to recapture the image described by the waiter of the couple sharing a meal. Perhaps it wasn't surprising that Caroline had told Lowrie about seeing Eleanor; her loyalty to her fiancé would be greater than her loyalty to her friend. 'And Eleanor never contacted you about her television project? Not even an email?' This was what he found most difficult to believe.

Another hesitation. 'Sorry, not even an email.' He turned away, so Perez couldn't see his face. If Lowrie was lying, what possible reason could he have?

They stood up to continue their walk.

'What's the talk on the island about Hillier and Gordon?' Perez asked. 'Your mother bakes for them and they buy your eggs, so you probably know them as well as anyone.'

'Are you saying that makes us suspects, Jimmy?' Lowrie's voice was suddenly hard and reminded Perez of Caroline.

'Of course not. But you'll have heard what people are saying about them.'

'A gay couple taking over the big house, do you mean? Things have moved on. We're not as bigoted as we used to be, even here in Unst.' Lowrie paused. 'There was some excitement because some folk recognized Charles Hillier from the television. He was quite famous at one time. One of those cheesy stage magicians. He did clever tricks, despite the dreadful patter. I was fascinated with them as a kid, got a magic set for Christmas. But most of us were just glad the house wasn't going to be allowed to fall into disrepair. None of the locals could have afforded to take it on.' He paused again. 'I only met them a couple of times, but they seemed fine men. I'm sorry that Charles is dead.'

'Does the name Monica mean anything to you?' Perez asked.

'In what context?'

'I'm not sure. Your father said that a mysterious woman turned up to your great-aunt Sarah's funeral. A daughter nobody had ever heard about. Could it have been her?'

Lowrie shrugged. 'I don't know anything about that. Sorry.' It was as if he was bored by the whole conversation. Perhaps, like Caroline, he wanted to get back to planning his new life in Shetland. Perhaps young Shetlanders had learned to let go of the past. Perez thought it was hard now to picture him as a young man obsessed with Eleanor Longstaff and desperately in love. Or even as an older friend who'd visited her in psychiatric hospital and listened to her troubles. He seemed cold and disengaged.

Chapter Twenty-Eight

THROUGHOUT THE INTERVIEW WITH the detectives Polly wanted to ask if they would still be allowed to leave the following day, but she felt it would seem selfish to press the point. She sensed the officers' disapproval already: they considered the group at Sletts as spoiled incomers whose lives were too affluent and too easy. In the end it was Marcus who put the question, when Perez and Willow were on their feet on their way to the door.

'Polly and I have to start home tomorrow. We need to be at work on Monday and we're booked onto the overnight boat south. I suppose that *is* OK.' Not tentative as she would have been, but breezy, confident. 'I mean, it's not as if we knew the man, and we're not even sure yet that it wasn't an accidental death.'

The detectives looked at each other. They seemed to have a way of communicating that didn't need words.

'Of course,' the woman said at last. 'We have no reason to keep you here. What time were you planning to leave Unst?'

'We told our landlady that we'd clear the house by one o'clock,' Marcus said.

Another look flashed between the officers and Polly sensed they were giving each other a deadline for making progress. Or for catching the killer.

'And you, Mr Longstaff?' Willow asked. 'Are you planning to leave tomorrow too?'

Ian paused for a moment. 'I don't know,' he said. 'It seems like a kind of desertion to go while there's still no news about what happened to Eleanor. But I can't stay at Sletts. There are other guests due in the house.'

He looked at Lowrie and Caroline, a plea for help. There was no immediate reply and Polly thought that the couple had already discussed this. She suspected Lowrie would have been happy to offer Ian a bed in Voxter for a few nights, but Caroline disliked the idea. Even now the woman remained impassive and there was a moment of awkward silence.

'So I'll probably go back with Marcus and Polly then,' Ian said at last. 'It seems as if I have no choice.'

They followed the police officers outside. The female detective drove off and Perez and Lowrie set off along the beach towards Voxter. Polly wondered what they might be saying to each other and thought again that if anyone was to find Eleanor's killer, it would be Jimmy Perez. Marcus and Ian wandered back into the house, to their laptops and their phones.

'You must be desperate to get away,' Caroline said to Polly as soon as they were alone. 'You've had a dreadful week. I've only sat in there for an hour and I feel so claustrophobic I want to scream. Perhaps it's the hill behind the house that makes this feel so shut in. I always think of Shetland as a place with long views and low horizons. That's what I love about it, the sense of space, and you don't really get that here. It's why I fell for our place in Vidlin – the fact that it's so light.'

'I do feel as if I'm going a bit crazy.' Polly wasn't sure how much she could say to Caroline, how much she should confide. Caroline wouldn't imagine girls in white dresses dancing in derelict houses. She was entirely sane.

'Why don't we escape for a couple of hours?' the other woman said. 'I'd planned to visit the gallery in Yell anyway and it has a nice coffee shop attached. We can have lunch and look at the art. Pretend we're back in London. Lowrie and I were given a voucher for the place as a wedding present. You can help me choose something for our new home.'

'Yes,' Polly said. She felt suddenly lighter, less depressed. For a couple of hours at least she could go back to the time before Eleanor's death. She and Caroline would look at beautiful things and drink coffee, and the talk would be of selling and buying houses, holidays and office gossip. And when they returned to Unst there would be just one evening to sit through and she could spend that time packing and preparing to go home. Life would be normal once more.

'Should we ask Grusche to come with us?' Caroline frowned. 'Of course there's no problem if you'd rather it was just the two of us, but she would love it.'

For a moment Polly was hurt. It seemed as if Caroline had already shifted her allegiance to her new family in the islands. Then she thought it would be good to take Grusche with them. If it was just her and Caroline they might end up talking about Eleanor after all. And she liked the older woman, with her sharp wit and laughter, her ability to sum up a character or a situation with a funny expression and a few words. 'Sure,' she said. 'Why not?'

It was the small ferry carrying them across the Sound to Yell, so there was no passenger lounge and they stood on the deck next to the cars. Grusche and Caroline chatted to the crew, calling them by name. Polly looked back at Unst. There was still a breeze and the water was chopped into small white-peaked waves. Back in the vehicle, waiting for the jaw of the ferry to open and let them out, Grusche and Caroline were still talking as if *they* were old friends – allies at least – and she was the stranger. Polly was sitting in the back of the car and Grusche turned to speak to her. 'The ferry boys said that Sumburgh's closed because of fog. It's hard to imagine, isn't it? That the weather down there could be so different.'

'Will the fog come here again?' Polly hated the mist and the way it shut everything down. The way it made her imagination run away with her.

'Who knows? It depends on the direction of the wind.' Grusche turned again and continued her conversation with Caroline about plans for the move. Polly wondered if she'd ever have that sort of friendship with Marcus's mother.

The gallery was new and built in the shelter of a small bay. The walls were of rough stone and rounded, so Polly thought of the sheep crus and planticrubs she'd seen on the hills at Unst. Of the place where Eleanor's mobile had been found. The owner was English, it seemed, and had made his money from a graphic-design company. This was his hobby and his indulgence. He'd brought a local potter in to run it for him, and she had her studio in the same building. Through a glass wall they could watch her at work. The owner was nowhere to be seen.

'No expense spared, apparently,' Grusche said. 'That's the way it is with some incomers. David and poor Charles must have spent a fortune at Springfield. That was such a big job, and they wanted it just so.'

They'd decided it was lunchtime and had found places in the cafe. Two elderly women were eating at the table next to theirs and Grusche greeted them and started talking about a mutual friend. The view from the big, curved window was of a pebble beach and hills beyond the bay. Inside there were examples of the gallery's art on the wall. Polly's attention was suddenly drawn to the painting of a young girl dressed in white. While the others looked at the menu, she stared at the painting, wondering if her imagination was playing tricks. The outline was misty, indistinct, and the background was all shadow. It was impossible to make out the features, but the dress and the ribbons in the hair looked horribly familiar.

'Who's that?'

'I'm not sure.' Grusche had noticed that Polly was staring. 'Though the name of the artist sounds familiar. Of course it doesn't have to be anyone local. The gallery stocks work by people from all over the country. That painting's rather old-fashioned, don't you think? Maybe something that's been done with the tourist market in mind.'

Polly thought there was nothing of the chocolate-box in the picture. The way the girl looked out at the viewer was disturbing, a kind of challenge.

'I think I saw that child.' Polly saw there was no escape from the nightmares even here. 'On the beach during the wedding party.' She looked at them, hoping for reassurance. Perhaps Caroline and Grusche, with their strength and their common sense, would have a rational explanation for her unease, her sense of being followed and undermined.

'You mean it looks like the ghost of Peerie Lizzie?' Caroline couldn't keep the mockery from her voice. 'Really, you can't let your imagination run away with you, Pol. It's being locked up in that dreadful house.'

A young waitress came with bowls of soup and bannocks and they began to eat.

Grusche frowned. Perhaps she thought Caroline was being unkind. 'There's only one painting of Lizzie Geldard and that's in the museum in Lerwick. She doesn't look anything like that girl, you know. I think you must be mistaken. All these dreadful things that have been happening . . . it's easy to let your imagination run away from you.'

'I've seen the portrait in Lerwick.' Polly thought Grusche was treating her as if she were a child who needed to be humoured.

'I always think the girl in the museum painting is very plain,' Grusche said. 'This lassie is quite different, don't you think? She's very bonny.'

'Do you believe in the ghost?' Polly looked up from her soup and waited intently for the reply, her spoon poised above the bowl.

'Not at all!' Grusche gave a little laugh. 'I've lived in Meoness for thirty-five years and I've never seen her. Though I have a sneaky suspicion that George is a believer. He claims not to be, but men who've worked close to the sea are terribly superstitious and he has some strange ideas. He doesn't talk about her, though. He thinks her death reflects badly on her family.'

'Why does he think that?' Caroline had already finished her soup and was spreading butter onto the remaining bread with brisk efficiency. Polly thought she'd never seen Caroline being dreamy or idle. Even her pursuit of Lowrie, when they were all students, had been carried out with a ruthless precision. She'd fancied him from the moment she first saw him and had decided she would make him ask her out. She'd just seen his infatuation with Eleanor in their first year as a challenge.

Grusche was answering. 'Because her nursemaid was Sarah Malcolmson, who was George's aunt, and she should have taken better care of the girl. There are different stories to explain Lizzie's death, but one of them is that Sarah was distracted from her duties, and her carelessness caused the accident. She was talking to her sweetheart, who worked in the garden at Springfield House, and didn't notice that the girl had run down to the shore in the mist. It's probably a pack of lies, but everyone loves a romance.'

'And she lived with her family in the house that's almost derelict now.' Polly was remembering her encounter with Charles Hillier and the strange smile on his face as he'd passed on the information. Looking back at the painting, she thought the girl in white had the same knowing smile.

'The house was called Utra,' Grusche said. 'We have photos of it before it fell into disrepair, if you're interested. George's mother as a young woman, just married, sitting outside it, knitting.'

'Why didn't they stay there?'

Grusche shrugged. 'Because it was so small. When old

George married he'd want his own space. Imagine them all crammed in together. Old George – that's Lowrie's grandfather – built Voxter before they started their own family.'

Polly pushed away her bowl and stood up to get a closer look at the painting. But as she got nearer, the girl seemed to disappear into the texture of the background. It was only when she moved back again that the figure became clearer, and once more there was another shock of recognition.

'Really, she does look just like the girl I saw on the beach outside the hall on the night of your party.' The words came out before she could stop them, and she gave a little laugh to show that she didn't really believe in the vision as a ghost. 'She has the same mouth and eyes. Some coincidence, huh?'

'Perhaps the child you saw was someone local,' Caroline said, 'and she acted as a model for the painting. Are you sure you don't know her, Grusche?'

Grusche stood up too to get a closer look, but shook her head.

Again Polly's eyes were drawn back to the painting on the wall. The background was of woodland and quite unlike Shetland. She knew she was being quite ridiculous. 'I thought I saw her another time,' she said. 'In the old house that's derelict. Utra. It was the night we'd all been to supper at your house. A girl dressed in white twirling round on her toes.' She snapped her mouth shut before she could say any more, but felt relieved that she'd told them about the visions. It felt good to have the words out in the open. She'd been wrong to bottle up her worries in her head. That way madness lay.

'You think you saw Eleanor's ghost-child in Utra?' Caroline looked at her strangely as if she was crazy already.

'Well, it obviously wasn't a ghost.' Polly gave a little self-deprecating smile, but really she wasn't sure. Perhaps that was what she *had* seen. The idea had been creeping up on her over the last few days, tugging at her reason, so she felt her rational thoughts unwinding like a hank of yarn. What other explanation could there be for the dancing child? A child whom nobody in Meoness recognized. She looked up at the other women. 'But somebody was inside.'

'That could have been anyone.' Caroline was dismissive. 'It must have been almost dark when you walked past. And we were all pretty spooked after Eleanor's murder.'

Not you! You've never been scared in your life. And I've been scared for most of mine. Not of being haunted, but of saying the wrong thing, causing embarrassment. Showing myself up. That's why I'm pretending now. Suddenly she longed for Eleanor, who would have listened to her without preaching or looking disapproving, whose solution to the ills of the world was laughter and another bottle of wine. 'I expect you're right. My imagination playing tricks in the weird light.'

Grusche gave her a strange look, but Caroline hardly seemed to hear. She'd wandered away to the gallery. Grusche followed, and Polly could hear them talking about curtains and colours, and whether an abstract painting inspired by Muckle Flugga would look well in a room with a polished wooden floor. 'I think that's the one Lowrie would prefer,' Grusche was saying. 'That's the one you should get.'

Polly heard the words, but they seemed to come from a long way off. She stood in front of the painting of the girl. There was an artist's signature in one corner. *Monica Leaze.* The name meant nothing to her, but she didn't need to make a note of it. She knew she wouldn't forget.

*

In the ferry on the way back to Unst they stood on deck once more and Polly felt a sense of foreboding as the island drew closer. She told herself that she just had to survive for one more night. When the vessel turned to inch its way to the pier she had a view south to Yell and saw a grey bank of fog on the horizon. It was as if the route of her escape had been closed behind her. By the time they'd driven back to Meoness the light had gone again.

Chapter Twenty-Nine

Willow and Sandy put together a scratch lunch in the kitchen at Springfield House. Willow was feeling restless. If she were on the Scottish mainland she'd be at the post-mortem by now. She'd know how Charles Hillier had died. Here, there seemed little to do but wait and she'd never been very good at that.

David had retreated to the walled vegetable garden. Earlier Willow had watched him from her bedroom window, digging and digging the uncultivated patch close to the shattered greenhouse, as if the activity would wear out his mind as well as his body and he'd stop thinking. She went outside to call him in for lunch, but even when she was right behind him he continued to plunge the spade into the sandy soil, then push it with his foot, his whole body straining to get the blade into the peaty soil, oblivious to everything else. She tapped him on the shoulder.

'Come in and get some lunch. You need to eat.'

He stopped. His face was red, and sweat ran down his forehead and into his eyes.

'Where is he?'

She didn't have to ask what he meant. 'Annie Goudie, the funeral director, has just arrived with a couple of men. Charles will be on his way to Lerwick soon. He'll be on the boat for Aberdeen tonight.' She paused. 'Do you want to see him? To say goodbye?'

'No!' He turned away angrily as if he intended to continue digging, then stopped, the spade dropped to the ground at his feet, and faced her again. 'I'm sorry, but I couldn't bear it. To see him so unlike himself. When he was alive he was never still.'

She nodded. A wheatear flicked along the wall that separated the garden from the open hillside. 'Is there anything I can get you? Tea? Water?'

He nodded towards a bottle of water standing on the path that ran around the garden. 'I'm fine. Really, it's very kind, but I'm better out here.'

Inside, Sandy and Perez had started to eat. Perez was making notes, methodical, just as when he'd transcribed Eleanor's scribbling. He reached out for a piece of bread with his left hand while he was still focused on writing with his right. Willow poured herself a glass of water from the tap and wondered how long they could continue to run the operation from Springfield House. This felt like an investigation from a different age, the three of them left to run the inquiry without outside interference. A Special Operations team during the war, perhaps a resistance group in a strange land. Soon she'd be under pressure to move back to the police station in Lerwick, where they'd have the technical support to investigate in a more orthodox way. And where her boss would insist on regular conference-call updates from Inverness. He was already worrying about the budget. 'Don't think you can claim overtime because you're staying out there. That's your choice.' When the three English people moved south they'd have no real excuse for being in Unst, so the following morning she'd hand Springfield House back to David and his memories.

She wondered what he'd do then. He had no real friends in the islands. Charles had been the sociable one, dropping into the bar occasionally in the evenings to chat to the locals. David had been happy to make things run smoothly behind the scenes. She suspected that he would sell up and move back to an anonymous flat in some small university town. He'd spend his days walking the hills and remembering with regret the only time he ever took a risk.

Perez looked up from his notes. 'How is he?'

'Angry,' she said. 'Trying to exhaust himself with digging. As if he could bring the man back by turning over the whole plot.' There was a clock on the wall and in the silence she heard it ticking, marking down the seconds until they would have to leave. The pressure felt tight around her head and she forced herself to breathe slowly. 'What have you got for me? Sandy, any news on the mysterious Monica mentioned in Eleanor's notes? We wondered if she might be Sarah Malcolmson's daughter.'

Sandy had his mouth full of smoked mackerel and bread and she had to wait for him to speak, and then he was full of apologies. Perez looked up from his writing again. 'Just get on with it, man!'

'Once Mary Lomax turned up to wait with the body, I went down to Voxter.' He looked anxious. 'You weren't here, but I thought that would be the best thing to do. I know you've talked to George already, Jimmy, but I thought he might know more about Sarah's daughter than he said. He would have met her at the funeral, so he'd have known her name at least.'

'Well? Was she our mysterious Monica?'

Sandy shook his head. 'Elizabeth. Her name was Elizabeth.'

'Sarah Malcolmson named her daughter after the child whose death she was accused of causing?' Willow couldn't make sense of that. It seemed like a strange kind of masochism. And hardly fair to the girl who'd remind her mother every day of why she'd been forced to leave the islands.

'Apparently.'

'Perhaps Sarah had been really fond of Lizzie Geldard.' Perez set aside his notes. 'In those days wealthy parents didn't do much of the real childcare, did they? Sarah would have been more like a mother to the girl. Perhaps the name was a way of honouring her memory.'

Willow wasn't sure about all that. It seemed a macabre thing to do. 'So we're still looking for the Monica who featured in Eleanor's notes. I don't suppose you've come across anything useful, like a phone number, Jimmy?'

'No.'

'So perhaps she hadn't tracked it down yet.' Willow took a ripe tomato from the bowl on the table and bit into it. The juice dribbled down her chin and she tore a piece of kitchen towel from the roll on the bench to wipe it away.

'Or maybe she knew it already. There's no surname, so perhaps Eleanor was friends with the mysterious Monica. Or had met her previously at least.'

Willow thought again that they didn't have time for this kind of speculation. She needed something concrete to give to her boss in Inverness. 'I want to track Charles's movements yesterday evening after he met Polly and Ian in the old house in Meoness. Did he go into the Springfield bar when the men were there, for instance?'

'Lowrie says not,' Perez said.

'Well, Lowrie's hardly an unbiased witness, is he?' Willow could hear the frustration spill out into her voice. 'He's an ex-lover of Eleanor Longstaff and a potential suspect.'

'Shall we look in Hillier's office?' Perez said. 'It might be a good time, while David's still outside. I'd be interested in any communication between Eleanor and Charles. Even if she just made one phone call asking about the history of the house and the Geldard family, why didn't he tell David? David was the historian, the expert.'

'And then I'd like to go to the derelict house where he met Ian and Polly.' Willow was already on her feet. Any action was better than sitting in this sad house waiting for inspiration to strike. 'Why would he go there? I don't buy the notion that he just drove around in the fog.'

'To meet someone?' Sandy had been following the conversation and was trying to help.

'Polly Gilmour, you mean? That could work. They'd arranged to meet and then Ian came along and surprised them.' But Willow couldn't see what possible connection there could be between a librarian from London and an ex-magician who ran a classy B&B in Shetland. It still seemed as if only Eleanor Longstaff linked all the people involved in the case. With her death they'd turned into a group of disparate individuals. And the encounter in the croft had obviously left Polly shaken. Would she have been so scared if the meeting had been planned?

★

The hotel office was a small room on the ground floor. Any money had been spent refurbishing the guest rooms and this work space was shabby. Flat-pack shelves had been put up in the alcoves and the desk looked as if it might have come from a charity shop in Lerwick. Willow sat at it and started the computer. Hillier hadn't logged off and she didn't need a password to get into the system or his emails.

'Nothing from Eleanor,' she said. 'Either they communicated by phone or he deleted the messages as soon as he'd read them.'

'Anything from the mysterious Monica?' Perez was working through the shelves, pulling out guidebooks and files. There was a box file full of receipts for the work done on Springfield House. He set it on the desk next to Willow.

'Nothing saved. But he seems to have been very diligent about deleting his emails. Mine go back for years.'

'More secrecy,' Perez said.

'But who would have access to this computer? Only David.' She was aware of Perez standing very close to her and looking over her shoulder. She imagined that she could feel his breath on her neck.

'That was the point, surely,' Perez said. 'Charles was involved in something to do with Eleanor's project and he knew that David would disapprove.'

'We'll take the computer with us when we go south tomorrow.' Again Willow sensed the movement of time as something tangible, like the tide or the wind. 'The geeks in Inverness should be able to track the email history. We might have some mention of your Monica yet.' She began to lift the receipts from the box file.

'Look at this! Hundreds of pounds for a set of bedroom

curtains. You can see why the couple were running out of cash.'
She wondered if David had sanctioned the expenditure or if
he'd closed his eyes to it because he knew the excitement of
renovating and decorating Springfield was all that kept Charles
in Shetland.

Perez had finished emptying shelves and turned his attention
to a painted cupboard that formed a window seat, the only
original piece of furniture in the room. It contained memora-
bilia of Charles's stage career, flyers and posters, a signed
programme for the *Royal Variety Show*, photos of Charles next
to men with wide lapels and women with big hair. He piled
the contents onto the floor. Then he stopped. He was on his
knees and was so still for a moment that it looked to Willow
as if he was praying. Then he pulled a pair of latex gloves
from his jacket pocket. She got down beside him and was
again aware of her body close to his. He reached inside the
cupboard and pulled out a small digital recorder, held it carefully in his fingers for her to see.

'It could be a coincidence.' Willow stood up. 'No reason at
all why it should be Eleanor's.' But she didn't believe in coincidence and she could hear the excitement in her own voice.
Here they could have found a definite link between the two
victims.

'Let's see, shall we?' Perez stood it on the desk and switched
it on. They heard an eager young woman talking about walking
along the path from Voxter after an evening with her relatives
and seeing the apparition of Peerie Lizzie.

'That's Vaila Arthur, telling Eleanor the story of her
encounter with Peerie Lizzie,' Willow said. 'Can we go right
back to the beginning and play it from the start?'

Perez pressed a couple of buttons. There was silence. Willow expected to hear Vaila's words again. Instead there was a child's voice. She was singing a simple melody; it was piping and a little flat on the high notes, but still moving somehow.

'What on earth is that?' She looked across the desk at Perez, whose face was white and quite still.

He waited a moment before answering. 'That,' he said, 'is Peerie Lizzie's song.'

Chapter Thirty

PEREZ RECOGNIZED THE SONG AFTER THE first few bars. Cassie had learned it at school and had come home singing it, over and over, to rehearse for the end-of-term show, until he and Fran had wanted to scream. And although Fran was still alive then, still a real presence in her own house, warm and strong and argumentative, he'd thought it wrong to teach Peerie Lizzie's song to the children. He'd understood the need for the bairns to be aware of their cultural heritage, the folk traditions, but this song had only been written twenty years ago, by Marty Thomson up in Northmavine, and it celebrated the death of a real child. But when he'd voiced his concerns to Fran she'd laughed at him and told him he was being daft and he'd spent too long as a cop. 'Kids love spooky stories. And most of them don't even listen to the words.'

His sense of her was so real that for a moment he imagined it was Fran sitting on the other side of the desk in the big house in Unst, and not Willow Reeves.

On hearing Willow's voice he was jolted back to the present, and felt the loss of his woman all over again. He felt he had to explain his reaction to the song, and as he did so his memory of Fran's laughter at his anxiety – at his notion that Cassie might be frightened – melted away. He'd wanted to focus on the memory, the sound that Fran's voice had made and the shape of her body with her head thrown back.

'A well-known local musician wrote it. It's a kind of ballad, using the story of Elizabeth Geldard's death. The children learn it in school – it's seen as part of their heritage, but the teachers also use it as a warning that the shore can be dangerous and the children have to be aware of the incoming tides.' As he spoke he was thinking there was something different about the song on the tape. It wasn't quite as Cassie had sung it. He considered asking Willow to play it once more, but was worried about the way he might respond. Perhaps he'd get emotional again, break down even, and he'd promised Willow that he was well now and perfectly fit for work.

'So why is it on Eleanor's recorder? Did Vaila Arthur sing it? More background to her story of seeing the ghost?'

'That wasn't a woman's voice,' Perez said. 'It was a child.' It was the one thing of which he was certain.

'So if we find out who the singer was we might know who else Eleanor met on the day of the party. Vaila only has a baby. It couldn't have been her.'

Perez didn't answer.

'We should ask Vaila,' Willow said. 'Come on, Jimmy. No time like the present.'

Perez felt her looking at him strangely and tried to concentrate on what she was saying, but he was thinking of the song and what was different about the recording from the version he knew. At last he got to his feet and followed her out of the house. They walked into the yard to pick up their car and found David sitting outside the walled garden, smoking.

'I gave up years ago.' He nodded towards the cigarettes on the bench beside him. 'These were Charlie's. He thought I didn't know that he'd started smoking again. I pretended not to, because I didn't want to nag. All these pretences and small lies. It seems ridiculous now. Why couldn't we just be honest with each other?' He sucked in the nicotine as if he hoped it would kill him immediately.

Vaila let them into her smart new bungalow. She had the baby over one shoulder and was patting her back. 'She's been crying all morning,' she said. 'Wind or colic. I'm not sure I'd know the difference, though.' And she looked at them hopefully as if they might be expert in the ways of small children.

Willow ignored her. 'I'm sorry to disturb you, but I've got a few more questions.'

Vaila put the kettle on, still holding the child. 'I'm glad to see you,' she said. 'My man's working away again and we all need adult company, don't we?' But her voice was cheerful; there was no evidence here of post-natal depression.

'I'll do this.' Perez nodded towards the cups and the teapot. 'You go and sit down.' He wondered what it might be like to hold a very small baby against your skin, how it might smell, and then thought again that he needed to pull himself together. With Fran gone, that was never going to happen.

In the lounge he poured the tea and offered milk and sugar as if it was his place. Willow and Vaila were already talking.

'We've found Eleanor Longstaff's digital recorder,' Willow said.

'You heard my piece then. What do you think it sounded like?' She looked at them, demanding their approval.

'Very good.' Willow smiled. 'Brilliant in fact.'

'So do you think they might still use it for the telly?'

'That's nothing to do with us.'

Perez could tell that Willow was starting to lose patience with the young mother. Eventually she'd come out with a sarcastic comment that would alienate their witness. 'There was something else on the recorder,' he said gently. 'A piece of music. Can you tell us anything about that?'

Vaila looked genuinely puzzled. 'Eleanor didn't play any music to me.'

'Did she ask you about Peerie Lizzie's song?'

'Marty Thomson's tune? No, nothing like that. Just about my story.'

'We're interested in the children who live in Meoness,' he said. He thought she would ask why they wanted to know, but she seemed strangely incurious about anything other than the possibility of appearing on television. 'Are there any kids aged between seven and twelve here?'

'There are bairns from the north of the island who come to the school, but nobody of that age living just around here.' She frowned with concentration as if she wished she could conjure them from thin air just to please him.

'You've got a climbing frame in your garden,' he said. 'Your Vaila's a bit young for that just now. Are you thinking ahead?'

She gave a little laugh. 'Kind of. Every day there's a change in her, and you know she won't be tiny for very long. But nah, we got that for Neil's boys. He was married before and they come to stay with us every other weekend.'

Perez thought about that. He'd assumed that a girl had been

singing on the recorder, but young boys' voices sounded very similar. Willow was looking at him, impatient for him to continue.

'When were they last here?' he asked. 'Were they here for Lowrie's hamefarin'?'

Vaila shook her head. 'Neil's a Yell man and he's no relation to Lowrie or his family. Grusche invited the boys out of politeness, but it wasn't their weekend for staying and they're kind of wild. I didn't need the added complication of keeping them under control. Neil's bringing them back for the weekend tonight with a peerie friend. That's the end of my peace for a few days.'

So it hadn't been either of her stepsons singing for Eleanor.

Willow stood up, eager to move on. Perez thought she'd been restless all day, anxious to have positive information to pass on to her boss to justify their staying in Springfield House. They stood in the front porch, ready to leave. The baby was asleep now and, on impulse, Perez reached out to touch her hair. It was as fine as down and he could hardly feel it. Her mother smiled at him – it was quite natural to her that he'd want to stroke her baby.

'Do you want a cuddle?'

'No!' He felt himself blushing. 'I wouldn't want to wake her.'

'Ah, once she gets off she sleeps like the dead.'

Vaila held out the sleeping baby as if she was a gift. Perez took her in his arms, felt for a moment how smooth and fragile she was and then handed her quickly back. He was worried he might cry in front of Willow. He'd always thought he and Fran might have a child, though it had never been discussed.

Outside Willow stared at him. 'What was all that about?'

'I've always been soft about tiny bairns.'

'Jimmy Perez, you never fail to surprise me.'

They left the car where it was and walked towards the old croft house. It was mid-afternoon and suddenly still and humid, with the smell of flowers from the in-bye land that was no longer grazed or cultivated. He was reminded of Fair Isle and wondered when he'd be brave enough to take Cassie to see where her mother had died. He'd promised they'd go before the end of the school summer holidays and he hadn't yet broken a promise to her. He'd wait for a still day like this, and they'd sail in from Grutness with his father at the helm of the *Good Shepherd*, so that Cassie could sit out on deck and watch the island get closer.

Willow was walking ahead of him and waited for him by the door. 'Well,' she said. 'What brought Charles Hillier to this place the day that he died?'

'Money.' Once the word was spoken it was obvious to him. 'He and David might not have had a conversation about how hard up they were, but both must have known that the business was failing. And they were desperate.' He imagined the men skirting around the subject, not wanting to face the difficult decisions that would have to be made, trying to be kind and not to blame the other.

'You think he might have tried his hand at blackmail?'

'Maybe.' But Perez had other ideas swirling around in his head.

'The English people all had the money to pay up,' Willow said. 'But what could Charles have that might hold them to ransom? Eleanor's digital recorder? All it tells us is that Vaila Arthur was telling the truth about being interviewed. And that a child sang a song about Lizzie Geldard to Eleanor Longstaff before she died.'

'Perhaps it wasn't the recorder at all.' Out at sea a flock of gulls followed a small fishing boat. 'Perhaps it was information. Perhaps he knew who'd committed the murder of Eleanor Longstaff.'

'He saw her being killed, you mean?'

'Or saw enough to guess.' Perez still wasn't sure how that might work out.

'So you think Charles had arranged to meet someone here?' Willow opened the door of the old house, but remained outside. Perez smelled damp stone and peaty soil. 'And Polly and Ian disturbed him?'

'It's possible.' In his mind he was running through a theory that seemed at once too elaborate and too simple.

'Shall we bring Vicki Hewitt back? See if we have evidence of a fourth person in the place?'

He was about to speak when there was a noise inside, something scrabbling and clawing, and a cry, piercing like a child's. Willow was about to go in, but he put his hand on her arm to stop her, and a creature shot past them.

'Feral cat,' he said. 'There are colonies on the cliffs throughout the islands. It probably got in down the chimney and couldn't get out. Trapped.'

His hand was still on her arm, which was downy like the baby's head. He could feel her shaking from the shock. A little embarrassed, he took his hand away.

Chapter Thirty-One

ON THE HILL NEAR THE SMALL LOCH where Eleanor Longstaff's body had been found, George Malcolmson stopped for a moment to watch what was happening in Meoness. This was a part of his daily routine. Every afternoon he'd walk the hill to check his sheep. Always in the same direction, quartering the hill in the same way, and always counting. It seemed there'd been another man killed. Another outsider. George couldn't pretend to be upset by that. He'd met the man a few times in the bar at the Springfield House, but didn't really know him. It wasn't like losing a family member. It wasn't enough to keep him away from the hill.

Now he looked down at Utra. He wasn't old enough to remember anyone living there, but when he'd been a boy the house was much as it had been left when the last inhabitant died. There'd been scraps of furniture inside and a couple of sheepskins. George's father had finally taken them to Voxter when it became clear that the roof was letting in water, and now one of the chairs stood in his and Grusche's bedroom. A car pulled up and two people climbed out: Jimmy Perez and the female detective who dressed a bit like a scarecrow. George thought professional people should be tidy. He'd enjoyed wearing his lightkeeper's uniform and it still hung in the cupboard at home. The two detectives stood in the door of Utra and looked about to go in, then stopped for a moment. He couldn't see why they hadn't just gone inside.

Then they disappeared into the house and the settlement was empty. George was about to continue walking when he saw a car pull up outside Spindrift, the new house built by Vaila's man. Neil was driving and then the kids got out of the back and chased round the house and started to swing on the climbing frame. Neil let himself into the kitchen. After a while the bairns went inside too – perhaps Vaila had called them in for their tea.

George thought back to the time when Lowrie was young. He'd never been a boy for shouting and chasing. Whenever George remembered him he was sitting at the kitchen table, doing his schoolwork. He'd always been fascinated by numbers and had shouted for Grusche to give him sums to do, just in his head, as if the quiz was the best kind of game there was. Sometimes when George came home from the lighthouse he felt like an outsider in his own house, because Lowrie and Grusche understood each other so well. They shared silly jokes that George couldn't understand. Then Grusche had told him that Lowrie had got his love of numbers from his father. 'I was always stupid about maths,' she'd said. 'He certainly didn't get that from me.' And that had made George feel better. Proud.

He shifted his gaze to Voxter. Caroline was in the garden, carrying a small wicker basket. She opened the door into the hen house and, though George was too far away to see, when she came out again he thought that the basket must now hold a few eggs. He wasn't sure what he made of his new daughter-in-law. Grusche said she was a clever woman and that she'd be good for Lowrie. George was just pleased that his son hadn't married Eleanor, with her long, dark hair and her secret witch's smile. He thought now it was a good thing that the woman was dead. She wouldn't be able to trouble the boy again.

Chapter Thirty-Two

SANDY MET LOUISA LAURENCE OUTSIDE the school. She walked through the yard carrying a smart briefcase and an armful of exercise books. A small red car was parked in the road outside and she stopped there when she saw Sandy.

'I'm afraid I have a few more questions.' He had the sense that she was in a hurry and his voice was apologetic.

'I can't stop now, Sandy. The carer leaves at five and my mother gets into such a panic if she's left on her own for too long.' She'd already tipped the books into the passenger seat of the car.

'Could I follow you down?' He could tell there was no point trying to talk to her here. Even if she stayed long enough for him to ask a question, she wouldn't concentrate on the answer. 'We could chat at your house. Once you've settled your mother.'

She paused for a moment and then she smiled. 'Why not, Sandy? I could use some adult company.'

★

Louisa's parents had retired to Yell when they sold their grocery shop in Lerwick's Commercial Street. Sandy seemed to remember that Louisa's mother, Mavis Laurence, had been born and brought up there, and that was why they made the move. The house had probably been specially built for them at the time, and he imagined it would have been the couple's pride and joy. It was a neat square bungalow with white render and a grey-tiled roof. The front door was locked.

'Sometimes she wanders,' Louisa said. 'It's a worry.'

Sandy followed her in, the pile of books in his arms.

The woman sat in an armchair looking out of the window over a tidy little garden and towards Unst in the distance. She'd been strong and fierce when Sandy had known her, running the business and acting as host in one of the halls at Up Helly Aa. Her husband had been a fine singer, Sandy remembered, and religious, but not in a strict or a hard way. Mavis Laurence had lost weight. She must have been middle-aged when Louisa had arrived, but now she looked very old and frail. Older, surely, than her years. A walking frame stood in front of her. She turned towards Louisa and gave a wonderful smile. 'Where have you been? I was just about to send your father out to look for you.'

'Father's not here any more, Mum. And I've just come back from work. This is Sandy. Do you remember him? Sandy, one of the Wilson boys from Whalsay.'

The woman turned towards him, her eyes kind of smeared and vague. 'Is this the young rascal that broke your heart? Your father threatened to beat his arse.'

Louisa blushed suddenly and deeply, and Sandy felt a stab of guilt and pain. He hadn't realized. He'd been so careless with his girlfriends when he'd been a young man, and now he was single and it served him right.

'You're confused, Mum,' Louisa said, giving a little laugh to hide her awkwardness. 'You're thinking of someone else. I was going to make Sandy a cup of tea. Would you like some? And maybe a piece of that ginger cake that we made together last night.'

Mavis clapped her hands as if she were a very young girl. Sandy sat with her while Louisa went into the kitchen to make tea. A sort of penance, and because he knew that Louisa would want him to.

'Your grandmother was Mima Wilson,' Mavis said. 'My mother knew her. She was wild too in her time.' Then she lapsed into silence. There was a bird table in the garden and feeders hung from it. She seemed to take great delight in watching the small birds come to take the seed.

'I used to come into your shop,' Sandy said. 'When Mima brought me to town for the day. I'd choose a bag of sweeties to take back on the bus.'

She looked at him as if she'd forgotten he was in the room. 'All the bairns came in for their sweeties.'

Then Louisa came back in again with a tea tray and slices of cake. She put a napkin over her mother's lap and cut the cake into small pieces so that she could eat it easily. Mavis ate a few squares and then seemed to drift off to sleep.

'So what questions do you have for me, Sandy?' Louisa seemed to have recovered her composure. She was sitting on the floor by her mother's side, her mug and plate on a small coffee table within easy reach.

'How do you cope with this?' He nodded towards the elderly woman. 'The stress of it. Every day.'

'We get on very well usually. Mother's in fine form today. Mischievous. As you noticed.'

'But with your work too. And all on your own. At school and here.' Sandy couldn't imagine what that could be like. Turning up to work every day and not finding colleagues and friends to chat with.

For a moment she didn't answer. 'It's easier than being in Edinburgh and worrying all the time about what was going on here.' Another pause. 'And I owe her, Sandy. Big-style.' She looked out of the window and he thought she was out of practice at making conversation with grown-ups. Then he realized that she intended to confide in him. 'I was adopted. Mum and Dad were middle-aged when they took me on. Not because they were desperate for a child. I don't think Mum was ever especially maternal. But because they heard about me through the kirk – about my mother being in a bad way in Aberdeen and not being able to care for me. And they took me into their home and loved me as if I were their own.'

'They wouldn't expect anything in return,' Sandy said.

'Of course they wouldn't, but it's a small way that I can pay them back for their love and their kindness. Do you see that?'

He nodded, but thought he'd never be able to give up his life for an old woman who hardly seemed to notice he was there. He'd end up resenting the demands she placed on him.

'So are you going to ask me those questions, Sandy?' Her voice was slightly impatient and he thought she was already regretting giving so much of herself away. When they were at school together she had never let on that she was adopted, even when the lads made fun of her older parents and the way they ran the shop.

'Peerie Lizzie's song,' he said. 'You know the tune written by Marty Thomson. Have the kids in your school learned it?'

'I haven't taught it to them. But then I don't teach music, and they might have learned it before I arrived at the school.' She was still sitting on the floor and looked up at him. 'Why is it important?'

'It probably isn't, but that old story of Lizzie seems to weave its way through the inquiry.' He knew he couldn't be specific, but still he valued her opinion. 'You don't believe in ghosts, do you?'

She laughed. He was glad to see it; he had the sense that she didn't laugh very often. 'Not the sort that walk through walls. But maybe I think that sometimes the past comes back to haunt us.' She paused and he knew better than to speak. He'd learned some tricks from Jimmy Perez. Louisa went on. 'Last year I was contacted by a social worker. My birth mother was trying to get in touch with me.'

'Did you meet her?'

'Once. But she was very needy. Still an addict, after all these years. Thinking that, with my good job and my settled life, I could help her get straight.'

Or fund her habit, Sandy thought.

'And I only have so much to give, Sandy. I had to make a choice. Between my birth mother and the mother who took me on thirty years ago.'

'You made the right decision.' He wished he could tell Louisa how much he admired her, but it was all he could think of to say.

'I'm sure I did, but it doesn't stop me thinking about the other woman occasionally.' She got to her feet. Obviously she'd decided it was time for him to go. 'This was the easy choice.

Running away north to be in my comfort zone. It feels a bit cowardly.'

'You made the right decision.' He repeated the words slowly, hoping that she might believe him this time.

'Is this all you came for, Sandy? To ask me about a children's song. You could have done that over the phone.'

'I was glad of the excuse to spend some time with you,' he said. 'And pleased to escape from the investigation for a while.'

There was another awkward silence, broken by the sound of Mavis's gentle snoring. He glanced out to the garden to see if her birds were still feeding on the table, but the mist had come in again and it was hard to make out anything other than grey shapes that looked more like bats than birds. Louisa walked with him to his car. There was a chill in the air and he thought some years there was no real summer at all.

'Does the name Monica mean anything to you?' he asked suddenly. 'It's cropped up in our inquiries. Maybe a character involved in the Peerie Lizzie legend in some way.'

Louisa shook her head. 'It doesn't sound like a local name,' she said. 'Not a traditional name certainly. I don't think anyone living in the islands at the time of Peerie Lizzie would be called that. Though I have a feeling that I might have heard it recently.'

'Will you get in touch if you remember where that might have been?'

'Of course, Sandy. You gave me your number when you were last at the school. I'll phone you if anything comes to mind.'

They stood without speaking again, frozen by a sudden embarrassment. 'I should go back,' Louisa said, 'just in case my mother wakes up.'

Sandy leaned forward and kissed her cheek. He thought he must look like one of the garden birds pecking at seed. 'Thank you. It was kind of you to see me. After I was horrid to you all those years ago. I'm sorry about that.'

She gave a laugh, very natural and giggly like a schoolgirl's. 'Don't flatter yourself, Sandy Wilson. It was never you that my father threatened to thrash for breaking my heart. It was Billy Leask. I told you that my mother gets confused.'

This time he was the one who was blushing. He got into his car and was just about to close the door when she said. 'Come back, Sandy. Whenever you need a break from your work. And don't go back to Lerwick without coming to say goodbye.'

Waiting for the ferry to Unst, he wondered what Jimmy Perez would make of his disappearing to Yell without telling anyone or asking permission. Then he thought that Jimmy would probably understand.

Chapter Thirty-Three

WILLOW AND PEREZ WERE ALONE IN the kitchen of Springfield House. Sandy had left a message to say that he was going to Yell to check with the teacher if any of the local kids had learned Peerie Lizzie's song as a party piece.

'I've heard back from an old colleague who works for the Met,' Willow said. 'He's been digging around into the financial affairs of Bright Star.'

'And?'

'You were right. Eleanor's company was on the brink of failure. It was only the ghost commission that persuaded the banks to give her some slack.'

'So she had that stress,' Perez said, 'as well as the loss of the baby.'

Willow didn't know how to reply to that. He always made her feel that she was cold, lacking in compassion. She wanted to talk to Perez about the case, not feel pity for a woman she'd never met. She was thinking about time, how it was slipping away from them, and her concern that at the end of the weekend they'd be forced to leave Unst and set up base in Lerwick.

Then there wouldn't be the same focus or concentration on the investigation. It would be a kind of failure. She'd just started trying to explain when David Gordon came in from the garden. He mumbled something that she could hardly make out: that he would take a tray to his room and wouldn't see them again that evening. He stood just inside the room and seemed set to grab a sandwich and run. There were smears of mud on his forehead and a rip in his checked shirt. The distinguished former academic had disappeared.

'Come in,' Willow said. 'I was just going to make some tea.'

'Is there any news?' Now David's voice was clearer – demanding, almost aggressive. 'Do you know who killed Charles?' He'd taken off his wellingtons at the door and wore thick white socks. He padded towards them and sat down at the table.

Willow didn't reply directly. 'Are you up to answering a few questions?'

'If it'll help.'

'We found a digital recorder in the office. It had belonged to Eleanor and we know that it was in her possession on the day of the party. Any idea how it got from Sletts to Springfield?'

'None. Unless Charles found it somewhere. It certainly has nothing to do with me.' He looked up at her. 'Could the woman have dropped it on the island?'

Like her phone. Willow couldn't believe that. Eleanor wandering round Unst and dropping things wherever she went. Too much of a coincidence. 'I suppose it's possible.' She poured tea and went to join him at the table. Perez was leaning against the bench. She thought again that he had the knack of making himself invisible. 'More likely, don't you think, that the two of them met up.' *Our two victims. Charles and Eleanor.*

Where did they meet, and what could they have had to say to each other?

'Charles had already told you he never set up a meeting.'

'And you told us that you thought Charles was making plans, keeping secrets from you.' Willow's voice was sharp. She wanted to jolt David Gordon into a response. 'Perhaps he was keeping secrets from us too, telling lies, and he and Eleanor got together on the afternoon of the hamefarin'. Are you sure she didn't come here? She had use of a car and it's not so far from Sletts.'

David shook his head. 'We were catering for a fortieth birthday that day. Lunch and afternoon tea, and lots of the guests stayed over. We were both busy for most of the afternoon. I don't think Charles would have had a moment to slip away to a meeting until late in the evening, and by that time of course the party would have been well under way in the Meoness community hall.'

'I don't suppose any of Caroline's family spent the night here?' Willow thought it would be the kind of place southerners might like to stay.

Again David shook his head. 'Caroline asked if we could put up a few of her guests, but we were already full. The birthday party.'

'And you weren't invited to the hamefarin'?' Willow thought that was odd. Grusche baked for them and supplied their eggs. This was a close community and usually everyone would be asked along.

'We were invited, but we didn't go. Charles said he might slip out later; he was always up for a celebration. The last thing I needed after a full day in the hotel was being dragged around the dance floor.' He gave a self-deprecating shrug. 'As you can imagine, I'm not much of a dancer. Not much of a party animal at all. Charles loved dancing and seemed to remember the steps when he'd only been told them once.'

'Do you think Charles could have called into the hamefarin' when you'd sorted out your visitors here?' Nobody had seen him, Willow thought, and he wasn't on the guest list supplied by Caroline, but he might have put in a brief appearance. Any proof that the two victims had met would give them something to work on.

'I don't think so. He didn't mention it.'

'Were you with him all evening?' But now, thinking about it in more detail, Willow couldn't see that Charles and Eleanor *could* have met once the hamefarin' got under way. The woman had been in full view of the other wedding guests, and later she'd been with her friends outside the holiday home. If Charles had been at the party, Ian and Polly would have recognized him when he turned up at the derelict croft. With his strange hair and his large hands he would have stood out.

'I worked for a couple of hours in the garden. I find it relaxing. An escape. I suppose Charles could have gone out then. I was inside by eleven-thirty, though, and he was certainly in the house when I got in. And if he'd been to the hamefarin' he'd have been full of it – the gossip and what everyone was wearing. He didn't mention it.' David looked up, startled. 'I can't believe that we won't have any more of those conversations. He was such an entertaining man. He delighted in trivial domestic details, things I would never notice if he hadn't pointed them out.' He paused. 'It feels as if my world's monochrome now. The colour has all drained away.'

And Willow thought he looked as if the colour had drained from *him*. He was a grey man. Burnt-out like wood ash.

'We're looking for a woman called Monica. Does the name mean anything to you?' Willow felt she was desperate, clutching at straws. A scribbled name in Eleanor's notebook. What could she possibly have to do with the murder of two people in Shetland?

David paused for a while. 'There's an artist who works in Yell. Came up from London a while back. Monica Leaze. But I don't suppose she could be the person you're after.'

Willow sensed Perez's interest. Nothing tangible, except a slight tension. She shot a glance at him, but there was no response.

'Could you tell us what you know about Ms Leaze?' she said.

'She held an exhibition in the gallery in Yell. We couldn't get to that, but I looked her up on the Internet. She paints. Interiors mostly. Interesting. She's based in London, but spends part of the year in Yell. I'd wondered if there was something that might suit here – we like to support local artists – but I felt that her work was too quirky and gritty for us. Our visitors expect something more traditional. Besides, we couldn't have afforded her. Then, about a month ago, we called in. The bulk of the exhibition had been moved, but there were still a couple of her pieces.'

'Did you meet her?' This was Perez, his voice so quiet that it was almost a whisper. 'If she stays in Yell, perhaps she was there. Talking about her work.'

'No, there was nothing like that. I wasn't even expecting them to have any of her stuff. We were going to Lerwick for shopping and called in on the way home. They do a good tea in the cafe, and we wandered around afterwards to look at the art.'

'Perhaps Charles met her on a different occasion?' Perez again, tentative, almost apologetic. 'If he liked her paintings . . .'

Willow wasn't sure where Perez was going with this. She couldn't make a connection between an artist in Yell, a hotelier in Unst and a film-maker from London.

For a moment David didn't answer. Willow even wondered if he'd heard. 'I don't know,' he said at last. 'And Charles was something of a philistine when it came to art. Leaze's stuff wasn't really his sort of thing.'

'But he might have met her in a different context?' Perez moved to the table and sat between them. His elbows were on the table and his hands cupped his face. He didn't look at David, but had obviously picked up some uncertainty in his response.

There was another moment of silence. Willow saw Sandy's car drive into the courtyard. She hoped he wouldn't come barging in. She sensed that this conversation between Gordon and Perez was important. 'Charlie was a good actor,' David said, 'but I knew him very well.'

'And you thought he might be pretending that he'd never heard of Monica Leaze?' Perez tipped his head slightly to the side to put the question.

'Not exactly that, but I'm not convinced that our calling into the gallery was entirely by chance. I wanted to come straight back. We'd had a long day and had bags of shopping in the boot. Charlie was insistent. "Let's give ourselves a bit of a treat. A real tea." He knew I'd never deny him anything that he really wanted. And then he looked at the paintings. I could tell immediately that they weren't his style, but he looked at them very carefully. Usually he would have been bored. He had a butterfly mind, in turn passionate and dismissive. But he took a sort of proprietary interest in them. As if they'd been painted by a protégée. Or someone that he knew.'

'Did you ask him if he knew Monica? If he'd met her perhaps in London?' Now Perez sounded like an elderly teacher, precise but encouraging. Willow wondered how he did it, how he seemed to know exactly what approach would work with a witness. He'd told her once, in a moment of weakness at the end of a case, that his ex-wife had called him 'emotionally incontinent' – too empathetic for his own good. Perhaps that was his secret.

Another silence. Sandy looked in through the window and Willow shook her head slightly. He walked away and round to the front of the house. At last David answered. 'I didn't ask him. I think we'd become so used to deceiving ourselves, about the business and our life here, that we'd stopped talking about anything important at all. And I was so afraid of prying, you see. We have a right to our own secrets, don't you think – our own privacy – even in a relationship? I thought if he wanted me to know what scheme he might be dreaming up, then he would tell me.'

Sandy must have gone to his room first and then waited until David Gordon had left the kitchen before coming in.

'Is that tea in the pot?'

He sounded cheerful, normal, and Willow thought that by comparison the rest of them were being affected by the nature of this case, becoming introspective and frustrated by ideas that seemed to dance away from them like shadows in the fog. 'How did you get on with your teacher?'

He seemed to blush slightly.

'Sandy Wilson, have you fallen for her? Do tell.' Teasing him as if he were a kid, because that was what they needed now. A bit of harmless fun.

'It's nothing like that.' He paused. 'We went out a few times when we were at school. I don't think I treated her so well.'

'Is she holding a grudge?'

He smiled. 'I don't think she is. She has a tough time at the moment. Her mother has dementia and Louisa is caring for her at home.' He paused. Willow decided he'd been thinking of this since he'd left Yell. 'Louisa was adopted. I'm not sure I could do all that intimate stuff for someone who wasn't my flesh and blood.' He looked up at them, realized they were both waiting for relevant information, and turned his attention to the case. 'She couldn't tell me anything useful, though. She didn't think her bairns had learned the song, but there's a specialist teacher who comes in to teach music. A guy called Joey Rickard. She gave me his phone number. I've just phoned him and he said he hadn't done the song with the Meoness kids, though it's the sort of tune they'd more likely get from parents and grandparents.' He poured himself tea and sat between them. 'How did you get on with David Gordon?'

'We might have found our Monica,' Perez said.

Willow was surprised by this. 'Really, Jimmy? There are lots of Monicas in the world. Probably a few in Shetland. It could just be a coincidence, don't you think? An artist, originally from London, with an exhibition in a gallery in Yell. There was no link with Eleanor, as far as I could see. And only a tentative one to Charles Hillier.'

She looked at him and wondered what she'd missed. What had Jimmy Perez picked up from the conversation?

'I went to the opening of the exhibition with Fran,' he said.

'It was held last summer, a few months before she died. The artist was a Londoner, who'd moved north for a while. There were a number of reasons, I think. A recent divorce, a sense that she wanted her work to move in a new direction and that Shetland might inspire her. Perhaps she was friends with one of the guys at Shetland Arts. We met her and talked for a bit. If I'd known her name I'd already forgotten it. Fran dragged me along to a lot of those occasions . . .'

He paused. Willow could see that he was remembering Fran Hunter, the love of his life. She had the uncharitable thought that no woman would ever compete with Fran in Perez's life. Fran would remain saintly and beautiful in his mind. She'd died before the couple had fallen into a boring rhythm of domestic chores and petty irritation, while the relationship was still fresh and exciting. Before Fran had developed wrinkles or middle-age spread.

'So tell me, Jimmy,' Willow said, pulling his attention back. 'Why do you think this Monica is the one mentioned in Eleanor's notebook?'

Chapter Thirty-Four

Perez tried to recreate the evening of Monica Leaze's exhibition in his head. He hadn't particularly wanted to be there; the discussion about the trip to the Yell gallery was the nearest he and Fran had come to a real row. He'd faced up to her in the small house in Ravenswick: 'I never know what to say to that arty lot, and I'm working an early shift tomorrow. You don't need me there.' He often felt awkward with her friends – shadowy, not a person in his own right. Sometimes they patronized him. But in the end he'd agreed to go with her. In the end he always did what he knew would make her happy.

'I'll drive,' she'd said. 'Then you can have a few glasses of wine, and anyway there'll probably be somebody there that you know.' And she'd run her finger down his neck, the promise of future compensations.

The gallery was new and seemed to rise organically from the pebble beach. One side was tucked into the hill, the other had a big window that enclosed the exhibition space and let in the clear northern light. The building had won an architectural award for its eco-design. They'd seen the artist outside on the way in. She'd been nervous and sneaking a quick cigarette before the public arrived. Fifty-something with wiry dark hair and button-eyes. Her nervousness had endeared her to Perez.

And so had her art. They were domestic pieces. Mostly interiors of ordinary rooms. Sometimes with a fragment of a person: a leg with a thick, wrinkled stocking and a slipper in front of an old-fashioned gas fire; a hand pouring milk from a plastic container in an untidy kitchen. In the paintings there was often an object that shocked. In an old-fashioned parlour set for afternoon tea – sandwiches with the crusts cut off, a tiered plate of iced fancies – a line of cocaine on an octagonal mirror. In an elderly woman's bedroom, on a dusty dressing table, a gun.

He'd been fascinated by the paintings, and while Fran caught up with her friends he'd stared at them. He'd decided they were like the photographs of crime scenes. Each piece held a narrative, a history of the room's owner. Then he'd come to the portrait of the child and he hadn't known what to make of it. At first sight it was a child from a different era. Dark hair twisted into loose ringlets and tied with white ribbons. A white dress. But the girl had a contemporary face. Knowing. A smile that might have been mischievous or complicit. Perez had stood and looked at it for a long time, and despite his reluctance to talk about art with Fran's friends – he was always anxious that he would show himself up in front of them – he'd sought out Monica to ask her about the painting. But Monica was standing with a glass in her hand, flushed and talkative, laughing a little too loudly, and he knew this wasn't a good time. So despite telling Willow that they'd chatted for a while, there'd been no real conversation. He'd stood on the edge of the crowd, listening, while she talked about her inspiration: 'I glory in the commonplace made weird.'

Instead the gallery owner had come up to him. Perez had met him once at a similar occasion, when Fran had turned out again to support one of her colleagues.

'What do you think of them?' The owner frowned.

'I like them.'

'I don't think they'll do well here. We sell mostly to tourists, and these are too urban. Or suburban perhaps. I'll keep a few pieces, though. Leaze is a big name after all. And the portrait of the girl. At first glance that's a traditional work and it might appeal to a grandparent. Something a bit odd about her, though, don't you think? Disturbing.'

Perez had agreed that there was. Then the evening was over and they'd driven to get the last ferry to Shetland mainland. And three months later Fran was dead. It occurred to him now, in a moment of complete madness, that the painting – so like the image of Peerie Lizzie described by the Sletts women – had somehow foreshadowed the tragedy.

He blinked quickly, dragged his attention back to the kitchen at Springfield and tried to describe the exhibition to Willow and Sandy. 'Monica Leaze made this painting of a child. White dress and white ribbons. Just like everyone describes Peerie Lizzie.'

'So you think she saw the ghost too? And painted her?' Willow leaned forward across the table and her long hair brushed his arm. He tried not to jerk his hand away.

That hadn't been the way he'd been thinking, but he considered the idea. 'Maybe. I suppose it's one explanation.'

'And Eleanor had tracked Monica down and arranged to meet her when she was coming north?'

'I think they must have met at some point,' he said. His mind was racing, chasing wild notions that refused to be pinned down.

'Eleanor must have had a busy afternoon the day of the party.' Willow sounded unconvinced. 'Vaila Arthur turned up to tell her story into the recorder; we think Charles Hillier might have tried to catch up with her at some point, either during the day or later in the evening; and now you decide that Eleanor and Monica had a meeting too. Just in the couple of hours that her friends took to walk along the cliff path. And knowing that they could come back at any time. It would only take a sudden rain squall to send them back to the house.'

They sat for a moment in silence.

'Maybe the party wasn't Eleanor Longstaff's first trip to Shetland.' This was Sandy, nervous that he might be making a fool of himself, looking up from his mug. 'I mean she was always travelling on business, wasn't she? So why couldn't she have come here? If she'd thought her husband would laugh at her for believing in Peerie Lizzie, she could have pretended she was in Brussels . . .' he paused, struggling to think of another suitable destination, '. . . or New York. Their only contact would be by mobile phone and the calls could come from anywhere.'

Another silence. Now that the words were spoken, Perez thought how obvious this was.

'Sandy Wilson, you're a bloody genius, and when this is all over I'm going to take you out and get you pissed.' Willow was laughing. 'Contact the ferry terminal and the airport. Let's see if we can track down if, and when, Eleanor arrived. She'd most likely have flown from London via Aberdeen to save time, and she'd have needed photo ID even for domestic flights, so she'd have used her own name. Then we track her movements. Who did she meet when she was here? And why have none of the buggers come forward when they heard about her death?' She stood up.

Perez thought he'd never seen her so excited. 'Where are you going?'

'I'm going to Yell to track down the mysterious Monica. And you're coming too.'

They knew it would be a rush to get there and back that evening. The last ferry north to Unst on a Friday night was always busy, so they'd want to avoid that. It would be full of kids who'd been to parties or down to friends in Lerwick. Couples who'd made the trek south for the sort of dinner out they'd not get in the North Isles. And late in the evening there'd be fewer ferries. The last thing they'd need would be to be stuck in Yell, or having to leave the car there and come back as foot passengers. And if Monica split her time between London and Shetland there was no guarantee she'd be there.

'Perhaps we're better leaving it until the morning,' Perez said. The only contact they had for Monica Leaze was at the gallery, and it was possible that nobody was there at this time. Of course Sandy should be able to track down a home address for them before they arrived in Yell. Mary Lomax would probably know. But Perez hated the idea of turning up at the artist's house, breathless and ill-prepared. She was crucial to the investigation, and she was famous. It seemed the worst kind of rudeness to barge in on a Friday night.

'We don't have time to wait,' Willow said. 'It has to be this evening.' He knew she was desperate to move the case forward before the soothmoothers left the islands. He saw that there would be no reasoning with her.

Still, in the car at the ferry terminal in Belmont he had another go at persuading her to put off the visit until the following day. 'Perhaps we should speak to Polly and Caroline first. Eleanor might have spoken to them about Monica. Or she might have dropped a hint that this wasn't her first trip north.'

But now he saw that Willow was caught up in the moment of the chase. She was enjoying the frantic drive to the pier, and the sense of movement was a reaction to the frustration of sitting in Springfield House running through the details of the case in her head. Perez thought again that she was obsessed by the passing of time; this was her attempt to stop the clock.

'We can't piss about, Jimmy. This might be our break-through.' Her eyes were gleaming. She was like a skua about to dive on an injured lamb.

By the time they arrived in Yell, Sandy had an address for them. Monica Leaze lived in Cullivoe, not too far from where the ferry came in. They turned off the main road and ahead of them the evening sky was red like flames, as if the sea was on fire. Everything was still. The banks on each side of the road were wild with flowers and grasses, the colours intense in the strange evening light. Willow was driving; she was too tense and fidgety to be a passenger.

When they found the house it was undistinguished, grey and small, a little ugly. There was no land attached, apart from a small square garden at the front, separated from the neighbour's by a slatted wooden fence. There were other, newer homes along the same road. A couple were squat bungalows and the rest were Norwegian kit houses in coloured wood. Willow pulled the car into a passing place and they climbed out. Outside Monica's front door stood a couple of terracotta pots, one containing mint and the other rosemary, but the lawn was overgrown. Willow opened the gate and knocked at the door.

No reply. Looking through the window, Perez thought the living room was too tidy. There was a Sunday paper neatly folded on a small table, but from the headline he could tell that it was at least a fortnight old. The cushions were piled symmetrically on the couch. It was oddly impersonal. No indication that an artist had lived here. No drawings on the wall. No paints. He stepped back a couple of paces and looked at the roof. There were Velux windows cut into the tiles, so perhaps Monica worked in the room in the attic.

An elderly woman was bringing in washing next door. She stood with a plastic basket at her feet, folding the clothes, but her eyes were fixed on the visitors. At last curiosity got too much for her and she came up to the fence. 'Can I help you?' She was all bone. Her face seemed to have been sculpted by the weather.

'We're looking for Monica Leaze.'

'Nobody's there. I haven't seen her for a couple of weeks. She comes and goes, though. It's more like a holiday place for her. I'm told she still has a house in London.'

Perez approached her. She'd probably respond better to his voice than to Willow's. 'Do you look after the place when she's away?'

'She never asked.' Perez sensed there was no love lost between the neighbours. Had Monica, tense and anxious and used to the anonymity of the city, resented the intrusion of a bored, elderly woman? 'Who are you?'

'We're police,' he said. 'Investigating the murders in Meoness.'

Her attitude changed at once to a manic excitement. 'Come in, come in. You'll take a cup of tea.' And they found themselves in her kitchen. The kettle already humming and some home-made flapjacks on a plate. Her payment for a story that would be retold by telephone to family and friends as soon as they left: *You'll never guess who was in my house this evening.*

'How long has Monica lived next door?' Perez was asking the questions. Willow was standing with her back to the window, trying to contain her impatience.

'She moved in about a year ago. She doesn't own it. It's rented from Johnny Jamieson in Lerwick, who bought it for holiday lets. I used to go in and clean for him once a week after the visitors left. He didn't pay much, but it helped out with the pension.'

Perhaps this was part of her resentment. With next door turned into a permanent rental, she'd lost her little job. She was continuing her story. 'I called round on her first day there, in case I could help at all. You know what it's like when you first move in – you can't find anything. She didn't even invite me across the threshold.'

'Does she rent it ready furnished?' That might explain the bland sofa and the bare walls.

'Yes, and that seemed kind of strange. If she was planning to live here full-time you'd think she'd want her own belongings. She didn't have much stuff at all. A couple of suitcases and a box with all her paints.' The woman sniffed. 'She calls herself an artist.'

'So you went round to see her,' Perez said. 'Can you tell us what she's like?'

'Kind of nervy. Skinny and a smoker. Dresses younger than she really is. All flowers and bright patterns.'

'Is it just her living there?' Willow interrupted. Perez saw her glance at the clock on the wall. 'No man or family?'

'I think she had a bairn here a couple of times. Young. Maybe a grandchild. But not living here full-time.'

'Boy or a girl?' Perez asked

The woman glared. 'How would I know? I don't snoop. I just saw them playing outside once.'

'But you might have some idea.' He smiled at her.

'I think it was a lassie. Though once she had a couple of lads to play with her too. They might have been local, because they didn't stay the night.'

'Can you remember when you last saw Monica? The exact date would be very helpful.' Perez again, coaxing her as if he was a favourite nephew.

'Exactly a week ago,' the woman said at last. 'So she hasn't been away as long as I thought.'

The day before the hamefarin'. Perez wondered if that had any significance.

'She might have been around since then, though,' the woman went on. 'I've been away at my daughter's down in Brae, so I wouldn't know.' A sniff. 'Not that Monica's bothered to cut the grass, if she has been there.'

'I suppose she locks her house when she goes out,' Perez said.

'I'm sure she does. She's never once asked any of the neighbours inside. I offered to go in occasionally when she was away, just to air the place, but she refused. "I value my privacy, Annie." It made me wonder at times what she has to hide in there.' The woman gave a theatrical shudder.

'Only we're a bit anxious about her,' Perez said. 'As she's not been seen for a while. It would put our minds at rest if we could take a look inside. And we'd prefer not to break a window to get in.'

'No need for that.' Annie gave a wide smile and paused for dramatic effect. She got to her feet. 'I've still got a key, from when I was cleaning for Johnny Jamieson. The woman might have been mad about security, but I doubt if she got round to changing the locks. Not even Monica would be that paranoid.'

She reached out and took a key from a hook on the dresser and held it out to them triumphantly.

Chapter Thirty-Five

THEY STOOD OUTSIDE MONICA'S HOUSE. Willow felt she already had an image of the woman in her mind: she'd be one of those people whose restlessness seems to generate impulsive action and creativity. When Willow was a child, Lottie, her mother, had been like that, fizzing with energy, firing up the family with her schemes, leaving them in turn exhilarated and exhausted. She'd worked in silver and enamel, made rings and bangles to sell at the local arts centre, but her whole life had been a piece of performance theatre. On a whim Lottie had invited a coach-load of tourists into the commune for dinner and had thrown together a meal for them in minutes. She'd needed a larger audience than the regular members of the Balranald community could provide. Now she was elderly and infirm, burnt-out and in her husband's shadow.

Perez had persuaded Annie, the next-door neighbour, to stay in her own house and keep a lookout for them. 'We wouldn't want to shock Monica, if she were to turn up and find strangers in her home.' He'd given her one of his special smiles and a card with his mobile number on it. Now the woman was glued to the window with the card in one hand and her phone in the other, feeling an essential part of the investigation. Willow wondered again what his magic was, how he managed to win people over. Perhaps it was something as simple as kindness. She would have been more brutal and would have told the woman to keep out of the way.

The key turned easily in the lock and they stood in a kitchen that had been updated as cheaply as possible, with chipboard worktops coated in a mock-granite plastic veneer. A Formica table had been folded against one wall. On the floor wood-effect laminate. Willow had already pulled on a pair of gloves and opened the fridge. An unopened bottle of supermarket Chablis, a packet of butter and half a dozen eggs. Which pretty well mirrored the contents of her own fridge, even when she was living at home. But she had a Sainsbury's just down the road and could shop every day.

'Looks as if she's cleared out most of the perishable things. Must have planned to be away for a while.'

The bin had been emptied. In the larder there were shelves of tins, olive oil, packets of pasta and rice, but there were no vegetables in the rack standing below the shelves. Monica was an organized woman, who hadn't left in a hurry. Perez stood in the middle of the room and seemed to be sniffing the atmosphere.

The living room was small and square. There was a post-war utility dining table, polished but scratched, again folded against one wall, a sofa and a television. An electric fire stood in what had once been an open fireplace. A postcard showing a picture of the Tower of London stood on the mantelpiece next to a bright-green china frog. Perez turned the postcard over to look at the message on the back and held it out for Willow to read.

See you soon, followed by a line of kisses. No name. The postmark was blurred. The address was M. Leaze c/o North Light Gallery, Yell. Willow wondered if that meant Monica was attempting to keep her home address secret. Various reasons suggested themselves: a bitter divorce had resulted in an abusive husband stalking her; debt; a desire for space and privacy.

On the sofa a line of red plush cushions had been arranged in meticulous order. The carpet was nasty and nylon. Willow wondered how an artist could live here, even on a temporary basis, and said as much to Perez.

He didn't answer immediately and, when he did, she wasn't sure that she understood him. 'I think this is just the sort of room that her art came from. She said she gloried in the commonplace made weird. And it is kind of weird, isn't it?'

On the other side of a narrow hall – more laminate flooring and an ornate gilt mirror – were the bedrooms. The landlord had obviously been determined to squeeze as many people as possible into the house, so there were twin beds in the larger room and a single in the box-room at the back. Willow thought they had probably been furnished entirely from charity shops. Perez opened the wardrobe in the big room. It was empty.

'We'll contact the landlord tomorrow and see if she's given notice. It looks as if she might have done a runner.' Though Willow thought that if *she* was planning to leave a place she'd have drunk the Chablis first.

In the box-room the bed hadn't been made up. Grey blankets were folded on a bentwood chair. There was no room for any other furniture. The wooden stairs to the loft were so steep that they were almost like a ladder. Willow went first and Perez followed. She was aware of him climbing behind her and could hear his gentle breathing. At the top she paused, with a sudden sensation of anticipation, fear even. The image of another body flashed into her mind. She pictured Monica Leaze, who was obviously tied into this case and had so much to tell them, lying dead on the attic floor.

But she knew she was being ridiculous. There was no stink of decay, no sign of a forced entry into the house. She hauled herself to her feet and looked around her. Here, for the first time, there was a sense that the artist had put her own stamp on the place. The floorboards were bare. No attempt had been made to sand or varnish them and in places there were splashes of paint. A big scrubbed pine table stood under one of the sloping windows and beside it there was an easel. From the window the view was out over a low-lying meadow to the water. There were no paints or brushes, and no cupboard where they might be stored. Monica must have packed them all away and taken them with her.

But she had left the easel. Perez had followed Willow into the room and was standing looking at it, his first point of reference. A piece of thick cream paper had been clipped to the easel and on it Monica had been making a pencil drawing. A woman lying on her back in a long, flowing dress. The background shaded. It was a sketch of Eleanor Longstaff lying dead in the loch at Meoness.

Chapter Thirty-Six

IN SLETTS, POLLY WAS PACKING. SHE WAS pleased to be in the bedroom away from Ian, who had already started drinking again. She supposed she should be tolerant, because a bereaved husband ought to be allowed to grieve in his own way, but his pent-up fury was becoming unbearable. And she wished that he didn't drink so heavily. It made him unpredictable and morose.

Her mother had been a Methodist and had disapproved of alcohol altogether. Polly worried occasionally that she was morphing into her mother, becoming middle-aged and anxious before her time. Sometimes Eleanor had teased her for being staid. 'Pol, just relax, won't you. You're still young!' Polly wondered how she'd cope without Eleanor to make her laugh, to tempt her to try new experiences. Would she turn into everyone's stereotype of a librarian, dull and officious? Then she thought that she had Marcus to bring adventure into her life, so perhaps there was still hope for her. She'd miss Eleanor's company, but recently the three friends had become more distant. Perhaps she'd already reached a new phase in her life.

When they were younger they'd been so close. Polly remembered the late-night conversations, the three friends squashed, half-sitting, half-lying, into a single hall-of-residence bed, a duvet tucked around them against the chill Durham night, drinking tea or chocolate or vodka, depending on the occasion. Then it had been a matter of honour that they had no secrets. They'd talked about all their dreams and fears in detail. Exposing their souls and their petty anxieties.

Now she was astonished at how far they'd drifted apart, how little of their personal lives they'd shared recently. Perhaps that had started with the move to London. London had demanded a gloss of sophistication and pretence. With their smarter clothes and their new friends, they'd developed different personas; suddenly they were competent, witty and self-sufficient. But now she thought that Eleanor and Caroline had always been actors, fitting into new situations in order to survive and excel. Perhaps they'd been performing as much in the draughty university bedroom as in the smart wine bars that had become their natural home in the city. It was likely that Polly, for whom the university experience had been a kind of magic, making her feel that she belonged with people of her own age for the first time, had simply been naive.

On the bed Polly laid out the bridesmaid's dress she'd worn to the hamefarin', folded it carefully and put it in the suitcase. She supposed that Eleanor's dress would be kept as evidence, and in the end it would be destroyed. She looked out of the window. It was early evening and the fog was drifting in from the water again, blurring the horizon so that it was impossible to see where the sky ended and the sea began. In the room next door she heard the men's voices. Marcus was being a saint. He hardly knew Ian, but he was supporting him, calming him, allowing him to talk. Allowing him to drink and to rant. Polly took a shirt from the wardrobe and folded that too.

She'd almost finished when Caroline and Lowrie arrived. She heard the door and their voices, wonderfully normal, and her mood lifted. The following day at this time she'd be on the boat south. Then she and Marcus would be alone in their own car for the drive to London. They could forget about Ian and dead people. Eleanor would have left Shetland without a second thought, in their situation. Polly had a tendency to be too introspective, and shutting herself away in her room wasn't helping. She opened the door and went out to greet her friends.

They were dressed almost as if it was winter, in anoraks and boots, and Lowrie carried a rucksack that clunked with bottles when he set it on the floor.

'You can't spend your last night in Shetland tucked away in here brooding,' Caroline said. Classic Caroline, prefect and social worker rolled into one. 'We've got a plan.'

It seemed that a friend of Lowrie's was a chef and he'd come across from Lerwick to set up a pop-up restaurant for the night in the boat club, in a settlement just down the coast. 'A couple of miles' walk to get us hungry,' Caroline said. 'Then great Shetland food, some good wine, and we'll roll back before it gets too late. What do you think?'

Polly thought that whatever they made of the plan, the rest of them would go along with it. Caroline in this mood was unstoppable. And although they teased her for being bossy, actually they were usually glad to have someone to make decisions for them. Without her they would dither and nothing would get done.

And it seemed that Ian was up for an evening away from the house, was even the most enthusiastic of them. They put on their outdoor clothes and set out on the walk. The path took them past the spot where Eleanor's body had been found, but nobody mentioned it. *We're so selfish*, Polly thought. *We care more about our own psyches than we do about our dead friend. We do what we must to survive intact.*

When they arrived at the boat club the party was already in full swing. It was in a modern wooden building looking over a small marina, where small motorboats were tied to a line of jetties and the occasional grand yacht was moored. The club room was on the first floor and they left their outdoor clothes in the cloakroom downstairs. From the room came the sound of laughter, a gabble of voices. Polly had a moment of panic. She was an undergraduate again preparing to attend a formal college dinner, hesitating outside, sick with nerves, certain that she'd use the wrong fork, would blush whenever anyone spoke to her; that she would break one of those unwritten rules that set the educated middle classes apart from the rest. Waiting to go into the club room, she had the same physical signs of panic – the racing heart and sweating palms, the same instinct to run. Then it had been Eleanor who'd arrived, linked arms and swept her into the hall before she could protest. Now it was Marcus, who gave a theatrical little bow, offered her his arm and walked with her up the stairs.

The room had been set out with two long trestle tables covered with white cloths and decorated with candles and flowers in glass vases. Boat-club members dressed in black were acting as waiters. It seemed as if everyone had been waiting for them, because there was a sympathetic cheer when they walked in, and Marcus – reading the situation immaculately as always – gave another, deeper bow. Caroline waved at people she knew. They were handed a small glass of whisky and took their seats at the end of the table. Lowrie pulled the bottles of wine from his rucksack. In the corner a young woman began to play a plaintive tune on the violin. Polly drank the whisky and found that her pulse had steadied. Food appeared on the table: fish and lamb, but in front of her a dish of roasted vegetables and a lentil-and-mushroom sauce, which, it seemed, had been cooked specially for her. The waitress even knew her name.

It took her a while to settle. She still felt that they were the centre of attention, and the inquisitive glances from other diners made her feel uncomfortable, thrown. As if she'd stumbled into a surprise party, only to realize that hers was the birthday being celebrated. She supposed the murders had made them objects of interest. Eventually, after a glass of wine, she began to relax and take in her surroundings. Marcus was having a great time. She saw that he viewed these social occasions in Shetland with the same clear, anthropological eye as when he'd shared supper with Berber villagers in Morocco. Perhaps he'd plan a trip here for rich American and German tourists, persuade the boat club and Lowrie's friend to recreate this dinner just for them. She wondered if there might be something slightly patronizing in his attitude to his hosts; he was an observer rather than a participant and she sensed that he found the local customs faintly amusing. But then she was an observer too.

Lowrie and Caroline seemed to know most of the people in the room. Polly recognized some of them from the wedding party. There was Lowrie's cousin, the chatty young woman with the baby, and her husband. All the talk was of the newly-weds' move back to Shetland and the new house in Vidlin. Nobody mentioned the murders. Perhaps the frenetic jollity, the too-brittle laughter, were an attempt to cover the awkward fact that the hosts knew they could be entertaining potential killers. In lulls in the conversation Polly heard Caroline and Lowrie gossiping about mutual friends, university politics and illicit love affairs. It was as if Eleanor hadn't died and normal life had been resumed.

Polly was sitting next to Caroline on one side and a large woman wearing a loose silk tunic in a vivid purple on the other. Caroline was talking to a friend across the table.

'So you work at the Sentiman Library?' The large woman in purple had a gentle voice, very musical and clear, despite the babble in the background.

Again Polly was thrown. How could this stranger know what she did for a living? Were Shetlanders all mind-readers? She had the sudden thought that she must be imagining the whole scene and that she'd dreamed the stay on Unst, from the moment of their arrival in the islands. Nothing here was real. Soon she'd wake up to find that Eleanor was still alive.

'I visited once,' the woman went on. 'It was quite fascinating. It must be a wonderful place to work.' Then she must have noticed Polly's confusion because she introduced herself as a historian from the museum in Lerwick. 'Simon, the archivist, said you'd been in to see us. I can see why you were interested in Peerie Lizzie. One domestic tragedy and a whole mythology grows up around it. We all have to find ways to explain the things that make us sad. Chance is never quite enough, is it?'

Polly wasn't sure how to answer, so she just smiled. But she thought the idea was interesting. Would Eleanor become part of the Peerie Lizzie myth; would the story mutate and develop to include a strange, dark woman from the south? A pretty teenage boy came to clear her plate. At the other end of the room three children had started to dance to the fiddle music. The historian turned away to continue a conversation with an elderly man on the other side of the table. It seemed that Polly wasn't expected to reply. She sat back in her chair and glanced outside. The fog was dense and grey and blanked out the light. The candles in the room glowed in the shadow. She looked again at the children dancing. Some of the adults had started to clap to the rhythm, cheering them on. The music got faster and the dancing more wild. The audience banged on the table to the beat. There were two boys and a girl. The boys had grey shirts and identical hand-knitted Fair Isle waistcoats. The girl was dressed in white and had black pumps on her feet. With a start, Polly realized that she was familiar. It was the child from the beach. Eleanor's ghost-child.

Chapter Thirty-Seven

SANDY WAS IN THE OFFICE AT Springfield House. He'd been working on the boring stuff, sitting at the computer in the hotel office checking the history of the people involved on the periphery of the case. Now he'd taken a break, made himself coffee and was thinking again about Elizabeth Geldard. He didn't understand how the death of a bairn so long ago could trigger a series of murders in the present, but Jimmy Perez was a great one for history, for digging into the past, and Sandy always wanted to impress him. At the same time, at the back of his mind he was thinking about Louisa. Of course he fancied her to bits, but he'd never been so choosy and he'd fancied lots of lasses, had been out with a few of them. This time it was different, though. He admired Louisa too. The job in the school, and caring for her mother and dealing with the complication of her family life with such dignity and good humour. Once this was over he'd find a way of taking her out. It must be possible to find someone to care for the old lady for an evening. He wondered where Louisa might like to go. It would be splendid to give her a treat.

David Gordon hadn't appeared downstairs since he'd taken a sandwich to his room. Sandy had the office door open so that he'd hear him if he was moving around, but the whole place felt quiet. Dead. He turned back to the screen. Five minutes later he was on the phone to Mary Lomax. 'Any chance you could come here for an hour? I need to pop out, but Jimmy and Willow are in Yell and I don't want to leave Mr Gordon on his own.'

'Are you expecting him to do a runner?' It sounded as if she was eating.

'Nothing like that. I just don't think I should leave him.'

She arrived twenty minutes later carrying a woven bag, with fine yarn and knitting needles sticking out of the top. He left her in the kitchen watching a period drama on the small television set there, the shawl she was working on spread over her lap.

In Voxter he found Grusche and George sitting in front of the same programme. There was no sign of Caroline or Lowrie, and Sandy was pleased about that. Having them there would have made things more complicated. The programme was coming to an end and he waited with them until it was finished; the grand house and the lord and lady with their servants reminded him of how Springfield House must once have been.

'How are you, Sandy?' George got slowly to his feet and rubbed his back. This time of year he'd be singling neeps on the croft and he'd be stiff and sore. 'Will you take a dram?'

Sandy shook his head.

'Tea then?'

'Fine, that.'

Grusche got up too and moved the kettle on the range. 'Look at that fog coming in from the sea. What a dreadful summer it's been for fog! Lowrie and Caroline are supposed to be flying south tomorrow, but I'm not sure the planes will go.'

'Where are they now?' Sandy was wishing that Grusche would leave the room. He would feel more comfortable talking just to George.

'Out with their friends from Sletts. It's their last night. They've walked along the path to the boat club. There's some sort of do going on there.' She sounded disapproving. Perhaps she thought it was disrespectful for the younger folk to be out when two people had died. 'I'll leave you to make the tea, George. There's some shortbread left in the tin. I have my spinning wheel set up in the other room and I'd like to get that fleece spun.' She walked away.

They both drank tea and sat across the table from each other.

'I'd been wondering about Elizabeth Geldard,' Sandy said.

George looked up at him, but said nothing.

'In those days it wouldn't have been so likely for a couple to have a baby when they were in their forties.'

'Not unheard of,' George said.

'I wondered if maybe they'd adopted her.' The idea had been rattling around in his head since he'd been talking to Louisa.

George said nothing.

'It was a long time ago.' Sandy drank tea and reached into the blue biscuit tin for some shortbread. 'We look at things differently now. No shame to having a child born out of wedlock.'

'It depends who the father was.'

There was a moment of silence. 'But the mother was Sarah? Your great-aunt and nursemaid at the big house?'

Another silence. 'That's the story in the family.'

Sandy thought that would make perfect sense. Sarah would

have been hardly more than a child when she got pregnant. Fifteen at the most. Probably ignorant about sex, and taken advantage of. And the couple in the big house were desperate for a child, so it would seem the perfect solution to pass the baby off as their own. The Geldards would spend a lot of their time in the south anyway, so nobody would be surprised if they arrived in Unst with a new baby. No doubt Sarah would have been spirited away to relatives in a different part of Shetland, once the pregnancy started showing. And when she returned the Geldards employed her to take care of her own child. Who better to look after the little girl? And it would explain why she was so upset when Lizzie died, why she felt she had to run away from the islands. And why she'd named her second daughter Elizabeth.

'Who was the father?' Sandy wasn't sure if any of this was important to the present case, but now he'd started he wanted the full story.

George was looking out of the window. 'There's no proof.' He gave an awkward laugh. 'No paternity tests in those days.'

'But there would have been rumours. The girl would have known.'

Another silence. George seemed to be weighing up how much to say. 'The story is that it was Gilbert Geldard himself. His taste was more for young things than for his middle-aged wife. Maybe that was why she never conceived a child.'

'He raped a young girl to give his wife a baby?' Even after all these years Sandy was shocked. He could see why the Malcolmsons hadn't wanted to talk about it. 'Or did Geldard pay for her services?'

George shrugged. 'Raped, seduced, bought. In the end it all amounts to the same kind of thing. All wrong. All violent.'

'Did Roberta ever know that her husband was the father of the child they'd adopted?'

Another shrug. 'If you look at the picture of the girl in the museum in Lerwick and the picture of the man in Springfield House they look kind of similar. You'd think the woman would have wondered.'

Sandy was trying to imagine how Roberta would have felt if she'd found out that Gilbert was the father of her adopted daughter. It would be one thing to take on the child of a local lass as a kind of charity. Selfish, of course. You'd do it because you were desperate to take a baby into your arms. But you could persuade yourself at the same time that it was a good thing that you were doing – rescuing her from poverty, from life with a single mother. Saving Sarah Malcolmson from disgrace. But how would it be if later you found out that it was the result of your husband's perversion? If the girl grew to look like the man you slept with at night. How would that make you feel? Would you still love the child? Or would you want rid of it?

George turned back into the room. 'I don't see why you want to dig all this up now. It has no relevance to the murder of two people from the south; they have nothing to do with our family.'

Sandy didn't know how to answer that. He wanted to say that murder was important even if the victims didn't belong to the islands. And that the murder of a ten-year-old child was important even if it happened years ago. Because he was starting to think that Peerie Lizzie had been murdered. Perhaps by her adoptive mother. And that both the Geldards had been happy to blame Sarah Malcolmson and see her move away. Then there would be nothing to remind them of the girl, and of the man's sexual violence. They could continue to convince themselves that they were good people, and to hold their grand parties. Except that the child had come back to haunt them, even if she only appeared in their dreams, and eventually they'd had to move away too.

George was looking at Sandy and was expecting a response. The place was so quiet that they had been able to hear Grusche's spinning wheel in the next room, the rhythm as soothing as a lullaby.

'I just wanted to understand,' Sandy said at last. 'The story as we'd been told it just didn't make sense.' He paused. 'Did Eleanor know the truth about Peerie Lizzie? Did Lowrie tell her the full background?' Because why wouldn't he? Lowrie was sophisticated and he lived in London. He wouldn't understand why George would feel awkward about the true story of the dead child being made public. He would probably have lost the Shetland islanders' habit of restraint and discretion. And it would make a great programme for Eleanor. A piece of detective work going back over time. Sandy could see that she would be excited.

'I don't think he would have told her about it,' George said. 'He'd grown up with thinking of it as something to keep in the family.'

But Lowrie might well have told his new wife. She was a family member too, an academic full of curiosity about unusual places and the people who lived in them. Perhaps Caroline had passed on the story to her friend. A gift. Something to cheer Eleanor up when she was depressed. Not realizing that it was any kind of secret.

The hum of the spinning had stopped. Sandy realized that if they had been able to hear the wheel, Grusche had probably heard every word of the conversation. She appeared now at the door, big and angular. She was wearing wide linen trousers and a loose fisherman's smock. She ignored Sandy.

'I'm going to phone Lowrie,' she said. 'Offer them a lift back from the boat club. In this fog I don't think it's safe for them to be walking back along the cliffs.'

George nodded and she disappeared again. They heard her speaking in the other room, but this time she'd closed the door and they couldn't make out the individual words. Sandy thought that he should go. He wanted to tell Jimmy Perez what he'd discovered, and he'd promised Mary Lomax that he'd only be away for an hour.

He got to his feet just as Grusche returned to the kitchen. 'They say they want to walk and anyway they don't know when they'll be done. They haven't finished eating yet.' She frowned. 'I hope they take care. We want no more tragedies here.' She flashed a sudden smile at Sandy. 'We mothers worry too much. You wait until you have your own child, Sandy. You'll understand then.'

Out in his car he saw that he had a missed call from Perez. There was a voicemail: 'We need to track down Monica Leaze, Sandy. There's been a development and we'll stay here for a while, though we'd like to get back to Unst this evening. Can you book us onto the last ferry from Yell?'

Sandy tried to phone back, but there was no reply. He drove to Springfield House. The fog was patchy and cleared occasionally to let bright shafts of sunshine light up the hills. Outside the hotel he paused, thinking about the girl who'd lived there, who'd led such a short and troubled life.

Chapter Thirty-Eight

PEREZ STARED AT THE SKETCH OF the woman on the easel in Monica Leaze's loft. Eleanor Longstaff was captured in pencil. Of course she looked like the body he'd seen in the tiny lochan, but this wasn't an exact representation. He felt just as he'd felt when he'd heard the child on Eleanor's recorder singing Peerie Lizzie's song: that there was a discrepancy, something not quite right. He continued to look at it and for a while found it hard to believe that the artist who'd made the disturbing and detailed interiors he'd seen with Fran in the gallery had sketched this too. Then he remembered that Leaze had also painted the little girl in the white dress and thought there was something similar in the tone of both figures. A jauntiness and a sense of mischief, which seemed almost blasphemous now. It was as if the artist was pleased that Eleanor was dead, was amused by the murder.

He became aware of Willow standing behind him. 'We have to talk to the woman,' she said. 'She must have seen Eleanor's body. At the very least she's a witness.'

Perez was about to contradict her, but stopped himself. At this point nothing was certain. Instead he went for a mild observation. 'There doesn't seem to be water in the background.'

'There's nothing in the background except a few pencil strokes.' The words burst out. He saw they were a release of her pent-up frustration.

He wished he could say something to make her calmer. Like this she reminded him of Cassie, panicky and on the edge of a tantrum. He calmed *her* by holding her to him, very tight. There was a brief moment when he pictured himself holding Willow, squeezing the stress from her, and then he remembered that he hadn't called Cassie that day. He never went a day without speaking to her. 'I have to make a phone call. Sorry. I'll be quick.' He climbed down the steep wooden staircase to the hall below, sensing Willow's displeasure tracking after him.

Cassie sounded pleased to hear from him. 'When are you planning to be back?' Her voice was even. She'd never been a child to make demands.

'Soon. Certainly by the end of the weekend.'

'Good.'

'We'll both be glad to get home,' Perez said.

'Will you take me to Fair Isle when you come back?'

'You have school,' he said, fudging it. 'It's too far to go in a day.'

'We could go for a long weekend. I asked my teacher. She said it would be fine to have a couple of days off. She thinks it's an important thing for me to do.'

'Then we'll go.' There was nothing else to say. 'The first weekend when the weather's good, when it's calm enough to take the *Good Shepherd*.'

She didn't reply, but he heard a gentle sigh at the other end of the line. Satisfaction because she'd got her way.

In the loft Willow was still fretting, but she was calmer. The yoga training perhaps. 'What do you think, Jimmy? How can we find Monica? This is the only address we have, and Annie's like Neighbourhood Watch on speed. If there was any gossip to be gained about the woman, then she'd have it.'

'We could try the gallery.' He thought he'd like to look at the painting of the girl in white again, if it was still there. He wasn't quite sure what good that would do, but it seemed important.

'Of course.' There was relief in her words because at least they had a plan of action. 'It'll be shut, but maybe someone nearby will have some information. We'll be able to track down the key-holder at least.'

Outside, she was set to drive off immediately, but Perez insisted on going next door to thank Annie.

'Did you find anything helpful?' The woman wanted to keep him there, chatting. She even had her hand on his arm. This was more about her being lonely than inquisitive.

'Not really. As you said, it looks as if Monica has moved on. We'll try her landlord. But you've been a great help all the same.' And then he had to walk away because Willow was flashing him evil looks from the driver's seat. Annie stood in the doorway watching until they'd turned the car and driven off.

He directed Willow to the gallery and left a message for Sandy at the same time. They drove through an empty hillside scarred with peat banks. In the gloom everything was dark and colourless. The gallery was so well camouflaged that Willow almost shot past, and when Perez pointed out the building she slammed on the brakes and had to back up to get into the car park. The door was locked, but there was a light inside and when they banged on the door a woman opened it to them.

'The gallery's not open in the evenings.' She had a European accent that Perez couldn't quite make out. French?

'We're police officers.' Willow was already holding out her warrant card. The woman stood aside to let them in. Inside the space was quite different from how Perez had remembered it, and the unreliability of his recall troubled him for a moment. How could it be so altered from the picture he'd kept in his head? It seemed smaller and more drab. Perhaps it had seemed grander on the opening night of the exhibition because of Monica Leaze's energy and the sense of occasion. Because Fran was there with him.

He saw the painting of the girl in the white dress on the far wall and went straight towards it, leaving Willow to engage with the woman. The murmur of conversation behind him didn't distract him. The girl in the painting at least was as he remembered her. There was the knowing smile, and the curls. She was just as Polly Gilmour had described the child she'd seen on the beach. He turned back to join the women.

'This is Catherine Breton,' Willow said. She frowned as if she resented his lack of attention. 'She's a potter. She has a studio here and looks after the place.'

'Do you know Monica Leaze?' Perez felt foolish as soon as he'd put the question. It was the first thing Willow would have asked.

'Of course. She's a painter. She exhibits here.' The woman was dark and heavily built, with muscular arms. There was clay under her fingernails. Perez sensed that she just wanted to get back to work.

'Do you have any idea where she is now?'

She shrugged. 'Monica has a complicated domestic life. I'm never sure exactly where she is.'

'Tell us about that.'

She must have realized that they wouldn't go away because she led them into her studio. At one end there was a beaten-up sofa and a low table. She sat them down there. A glass wall showed through to the gallery.

'This must be like working in a goldfish bowl,' Willow said.

'It's part of the deal. I get to live in Shetland, and the studio comes for free.' Catherine paused. 'And in winter we get few visitors here.'

'So tell us about Monica.'

'She's a painter from London. A good painter, and recognized. She has a . . .' the woman paused, seeking the right word, '. . . turbulent relationship with her partner. A couple of years ago she decided that she couldn't live with him full-time. He bored her.'

Perez's thoughts were racing. He remembered his conversation with Cilla, Eleanor's mother. Cilla had said that Ian would bore Eleanor eventually. Perhaps Eleanor and Monica knew each other from London. Perhaps they were friends. If Eleanor already had Monica's contact details that would explain the lack of family name or phone number in the notebook. He looked up at the potter and kept his voice calm. 'So she moved to Shetland.'

'She rented a house in Shetland. But she doesn't live here all the time. She has a daughter. Grandchildren. And she still maintains a relationship with her husband. So it's a kind of semi-detached attachment that she has with the islands.'

Another complicated family, Perez thought. *Like me and Cassie and Duncan. But perhaps it's a good thing that families have changed over the years. I think my mother suffocated in her marriage. And I kind of suffocated as a result. Now we let some air and space in and give individuals a chance to breathe and grow.*

'When did you last see her?'

Catherine considered. She was a very precise woman, Perez could see. 'A week ago. On the Friday morning.'

The day before the hamefarin'. The day before Eleanor's murder.

'Could you tell us about the meeting?'

'Monica called in here. There'd been some family crisis in London, she said. One of the grandchildren was ill. She'd decided to go home. She asked if I could let the owner of the gallery know. She'd agreed to run a workshop here later in the month and she wasn't sure that she'd be back in time.' Catherine looked at her watch. It was clear that she felt reluctant to spend any longer with them. 'She seemed pleased to be going back to London. Almost excited to be leaving. She claims to love Shetland, but she misses the city, I think, and her friends there.'

'Does Monica have any friends in Yell?' Perez thought the woman he'd seen in the gallery with Fran had been sociable. She'd enjoyed an audience. Monica might find Annie's questions too intrusive, but he couldn't imagine her leading an entirely solitary life while she was in Shetland.

'She's very close to Jen Arthur and her parents.'

'And they are . . .'

'Jen's a musician, a songwriter. She has a young family. Divorced.' Catherine allowed herself a brief smile. 'She found her husband very boring too. They met at school. Married too young, according to Jen. She had two sons with him, then decided that she'd be better on her own.'

'Is her ex-husband Neil Arthur? Lives in Meoness in Unst?

He's a plumber.' Willow interrupted with the questions, suddenly excited. It took Perez a moment to make the connection. Neil Arthur's second wife was Vaila, Lowrie's cousin. They had Neil's sons to stay with them every other weekend. Another complicated family trying to make things work. And Vaila claimed to have seen the ghost of Peerie Lizzie. She'd also met Eleanor on the afternoon of her death.

'That's right.' Catherine stood up. She'd been barely polite throughout the conversation and now she was making it clear that she wanted them to leave.

Willow and Perez got to their feet.

'Do you like Monica?' He asked the question without really thinking about it. There was a pause and he expected a bland and conventional answer. Instead the response was surprising and honest.

'Not much. She's self-centred. Unpredictable. A little arrogant. She doesn't care about hurting people if they get in her way.' Catherine paused for a beat. 'But I think she would be a loyal friend. You wouldn't want Monica as an enemy, but if she was your friend she'd fight for you until the end.'

They left the studio and returned to the main body of the gallery. Perez was drawn again to the portrait of the child in white.

'Do you know the model for the painting? Is it her granddaughter?'

Catherine shook her head. 'It was painted a long time ago. Monica had kept it and only brought it up for the exhibition last year. Then Roland, the owner, persuaded her to leave it. It does his credibility good to have a Monica Leaze in the gallery, even though he knows it's unlikely to sell at the price he's put on it. That's Freya, Monica's daughter. Monica was happy to hang it here because she says the girl was conceived in Shetland. She made it sound like a kind of joke.'

In the car back to the ferry terminal Perez was on the phone to Sandy. More requests. 'Can we rouse someone at NorthLink and Flybe and see if Monica Leaze left Shetland on the day of the murder. Or the day after. The Sunday. It'd also be great to find out if Eleanor met her on her flying visit to Shetland the week before. I think Monica is friendly with the director of Shetland Arts, so Mareel might be a logical place for them to meet. Do you know any of the kids who work in the bar there? See if they remember the two women meeting. They'd have stood out. Both English, both stylish.' He paused for breath and imagined Sandy jotting down notes, rather slowly, on a scrap of paper. 'Did you get all that, Sandy?'

'I went to see George Malcolmson,' Sandy said. 'I had an idea.'

'What idea would that be, Sandy?' Perez was glad that *he* was on the phone. The mood she was in, Willow would already have lost her temper with the younger man.

'I was talking to Louisa about the fact that she was adopted. I wondered about Lizzie Geldard.' He paused and Perez didn't make any attempt to hurry him. Sandy would need time to gather his thoughts. 'It seems she was the natural child of Sarah Malcolmson. Story is that Gilbert Geldard seduced the girl when she was only fifteen. Roberta took in the little girl, not knowing the history. I wondered how she'd feel about the girl if she found out the truth.'

'You think Roberta might have drowned Lizzie Geldard?'

'I don't know.' Sandy sounded anxious and worried that he was making a fool of himself. 'What do you think?'

'I can see how that might happen.' Perez thought that an angry woman might blame the child, rather than the man she would be forced to stay married to for appearances' sake. If Gilbert had loved Lizzie because she was his daughter, to kill her would be a terrible act of revenge. And a denial – a way of eliminating the proof of her husband's flaws.

'I don't see how it could have any relevance to this case, though,' Sandy said.

Perez didn't answer. He was thinking that the heart of the investigation lay in complex families trying to survive.

'How have you and Willow got on?' Sandy asked. 'I booked you onto the last ferry. Are you heading back now?' He sounded nervous.

'It was very interesting,' Perez said. 'We'll fill you in when we get back. We're hoping to get the earlier ferry, so we should see you soon.'

Willow was driving like a maniac down the narrow roads. The fog had settled again and visibility was poor. Occasionally house lights would swoop at them out of the gloom, or headlights would appear straight ahead of them so that she had to swerve onto the verge. But Perez didn't ask her to slow down. Like Willow, he was desperate to get back to Unst. He couldn't bear the idea that they might have to wait an hour for the last ferry. He sensed that they'd soon reach the end of the investigation and they needed to be on the most northerly island of the archipelago before there was another tragedy.

★

Sandy was looking out for them. It was nine o'clock. As they opened the main door to the Springfield House the long-case clock in the hall chimed the hour. He had the light on in the kitchen and had been peering out at the shadowy courtyard to check that the car he'd heard belonged to them. He'd looked like an anxious child, left alone in the house for the first time, waiting for his parents to return.

'I need tea.' Willow slumped in one of the chairs and took off her shoes. Perez saw that there was a small hole in the toe of her hand-knitted sock.

Sandy switched on the kettle. 'So, did you find Monica?'

Perez explained about the empty bungalow and the visit to the gallery.

'So you think she was away before the killings?' Sandy said. 'I can't confirm that. Nobody from NorthLink or Flybe will be available until seven tomorrow morning.'

'She can't have left on the Friday.' Willow had her hands cupped round the mug of tea and Perez thought she looked exhausted. 'She saw Eleanor's body.' She explained to Sandy that they'd seen a sketch of the dead Eleanor in Monica's house.

'That's not necessarily true, is it?' Perez had been thinking about that. 'She didn't need to see Eleanor's body to make the drawing. She just needed to know that it would be there.'

'The murderer confided in her beforehand, you mean?' Willow looked up sharply. 'If you've got a theory about this, Jimmy Perez, now's the time to share it.'

Perez hesitated. He wasn't sure what to say. His phone started to ring and he took it out of his pocket. Cilla, Eleanor's mother. He'd saved her number when he was in London.

'Inspector Perez.' She sounded very old and her voice was

302

slurred. She'd been drinking. 'I've been thinking about our conversation.'

'Yes?'

'I wasn't entirely honest with you.' She paused. He imagined her in the room in Pimlico, looking out at the small garden, a large glass in her hand. Mourning her daughter in the only way she could. As far south as London it would already be dark; moths would be attracted to the light in the window. Perez wondered whether he should prompt her again, but at last she continued. 'I think I know why Nell wanted to talk to me that day before she set off for Shetland. I know what was on her mind.'

Chapter Thirty-Nine

WILLOW COULDN'T WORK OUT TO WHOM Perez was talking on his mobile. The Shetlander got up suddenly and walked away from her. He opened the kitchen door and continued the conversation there in the doorway, facing outside. She could only see his back, which was hunched slightly. The open door let in the chill air. The call would be about Cassie, Willow decided. She was the love of his life, these days. Fran reincarnated, another kind of ghost. It was a lot for the girl to live up to.

Sandy was talking and he pulled her attention back into the room. 'I'm pretty sure that I have proof Eleanor was in Shetland before, and that she met up with Monica Leaze.'

'How do you know that, Sandy?'

'I did as Jimmy suggested and talked to a friend who works at Mareel arts centre. She couldn't help, so I contacted the manager at the Hay's Dock, the restaurant at the museum.'

'And?'

'She knows Monica Leaze. She remembers Monica having lunch there with three other people. One of them was a woman with dark hair. I emailed my mate the photo that Polly Gilmour let us have and she confirmed that it was Eleanor.'

Willow forgot about Jimmy Perez for a moment. Monica Leaze *must* be the 'Monica' of Eleanor's notebooks. 'Did your friend recognize any of the other people?'

Sandy shook his head. 'Two men. That was all she said.'

'I don't suppose the restaurant manager overheard any of the conversation?'

'No.' Sandy was disappointed because he couldn't contribute more. 'The women seemed like good pals, though, and greeted each other like old friends. It didn't look like the first time they'd met.'

Willow wasn't sure that meant anything. She had arty friends too and their natural form of greeting, even to a stranger, was a hug, kisses on both cheeks, exclamations of delight.

'Monica had a portfolio with her,' Sandy went on. 'The group looked at some paintings. Had them spread over the table.'

'Then what?'

'They went outside. They'd had wine with their meal and they were laughing. Like it was a sort of celebration. My friend was looking out of the window a bit later and saw the group taking photos of each other on that decking between the museum and the dock.'

Willow's brain was fizzing with ideas and snatches of memory. She fetched her laptop and fired it up. 'This is a scrap of a photo found on the hill near Eleanor's body. Look at the blown-up image. Could that be the outside of the museum, do you think?'

Sandy stared at it, frowning. 'Yes,' he said at last. 'It's hard to tell, but yes, I think it is. But why would that picture make someone commit a murder?'

ANN CLEEVES

'If we knew that, Sandy, we'd have the case closed and be on our way home.'

Willow looked towards Perez to share the news, but he wasn't there. He'd finished his call, wandered out into the courtyard and was standing quite still. The public bar was closed as a mark of respect following Charles Hillier's death, so there were no lights to shine on the yard. Through the window Willow saw his silhouette. He seemed lost in his own world. Again Willow thought there must be some domestic crisis concerning Cassie. *Anyone who took on that man would have a whole heap of baggage to deal with too.*

She heard a sound from inside the house, a door being quietly shut, the rustle of clothing, and she walked through into the grand lobby. The only light came from a long sash window next to the front door and was milky, filtered by the mist. David Gordon stood at the top of the curved staircase. He was still in the clothes he'd been wearing during the day and it seemed that he'd made no attempt to sleep. She wondered how long he'd been there and if he'd heard any of the conversation.

'David, are you OK? Can I get you anything?'

He muttered something that she couldn't make out and turned away. It was only then that she saw that his hair was covered with fine droplets of water and there were wet footprints on the parquet floor where she was standing. David had been outside. She imagined him standing on the terrace and looking down over the shore to the spot where he'd found his lover's body. Willow was about to ask where he'd been, but he'd already disappeared back into his room. She hesitated, unsure whether to follow him, when she heard Jimmy Perez come back into the kitchen. Willow thought how disengaged

306

he seemed. She had an urge to shake him. *Leave the past behind, at least while you're working.* In the end it was Sandy who asked who'd been on the phone.

'Eleanor's mother, Cilla,' Perez said. He frowned and Willow saw that the content of the call had been preoccupying him. So she'd been wrong. He was entirely focused on the case. She felt a twinge of guilt.

'Anything useful?'

'It could be.' But he didn't seem happy or excited. This was a different Perez from the one who'd sat beside her in the car in Yell, urging her on down the narrow roads to look for Monica Leaze and then to catch the ferry.

'Perhaps you could tell us what she wanted then, Jimmy. It's getting late.' Willow was losing patience once more. This wasn't the time for games. She thought she needed a large drink and remembered there was a bottle of Chablis in the fridge. Monica's tipple. She set it on the table with three large glasses. 'Come on, Jimmy. We won't be going out again tonight. Pour us both some wine and tell us what this is all about. We have important information too. There's a lot to discuss.'

'Cilla has been having an affair,' he said. 'She thought Eleanor had found out about it, suspected *that* was why she'd asked Cilla to meet her for lunch the day before they all set off for Shetland.'

'And Eleanor was upset? I don't quite see how that's relevant to her murder.'

'The affair was with a younger man.' He turned so that he was staring out of the window again. Willow hoped he wasn't going to go moral and God-bothering on her. With Perez she never knew exactly how he would react. He looked back into the room and directly at her, weighing his words. 'With Marcus

Wentworth. Cilla's field of expertise is Middle Eastern and North African art. He runs occasional cultural tours. That was how they met. The fact that Polly and Eleanor were friends was just a weird coincidence.'

'But he must be half her age!' Sandy sounded horrified.

Suddenly Willow felt wide awake, and she thought again that they could now look at the facts of the case from an entirely new perspective. 'Well, that gives us a very strong motive, doesn't it?'

Perez nodded. 'I think Marcus was the man Eleanor met in the Bloomsbury restaurant. She was trying to persuade him to end the relationship with her mother. She knew how upset Polly would be if she found out. And Eleanor took a phone call from him when she was in the Sentiman. Again she was telling him to sort out the situation.'

'Marcus has got Polly all lined up for the role of wife and mother,' Willow said. 'The woman to step into his mother's shoes and become lady of the manor. Very aristo. He's not going to be best pleased if Eleanor threatens to spill the beans to her best friend.'

'I'm not sure how Polly would respond to the news, either. She seems fragile already.'

Willow looked at him sharply, uncertain exactly what Perez meant by the comment. She breathed deeply. 'For the first time we've got a credible motive in this case. We'll bring Marcus in first thing in the morning.' She felt a rush of relief. In the end this would turn out to be an ordinary case with a human motive. Peerie Lizzie had nothing to do with it. 'I feel like celebrating. Let's have that glass of wine.'

But as she reached out for the corkscrew and the bottle, her mobile rang. It occurred to her again that this was like the operations room of a wartime mission. Phones ringing constantly from different agents in the field. New information arriving all the time and needing to be assimilated. Her caller was breathless, female and English. Willow recognized the clear tones and the academic precision. Caroline, Lowrie Malcolmson's new bride.

'We need your help, Inspector. It's Polly. She seems to have disappeared.'

Chapter Forty

IN THE BOAT CLUB, AT THE end of the meal, Polly couldn't take her eyes off the dancing girl. It was as if she and the child were frozen in time and space and all the other guests were whirling around them until they became a blur of speed and colour. Then the music slowed and stopped and everything became normal once more. The child seemed to be aware of Polly's eyes on her, because she stared back. Her eyes were blue and unblinking. Not rude, but curious.

Polly stood up to walk around the table to speak to her. She would feel less disturbed if she discovered the child's name, if she got to the bottom of the apparent haunting and spoke to this strange girl, who appeared only to her and to Eleanor. But everyone was standing up to leave now and in the narrow gap between the trestle tables and the walls there were people struggling to their feet, kissing farewell, catching up on last-minute gossip. Words spoken in an accent Polly could scarcely decipher, adding to her sense of panic. An elderly woman with a walking frame was blocking her route. When she finally did squeeze past, the girl and the two boys had disappeared. So once again she was left questioning her judgement. Had her imagination been playing tricks once more? Was the dancing child like a shadow in the mist?

She pushed her way back to the door and down the stairs, thinking there might be a queue for the cloakroom and the girl might still be there. No sign of her. Polly grabbed her jacket and walked out into the night. The fog was so thick that it seemed she could taste it. It was salty like seaweed and dense on her tongue. A soup made of sea water and sulphur. The wall lamp outside the boat club bounced light back from the screen of grey. Somewhere at the mouth of the harbour a red buoy flashed very dimly. In the car park people were banging doors and shouting goodbye and words of warning about the journey home. Polly could make out some silhouettes, but there was nothing that could be the girl in white.

I'm becoming obsessed. I should leave it and find the others. Walk back to Sletts and finish packing. Tomorrow I'll be on my way home and this will be just another story. Everything I've done here can be forgotten.

Then she heard a child singing. The words were high-pitched and clear:

> *Little Lizzie Geldard died today*
> *The tide came in and drowned her.*
> *The water swept the girl away,*
> *It was night before they found her.*

The words seemed to be mocking Polly and pulling her towards them. They weren't coming from the car park, which was almost empty now, but from the footpath where she'd walked with Marcus and Ian earlier. Polly knew she should find the others and persuade them to listen to the song and help her to find the singer. For her own sanity she needed witnesses. But the words were getting fainter and seemed to be taunting her, calling her forward. *It was night before they found her.*

There was a torch in her jacket pocket and she set off after the girl's voice. She hoped the others would realize that she'd left and would follow, then thought that they might be anxious if she just disappeared. As she walked she pulled out her phone, but the signal was very faint. Marcus answered, but when she spoke to him she wasn't sure he'd heard what she'd said. Then the connection was lost. She still had a signal, but it had been cut off at the other end. It occurred to her that Marcus had deliberately switched his phone off.

Marcus. Unbidden, thoughts of her last conversation with Eleanor forced themselves into Polly's head. She was back on the deck the night of the hamefarin'. Both the men were asleep and it was just the two girls, like the old days in Durham. Polly had gone outside again to find Eleanor wrapped up in her theatrical velvet gown, looking like a character in a Victorian melodrama. Polly had fetched her quilted jacket and joined her. A new bottle of wine on the table between them. The fog coming and going and swirling in weird shapes over the shore. Just like tonight.

And then Eleanor had started spilling out her story, her weasel words and excuses. 'I'm so glad of the chance to talk to you on your own, Pol. This has been tearing me apart.' And for a brief moment Polly had thought she was about to admit to an affair with Marcus. She couldn't understand how they might have met, but she could see that there would be an attraction. Two beautiful people, both dark and handsome.

Both intelligent. Polly was accustomed to playing second fiddle to Eleanor and might even have got used to that. The woman was easily bored and would have moved on very quickly. Marcus might have settled for Polly in the end. But that wasn't what Eleanor had wanted to say at all.

'You should know that Marcus is having an affair.'

'With you?' Keeping her voice even, because although she loved Marcus to pieces, her friends were still more important to her than he was. They'd rescued her when she was frightened and alone and had first left home. They'd kept her going in a strange and intimidating city when she'd moved to London.

'Of course not with me.' Eleanor's voice was amused, with that touch of arrogance that never really left her. 'I don't want anyone other than Ian, these days. You know that, Pol. I'm a married woman. A reformed character.'

'Then who?'

There'd been a silence and Polly had thought again that she'd glimpsed a white figure moving along the edge of the tide. A figure with a strange silhouette, hair peaked at the front like a bird's crest.

'With Cilla. My mother.'

And that was when something had broken inside Polly. Because Cilla was old and snooty, and always treated Polly as if Eleanor was doing her the hugest favour in the world by befriending her. How could Marcus have anything in common with a woman like that?

Eleanor continued to speak and seemed comforted because she no longer had to keep a secret. She'd probably convinced herself that she was really doing Polly a favour. 'They met in Jordan when he was leading a group and she was on a field trip. Lust at first sight. For her at least. I saw them at an exhibition together and she introduced me. When you showed me his photo I recognized him at once.' And Eleanor had paused and taken a swig of wine straight from the bottle and seemed to have no understanding of the effect she was having on Polly. Or seemed not to care. Then she looked up. 'I did try to stop it, Pol. I tracked Marcus down through his website. I did tell him to stop it.'

On the cliff, lost in the fog now, Polly closed her eyes to blink away the memory of that conversation. She'd decided then that it couldn't be true, that Eleanor was just stirring up trouble to create a drama. Of course Marcus wouldn't make love to a woman nearly twice his age. Of course he wouldn't betray her. Her phone rang, the shrill noise startling her and bringing her back to the present.

When she'd finished the conversation Polly felt sane again. There was no singing, just the distant sucking of waves on the shore at the bottom of the cliff. A faint murmuring that might be the call of seabirds. Then a child's laughter.

Chapter Forty-One

WHEN WILLOW, PEREZ AND SANDY ARRIVED at Sletts, Caroline was the only person there. The men were still out looking for Polly. It was properly dark now, past midnight, and the fog was as thick as ever. Caroline was sitting in the window of the cottage looking out for them. Sandy thought that she would have organized the search, and the men would have done as they were told. She was like some of his school teachers who never shouted, but scared the kids shitless all the same and always got the respect they felt they deserved.

In the car he'd wanted to ask questions. About the phone call from Eleanor's mother and the men who'd met Eleanor at Mareel, and what Jimmy made of it all. But he'd kept quiet. On their way out Willow had said he should stay in Springfield House in case David Gordon did something daft. She said that the man had wandered away once and she wouldn't put it past him to just walk into the sea and drown. But Jimmy had told her they'd need as many people as possible to search for the Englishwoman and they could get Mary Lomax in as a babysitter, so Sandy had been allowed along. But he knew he was there on sufferance, so he just sat quietly while Willow did the driving, and he kept his questions to himself.

In Sletts, Willow took charge. She and Caroline were two strong women together. Jimmy and Sandy let them get on with it.

'You'll have tried to phone Polly?'

Caroline nodded. 'Of course, but we're getting no answer. She made one call to Marcus while we were waiting to collect our coats, but then his phone cut out. You know what the reception's like here.'

'What did she say?' Willow asked.

'Marcus couldn't really make any sense of it. Something mad about looking for Peerie Lizzie. There was such a noise all around us in the boat club. He tried to call her straight back, but he couldn't get through.'

'Tell us what happened this evening.'

'It was their last night in Shetland,' Caroline said, 'and we wanted to mark it in some way. There was a charity dinner at the boat club. Food and music. We thought it would be better than letting them sit in here, brooding. And local people had wanted to express their sympathy, so we knew they'd be made welcome. That they'd be treated with proper sensitivity.'

'You walked?'

'We took the path along the cliff, yes. It's not very far.' Caroline shifted uneasily in her seat and Sandy thought the walking had been her idea. She'd be a great one for the benefits of exercise and fresh air.

'Did you think that was safe in the fog?' Willow kept the question polite, but Sandy could sense the hostility between them. It crackled like electricity. Two strong women, but otherwise different in every way. Willow would have been the rebel at school and Caroline the perfectly behaved head girl.

'It wasn't so bad when we set out. Besides, Lowrie has been playing on the cliffs here since he could walk. He wasn't going to get lost.' As if Willow was stupid for suggesting there might be any danger.

'But Polly *did* lose her way?'

There was a silence. Caroline couldn't seem to explain the fact that Polly was missing. 'Polly ran off on her own after the meal,' she said at last. 'We couldn't have expected that. Marcus thought it was some sort of panic attack. She was there watching the musicians and then she'd disappeared. Eleanor's death has made her kind of flaky.' Sandy thought the woman had already picked up some of the accent. She'd turn into one of those soothmoothers who became more Shetland than the Shetlanders. He imagined her as a member of the parish council, fighting on behalf of the other crofters. A pillar of the community.

'You're sure she went of her own volition?' Willow asked.

'Well, she wasn't kidnapped in front of an audience of fifty people!' Caroline's voice was sharp. The prefect was reasserting her authority.

'Did you see her leave the room?'

'No.' Caroline looked up at Willow. 'None of us did. It was a bit of a scrum at the end. As soon as the music stopped everyone got up to leave at once. The weather was so bad then that people wanted to get home. Folk who hadn't been able to make the hamefarin' came to congratulate Lowrie and me on their way out, so we were among the last to go. Marcus met us at the cloakroom downstairs, but Polly's jacket had already gone. We thought she'd be waiting outside, but there was no sign of her.' Another silence, then an admission. 'It was a bit spooky actually. As if she'd disappeared into thin air. Just like the night that Eleanor went missing.'

Perez had been looking out of the window during the conversation. Now he turned back into the room. For a moment Sandy thought he was going to make sense of all this, to tell them what lay behind the killings. Because Sandy thought that Jimmy had an idea. He'd been working it out in his head since Eleanor's mother had phoned. Instead Perez said, 'We should look for her.' Just those words. Forceful, as if Polly wasn't only a potential victim, but was essential to the solving of the case.

They all looked at the inspector, but nobody moved.

'We should look for her.' Perez said the same words, but they were even more urgent this time.

'The boys went straight back out when we got here and there was no sign of her,' Caroline said. 'I waited in the house to call you.' She paused. 'They haven't found her yet. I've just spoken to them. They walked together along the cliff path back towards the club in case we just missed her, but now they've split up. Lowrie's taking the cliffs because he knows them best. The others will search inland.' Another hesitation. 'Marcus said he'd look at the lochan where Eleanor was found.'

Perez was on his feet and they were all looking at him. Now he was in charge. 'We'll check Meoness then, if your men are looking along the cliff path. Willow, will you do the beach between here and the hall? Sandy, you go to Voxter. Not along the road, but by the path that takes you past the planticrub where we found Eleanor's phone. Check the fields and the ditches on either side of the path, in case Polly has tumbled. Then chat to George and Grusche and see if they noticed anything unusual this evening.'

Caroline interrupted quickly. 'There's no point in going to Voxter. I've only just spoken to George to explain why we'd be late back. He didn't mention anything.'

'Was Grusche there?'

'I presume so. George didn't say.'

'Go all the same, Sandy.' Perez's voice was firm. Sandy thought how splendid it was to have the old Perez back. There'd been a time following Fran's death when he'd thought he'd be lost to them forever. 'Anything out of the ordinary, report back to me.'

None of them asked where Perez intended to search. They had the sense that he wouldn't have told them anyway.

Outside, Sandy thought that the fog was lifting a little. They'd passed the darkest point of the night. He walked away from Sletts, first onto the road and then by the path that led above the beach towards Voxter. His mind wandered. A week ago the Malcolmsons would have been preparing for the hamefarin', the house full of activity and the smell of baking. Friends and family would be turning out to help make bunting and decorate the hall. Caroline would be in her element directing proceedings. Then he wondered if *he* would ever marry, and that led him on to thoughts of Louisa.

The sky was definitely lighter now, but still he shone his torch and shouted Polly's name. If she'd fallen she might see the pinprick of light in the gloom. He imagined finding her alive and well, and thought how pleased Jimmy would be then. At the planticrub he paused. But there was no sign of Polly here. No phone lying on the grass to be discovered. He looked down towards the sea. The sky was brighter still. A faint glimmering line along the horizon. There was a sharper point of light, which he assumed to be from Willow's torch as she searched the beach. He walked on down the bank towards the Malcolmsons' croft, shouting the woman's name, thinking he must look like a madman, howling into the darkness.

He'd just left the crub when his phone rang. He answered without seeing who was calling. 'Jimmy? Is that you? Any news?'

But it was a woman's voice on the other end and it took him a moment to work out who was there. Mary Lomax.

'Sandy, I'm really sorry.' She seemed distraught, on the verge of tears.

'What's happened?'

'David Gordon has done a runner. I didn't realize until I heard the sound of the car starting. He must have come down the back stairs. I tried to run out to stop the car, but I was just too late.'

'You should tell Jimmy Perez.' Sandy didn't know what else to say. He didn't want to take responsibility for the missing man. And Jimmy had told him to check on Grusche and George, so that was what he intended to do.

The buildings at Voxter were darker shapes against the sky. Chickens stirred in the hen house as he passed. He stopped outside the house and looked in through the window. The light was still on in the kitchen. There was no sign of George in the chair, where Sandy had left him earlier in the evening, though a nearly empty bottle of whisky and a glass remained on the table. No sign of Grusche, either. Sandy thought if they had any sense they'd both be in their bed. Caroline had said she'd spoken to them when she'd phoned Voxter about the missing woman, but that might have been a while ago. Sandy wondered if George was outside helping in the search. He tapped on the window, but there was no response, so he walked round to the front door. He switched off his torch because there was light from the window and his eyes were accustomed to the dusk now. The door was unlocked and he went inside.

There was a rush of sound and a white figure appeared in front of him. It was Grusche in an old-fashioned cotton night-gown and a shawl wrapped around her shoulders. 'Who is it? Lowrie, is that you?' She sounded older than Sandy remembered, panicky and frail. He realized that if she'd come out of a lit bedroom, he would be just a shape to her.

'It's Sandy Wilson. The detective from Lerwick.'

'Sandy, what are you doing here at this hour of the morning? You scared me.' She reached out for a switch and suddenly the room – a small scullery with space for boots and coats – was full of light.

He blinked. 'Polly Gilmour is still missing. Jimmy Perez sent me here to see if she'd wandered this way.'

'We'd have told you if she was here, Sandy. Of course we would. Caroline phoned earlier to say she was missing.' She paused. 'These have been terrible times. I'll be glad when the English people go south again. They've brought nothing but trouble.'

Sandy thought that Caroline was English too, but perhaps Grusche already counted her as local.

'Could I speak to George?'

She hesitated for a moment. 'He's asleep,' she said. 'He'd been drinking all evening and I sent him to bed.' Her voice was bitter. Sandy decided you could never tell what went on between a man and his wife. The picture they showed to the world could be quite different from what went on in the home. It started with the wedding – all music and smiling, a kind of performance – and then unless you were lucky things started to crack. Maybe Grusche was so eager for Lowrie to move back to Shetland because George provided no companionship for her at all.

She stood where she was, poised between the bedroom and the kitchen, as if she was unsure whether to go with him or back to her bed. In the end she wrapped the shawl around her head and led him into the kitchen.

'I should try to wake George,' Sandy said. Perez had told him to speak to the man.

'You'd be wasting your time,' Grusche replied. 'You'll get no sense out of him when he's like this.' She stood blocking the door and he saw she was adamant that her husband shouldn't be disturbed.

'Does it happen often?'

She shrugged and moved to the Rayburn and lifted the kettle onto the hot plate.

'Often enough. He needs help, but I don't think he really wants to change. He's not been the man I married since he left the lighthouse service.'

'It must be hard living with him.' Sandy couldn't see how this had anything to do with the two murders, but he knew that Jimmy Perez wouldn't walk away if a witness was just about to speak to him.

'Not really. He's a good man. He works hard and he's always been a good father to Lowrie. He can be the life and soul of a party. He just needs a drink before he can face new people or difficult situations, and then he can't stop drinking when he's had a few drams inside him. There are lots of Shetlanders who are just the same.'

Sandy thought that was true too.

The kettle on the hob whistled. Grusche made the tea.

'What do you think happened to Polly?' she said. She put a mug of tea on the table in front of him.

'I'm not sure.' Sandy sipped the tea. 'It was very foggy. It's easy to lose your way.'

'She'll maybe have been chasing after Eleanor's ghost-child,' Grusche said.

'What do you mean?'

'She thought that she'd seen Peerie Lizzie. It seems the spirit appeared to her on the night of the hamefarin'. And then again on the beach the next day.' Grusche paused. 'Caroline and I took her out for lunch in Yell and I thought she was kind of obsessed with all that nonsense. I suppose if your best friend is killed, you lose your perspective. It'd be easy to start believing in the spirit world. And she was determined to track the lassie down.' She paused. 'Polly seemed rather mad to me, Sandy. I don't think she's entirely safe to be left alone. You need to find her.'

Sandy wasn't sure what he made of that, but he supposed that Willow and Jimmy would be interested in Polly Gilmour's state of mind. 'You've known her for a long time?'

'She was one of Lowrie's friends since they started at university together.'

'And what did you make of her?'

'She was a quiet little thing,' Grusche said. 'Always overawed by Caroline and Eleanor. Grateful for their attention. They loved having an admirer, of course. It was very good for their egos to have Polly hanging on their every word. I knew that she'd do well, though. She worked very hard. And she wasn't one then for weird imaginings.'

'But that last time you saw her, when you took her out to lunch, you thought she was a bit flaky?' Sandy asked.

'She said she didn't believe in the ghost, that there'd be some rational explanation for the girl she'd seen, but I think she was trying to convince herself as much as us. It'd be easy enough to frighten Polly and tip her into a panic.' Grusche stared at Sandy as if she was telling him something important. 'If that was what you wanted to do.'

'Caroline said Polly had a panic attack at the dinner tonight and that's why she ran out.' Sandy finished his tea and thought he should get back to Sletts and see if there was any news of the woman. He shouldn't sit here in the warm gossiping, though it was pleasant to be inside.

Grusche stood too and led him back to the front door. 'They should never have dragged her and the others out to that dinner. It was Caroline's idea. Lowrie was all for leaving them alone last night.'

'Caroline's a strong woman,' said Sandy.

'She is.' Grusche allowed herself a smile. 'But she loves my boy to bits, and in the end that's all that matters.'

Sandy didn't quite believe that. He thought Caroline might turn into one of those bunny-boilers, very jealous and posses- sive. He wondered how Lowrie would be in twenty years' time. Would he be asleep in his bed after too much whisky and a day of being nagged by his strong woman? He thought Grusche wouldn't have been an easy person to live with, either. Perhaps George could deal with her better when he was still working his shifts in the lighthouse and there was an escape for him every month. Perhaps she'd been happier then, when she just had Lowrie to keep her company. Caroline and Lowrie would be working and living together every day, though. Sandy couldn't see how that arrangement could work successfully.

'I should go and see what's happening,' he said. 'Polly might be back at Sletts now and we could be worrying over nothing.'

'Aye, maybe.' But he could tell that Grusche wasn't convinced. As he left the house, the cockerel in the hen house began to squawk and he saw that it was almost morning.

Chapter Forty-Two

WILLOW MADE HER WAY DOWN TO the beach and felt a sudden spurt of anger. *What the shit am I doing here? I'm the senior investigating officer in this case, not a rookie plod to be ordered around by the great Jimmy Perez. He wouldn't have spoken to a male superior officer like that!*

The anger was directed first at herself, because she hadn't taken charge of the search when she'd had the chance. Because she'd allowed the man to walk all over her. Then it was turned towards Perez, who'd been cold and uncommunicative since they'd left Springfield House. What was it about the man that turned her into a pathetic girl, unable to assert her authority for a moment?

The tide was out and she walked on the damp sand, which was ridged, hard under her feet. Here the fog was patchy; sometimes it was so dense that she lost all sense of direction and wandered towards the water, and occasionally it lifted so that she could make out the lights in Sletts. She was shouting Polly's name and swinging her torch in an arc so that it would be seen from all directions, but she felt this was pointless. Why would Polly be on the beach, when the holiday house and safety were close by? Surely there would be nothing in Sletts to scare her. No, Jimmy Perez was going it alone again, playing the hero. This was more about his ego, and proving to himself and to the world that he was back at the top of his game, than saving a young woman's life.

There was a sudden breeze from the sea, which swirled the mist in strange patterns and she thought she saw a figure standing near the water. She told herself that she was dreaming or the faint light on the horizon was playing tricks with her imagination, but all the same she felt chilled, suddenly scared. As she got closer to the tideline she saw that it was no Peerie Lizzie, no young girl dressed in white. This was an adult clothed in a waterproof jacket and a hood. The fog thickened again and the figure disappeared. Willow screamed Polly's name and ran towards the shadow, but on the flat sand directions were deceptive and she thought she could be running in completely the opposite direction. She stood still and listened. The tide must be turning now. She heard soft waves breaking. On a morning like this Elizabeth Geldard had slipped away from her adoptive mother, or had been led into danger by her, and been drowned as the water slid down the voe and filled the gullies behind her, cutting off her escape back to the shore. For the first time Willow realized how easily that could have happened.

There was another sound. Human, not supernatural. Choked sobs.

'Polly!' Yelling as hard as she could. But it was like screaming in a dream, when no sound comes out. Her voice was lost in the wide expanse of the beach and there was no response. 'Polly, come away from the water, it's dangerous there.' She wondered if the woman had had a real breakdown, or had been attacked and left wandering on the shore. She listened again, but now there was silence, apart from the splash of the waves.

Then, like a curtain rising, the mist ahead of her cleared and she saw the figure clearly, still some way off to the north of her and on the part of the beach that was closest to the Meoness community hall. The water had already come up to the figure's calves. Willow was reminded of a series of sculptures that she and her mother had visited on a beach in Merseyside. Antony Gormley's cast-iron figures, which had been moulded from his own body, planted in the sand and covered twice a day by the tide. Each of them had seemed entirely lonely as the water covered them, and Willow had watched, fascinated, as they disappeared a little at a time under the sea.

She ran across the shore, determined to get there before the fog returned. Then she realized that the figure was too tall to be Polly. This was a man, standing motionless and waiting to be swallowed up by the tide.

'David.' Still the water came. He was wearing wellingtons and the water had started to spill inside the boots. 'Come here. You'll catch your death.' She didn't approach him because she wasn't going to risk wet clothes until there was no alternative, even in midsummer, and he was so distraught that she worried she might spook him, so that he'd walk away from her and deliberately drown.

He turned slowly and, for the first time, seemed to see that she was there.

'Come away from the water, David.' No response. 'Do you want to talk?'

He gave a deep breath, half-sob and half-agreement, and walked towards her. On the sand, under the Meoness community hall and just above the tideline, someone had built a bonfire, perhaps in preparation for a beach party. A pile of driftwood and dry garden clippings from shrubs and bushes, some rotten fence posts.

'I don't suppose you've got any matches.' Whoever had built the fire would be hopping mad if they used the wood, but she didn't want to take Gordon back to Sletts, where Caroline would be waiting, and he needed to get warm.

He felt in his pocket. 'This was Charlie's spare jacket. I thought I'd feel closer to him wearing it. Quite ridiculous!' He pulled out a lighter.

She lit the scrub at the base of the fire and it flamed immediately. They sat on the powdery sand and stared into it. 'What on earth do you think you were doing?'

'I lied to you about the night of Eleanor Longstaff's murder,' David said. 'Charles was here in Meoness when she died. I followed him.' He turned and the orange glow from the fire caught his face. 'Do you think he killed her? I've been going over and over it in my mind. It might explain why somebody wanted him dead.'

'What reason would he have for murdering Eleanor?'

David looked into the fire. 'Money,' he said. 'We both knew that the business was on the brink of disaster, and neither of us was prepared to admit it.'

'You think somebody paid him to kill Eleanor Longstaff?' She couldn't keep the incredulity from her voice. The thought of the ex-magician as a paid hitman seemed ludicrous.

'No! At least I don't think so.' David stretched out his hands towards the flames. 'But I'm going crazy. While I was in the garden this afternoon I was going over it all in my head. I'm ready to believe almost anything.' He paused for a beat. 'Charles was here on the night of the hamefarin' and he lied to me. Why would he do that?'

She couldn't give him an answer, but could see that he wouldn't rest until he got one. 'What *did* he do? What makes you think he was caught up in all this?'

David leaned forward. His damp jeans were steaming in the heat and his face was flushed. 'Charles had been behaving oddly for weeks. There'd been mysterious phone calls and sudden trips to Lerwick. When I asked him what was going on, he said he was investigating a project that might provide extra income for the business. He'd tell me when everything was settled.' He paused again. 'That night we'd decided that we wouldn't go to Lowrie's hamefarin' and I went to bed early. Then I heard Charles go out, the engine of his car starting. I followed him to the Meoness hall in my own car. He parked there, but he didn't go inside. He walked up the road a little way and met someone. It looked as if they'd arranged to meet.'

'Did you see the person?'

'It was a woman. That was a relief of a sort. I suppose I'd imagined that he'd found someone else. Another man. I didn't see any detail. There wasn't much light and I was worried about getting too close.' David paused. 'The last thing I wanted was for Charles to think I was spying on him.'

'Could it have been Eleanor Longstaff? Tall and dark.'

'She was certainly dark-haired. I'm not sure about anything else.' David was calmer now and focused on getting the facts right. 'They spoke for a minute and then they walked down here to the beach. They seemed very easy with each other, looking out over the water. Then other people came out of the hall – I suppose a dance had finished and everyone wanted fresh air or a cigarette – and I left. I didn't want to be seen and dragged in to the party.'

'Did Charles leave at the same time?' Willow was trying to work out a timeline for this. Even if Eleanor was Hillier's companion on the beach, it didn't turn him into a murderer. She was still alive to go back to Sletts with the others, to sit on the deck and drink more wine.

'No, when I left they were still talking.'

'What did you do when you got home?'

'I went back to bed. As I say, the last thing I wanted was for Charles to know I'd been following him.' David took off his wellingtons and wrung out his socks. His pale bare feet looked pink and fleshy in the firelight. A piece of pitch pine fell into the hottest part of the blaze and sparks floated upwards.

'What time did he get back?'

The fire had taken Willow back to parties on the beach close to Balranald. Sometimes the whole commune had been there; middle-aged hippies sang the folk songs of their youth to acoustic guitars. Sometimes it was the wild boys of the island, steaming with drink because they were bored out of their skulls and that was the only excitement they could get.

David was taking a long time to reply and she prompted him. 'Were you asleep when he got in?'

This time the answer was immediate. 'Of course not! But I pretended to be. I was scared that he might be planning to run away, that stress about the business had finally pushed him over the edge. I kept looking at the clock and wondering what could have happened to him. I told myself he'd just have joined the party, had too much to drink and would be walking home. But I couldn't quite believe that. Then I thought maybe he'd had an accident, and I imagined him lying at the bottom of a cliff somewhere. Eventually I heard his car. I almost wept with relief.' He turned to her. 'This must seem so foolish to you. An overreaction. But it was the first real relationship of my life. I was desperate not to lose him.'

'What time did he get in?'

'Ten to three. I looked at the bedside clock when he pulled into the courtyard.'

So that would have been after Eleanor had sent her email to Polly. She might even have been dead by then. Looking out to sea, Willow saw that the mist had almost cleared. 'Did he give you any explanation for why he was so late?'

'I've told you: I pretended to be asleep. And I really was tired by then. It was the worry – heading out after him to Meoness when I was already shattered. Besides, we had guests staying and I knew I'd have to be up early to make breakfast. It wasn't the time for a meaningful discussion.'

'Did you talk to him about it in the morning?'

David shook his head. 'If Charles had secrets, I wanted him to share them when he was ready. I didn't want to pry.'

Which was all very well, Willow thought. All very adult and civilized. But it didn't really help her track down the killer. 'And Charles didn't give any hint that he'd been out that night, or what he might have seen or done?'

'No.' David hesitated. 'He seemed excited, pleased with himself. And then Sandy phoned with news of Eleanor's death and to ask if your team could stay at Springfield House. I took the call and said we had space. All I was thinking of was the money and how useful it would be.'

'How did Charles react when you told him that one of the hamefarin' guests had been murdered?'

'It was as if he couldn't believe it. He asked me to repeat what I knew and pressed me for details that I couldn't give. Then he was on the phone to Grusche, in case she knew more about it. He's always been a gossip and I thought he was excited about Springfield being the base for a murder investigation, but I think there was more to it than that. He was desperate for information.' David turned his face away from the fire and towards her. 'Charles didn't kill Eleanor Longstaff, Chief Inspector. The news of her death came as a surprise to him.'

Willow thought that was probably true. But she also thought Charles had seen something when he was out in Meoness that night, something that seemed important in the light of Eleanor's death. And that knowledge had probably killed him.

Chapter Forty-Three

PEREZ SENT SANDY AND WILLOW OUTSIDE to search for Polly, but though he went to the door to see them out he remained inside the house. He was thinking of Polly, anxious and fraught, desperate. Caroline had moved to the window and was staring at the beach, as if her friend might suddenly appear through the mist. For a while Perez said nothing. He was glad of the chance to think. Then he moved further into the room and took a seat by the wood-burner.

'I have a question,' he said. Caroline turned back to face him, startled. Perhaps she thought he'd gone out with the others. 'You saw Eleanor with another man in a restaurant in Bloomsbury. Who else did you tell about that?'

'I only talked to Eleanor about it.' Caroline's voice was clear and certain. 'I don't really do gossip. I have enough to think about without that.'

There was a brief silence. Perez supposed he should be panicking and out searching with the others, but in this room he felt quite calm. The worst thing in the world that could happen to him had already occurred when Fran died. He thought he wouldn't panic ever again. Unless someone threatened Cassie, and now he couldn't let himself think about that happening. 'That's not entirely true, is it? For instance, you told your husband that you'd seen Eleanor with the man.'

'Lowrie doesn't count.' She gave a little laugh. 'We share everything.'

Really? I don't think I shared everything with Fran.

'But he might have spoken to someone else,' Perez said. 'His friend Ian, for example. Perhaps he'd think it was his duty to tell his friend that his wife was seeing someone else. Lowrie knew what Eleanor was like, after all. She'd messed him around big-style when he was a student. Perhaps he saw an opportunity to get his revenge.'

The silence stretched, so he thought she might be considering the matter seriously, but when Caroline spoke her voice was dismissive. 'Lowrie got over being dumped by Eleanor years ago. We were students. That's how students behave. He's with me now. I was happy enough when we were just living together, and he was the one who wanted the wedding and the hamefarin'. He wanted to be married to *me*.' She tapped the palm of her hand on the windowsill to make her point. 'Honestly. He's the one who cares so much about family.'

Perez thought about that. About all these complicated families. About Lowrie, who'd threatened to kill himself over a dark and exotic woman from the south. And about Polly, who had nobody but the man and the friends who'd come with her to Shetland. He was still thinking when he got to his feet and left the house without speaking to Caroline again. He stood outside, just where the track began, and listened. Nothing. He waited for his ears to tune into the tiny sounds all around him. He still had Caroline's hard English voice in his head, and it took him a while to hear through the silence. The first sound to emerge was water. Always in Shetland there was the background noise of water on the shore or falling as rain. During the day you could usually hear sheep too. And wind, but tonight there was no wind at all.

His phone buzzed, shattering his attempt to listen properly. He moved further up the track. Despite what Caroline had said about despising gossip, he wouldn't put it past her to eavesdrop through the door.

It was Mary Lomax and her words were tumbling over themselves, so for a minute he couldn't make out what she was telling him. Then she became more coherent and explained that David Gordon had run away and she didn't know where he'd gone. Perez thought this was a complication he could do without: all these people wandering around in the dark, all tense and jumpy. But there was no point blaming the police officer, and he cut into her apologies.

'I'd like you to do something for me, Mary. Make a few phone calls. I know it's late, but I think these folk will be awake. This is what I'd like to know.' He spoke carefully and sensed that she was steadying on the other end of the phone. 'There's no need to ring me back. Just send me a text with your answer. Is that OK?'

As he switched off his mobile he thought he could hear children singing, but the tune faded away immediately and it could have been his imagination, or a strange echo from the phone.

Then he was still, waiting for his eyes and ears to adjust again, as he tried to put himself in the footsteps of the killer.

He climbed the bank behind the house to the overgrown bones of the farmstead close to the loch where Eleanor's body had been found. He'd seen George Malcolmson standing here when he and Willow had gone to look inside Utra. From there Perez thought he'd get a sense of the space all around and, when the sun rose, he'd have a view north along the shore. As he watched he saw flames. Someone had lit a bonfire on the beach, probably to celebrate midsummer and the tilting of the year towards winter. Sparks were shooting into the sky like fireworks or an emergency flare. Perhaps people who had been eating in the boat club had decided they would carry on partying. The thought reassured him. If there were other people around, then there was surely less danger of another murder.

His phone buzzed. A text from Mary with the answer to his questions. The words seemed domestic and normal in this wild setting.

Then he heard footsteps. Heavy. Someone wearing boots on the rocky path. Perez moved into the corner formed by two walls so that his silhouette wouldn't show up against the lightening sky. There were still occasional flagstones on the floor, with cotton grass growing between them. He crouched in the corner and waited, feeling slightly ridiculous, reverting to childhood and hide-and-seek with his cousins. Around him suddenly there was movement. It was as if the wall was alive and shifting. There was a murmuring, the softness of wings against the air. Storm petrels, bat-like and gentle-eyed, which had nested in cracks in the wall, were flying out towards the sea.

The footsteps got closer and now Perez saw torchlight. Very faint, as if the battery was low. No other sound. No one was shouting out for Polly. If this was a searcher, then perhaps they'd lost heart. Perhaps. Still there wasn't enough light to make a positive identification.

Standing in the shadow, Perez was thinking about all the people he'd met since he'd come to Unst the week before, and in his head he saw them moving around as if they were actors on a giant stage. But now he'd lost control of their moves. He knew they were scattered around Meoness, on the cliffs and the shore, but didn't have precise positions for them and that made him nervous. He was a director whose players were taking no notice of him. He'd lost control of the action.

The figure moved on down the path towards the settlement of Meoness and paused briefly to look over the loch, where Eleanor had been lying in her smart silk dress, pointing the torch around the grassy banks as if looking for something specific. It was impossible to tell if the walker was male or female, but they were fit and moved easily down the steep path. Perez waited for a while, indecisive. He still thought Polly might come this way. The fog had cleared above him and, in the last of the darkness, the sky was suddenly filled with stars. He saw the Milky Way as defined points of light and all the space made him feel giddy, made him forget for a moment what he was doing there. Then he came to his senses and followed the figure further down the path.

On the road leading towards the Meoness community hall the torch was switched off. Perez found it more difficult to track the person then. If they stopped in the shadow, he might get too close and he didn't want to give away the fact that he was following.

Utra, the house where Sarah Malcolmson had grown up, appeared as an indistinct silhouette beside the track. Perez stopped and listened. Nothing. Now the footsteps were so far ahead that he could no longer hear them. There was another moment of indecision. Should he run on and try to catch up, or go inside? Polly was the most important person in all this. He still wasn't sure whom he'd been following. This place was central in the Peerie Lizzie story, and Polly might have been attracted inside for another look. He pushed open the door.

In the old house the darkness felt viscous, like melted tar. Perez imagined that he would have to wade through it to get beyond the lintel. He turned on his torch and walked past the scullery to the bigger room and a smell of damp and decay. He was distracted, remembering his last visit to the house and the feral cat that had shocked Willow, the way her arm had felt under his hand, how the touch had been like an electric shock all the way to his shoulder. Then they'd both been disturbed and he thought they hadn't searched the place properly. He was torn, aware that the figure he'd been following would soon be lost to him altogether, but curious. Something here had pulled in Polly Gilmour and Charles Hillier. He shone his torch into the corners. The room seemed quite bare. He opened the stove, which stood in one corner. A piece of half-burnt peat. Then as he was leaving he saw, caught on a sharp corner of the metal stove, a scrap of cloth. White. Like the dress worn by Peerie Lizzie every time she'd appeared. The dress, at least, was real and not imagined. In the dust on the floor he saw two long, thin rectangular shapes. Something had been placed here. Or lain here.

In the distance there was the sound of a car engine. Perez went outside, saw the headlights just before they were switched off and thought he could place them in Meoness with some accuracy. He ran down the track and away from the ruined house. As he was running his phone rang. He slowed to take it from his pocket, but continued walking fast.

'Jimmy!' Sandy had his panicky *I'm out of my depth* voice. 'I'm just on my way back to Sletts and I heard a scream.'

'From inside the house?' He didn't need to ask *which* house. He knew now where the focus of the investigation should have been from the start.

'I'm not quite sure. From near the house at least.'

'I'm on my way.' He paused. 'Sandy, don't go inside. Wait for me.'

Outside, after the dense darkness of Utra, it seemed that dawn had arrived. There was that cold, grey sky and the stars had disappeared. Birds were singing. Perez ran on. He'd been infected by Sandy's anxiety and by the thought that he'd misjudged the situation. He'd been following the wrong person all the time and hadn't considered that he should be looking out for a car.

Sandy was waiting for him, curled into the hillside, so well camouflaged that when he moved, unrolling his body until he was standing, Perez was startled.

'Willow's on the beach.' Sandy's voice was low, a whisper, though from inside the house surely nobody would hear. 'With David Gordon. I saw them from the hall.'

Perez nodded. One less thing to worry about. 'What did you hear?'

'A scream. A shriek. High-pitched.'

'Man or woman?'

'Woman, I think. But hard to tell. And because we're looking for Polly Gilmour, I assumed it must be her.'

'Of course.' Expectation altered perception. That was how magicians could so easily confound their audience. 'That's natural—'

He didn't finish his sentence. There was another scream.

Terrified, and still impossible to identify as male or female. Perez found it unbearable. 'Wait here. Stop anyone who leaves. Whoever it is. And don't let anyone else in.'

Bent double, he ran round Voxter, past the hen house and the shed where George Malcolmson kept his old tractor. The man's car was parked outside. Perez touched the bonnet and felt that it was still warm. From this side of the house he had a view into the kitchen through a small window in the back door. There was no sign of George.

Inside stood Polly Gilmour. She looked pale, but strangely calm. Even with an arm around her neck and a knife to her throat. Even when she opened her mouth and screamed again, her nerve cracking and tears running down her cheeks.

Chapter Forty-Four

INSIDE THE VOXTER KITCHEN POLLY THOUGHT she was melting at the edges. She decided she must look as Eleanor had done when she'd sat on the deck, the last night of her life, when the mist had eaten into her and made her slowly disappear. If Eleanor had come inside then, after sharing those silly stories about Marcus, everything would have been well. Her friend would still be alive. The malicious man from the hotel would still be alive. And Polly wouldn't be here in this strange house by the sea, hardly able to breathe, a knife at her throat.

She thought again that this was like being in the middle of a terrible nightmare and soon she would wake up and everything would be well. As the arm tightened around her throat, she began to slip into unconsciousness and the events of the evening drifted through her mind, very slowly, like shadows in the fog. She watched the action as if from a great height, as if she was Eleanor filming it in a wide-angle shot for her show.

The five of them had walked along the cliff towards the boat club. Ian had been striding out ahead of them, as if he wanted to pretend they weren't there, that he was quite alone. Marcus had been strangely silent. Polly had turned to him. 'Is anything wrong?' She'd been frightened that he might tell her the relationship was over and that he preferred Eleanor's mother. Because deep down Polly knew that Eleanor had been telling her the truth about the affair. Behind them Lowrie and Caroline were quiet too, as if Marcus's mood was contagious.

Then the scene in her head shifted to the boat club, and the tone was quite different. Here everything was music and partying. It had felt as if the whole room was celebrating Eleanor's death, that Polly was the only person there sad that she'd gone. And then she'd seen the girl dancing. Peerie Lizzie, who couldn't be a ghost, because Polly had heard her singing. She'd been captured as if in a spotlight, as if the camera had zoomed in on her and all around her the scene was blurred. Polly had followed her out into the night and the fog had come down. For a moment she had thought seeing the girl had been a warning, a premonition. Perhaps Polly would drown too, like Elizabeth Geldard, and her body would be washed up on the shore. And nobody would care. Not even Marcus.

At the worst point of the panic, when she was remembering the night of Eleanor's disappearance, Polly's phone had rung and a sensible voice at the other end had come to her rescue. 'Don't you dare try to find your way back along the top of the cliff. Not in this weather. Walk back along the track to the boat club and we'll come along and pick you up in the car. It might take you a while but that's the safest thing.'

And now, as the life was being squeezed from her and the point of the sharp knife was pricking her skin, she relived her relief as the car drew up. Lowrie's father George had leaned across and opened the door for her, and she remembered that first time they'd danced together, the strength in his arms as he'd almost swung her off her feet, the tingle of excitement when the music had stopped.

'Come along in out of the cold,' he'd said. 'You must be frozen. Grusche says I'm to take you back to Voxter. She has some soup on the stove for all of you. She'll let the others know, and you can have some supper with us before you go back to Sletts.'

But when they'd arrived back at Voxter there was no sign of the others. There was just Grusche in the kitchen wearing a strange white nightdress, with a hand-knitted shawl tied around her shoulders. And George disappeared, saying something about needing to get to his bed. And suddenly Grusche was standing behind her, muttering about Eleanor and Lowrie, and the arms that had gained their strength through lifting sheep and kneading dough were holding her as if she were in a vice, and Polly began to scream and at last everything went black.

She regained consciousness briefly and thought she saw a figure at the window. Perhaps it was Peerie Lizzie coming to fetch her into the water. But when the door opened, it wasn't Lizzie standing inside, but the detective with the wild black hair. Polly had thought that sometimes he looked haunted too.

He walked up to Grusche and his voice was gentle, as if he was talking to a child. 'This won't do now, will it? You don't really want to hurt Polly. What has she ever done to you?'

Polly felt the grip on her neck relax a little.

Then an inside door was opened. George stood there. 'Woman, let that lass go!' His voice was as clear as a foghorn and roused Polly completely. Grusche turned to face him. Polly felt the movement of Grusche's body against her shoulders and again a slight release of tension.

'It was for Lowrie,' Grusche said.

'Was it?' This was the detective again. 'You've always been honest. That class you did with Fran. The final assessment. She said your art was uncompromising, truthful. Didn't she?' He paused briefly and when he spoke again his voice was easy, conversational. 'So let's be honest now, shall we? This was about you. About not wanting to end up a lonely woman. Needing Lowrie and Caroline for company and conversation. I know about loneliness. I can understand that. But it has to end here.' He held out his hand. There was a moment of hesitation, a sudden tightening of the hold on Polly's neck, then Grusche reached out, twisted her wrist so that the handle was facing the detective and dropped the knife into his palm. Polly saw that his skin was dark, as if he'd been in the sun, and his hand was bony like Marcus's.

Then Willow Reeves was there, wrapping Polly up in a blanket and asking if she was all right, or if they should get *Oscar Charlie*, the rescue helicopter, to take her to hospital. Saying they'd take her back to her friends in Sletts. Polly turned for a moment and saw Grusche staring at her with eyes that were still full of hatred.

Chapter Forty-Five

In Springfield House, Willow sat in the corner of the yellow morning room and watched the conversation between Jimmy Perez and Grusche Malcolmson. Sunlight was streaming through the window and outside there was the sound of birdsong. Jimmy had rustled up coffee from somewhere and the smell of it filled the room. On a plate was a pile of little round biscuits dusted with sugar. They'd probably been made by Grusche herself.

'Why did you kill Eleanor?' The inspector's voice was so soft that Willow strained to hear.

They'd allowed Grusche to get dressed. She was wearing wide linen trousers and a hand-knitted sweater. Willow thought that she herself would probably look very similar to Lowrie's mother when she was in her sixties. She would be tall and angular and would wear charity-shop clothes.

Grusche looked up sharply. 'She was evil. You know that, Jimmy. She was flirting with Lowrie, trying to steal him from Caroline, trying to steal him from *me*.' The voice suddenly very sharp and shrill.

'I don't think she was doing that, Grusche. She was faithful to her husband. Always had been.'

'No!' The word exploded from her like a gunshot. 'I had proof. The two of them were here in Shetland together just a week before Lowrie's wedding. I saw a photograph on his laptop, the day of the hamefarin'. It was of Lowrie with his arm around that woman, and the museum in Lerwick behind them.' She stared at Perez, her eyes like steel, forcing him to understand the implication of her words. 'That afternoon Lowrie was in his room, staring at the picture, when I took in his clean shirt for the party. He shut his computer, but not before I'd seen the image.'

'You printed it out,' Perez said, 'on photographic paper.' Willow thought none of this was coming as a surprise to him.

Grusche nodded. 'While he and Caroline were hanging up bunting in the hall. Think of what it meant, Jimmy. Think of the spell that woman must have had over him. He was only married for a week, and yet he was obsessed by the photograph of himself with another woman. She must have been some kind of witch.'

'So why did you print out the photo, Grusche?' Perez took a little sip of coffee and seemed to savour it.

'I wanted to confront the woman. To prove to her that I knew what her game was. I wanted something in my hand – something concrete.' The German woman paused as if she was looking for the right words, as if she was desperate for Perez to understand. 'Something real. I couldn't carry Lowrie's computer across the sand to Sletts now, could I, Jimmy?'

'Why don't you tell me what happened,' Perez said. He leaned back in his chair and waited. Outside a curlew flew overhead, calling. He shut his eyes and for a moment Willow wondered if he was drifting off to sleep.

'I had to speak to Eleanor Longstaff, to make her see what she was doing. All that evening, while she was dancing and laughing and flirting, the truth was eating away at me. She was going to make Lowrie unhappy again. You must see, Jimmy, that I had to do something. You'd be the same if anyone treated Cassie badly. Eleanor would ruin my son's marriage and he'd become ill and depressed. He might disappear south with her, and then I'd never see him again. I could tell that *she* would never consider living in Shetland.'

Perez had his eyes open and leaned towards her. 'Eleanor never planned to steal your son from you. You must know that now.' But it was spoken in a whisper, almost to himself.

Grusche didn't seem to hear him and continued talking. 'After the party we tidied up a bit and then George went to bed. He'd been drinking all night and I knew that he wouldn't wake up until the morning. I could hear him snoring, like a great big bear. Then Lowrie and Caroline went off too. I let myself outside and walked down to the beach. I could see all the people from Sletts sitting on the deck. They were talking and laughing. After a while the men went inside. Then a little later Polly disappeared too, and only Eleanor was left. And that seemed like a sign that I should go and talk to her. It was just getting light and she saw me coming. She waved to me. "Can't you sleep either, Grusche? Shall we go for a walk?" Not waiting for an answer. I don't think she ever really listened to what people said to her.'

There was a moment of absolute silence in the room before Grusche continued.

'I didn't know where we were going until she said: "Do you

348

believe in ghosts? Do you think Peerie Lizzie exists?" That was like another sign. I said I'd show her where Vaila had seen Lizzie, and I led her up the footpath to the standing stone.'

Another silence. Perez drained the coffee in his mug. 'Were you planning to kill her at that point, Grusche? Please tell us. It is important that we know.'

'No! I wanted to make her see that she had to leave Lowrie alone.'

'So you're walking up the footpath towards the standing stone and it's just getting light.' Perez gave an encouraging smile. 'What happened then?'

Willow felt as if she was almost dozing. She'd had very little sleep in the last few days and the tension had drained from her. The sun was strong now and the room was very warm.

'We sat close to the cliff edge,' Grusche said. 'We talked. She said she hadn't been this happy for years and at last it seemed that everything was going right for her. Perhaps she'd been silly to place so much importance on having a baby. She'd finally found the man she loved and nothing else seemed important.'

'You thought she was talking about Lowrie?'

'Who else could she be talking about?'

'Her husband,' Perez said. 'I think she was talking about her husband.'

'I showed her the photograph.' Grusche was almost screaming. Willow thought she didn't listen much, either. 'I laid it on the grass. I demanded to know, Jimmy, what was going on here. I had that right. What had she been doing in Lerwick with my Lowrie the week before his wedding?'

'And what did she say?'

Again Willow had to strain to hear Perez's words.

'She said it was a secret. "But don't worry, Grusche, I don't really have designs on your son. Besides, he's quite grown-up now. He doesn't need you to look out for him." Then she laughed. As if I was ridiculous for caring what happened to my boy.'

'So you killed her,' Perez said, as if it was the most natural thing in the world. 'Talk me through exactly how that happened, would you, Grusche? For the record.'

'I wanted to stop her laughing,' Grusche said. 'And I wanted to be sure that she'd never make Lowrie so unhappy that he wanted to kill himself again.'

She paused and Willow listened carefully, imagining how the scene might have played out. They were recording the interview, but this first telling might help her to understand.

Grusche continued, 'We were sitting at the top of the cliff, Jimmy. There was that strange early morning light, which you only get at this time of the year. There was so much noise. All those seabirds shrieking around our heads. But I could still hear the woman laughing. I picked up a boulder and I hit her with it.' Another pause. 'She fell awkwardly and seemed somehow crumpled and disfigured. I like lovely images. You know that, Jimmy. You know I could have been an artist myself. Fran always told me I had great potential, but I was happy to sacrifice that for my son. I dragged Eleanor into the middle of the loch, so that she looked like a picture. Someone might take some pleasure from the striking image, at least. She was a beautiful woman.'

'What did you do then? After you'd thrown her cloak and shoes over the cliff and you'd torn the photograph into little pieces.'

'I went home,' Grusche said. 'I lay next to my snoring husband. I went to sleep.' She reached out and took one of the biscuits, then nibbled it as if she was judging its quality. Willow was astonished at how calm she seemed. There was another minute of complete silence.

'Did you tell Lowrie what happened?' Perez's voice was sharper now. 'I mean, has he known for the last week that his mother is a murderer?'

'No!' The same explosive retort. 'Of course not.'

'But you must have asked him what he was doing with Eleanor in Lerwick. You would have wanted to know.'

For the first time Grusche seemed less sure of her ground. 'He said he was there as a friend, helping Eleanor with some project at work. I told him that he must keep that secret, that you would suspect him of killing her if you knew that he'd met her in Lerwick without telling anyone.'

'And Lowrie did what he was told,' Perez murmured. 'Of course he did. First you and then Caroline making decisions for him. He'd never had to think for himself.'

Willow wondered if Lowrie had guessed at his mother's involvement in Eleanor's death. Perhaps she was so perfect in his eyes that he couldn't contemplate the possibility of her being a murderer. Certainly he hadn't asked Grusche any awkward questions. Willow was reminded of the way that Charles and David had kept their relationship intact by ignoring unpleasantness – anything that was difficult or uncomfortable.

'What about Hillier?' Perez was saying. 'Why did he have to die?'

'He was there that night,' Grusche said. 'He saw me walk up the path with Eleanor. And come down all alone.'

'He was blackmailing you?'

'And that shows just how ridiculous he was!' Grusche spat out the words. 'As if we'd have any money to give him.'

'Did Hillier tell you that he was in Lerwick for that meeting in the museum? With Lowrie and Eleanor and Monica Leaze?'

She nodded reluctantly. Willow had no idea what Perez was talking about. He seemed to her like a magician himself, fanning random cards on the table until they made sense, at least to him. But she knew better than to interrupt. Let him explain to her later.

'So you'll know that Eleanor was telling you the truth,' Perez said. 'That there was no affair. Lowrie was there as her friend.'

'That wasn't how Lowrie saw it.' Again she was almost screaming. 'You didn't see the way Lowrie stared at that picture. He would have done anything for that woman. He was as infatuated now as when he first met her.'

'Even if he was,' Perez said and his voice was sad, 'I don't think it was your place to interfere.' Then he changed his tone. 'Hillier. Tell me what happened.'

'I arranged to meet him on the shore at Springfield. I said I had some savings, a family inheritance, and we might be able to do a deal. I went to the book club in Baltasound as usual that night, but I stopped at Springfield on my way home.'

Willow was tempted to ask what the book group had been reading. She was feeling light-headed and a little giddy. She'd believed that Grusche was a dignified and intelligent woman. She hadn't recognized the obsession that had gripped her.

But Grusche was still talking. 'Hillier was waiting for me on the sand. The mist was coming in again. It wasn't hard to dispose of him.' Then she snapped her lips shut. 'I'm not talking any more, Jimmy. Not to you, and not in this place. I know my rights. You can take me to Lerwick now, and Lowrie will find me a lawyer. Lowrie will look after me.'

Chapter Forty-Six

'I STILL DON'T UNDERSTAND WHY THE Malcolmson woman went after Polly Gilmour,' Sandy said. 'And that stuff about Peerie Lizzie. Was the lassie on the sand just a figment of the English folk's imagination?'

They'd stopped in the North Light Gallery for lunch on their way south through Yell. Willow's idea. Perez would have preferred to go straight back to Lerwick so that he could be home when Cassie came back from school. The painting of the girl in the white dress was still hanging on the gallery's wall. Catherine Breton was in her glass bubble making pots. The gallery with its cafe was unusually quiet. It was a breezy day, with the wind blowing cloud-shaped shadows across the water outside and loose sand against the windows.

He was about to answer when the door opened and a woman walked in. Perez thought Willow had been expecting her, that this was a pre-arranged meeting. The newcomer stood just inside the door, then approached them. She was wearing a bright-red coat, heavy brown boots and carried the smell of cigarettes with her.

'I went to the police station this morning as soon as the ferry came in.' Monica Leaze had the same nervous energy that Perez remembered from the launch of her exhibition. The same wiry hair and chestnut eyes. 'They told me to talk to you here.'

'So now we're in a position to explain to Sandy about the ghost.' Willow's voice was light until she turned to the artist. Then she was fiercer than Perez had ever seen her. 'If we'd understood earlier that you were involved, we might have prevented Hillier's death.'

'Of course I should have come before.' Monica was playing with a napkin on the table, folding it into smaller and smaller squares. 'But when I left Shetland I didn't know Eleanor had died, only that she was missing, and that was always part of the plan.' She turned to stare out of the window. A waitress brought coffee without her noticing. 'It started out as a bit of a hoot, and a way to get Nell out of a financial mess. Nobody was really supposed to get hurt.'

'Perhaps you could talk us through what happened.' Perez thought he knew most of it, but Sandy was sitting on the other side of the table looking bewildered. The man had worked well on this investigation and his own version of the real Peerie Lizzie story was probably close to the truth. He deserved some answers to the make-believe one. 'You met here in Shetland a couple of weeks ago. You and three others.'

'Well, I'd known Eleanor for ages. We moved in the same arty circles, I suppose – my husband's a director. I hadn't come across Charles or Lowrie before. We came together that day; we were Nell's team, her secret weapon. The four of us had lunch in the Hay's Dock. It seemed like great fun at the time, a bit of a party, as if we were on some kind of secret mission.' Monica paused. 'That was the last time I saw Eleanor. Lowrie and Eleanor had flown in on separate planes, very cloak-and-dagger – Lowrie from Edinburgh and Eleanor from Glasgow, though they both started off in London. I was already here in Yell and Charles Hiller gave me a lift down to Lerwick.'

'And what was the meeting about?'

'To arrange the scam, of course: the Peerie Lizzie haunting. Nell needed her documentary about ghosts to be a big success. The company, Bright Star, had been leaking money – there'd been a couple of poor shows, and Eleanor was distracted when she lost the baby. Not on top of her game. This was the last chance to avoid bankruptcy. She wasn't prepared to take any chances.'

'And you?' Perez asked. 'What would you get out of it?'

She seemed startled for a moment, as if the answer was so obvious that it needed no explanation. 'Fun,' she said. 'Like I said. And Nell was a mate who needed help. Besides . . .' She paused again.

'You glory in the commonplace made weird,' Perez said.

'Yeah. Something like that.' She gave him a strange look. 'I suppose I was thinking about it almost like a piece of art.'

'So you manufactured a ghost.'

'Not to mislead the television audience,' Monica said sharply. 'Eleanor would never have stooped to that. She was honest about her work and took it seriously. But to show how educated and rational people might become suggestible in certain situations. She wanted to persuade her friends of the reality of Peerie Lizzie and use their experience as an example in her documentary.'

'Why did she involve Hillier and Lowrie?' Willow stood up and stretched. The gallery ceiling was so low that she almost touched it. There was a sudden shower and the rain hit the window hard, like stones. The room became very dark.

'Eleanor always liked a gang,' Monica said. 'Especially a gang of admirers. But there were practical reasons too. Lowrie knew the layout of the land. He'd grown up in Unst. Hillier's partner had researched the background to the Peerie Lizzie story and Charles could throw in the details that might make it seem authentic. Besides, he'd been a stage magician. He had skills that we could use.'

Hillier would have loved that, Perez thought. *And the chance to appear on television again.*

'And you?' Willow asked. 'What was your role?'

'I was the set designer and the theatrical assistant. When we met for lunch I brought along some drawings. One was of Eleanor looking like Ophelia in her bridesmaid's dress – you found that in my house in Cullivoe. We weren't sure how we'd use them, and it was all very cheesy.' A pause. 'But mostly I was there because I could provide the ghost.'

'Your granddaughter.'

'Grace, yes. Her mother finds her a tricky child and I don't think London suits her. She's got too much energy. She spends some of her time here with me.'

Perez was looking at the painting of the girl on the gallery wall.

'That's my daughter,' Monica said, 'but the resemblance is uncanny. It's a while since I've seen that and I hadn't realized quite how alike they look, now that Grace is getting older.'

I can see how Polly was so disturbed by it, Perez thought. *How she started to question her sanity.*

'You got Grace to record Peerie Lizzie's song,' he said. 'But of course it didn't sound right. She's spent a lot of time in

Shetland, but she hasn't picked up the accent yet.' He paused. 'She and the Arthur boys were singing it the night Polly was lost in the fog and must have freaked her out big-style.'

'When I went south, Grace wanted to stay with Jen Arthur and the boys and I thought another week off school wouldn't do her any harm. Jen was happy to have her, and it's an education in itself, isn't it, living in Shetland? I didn't know then that Eleanor had been killed and there was a murderer on Unst.'

'It must have been in the papers in the south,' Sandy said. 'Once Hillier was killed too. Why wait until today to get in touch?'

Monica still looked out at the grey water. 'I was scared. If you knew I was there the night Eleanor was killed – if you found my painting – you might accuse me of murder.'

'Not if you were innocent,' Sandy said. 'You'd have nothing to fear, if you told us the truth.'

She turned back to face him. Her words shot towards him like the rain on the window. 'Really? When I was a student I was assaulted by a lecturer. I went to the police that time. They believed a respectable lecturer over an unconventional art student and threatened that I could be charged with wasting police time if I didn't withdraw the allegation. I wasn't prepared to take the risk now.'

The room went very quiet. Behind the counter the coffee machine hissed.

'Let's go back to that meeting at the Hay's Dock,' Perez said. 'Did you take photographs afterwards?'

'Yes, Eleanor wanted some publicity images that we could release to the media before the show.' Monica looked up. 'She was already planning features in the broadsheets. *How four metropolitan thirty-somethings believed that they'd seen a ghost.*'

'And one of the pictures was of her and Lowrie?'

'Yes, Lowrie asked if he could have it. I emailed it to him. Why? Is it important?'

Perez didn't answer. This was the photo that Lowrie had been staring at when Grusche went into his room before the party. The photo that had triggered Eleanor's murder. 'Tell me what happened the night of the party.'

'Grace and I went into Unst on the ferry.'

'You were seen by the Meoness teacher.' Sandy seemed to wake briefly, then to settle back with his arms on the table. They'd all been awake all night. He looked like a nursery child ready to take a nap.

Monica ignored the interruption. 'We left our car at the hall. There were so many vehicles parked there that nobody would notice. Then we camped out in the old house, Utra. Lowrie had told us we could use it, and Grace got changed there. For her it was just a game. Staying up late. Putting on a party frock. Dancing on the beach. She's like all the women in our family – given to exhibitionist tendencies. I met Charles on the beach. We had a smoke and watched the performance. Afterwards Grace and I lit a fire and rolled out our sleeping bags on the floor, just waiting until it was time for the first ferry to Yell. Early the next morning I dropped Grace at Jen's and drove on south.'

'Polly thought she saw the girl on the beach and in the house at other times.' It was Sandy again. Perez could tell that he thought this artist, with her paintings of dead women, her camping out all night in a ruined house, wasn't fit to have care of a child.

Monica shrugged. She seemed fidgety and uncomfortable. Perhaps Sandy reminded her of the cops she'd met in the Met.

Perhaps she just wanted to go outside to smoke. 'Maybe Jen took her and the boys to play at their father's house. He lives with his new wife in Spindrift, that hideous bungalow in Meoness. They've been divorced for a while, but it's all quite amicable. The boys like to see the new baby.'

Or maybe, Perez thought, Polly conjured her own ghosts out of the air. She'd been told that her lover was having an affair with an older woman and she was emotionally frail to start with. He could imagine that she might be haunted by dreams and demons.

'Who sent the email saying the group wouldn't find Eleanor alive?' Willow broke into his thoughts.

'The plan was for Eleanor to write it, and for me to take her phone and find somewhere with a good signal to send it,' Monica said. 'Grace was fast asleep, so I slipped out of Utra and sent the message. We'd arranged that I'd leave the phone in the planticrub, where Eleanor could pick it up later.'

'And then Eleanor was supposed to disappear?'

Monica nodded. 'Charles was waiting with his car. He was going to take her back to Springfield House. There was a small room waiting for her.'

But Eleanor kept being interrupted. First by Polly, who'd joined her straight after the men went to bed. Then by Grusche. And in the end Hillier went back to the hotel alone. When Eleanor's body was discovered, he remembered seeing Grusche coming back from the cliffs alone and knew who must have killed her.

Monica was on her feet. 'I'm going to fetch Grace and take her home. I thought this was a good place for her to spend part of the year, but I think perhaps London is safer after all.' At the door she stopped and turned back to Perez. 'Don't I know you?'

'I met you here,' he said. 'At a party for the opening of your exhibition.' He paused. 'My partner was an artist. Fran Hunter.' He was pleased with himself because the words came easily.

Monica nodded as if she recognized the name and then she left.

Later they ended up in Lerwick, in the house by the water that Perez hadn't quite got round to letting out. He'd arranged for Cassie to stay one more night with her father. Perez wasn't sure exactly what time it was. Or even what day. He'd be glad to be back in Ravenswick with just Cassie's chat as the background to his thoughts, and the routine of getting her to school and himself to work to keep him straight. But now they were drinking coffee, and Willow had managed to find an unopened bottle of single malt from the top of her bag. There were fulmars sailing past the window and no trace here in the town of fog. And then he saw the *Hjatland*, the big ferry to Aberdeen, pass down the Sound and so he knew it was just past seven o'clock in the evening. In twelve hours the three visitors from Sletts would be back on the Scottish mainland. He wondered how things would be between Polly and Marcus. Would the man give up his glamorous older woman, and would the timid librarian be able to forgive him? She seemed to have a knack of seeing the world as she wanted it to be. He thought it would be easier for Ian Longstaff to come to terms with his wife's murder now that there was some resolution.

'That scheme of Eleanor's seems an awful lot of bother to have gone to.' Willow was sitting on the floor and her long hair fell over her knees.

'She was desperate,' Perez said. 'As Monica said, her

company was on the verge of bankruptcy. She needed something new and dramatic to make the show a hit. Persuading a group of graduates that they'd seen the ghost of a child who'd died in 1930 would do that. And maybe Eleanor saw the hoax as a kind of retribution. She thought that Ian had been unfair in the way he treated her after losing the baby.'

'They must have had a weird kind of relationship.' Sandy seemed dreamy and lost in thought. By now the lack of sleep was catching up with them all. Perhaps he was thinking about his Unst school teacher and planning another meeting with her.

'It makes a kind of sense to me,' Willow said. 'They both liked a drama – the fights, the falling out, the reconciliation. I can understand how Eleanor would have enjoyed the challenge of convincing Ian that something supernatural was happening in Unst. She'd be able to mock him for the rest of their life together. And her whole existence was a theatrical production, so she'd have relished setting up something like this.' She paused. 'In her documentary I guess she wanted to prove that we need to believe in something other than the everyday world, to show that we're looking for an explanation for random events. It doesn't seem too daft, as theories go. Folk were always turning up at my parents' commune searching for answers.'

Perez thought this story had started with a deception and it was all about illusion and distorted perception. Strange shadows and half-spoken lies. 'I was never convinced when Lowrie said Eleanor hadn't discussed the project with him. That defied belief. She knew he'd do whatever she asked him to. He was Eleanor's champion, her knight in shining armour, charging to the rescue of her failing company.'

Willow reached out and poured herself another dram. For all that she was lanky and awkward to look at, Perez thought there was a grace about the way she moved. He looked at the water again. The *Hjatland* was already out of his line of sight.

'Why didn't Lowrie tell us all about the hoax, when Eleanor's body was found? There was no reason to keep it secret after that.' It was Sandy again, full of common sense.

'Because Grusche persuaded him that it would be a mistake and his involvement might turn him into a suspect. He wasn't exactly in the right frame of mind to make a rational decision. Bullied into marrying Caroline. Convinced by two strong women that his future lay in Shetland. And imagine the shock of finding Eleanor dead! The love of his life. His adolescent sweetheart. He'd grown up doing exactly what his mother wanted him to. This wasn't going to be the time when he'd stand up to her.'

'Do you think he guessed that Grusche was a killer?'

Perez hesitated. It was something he'd been thinking about since they'd first interviewed the woman. 'Maybe. Deep down. But it wasn't something he could afford to admit to himself.'

'I still don't quite understand what happened last night. All that unnecessary melodrama.' Willow was lying flat on the floor now, and fibres from Perez's shabby carpet had clung to her sweater. 'Why did Grusche attack Polly? Where on earth did that come from?'

'Lowrie had been convinced by his mother that the Peerie Lizzie scam must be kept secret at all costs. Grace was often knocking around in Meoness and it was freaking Polly out. The poor woman was really starting to believe in ghosts. And of course the girl was at the dinner in the boat club with Vaila and Neil and his boys. Polly must have thought she was going mad by that point, especially as Grace was in the dress she'd worn on the beach.' Perez paused and pulled together the timeline in his head. 'Grusche phoned Lowrie to offer them a lift back from the boat club, so that they wouldn't have to walk in the fog. The sight of Grace was already making him jumpy and he told Grusche that she was there.'

Perez spoke slowly, explaining the events to himself as well as his audience. 'The sight of the girl in the same room as Polly would have sent Lowrie into a panic. *What shall I do? What will happen if Polly sees the girl, and Grace tells her everything? The police will want to know why I've been lying to them.* And there might have been recriminations too: *I should have gone to Jimmy Perez right at the start. I should have explained.* Implying that all this was his mother's fault. And still Grusche would have been strong and reassuring: "Don't worry, son. Leave it to me. I'll sort it out." Then Lowrie made another phone call to Voxter, after Polly went missing, and the tension increased. Grusche would have heard the fear in her son's voice. "Polly's disappeared. She chased after Grace. She just phoned Marcus to tell him what she was doing, that she's seen Peerie Lizzie." And again Grusche would have reassured him. She'd always looked after him and she would always provide the answers.'

Perez's thoughts rushed back to the house by the shore, where he'd lived quite happily until Fran had swept him away to her home in Ravenswick, like flotsam on a big tide.

'Grusche phoned Polly on her mobile and told her to go back to the boat club, where George would pick her up. That's where George was, Sandy, when you went to visit Voxter. He wasn't asleep in his room, but driving through the fog to do what his wife had told him. Half-asleep and more than half-drunk.' A pause. 'And by then Grusche thought she was invincible and that her only role in life was to protect her son.'

'I'd wondered if Polly Gilmour was the killer,' Sandy said. 'She seemed so weird and distant most of the time. Spending her days reading old folk tales and legends. I thought it might have twisted her brain. It didn't seem like a real job for a grown woman.'

'Not like teaching, you mean?' Willow gave an innocent smile, but Sandy blushed to the roots of his hair.

Perez grinned. Sandy got awkwardly to his feet. 'I'm away home to my bed.' He shambled out of the house without looking back. The house was quiet again.

'What are your plans?' Perez felt suddenly uncomfortable, with Willow lying almost at his feet. It was as if Sandy had left them alone on purpose, a tactless kind of matchmaking.

'I'm booked on the first plane in the morning.'

There was an awkward silence and Willow broke it first.

'When did you know, Jimmy, that Grusche was the killer?'

'I didn't *know* until I saw her in the kitchen at Voxter with her arm round Polly's neck.'

'But you suspected. You had a very good idea.' It wasn't a question.

'Grusche was a kind of friend,' Perez said. 'She was always talking about her son, and there was nothing wrong in that. I thought it a splendid thing that she was so proud of him. Then, this time, the way she looked when she was speaking about him made me feel uncomfortable. It was as if she was living her life through her boy. She was too intense.' *And that's a lesson for me, perhaps.*

'You could have talked to me, Jimmy. There was no need

to wait until you were certain you were right. That's what colleagues do. Share their uncertainties and their ideas. I don't like feeling shut out.'

'I'm sorry,' Perez said. 'I was trying to work it all out in my head. I didn't want you to think I was a fool. All that stuff about ghosts was making me a peerie bit paranoid too . . .'

Willow got to her feet. He wondered if she was going to walk out on him, just as Sandy had done. Without looking back. Then she laughed. 'Put the kettle on, Jimmy Perez. Let's have some more coffee and another dram. We're at the end of this investigation and we've plenty to celebrate.'

Chapter Forty-Seven

THE NEXT MORNING PEREZ AND CASSIE gave Willow a lift to Sumburgh. They dropped her at the airport and she swung her bag out of the boot and walked away with just a little wave. Cassie jumped into the front seat beside Jimmy, because it was only a short drive from there to the pier at Grutness, where the *Good Shepherd* would arrive from Fair Isle. Perez had slept well and felt rested and oddly calm, better than he had since Fran's death. He and Cassie climbed the low headland together and watched the boat approaching from the south.

They were the only passengers. The *Shepherd* had a reputation for making folk seasick and most visitors into the Isle chose to fly these days. But there were provisions for the shop to load and some equipment for the bird observatory. Perez helped the crew and Cassie waited, very serious and a little apart, until his father, the skipper, called her aboard.

'Will you come into the wheelhouse with me and Jimmy, lass? We've only had one female crew member before, and I'm thinking that it's about time that we had another. And this is a bit special, isn't it?'

So she stood between them and watched the misty outline of Fair Isle become clearer, until they could make out the North Lighthouse and the wedge of Sheep Craig. James told her what he was doing and the hours passed very quickly. Then they were so close to the cliffs that they could make out individual kittiwakes and razorbills and they rounded the headland into the North Haven. And the whole island was there to meet them.

Chapter One

THE LAND SLIPPED WHILE JIMMY PEREZ was standing beside the grave. The dead man's family had come from Foula originally and they'd carried the coffin on two oars, the way bodies were always brought for burial on that island. The pall-bearers were distant relatives whose forebears had moved south to England, but they must have thought the tradition worth reviving. They'd had time to plan the occasion; Magnus had suffered a stroke and had been in hospital for six weeks before he died. Perez had visited him every Sunday, sat by his bed and talked about the old times. Not the bad old times, when Magnus had been accused of murder, but the more recent good times, when Ravenswick had included him in all their community events. Magnus had come to love the parties and the dances and the Sunday teas. He'd never responded to Perez's chat in the hospital, and his death had come as no surprise.

The coffin was lowered into the grave before the landslide started. Perez looked away from the hole in the ground, as the first earth was scattered on the coffin, and saw the community of Ravenswick stretching away from him. He could see Hillhead, Magnus's croft, right at the top of the bank next to the converted chapel where Perez lived with his stepdaughter Cassie. Nearer to the coast was the kirk and the manse that had been turned into a private home, much grander than the kirk itself. There were the polytunnels at Gilsetter farm and a tiny croft house hidden from the road. He didn't know who stayed there now. The school where Cassie was a pupil was further north, not visible from the cemetery; and hidden by the headland was the Ravenswick Hotel and a smart holiday complex of Scandinavian chalets. This was his home and he couldn't imagine living anywhere else.

The view was filtered by the rain. It seemed it had been raining for months. There'd been talk of cancelling Up Helly Aa two weeks earlier because of the weather, but the fire festival had never been stopped in peacetime and had gone ahead, despite the storm-force winds and the downpour. Now Perez turned his attention back to the minister's words, but at the same time he was remembering Fran, Cassie's mother and the love of his life, who was buried here too.

The landslide made no noise at first. The hill had been heavily grazed all year; sheep had tugged at the grass, disturbing the roots, exposing the black peat beneath. Now, after months of deluge, water had seeped under the surface, loosening the earth, and it was as if the whole hillside was starting to move. The contour of the landscape changed, exposing the rock below. But at this point Perez had turned back to look at the grave where Magnus Tait had just been laid to rest, and he had no warning of what was to come.

The rumbling started when the landslide picked up speed

and gathered boulders and the stones from field dykes. When it crossed the main road it missed a car but ploughed into the small croft. Relentless as a river in flood, the mountain of earth moved with a power that flattened the outhouses of the tiny croft house and forced its way through the main building, smashing windows and breaking down the door. Perez heard the noise when it hit the house as a roar, and felt it as a vibration under his feet. He turned at the same time as the other mourners. In Shetland, cemeteries are located by water. Before roads were built, bodies were carried to their graves by boat. The Ravenswick graveyard lay on flat land at the bottom of a valley next to the sea, in the shelter of a headland. Now the steep valley was filling with mud and debris and the landslide was gathering speed as it rolled towards them. The sound was so thunderous that the mourners had warning of its approach. They paused for a second and then scattered, clambering for higher ground. Perez put his arm round an elderly neighbour and almost carried him to safety. The minister, a middle-aged woman, was helped by one of the younger men. They were just in time. They watched as headstones were tipped over like dominoes and the landslide rolled across the pebble beach beyond and into the water. Fran's headstone was simple and had been carved by a friend of hers, a sculptor. It was engraved with the image of a curlew, her favourite bird. Perez watched the tide of mud sweep it away.

Perez recovered his composure very quickly. There was nothing of Fran left in the grave and he didn't need a stone to remember her by. He turned to check that everyone was well. He wondered what Magnus Tait, who had been a recluse for much of his life, would have made of the drama at his funeral. He thought Magnus would have given a shy grin and chuckled. He'd suggest that they all go back to the community hall for a dram. *No point standing out here in the wild, boys. No point at all.* Because, except for the minister, the mourners *were* all men. This was an old-fashioned funeral and women didn't go to the grave. They were a small group. While people had made more of an effort to get to know Magnus towards the end of his life, he had few contacts outside Ravenswick. Now they stood, shaken by the power of the landslide. From a distance they would have looked like giant sheep scattered over the hillside, aimless and lost.

Perez stared back up the bank. He was thinking that if the landslide had started a mile further north, the Ravenswick school would be as devastated as the croft house, which looked as if it had been smashed by a bomb. The slide had missed the farm at Gilsetter and the old manse by less than that distance. He looked at the ruin.

'Who lives in there?' He couldn't believe that anyone inside would still be alive. They'd be smothered by mud or crushed by the debris caught up in the slide. But he couldn't remember anyone living in the croft since Minnie Laurenson had died.

'I think it's empty, Jimmy. Stuart Henderson's son stayed there for a while, but he moved out months ago.' The speaker was Kevin Hay, a big, middle-aged man who lived at Gilsetter and farmed most of the Ravenswick land. Perez couldn't remember the last time he'd seen Hay in a shirt and tie. Probably at the last Ravenswick funeral. His black hair was so wet with the rain that it was plastered to his forehead. It looked as if it had been painted on.

'It hasn't been let out?' Accommodation was still so tight that at this time of year even holiday homes were rented to oil or gas workers. There were few empty houses in Shetland.

'Not as far as I know.' Hay seemed less sure now. 'I haven't noticed anyone in there. No cars parked outside. But the sycamores and our polytunnels mean we can't see it from the house.'

'Unlikely that it's occupied then,' Perez said. It would be hard to manage so far from town without a vehicle. The other mourners were now gathering together around the minister. She was calm and composed and seemed to be taking charge. He supposed they were making plans for getting home. The cemetery car park was on higher ground and their vehicles were undamaged, but some lived on the other side of the slip. 'I'd like to check it out, though.'

There were sheep tracks running up the valley slopes and Perez and Hay followed one of these. They looked down on the ruined house from above. Now the landslide had passed through, there was no sound but the rain. A strange eerie silence after the reverberating noise caused by the slip. People had already called the emergency services and soon there would be fire engines and police cars, but not yet.

The main walls of the croft house were almost intact, but the surge of the slide had weakened the inside walls and the roof had collapsed over half of the house, giving glimpses of the interior. Everything was black, the colour of the peaty earth. Perez slid further down the bank so that he could get a better view of the exposed rooms.

Hay followed, but put a hand on Perez's shoulder. 'Don't get too close, Jimmy. The hill's not too stable. There could be another slide. And I don't think there's anyone to save in there. No point putting your life at risk.'

Perez nodded. He saw that the mourners had reached the car park and people were driving away north, carrying with them friends who lived to the south of the slide. He supposed they'd be moving on to the community hall. The women would have a spread laid out. No point wasting that, and they'd all be ready for a hot drink.

'We should join them, Jimmy,' Kevin Hay said. 'Nothing we can do here.' In the distance they heard the sound of sirens. He looked back at the hill, worried about another landslide.

'You go. I need to stay anyway.' Perez looked beyond the house. There'd been a lean-to shed on the back of the kitchen and that had been completely destroyed: glass and the corrugated iron roof would have been swept into the mud. Beyond it, though, a stone wall that separated the small garden from the open grazing beyond was almost undamaged; it seemed to have funnelled the landslip through a gap where a wooden gate had once been. Nearest the space, the edges of the wall were ragged, eaten away like unravelled knitting, but beyond the gap on each side they were quite solid. The tide of earth had deposited debris there, thrown it up on its way through. Perez saw a bedhead, a couple of plastic garden chairs that must have been stored in the lean-to. And something else, bright against the grey wall and the black soil. A splash of red. Brighter than blood.

He scrambled down the bank towards it. A woman's body had been left behind by the ebbing tide of earth. She wore a red silk dress, exotic, glamorous. Not the thing for a February day in Shetland, even if she'd been indoors when the landslide swept her away. Her hair and her eyes were black and Perez felt a strange atavistic connection. She could be Spanish, like his ancestors of centuries ago. Kevin Hay was already walking back to the cars and Perez stood alone with her until the emergency services arrived.

Chapter Two

THE LANDSLIDE CAUSED CHAOS. THE MAIN road from Lerwick to Sumburgh Airport would be closed for at least the next day, and just where the slip had been there were no roads to set up a diversion. Flights into Sumburgh had been diverted to Scatsta Airport in North Mainland, which was normally only used for oil- and gas-related traffic, but was now stretched to capacity. Business people fired off emails of complaint to the council, as if *they* could influence the elements, and then booked themselves onto the ferry. Power lines were down – the slide had snapped poles and dragged them from their foundations. In the south of the island, people lucky enough still to have them reverted to the little generators they had used before mains electricity, and which they kept for emergencies. Others made do with candles and paraffin lamps.

The day after the incident Jimmy Perez was busy. He was the boss, so it was mostly meetings: with the council, to work on getting the road open as soon as possible; with social services, to check that the vulnerable and elderly had food delivered to them and that their houses were warm. Not exactly police work, but in the islands it was important to be flexible. He disliked being trapped in the police station and in endless discussions. And still it rained, so he looked out at a grey town, the horizon between the sea and the sky blurred with cloud. Today it hardly seemed to get light.

The main focus of his colleagues was to identify the woman who'd been killed in the landslide. As far as they could tell, she'd been the only casualty. There were no pockets in the silk dress and no handbag had been found. So there was nothing to identify her, no credit card or passport. The fire service said it was too dangerous yet to get into the ruined house to search for belongings. The bottom of her face, her jaw and her nose had been damaged beyond recognition and there were wounds to the back of her head; Perez thought she'd been gathered up by the moving hillside, tumbled and battered until she'd been left adrift at the stone dyke. Yet her forehead and her eyes had seemed oddly untouched. There were scratches and tears in the skin, but the structure of that part of the face had been left intact. Her dark eyes had stared out at him. Perez hoped that the first impact had killed her, knocked her out at least, so she'd had no knowledge of what was happening to her. He still felt the weird and irrational attachment that he'd experienced at the scene.

They assumed she must have been staying in the croft house that had been half-flattened and filled with black earth. On holiday perhaps. Yesterday had been the eve of St Valentine's, and in Perez's head she'd been trying on the red dress for her lover. Making sure that she would look good for the following evening. Perhaps she'd planned to cook him dinner. Something spicy and Mediterranean, made with peppers and tomatoes as red as the dress. Perez knew all these were fantasies, but he couldn't help himself. He wanted a name for her.

They still hadn't tracked down the owner of the house, though they did have a name for *it*: Tain. Apparently it had been inherited by a woman who lived in America, from an elderly aunt. Word in the community was that she rented it out on an ad hoc basis. She had plans to do it up and didn't want to let it out long-term. Robert Henderson, whose brother had been the last tenant, was enjoying a Caribbean cruise, and the brother himself was working in the Middle East. It was all frustrating and unsatisfactory. Perez knew there would be a logical explanation and that soon somebody would come forward to identify her, but at present the dead woman remained mysterious, fuelling his imagination and making him feel ridiculous.

Her body would be sent by ferry to Aberdeen for the post-mortem and Perez hoped they could get a name from dental records, once the pathologist James Grieve had started his work, but that could take days. And they needed some idea who she was before they could find her dentist. Perez didn't think there was any point checking in the islands. She wasn't local. He would have seen her in town or heard about the dark lady who lived on the edge of his community.

Now he was between meetings. He'd made coffee and stared out of his window towards the town hall. Its bulk was a shadow against the grey sky. Sandy Wilson knocked and came in.

'I've spoken to most of the estate agents in Lerwick. None of them managed the Ravenswick house or rented it out.'

'We need to track down the owner then.' Perez continued looking out of the window at the rain. 'The dead woman might have been their friend or relative. Do we still have no idea who it belongs to?'

Sandy shook his head. 'The person who might have had an idea is dead.'

'What do you mean?'

'Magnus Tait. He would have grown up with Minnie Laurenson, the old lady who used to live there. He might have been able to point us in the direction of the niece who inherited it.'

But Magnus had died after a stroke at the age of eighty-five and Perez suddenly realized that he still needed to grieve for the man. Magnus had been a part of his life for the past few years. The landslide cutting short the funeral had disturbed the natural process of mourning. At least Magnus had been laid to rest with some dignity, lowered into the ground before the cemetery had been inundated with mud.

Perez had first met Fran, his fiancée, because she'd been Magnus's neighbour, and the crofter had arrived at Perez's door soon after *Fran*'s funeral. Looking as awkward as a shy child. Clutching in his hand a bag of the sweets he knew Cassie loved. *For the bairn. Yon wife was a good woman.* Then he'd turned and walked down the bank to his croft, making no other demands, not expecting Perez to chat or to invite him in.

'The woman in the red dress couldn't have been the owner?' After all, why not? Perez thought. He'd imagined the dead woman as exotic and Spanish, but perhaps an American woman would wear red silk too.

Sandy shrugged. He didn't like to speculate in case he got things wrong.

'And you're sure that nobody has been reported missing?' Perez thought the woman couldn't have been staying in the house alone. Or if she was there alone, she had known people in the islands. February wasn't the time for a walking holiday or sightseeing. And if she was that sort of tourist, she wouldn't be dressed the way they'd found her. She'd be wearing jeans and a sweater, woollen socks – even indoors. 'When will they go in?'

'Soon,' Sandy said. 'Before it gets dark. They've got a generator set up, but they'd rather start during daylight.'

Perez nodded. 'You be there, Sandy. But before you go, talk to Radio Shetland about putting out a request for information on this evening's show. A phone number for the owner, or a contact. She'd have somebody to clean the place between visitors and to hold the keys. And a description of our mysterious woman.'

'We weren't in time to get the dead woman onto yesterday evening's ferry,' Sandy said, as if he'd just remembered and this was something Perez should know. 'She'll be going south to Aberdeen tonight. James Grieve is ready for her.'

'It would be good to have a name before James starts the post-mortem,' Perez said. 'I'd like to tell the relatives what's happening, before he begins his work.' His phone rang. He was expecting a summons to another meeting, but it was Kathryn Rogerson, the young woman who'd recently taken over as the teacher at Ravenswick School.

'I'm afraid we're closing the school today, Mr Perez. The engineers' department wants to survey the hill all the way along to Gailsgarth. It might need shoring up from the road. If there was another landslide there, the school would be right in its path, and we've been advised we have to get all the children away.' She still sounded like a child herself, rather earnest and desperate to do the right thing. Perez knew her father, who was a lawyer with an office just off Commercial Street. 'I know Maggie Thomson sometimes cares for Cassie when you're at work, but she's away at her sister's and her flight's been cancelled.'

So now he'd have to start ringing round to sort out childcare. The last thing he needed. Duncan Hunter, Cassie's natural father, was in Spain, apparently making out a deal with a company supplying holiday villas for the rental market. In practice, avoiding the most miserable of Shetland's weather. This was the time of year for islanders who could afford it to take their holidays.

'I wondered if you'd like me to bring Cassie back to Lerwick and she can spend the afternoon with me.' The teacher sounded hesitant, as if the offer might be considered impertinent. 'She'd be no bother, and at least you'd know she'd be safe in town. We're nowhere near the danger zone.'

'Are you sure? It sounds above and beyond the call of duty to act as childminder to your pupils when the school's closed.'

'Not at all!' Perez could picture the teacher in the little office in the school. She was small and tidy and had a pleasant manner with the bairns, but she stood no nonsense. Cassie adored her. 'We'll probably be shut at least until after the weekend, so if you need me to have Cassie on any other day, just let me know.'

'That's very kind. I'll try to sort out something else for later in the week, though.' Perez felt uncomfortable. Partly because he thought he couldn't take advantage of the woman's good nature. Partly because he hated being in emotional debt. He'd never been very good at accepting help. 'I'm not sure what time I'll be able to pick Cassie up this evening.'

'Have supper with us,' Kathryn said. 'My mother always cooks enough for an army.'

Perez was still trying to think of an excuse that didn't sound rude when the teacher ended the call.

THE COMPLETE SHETLAND SERIES

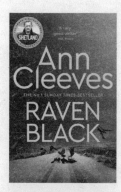

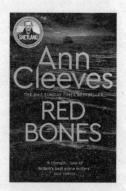

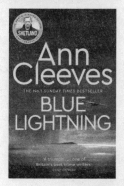

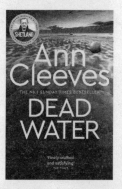

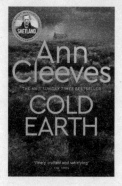

THE VERA STANHOPE SERIES

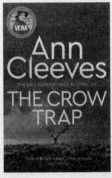

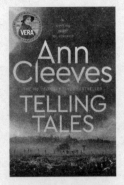

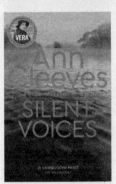

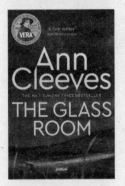

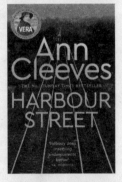

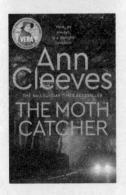

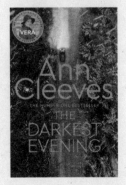